THE GHOST WHO CAME HOME FROM THE AUCTION

Dolores Stewart Riccio

ISBN: 1497320100
ISBN 13: 9781497320109

Also by Dolores Stewart Riccio

Spirit, a romance of past and present lives
Circle of Five
Charmed Circle
The Divine Circle of Ladies Making Mischief
The Divine Circle of Ladies Courting Trouble
The Divine Circle of Ladies Playing with Fire
The Divine Circle of Ladies Rocking the Boat
The Divine Circle of Ladies Tipping the Scales
The Divine Circle of Ladies Painting the Town
The Divine Circle of Ladies Digging the Dirt

To my BFF Joan Bingham
who shares my passion for auctions
and my fascination with haunting events ...

And to my own favorite ghosts
who are always near and dear

Thank you ...

to Joan Bingham for her graceful, meticulous proofreading and editing,

to Lucy-Marie Anderson Sanel for technical advice,

and to enthusiastic first readers Leslie Godfrey and Donna Austin. Your interest, comments, and reactions are so very helpful to my understanding of how this work will be perceived.

MARCH 13
Things to Do Today

Call Jamie re: auction
Don't forget magnet, magnifying glass, notebook, checkbook,
sandwiches
Libr, return Mr. Right, Right Now, *and* How to Land the
Loaded; *borrow* Zen and the Art of Portfolio Management
Reassess life goals—make 5 yr plan for financial independence

Something about the woman's smile—a vivacious, eager, hopeful smile—drew Olivia into her world. A white-gold blonde, showgirl-pretty, slender enough to model with elegance the trim fox jackets, sable wrap, and white mink coat that were laid out on the bed for viewing. Her likeness, in a variety of poses, smiling at Olivia from expensive frames that were also for sale, seemed to go unnoticed by the crowd shuffling through the auction preview.

"Look how many photos there are of the same woman," Olivia said to Jamie.

Jamie Andrews, a Rubenesque gal with a barely tamed mop of flaming hair, ran her hand over the bust of a staunch, helmeted Roman warrior. "Hmmm. Is this really bronze, do you think? Want to check out the jewelry, Liv?"

"No, you go ahead." Olivia took out her magnet and laid it against the warrior's head; it fell off, no magnetism. "Yes, probably this is bronze."

"Oh my Gawd—a magnet! Are you organized, or what! I suppose you've brought your jeweler's glass, too?"

"No, but this will do as well." Olivia removed the chain and pendant magnifying glass from around her own neck and hung it over Jamie's.

"Cool. See you later." Jamie headed for the glass case that protected the valuable jewelry, leaving Olivia, notebook and pencil in hand, to browse dreamily through the accumulations of the unknown woman's life.

Those quirky collections on display somehow made the dead blonde seem still alive, still vulnerable—the ceramic roosters, cats, pigs, and elephants, the carousels, perfume bottles, music boxes. The ginger jars, painted screens, snarling Chinese dogs. The stained-glass window panels (how many windows did she have?) The dolls still in their original boxes. The watches, earrings, miles of costume beads. The massive mahogany fifteen-piece entertainment set, the elaborately carved bedroom set with mirrored headboard. Apparently, this woman had lived to the beat of *shop till you drop.*

She'd probably loved every last cat and rooster, remembered where she'd bought many of them, or who had given this one or that one. In dozens of elaborate frames, she was sometimes alone, sometimes cheek-to-cheek with a rotund balding guy, or leaning against him—full-length poses, stiletto heels, nice legs—often in a party setting. Her husband? Boyfriend? Daddy? Lawyer? Furrier? She had an ageless quality, as if she'd been born at thirty-five and remained there until she died. With so many photos of this one person, the few other, older faces must be her family—parents, grandparents, aunts—

scooped off her shelves by the hungry auctioneer, all bunched together into three box lots. And those weren't all of them. A small selection of valuable silver frames and a Victorian red velvet album were listed separately.

A forgotten woman with no heirs, or heirs so remote that no one cared to keep her photographs, even some of them, for old times' sake. To Olivia Andreas, divorced and childless, this was a shivering gaze into her own future. True, she would never frame so many photographs of herself, certainly not in such glamorous poses—but who would want to keep the albums she does have, the record of her growing-up years, the baby pictures, the high school friends, the dates? How quickly some junk dealer of the future would consign those to the dumpster!

It was an appalling sale, a heartbreaker, as if all these people oozing over their wooden folding chairs and wolfing down limp French fries from the Grange Hall kitchen in Milton were in fact grave-robbers, no better than thieves ravaging Egyptian tombs.

Weird prickles of ice traveled up Olivia's neck and flowed over her scalp—a feeling that would have made her mother say, "someone is tiptoeing over my grave." Well, Olivia prided herself in being far too sensible for such superstitions. She shook off the sensation, at the same time aware that she'd been standing and staring into space for who knows how long? It was time to settle into the aisle seats she and Jamie had saved by laying their raincoats across them.

At six-thirty, the auctioneer tapped his mike, listened to its satisfactory squeaks, and set a cup of hot coffee and a glass of cold water nearby. "Ladies and gentlemen, this auction is unique in Byatt's history," he said with a broad, inclusive grin and a knowing nod to regulars in the first row. "All items here are from one estate and very few items are older than fifteen years. This lady had some fine possessions. All top quality merchandise, exceptional collections, valuable jewelry, treasures for every taste—many of you will be taking home some real prizes. Everything and I mean everything, has to be sold and moved off the premises tonight, so *let's have an auction!*"

"Must have been some wild fifteen-year shopping spree! How was the jewelry?" Olivia whispered as brisk bidding began on a blue and white china Fu Dog with a pug-ugly face.

"Maybe she won a lottery and went straight to the nearest mall, just as I surely would have done. Some really nice rings in the glass case. I didn't fit into that cute fox."

"Fur is no longer politically correct," observed Olivia, sorry to have missed the sight of her zaftig friend trying to wedge herself into the petite jacket.

"They found all this stuff crammed into a five-room apartment in Boston," said a voice in the row behind them. "Can you imagine? She must have stacked those tables one on top of the other. Talk about a pack rat."

Olivia glanced back. The two women had a satisfied air. They didn't look as if they were friends of the slim, well-groomed woman in the photographs. They looked like refugees from a tabloid talk show. The tables they spoke about were marble-topped or inlaid wood or beveled glass, all pristine and expensive—too elaborate for Olivia's taste, except for the dining room table, a pure unblemished oval of mahogany. Displayed on it, a cobalt and gold dinner service for twelve. Sterling silver in a velvet-lined case. Nearby, a red satin Victorian fainting couch (reproduction) was too stiff and perfect to sit on, let alone lounge.

Having inspected the primitive bar, Jamie came back with two gins-and-tonic to wash down the cheese and chutney sandwiches, "ploughman's lunch," Olivia had packed.

"I wonder what possessed Bill Byatt to hold an auction tonight," Jamie said.

"What's wrong with tonight?" Olivia asked.

"It's Friday the Thirteenth, girlfriend. I almost decided to stay home. We're tempting fate, you know."

"I'm not superstitious, Jamie. Same as any other Friday to me."

"We'll see," Jamie said with a knowing smirk.

The impeccable dinner set, purchased by a woman in the next aisle, was a steal at six hundred. The three box lots of framed photos went to a man in the back row for a song. When the single frames came up, he bought those, too. Olivia turned around to have a better look, he was already moving toward the cashier's table to pay for his purchases. This confirmed her notion that a caring relative had come to light at last, or perhaps a sentimental boyfriend who had loved and lost the gorgeous blonde.

Jamie won the bid for a lot of five watches, sixty-five dollars, but lost her nerve on the diamond and sapphire ring. Consulting her notebook, Olivia bought a small Italian chest with a curved lid, inlaid woods in a pattern of lilies, for fifty-five dollars, nine cobalt goblets for thirty, and the Victorian album for twenty. Then, impulsively, she waved her numbered card in the air for an art deco frame decorated with a spray of leaves, fifteen dollars (really cheap for good silver!). The old beau must have missed that one. And a few others that were sold later in the evening. Well, he'd certainly disappeared with plenty of stunning poses to remember her by.

Possibly Olivia wouldn't even remove the smiling woman's photo from her art deco frame. Not a very sensible notion—a whim, really—but the woman seemed much too alive to be tossed out, even by a stranger. At least Olivia would leave her there until there was a darned good reason to replace her, such as wanting to frame a new man in her life. The possibility of a lover showing up any time soon seemed rather remote, but *Mr. Right, Right Now* counseled a confident attitude—you go, girl! "Your dream man in six weeks."

Now, what about the album? Pictures of dead relatives (and she didn't even know whose) in ramrod poses. What on earth would she do with that?

"She sure loved lilies," Jamie commented.

So Jamie had noticed the sale's strong personal aura after all, the lily theme repeated in several places. The designs for two of the stained glass windows depicted white lilies and red roses as rich and deep as fresh blood.

After the auction, Olivia drove Jamie home to *The Willows*, where, in a town house with full amenities, her friend enjoyed a lifestyle untroubled by spiteful old appliances and gardening chores. Mike, Jamie's twelve-year-old son, was just being dropped off to spend the weekend by her ex number one, Mitch Moody. Olivia waved at the boy, got a big grin back, and felt a serious twinge of envy. *Best of all worlds*, she imagined as she drove home. *I bet Mike will keep photos of Jamie forever, and his children after him.*

Somehow her own familiar rooms seemed too quiet for a Friday night. She inserted a CD in the player—*Phantom of the Opera* at full volume—then carefully washed and dried the cobalt goblets, arranging them in her china cabinet, while she belted out "Music of the Night" at top voice along with the opera's love-starved baritone. The elegant Italian chest looked perfect on the tall bureau in her bedroom. Not for jewelry, though; there were specially fitted drawers in her vanity for that. Olivia liked everything to have its proper place, to be taken up and put back there, as regular and secure as the stars in their orbits.

Olivia ran her fingers across the soft red velvet of the album. It was a beautiful thing, *Our Family* embossed in gold, each moss-green cardboard page holding photos framed with scrollwork. She laid it reverently between tablecloths in the bottom of her china cabinet. She'd give the living room furniture a good polishing before displaying the album. *Now that's what I call a coffee-table book!* Olivia said to herself.

After carrying the photo in its heavy silver frame upstairs to her office, Olivia stood it on the long white shelf with her own family pictures. A smiling blonde whose name she didn't know. (Later, Olivia wished she had asked someone.) The flamboyant stranger certainly didn't fit in with Olivia's relatives. Not even with the photo of her handsome father leaning on his new Chevy, gazing through dark-framed glasses with an enigmatic smile for the photographer, probably her mother. That picture had been taken many years ago but it's all she had to remember him. A bank officer, Philip Andreas had been tempted by a dormant trust fund into embezzling a sizeable sum. In danger of being discovered, he'd fled from their home in Cleveland to an undisclosed location, presumably where the United States had no jurisdiction, leaving Olivia's mother Cecelia to deal with their five-year-old daughter and a mess of legal questions. As the years passed, Olivia's memories of her dad became as bleached, smooth, and characterless as a shard of sea-washed glass. Now that time had worn away his imperfections, Olivia would readily forgive him, if only he could be found.

Not so her mother, whose sense of abandonment sharpened with the years. The unfairness, the anguish of her situation grew deeper and wilder inside her, and so did an untidy mass of fibroids, leading to an early hysterectomy. The ill-humor and fault-finding that followed her mother's operation-induced menopause never ended. Photos of Cecelia showed increasing dissatisfaction with whatever she was looking out at, including Olivia. Through all of her growing up, Olivia was nearly starved for approval but had found comfort in approving her own orderly adult life.

The lively blonde, who had owned all those fur coats, one of them falling in lush folds to her slim ankles, was a pleasant addition to Olivia's office shelf, helping to fill in where the discarded pictures of ex-husband Hank and their wedding photo had left empty places.

LILY

Take it from One Who Knows, Hon—being a ghost sure has its advantages. First thing I noticed, I can be anywhere, anytime, just by thinking about it. All I got to do is imagine myself, say, in Vegas, and Flash! I'm there! Lounging around the Mirage penthouse or even some high roller suite at the Venetian (better yet, the old Glory Days when the Venetian was the Sands. Yes, Hon, I can pick my own time.) Picture me sweeping down that grand staircase into the casino on the arm of some Hot Italian Guy. You bet, Hon, I can feel alive That Way anytime I want. As they say, The Possibilities Are Endless. The shows, the parties, the gambling. And yes, I can win, too. I can win so easily, it kinda spoils the fun, you know what I mean?

Another thing, I can look in on the people I used to care about without worrying how the hell they're Screwing Up. When my third cousin Bobby Ray is about to do some coke and boogie his way through an all-night rave followed by a stumbling fry-up of Mexican eggs that will set fire to his mom's kitchen, I no longer feel the need to warn him off the stuff. I'm free at last from trying to save a Living Soul from himself.

Even if I wanted to, though, it's No Cinch to make a Live Appearance among my former nearest and dearest. Easier to Ping *or* Ping Ping *the wall or murmur a suggestion than to Make an*

Appearance. But I've been warned it's a real Dumb Idea to try to connect through one of those phony, money-grubbing Ghostbusters, with or without the clerical collar. Unless, of course, there's a Life-or-Death Reason.

Ghost, by the way, is not exactly the right name for me. The same goes for Specter, Spook, Phantasm, Revenant, or Demon. The correct term for what I am—which they tell me here is something between the Eternal Energy and Memory—doesn't exist in any known language. (Not including dolphins, who do have a whistle sound that comes close.) So I'm using the word Ghost as John Wayne might talk about a Great White Bird to a bunch of Indians who never saw an airplane.

And there's one more advantage to my Present State, if it isn't a disadvantage. I no longer positively hunger for a box of chocolate truffles, a double Jack Daniels on the rocks, or a joint. I can have them, of course—nothing harms the sort of Hologram Body I am these days—but I hardly bother about indulging myself when I have So Much Else to do. And I'm not talking about partying in That Great Casino in the Sky.

You see, Hon, my Chief Desire now is to find out why I am here when I could be Moving On to this Better Place I've been hearing about. But apparently Something Unfinished about my death keeps me hanging around. Sorry ... I can't quite recall the nitty-gritty details.

All I remember about Before is being in my apartment, kinda sloshed on sloe gin fizzes as I was into Deep Mourning for my Frankie Boy, when two wiseguys busted in on me and demanded something I wasn't supposed to give them. That part's a bit hazy, too. The next thing I knew, one of those bozos was dangling me, screaming, over the stairwell in the hall. I can sure recall the Scared-Shitless feeling I got when he lost his grip. I guess maybe I squirmed around too much. I'm a dancer, you know, so I got some really Powerful Moves in me.

Anyway, somehow, I was Out of My Body in a sec, looking down at myself lying prone on the entrance hall floor, the one with the classy black and white marble squares. Only now there was a pool of red blood running across it. Talk about Totally Flabbergasted— that was me!

Then there was this sound/feeling like a Giant Whoooosh, and I was pulled out of my apartment building into an apple tree full of brown-spotted buds and buzzing bees. My second cousin Evelyn's dying orchard in Harvard. I could see her house through the branches. It looked less crappy from a distance. I heard Bobby Ray revving up his motorcycle in the driveway, the Fancy Ride he'd bought with the tuition money I gave him at graduation, the bum. But thinking of my Plunkett cousins, the Whole Motley Crew of them, I felt more love than annoyance for the first time in memory.

I jumped down beside Bobby, but he didn't seem to notice. He hadn't paid that much attention to me in life, either, despite the constant urging of his dad "be nice to Cousin Lily." Cousin Lily who had no children of her own to inherit her hard-earned fortune. Maybe I was there to say good-bye to him and his mom, I don't know. Whatever, it sure didn't work out right.

And I still don't know what I'm doing here tonight. I remember riding on top of the Byatt's Auction House truck that carted away My Beautiful Things. Then I was in this hall where a bunch of people were buying all the stuff that used to be mine. That shouldn't be allowed, you know, Hon. I'm going to Speak to Someone about that. They tell me here that in Egypt a few millennia ago, I could have taken all my good jewelry and sterling silver with me. My sable and white mink, too—especially that white mink.

Next thing, the grab-bag was over and I went home with someone I sort of took to. I guess I was drawn to her because she actually thought about me while the Greedy Ones were busy pawing through my belongings. And when I whispered to her, "buy that silver frame with the spray of leaves," she did. Like, maybe she might be able to help me in some way. I'm just not sure yet how or why.

MARCH 25
Things to Do Today

Appt locksmith
Where is dog pound? Hours?
Defrost cellar freezer, list contents
Buy moisture-resistant labels

Olivia found a particular satisfaction in writing her daily To-Do list. Without a list, she might have frittered away hours just rearranging pantry shelves or browsing through quarterly reports and earnings statements. She wrote out each list just before going to bed, when the previous day had been shot to hell but the next was still a blank page of possible accomplishments.

Olivia started listing right after she got a court order forcing Hank to vacate the premises a year ago last fall. Only he hadn't moved far enough, just a few streets away. He still hovered in her sphere of annoyance and responsibility where she could run into him at any time. One look at that lean, hungry face might tempt her to cook those stuffed peppers he loved so much, and maybe leave them in a covered dish on his porch while he was at work selling "starter" homes with walls like eggshells to gullible newlyweds. Stuffed peppers (unless yellow) are as indigestibly close to poison as you could feed someone legally. Olivia would use the green ones. Let his heart burn for a change.

No, she would *not* whip up a casserole for Hank ever again! She ought to stop cooking so much, or even cooking at all. The trouble was, she enjoyed it. Unlike her day-to-day life, cooking was non-cerebral and unpredictable. You never knew how fresh ginger was going to taste in lentil soup unless you tried it. From the day she'd packed up Hank's stuff and stacked it out on the lawn, her freezer had begun to bulge with foil-wrapped packages, recipes she couldn't resist trying, and her own improvisations—carefully labeled and dated. Unfortunately, the labels had curled off at the first hint of moisture and now lay like puzzle pieces at the bottom of her cellar freezer chest.

Although she'd changed the locks before Hank's tracks were cold in the driveway, Olivia was convinced that her ex had broken into the house two days ago while she was at South Shore Savings organizing her final report. He was probably looking for his back-up zip discs, which she'd trashed after reading the contents and finding it contained, among business-related files, an address book labeled "Pussies." Hank was a hunk, as well he knew. Time for a new lock. Time for a new life.

Or maybe the break-in hadn't been Hank. But who else would it be? What could he (or she!) have been looking for—a neat search, but unmistakable to someone who color coded her trouser socks and alphabetized her canned goods. If a stranger, maybe he had her mixed up with someone else. *A jewel thief with a cache of stolen diamonds? A call girl with a compromising little black book?* What did Olivia own or know that anyone would want to possess? Nothing. Zero. She was a completely unimportant person. How mortifying. *There'll be some changes made here*, Olivia vowed.

Meanwhile, she was going to buy a dog, a mean junkyard dog, and teach him not to make friends with Hank (who disliked animals anyway). Training a dog couldn't be all that difficult. It just took patience, persistence, and all those hard-won virtues that Olivia had in abundance.

The best part of writing a To-Do list was when Olivia got to cross off tasks with a gratified *There, now! That's done.*

THE OFFICE

Rosario Benedetto was spitting mad, literally. And when "The Rose" lost it, everyone at the Benedetto Fruit Company, a wood-framed, two-story building on King Street near Haymarket, tried to stay out of the boss's way. Right now he was banging his fist on the dusty littered desk. The mobile phone shook off its receiver. Framed photos that had been pried apart with a screwdriver flew off in all directions. Spittle gathered in the corners of The Rose's thin lips.

"Shit! Shit! This is all shit," he screamed waving a printout of the March Byatt auction. "That idiot must have missed something. I want that *stupido* and his dumb-ass brother brought in here so I can get it through their thick skulls what I'm looking for." The permanent scowl on The Rose's face, perhaps formed by the smoke of a cigarette forever dangling from his mouth, became even more menacing.

Despite his rage, Rosario Benedetto wasn't about to spill his real fears to any of his underlings, even a close relative. While The Rose was undisputed boss of King Street, if this mess wasn't contained, he was going to have to answer for it to someone else. Failing to protect the family through his errors in judgment would not be tolerated. A sobering thought that brought with it an icy calm. The Rose stopped bellowing and resumed his usual sangfroid.

"Let's get some air, Junior," he said to the good-looking young man with the cleft chin, square jaw, and shock of black curly hair who'd been lounging on the cracked leather sofa, wishing he were elsewhere but trying not to betray his anxiety.

"They swore they bought every fucking frame at the Byatt auction ..." Junior began tentatively.

Moving across the room with a speed belied by his size, The Rose made a quick cutting motion across the young man's throat. Junior stopped talking in mid-sentence. The Rose knew he had to watch out what was said indoors in case the office walls sprouted ears. It had been known.

Stuffing the printout into his pocket, The Rose slapped an old felt hat on his head. After being in a shrouded office all morning, as he stepped outdoors, he blinked and squinted in the sunshine. Shielding his eyes with one hand, he chuckled darkly and waved at the top floor of the shabby medical building across the street.

The two men—one short and powerful as a bull, the other tall, slim, dark, and deferential—started down King Street past small shops and restaurants. Owners, workers, and passersby nodded respectfully as they passed. The Rose held up one hand in greeting and twitched his mouth into what passed for a smile on his deeply-lined face.

Calmed by this ritual stroll, he spoke to his nephew in a low confidential tone. "That motherfucker Frankie R., I trusted that son-of-a-bitch. And all the time he was stashing away a little insurance policy. Stuck the key to it behind a photo at his broad's place. A good thing her coke-head cousin overheard him, the little weasel."

"Yeah, lucky break, that," his nephew agreed.

"Should have been. Should have been, Junior. If Idiot Number One hadn't let Frankie's broad drop down the stairs before he could get her to tell him which photo. Then Idiot Number Two let some of those pictures slip right through his fucking fingers. I'm surrounded by fucking incompetents. Shit!"

"What about that red velvet thing they lifted for you? Wasn't so dumb, them following up on the sale, finding out who bought the album. Full of pictures, wasn't it?" Junior asked.

"It was red, all right. Damned red herring. Full of fucking Frankie's relatives and nothing else."

"So, Uncle. Want me to straighten this out for you? Be my pleasure," Junior said.

"Okay. Okay, you do it, because I swear if I see those two guys myself, I'm going to rip off their faces. Their own mothers won't know them when I get through." The Rose swept off his hat to a startled priest coming out of St. Anthony's.

Junior saluted the Father as politely as his mentor had. "Consider it done, Uncle. Let me have that print-out, and I'll get right on it."

"Good, kid. And get those retards to help you. Keep your own hands clean. I don't want no grief with your papa. Better I should have squeezed the truth out of fucking Frankie R. before he was hit, and we could have avoided all this shit. So remember, I'm counting on you to get what I'm looking for." The Rose clapped his hand on Junior's shoulder. His stony eyes bored into his nephew's in a meaningful way. Junior understood.

On their way back to the office, the deli owner emerged with a bag of the robust, spicy sandwiches known to be The

Rose's favorites, which he presented with a genteel bow. The scent of soppressata salami, well-aged provolone, and hot peppers perfumed the air. The Rose sniffed appreciatively and shook hands with the deli owner, murmuring his thanks.

As they walked back to the office for lunch, The Rose held forth sagely to his nephew. "Mikey D'Amico. Remember the name, Junior. He never disappoints me. It's good to have friends who never disappoint. Machiavelli said it. 'A man can always defend himself by good troops and good friends. And he will always have good friends if he has good troops.'"

Junior struggled to remember. "Machiavelli? Chicago connection, was he?"

His uncle sighed. "You got a lot to learn, kid, but you're family. Family and friends—that's what life is all about."

MARCH 26
Things to Do Today

Libr, return Zen, get dog training
Lunch with Jamie
Gentle Folk Intro Serv?
List 12 desirable qualities in Mr. Right

Olivia had the strong, broad-shouldered build of a long-distance swimmer, the expressive hands of an actor, and the serene eyes of a Madonna, but she was none of these things. She was a records expert, a fact-checker, a list-maker, an organizer, and a budding stock trader—nearly a perfect Virgo type, although she herself didn't believe in astrology and never even peeked at her daily horoscope. Few people would have called her pretty, but with her strong Athenian features and glowing olive skin, some would find her beautiful. Her glossy black hair—she called it "brownish"—was sheered off like Joan of Arc's. Her sea-green eyes were hidden behind no-nonsense glasses, although at age thirty-four her myopia had improved a great deal. With or without her glasses, however, Olivia didn't miss much.

The Hawthorne Library was one of Olivia's favorite places, a gracious gray stone building never ruined by modernization.

Just wandering through its pleasant old rooms on a weekday morning gave her a feeling of peace and privilege—the smell of printer's ink and dust, the golden oak furniture sturdy and reassuring, the unblinking computers like a row of shut eyes, the shelves packed with promises of excitement, escape, or at least, erudition, more books than any one person could read in a lifetime. All this acted on her psyche the way an extra-dry martini with three olives affected her friend Jamie. It made her good-humored for several blissful hours afterwards. That was the greatest thing about being a temp consultant—the down time between assignments when she could enjoy inexpensive delights.

"Hi, Olivia," the woman at the circulation desk greeted her. "I'm not really supposed to let you take out three books on one subject...but...just this once. I didn't know you had a dog."

"I don't," said Olivia, packing up *Seven Days to a Perfect Pet, Training Your Guard Dog Like a Pro*, and *All Dogs Are Good Dogs*—none of which were noted on the computerized list of *Books I Want to Read* that Olivia kept in the tote she always brought to the library. Dog training, like landing Mr. Right, was an entirely new territory.

The blustery first days of spring invigorated Olivia. Last year's brown leaves scurried away from her brisk, confident steps like old worries swirling to oblivion. The minaret buds on the magnolia trees outside the library were softening, turning from gray to mauve, getting ready to burst out in ruffles. For no good reason at all, a sense of hope and adventure lifted Olivia's spirits. Perhaps she'd enroll in the Gentle Folk Introduction Service. No druggies. No smokers.

Jamie was sipping her favorite mood enhancer in a frosty oversized cocktail glass when Olivia slipped into the seat opposite her at the *Rue de Bonheur*, a pseudo-bistro where the pesto was gritty and bitter but the cocktails were outstanding. Depending on the hours they were working, Olivia and Jamie tried to go out for lunch or dinner somewhere every week. And they went to auctions together whenever possible. They both loved the action, but for different reasons. Jamie enjoyed the combination of theatrics and gambling, the glamour of bidding. Olivia prided herself on having a good eye for value, carefully choosing which items to bid on and how high to go, then acquiring some lovely thing at a sensible price. It was the same with the stock market. They both traded but from different perspectives.

They'd met at Beaumont High School in Cleveland, having been thrown together as partners for alphabetical reasons (Olivia Andreas, Ella Jamison Andrews) in Home Ec and Chemistry. Sensing Jamie's culinary desperation, Olivia had produced velvety white sauce for them both, and Jamie returned the favor by completing both sets of Chem experiments. Jamie's parents being hospitable and good-humored, unlike Olivia's embittered mother, the two girls often hung out at the Andrews' house. "Always room for one more pretty girl," Jamie's father Artie would say as he carved the Sunday roast, beaming at both of them. Olivia basked in their welcoming warmth.

Despite the differences in their home lives, both girls wanted to get out on their own right after graduation, far away from boring old Cleveland. Jamie had gone on to the University of Massachusetts's Nursing School and Olivia to Boston University. After college, they'd remained friends through three failed marriages (two for Jamie, one for Olivia), two miscarriages (Olivia's), one childbirth (Jamie's), and all the minor triumphs and disasters along the way.

When Jamie moved to Massachusetts' South Shore with her first husband and young son, Olivia visited often enough to discover that the sight and scent of the ocean were slightly intoxicating to her. Her summer tan took on a sea-glow. Her thoughts, like sun-burnished gulls, veered away from earthly matters. Her steps grew light as a dancer's. In that state of constant mild inebriation, it's no wonder that she fell for Hank as easily as a stone disappears into water.

And what a blessing it had been to make a final break away from her mother in Cleveland. Now Olivia called home once a month, religiously sent birthday and Mother's Day cards, and wrestled with her conscience to escape holiday visits. Soon after the divorce, Olivia had made the mistake of mentioning her loneliness and dismay to her mother. Cecelia declared that Olivia should never have broken up with Hank, but now that she had, the sensible thing would be to move back to Cleveland where she would be safe. Olivia pleaded problems in finding suitable consulting jobs.

Like Olivia, Jamie enjoyed a certain amount of flexibility in her career as a private nurse who was both sought after and choosy. Jamie, whose bright auburn hair often escaped its neat coil and who filled out her white uniform with delicious curves, more often than not chose to nurse unmarried males among the locally rich and famous. "The older, the better," she confessed to Olivia. "They always fall for their nurses. Someday ..."

But Someday hadn't arrived yet, and Jamie was between prosperous sick old duffers, hence available for lunch. Olivia ordered a glass of Pinot Grigio, and after the waitress left, leaned over and whispered, "Listen, Jamie—I don't know what to make of this. Someone broke into my house a few days ago, while I was at South Shore Savings. My last day, organizing my final report. Whoever did it searched everywhere. I wondered what he could have been looking for, and then I discovered something missing."

"Oh my Gawd! That bastard Hank. Was it a terrible mess? Why didn't you call me? I would have helped you clean it up."

"No, it was all right, really. He was very neat—or she, or they. But I'm a noticing kind of person. Everything was a little disturbed, know what I mean? My folded turtleneck shirts were in the wrong order. Some of my books were pushed back instead of flush with the shelves. What bothers me most is that the one thing missing was the lovely Victorian album I bought at the auction—you remember? I was meaning to display it in the living room, but I hadn't got around to that yet. I wanted to polish the coffee table first. So the album was still stashed where I put it the night we got home from the auction. In the dining room sideboard, between table cloths."

"Wow! That doesn't sound like Hank at all. And you're absolutely sure nothing else was missing?"

"No, the burglar didn't take any of the obvious things. I always keep a little cash on hand so I don't have to hit the ATM, and it was still in my desk drawer. You know I own a few gold pieces, too—earrings and a necklace. TV, VCR, laptop—everything is still in its place. Isn't that weird?"

"Gawd, Liv—*cash!* Are you crazy? They didn't take *anything* but a moldy old picture album? What do you suppose …? Have you called the police?"

"Yes, of course. No signs of forced entry. I actually hoped it *was* Hank rather than some hairy pervert pawing through my underwear. The officers who came to interview me seemed to think, as I did, that it was probably my ex looking for his favorite golf shirt or some old bonds he could cash or anything I might have screwed him out of."

"So ..." Jamie took a long appreciative swallow of her liquid Prozac. "What were they like? Any cute ones? Did they dust for fingerprints? Are they going to talk to Hank?"

"Well, first there was a young cop from Scituate PD. Then a couple of investigators from the Plymouth Detective Division. One of those guys was ... not too bad. Dave Lowenstein. I guess they didn't dust because nothing appeared to be stolen. I hadn't reported the bizarre theft of the album because I hadn't discovered it yet. The detectives had a talk with Hank right away. But Hank was in Braintree all that day with a full schedule of appointments, verified by his boss. There's no way he could have searched my place between clients. In fact, he closed some deals, down payments signed and sealed. Two more young couples who think they're going to get the landscaping and paved roads the Castlebridge brochure promises them."

"The important thing to remember about salesmen is, once they get your signature on the dotted line, they couldn't care less about your hopes, dreams, and reasonable expectations."

"If you're trying to warn me not to marry a salesman, you're too late."

When Olivia was being courted by charming Henry ("call me Hank") Robb, he was so lavish with affection, attention, and approval that Olivia had felt quite full for the first time in her hungry life. Not long after they were married, however, Olivia realized that everyone in Hank's acquaintance got that special attention, particularly good-looking women. Besides being a born salesman, Hank was an incorrigible chaser. As if that weren't bad enough, Hank's wasteful ways and reckless schemes kept their finances constantly on the brink of chaos. Olivia stuck it out for eight and a half years before escaping with her credit in tatters and a second mortgage hanging over her head.

"I won't say I told you so, but I did strongly hint that Hank was not husband material." Jamie signaled the waiter for another round of drinks. "If it wasn't Hank who broke in, what are you going to do? How are you going to protect yourself?"

"I'm getting new locks, real ones—deadbolt, or whatever they're supposed to be. And a guard dog."

"A *dog*? A state-of-the-art alarm system would make more sense. Or a gun. One of those sportsman's assault weapons that shoots a hundred bullets a minute. Gawd ... what fun!" Jamie pointed her finger at nearby diners and made soft *rat-a-tat-tat* sounds.

"I'm afraid of guns. I've always been. And alarm systems cost the earth and only deter amateurs. No, I'm going over to the Shawmutt Pound and rescue the meanest dog on death row. It's a logical solution."

"The way your flawless logic leads you astray never ceases to amaze me. A dog is going to be *way* more trouble than a nice little security system with a motion sensor, a number code keypad, and a panic button you can wear on your wrist. You could even get a surveillance camera. The newest systems will foil even the professional thief."

"Unless I manage to 'land the loaded'—yes, I did read that book you recommended—I doubt I can afford anything so elaborate. Motion sensor? Surveillance camera?" Olivia laughed merrily. "No, thanks. Just give me a good guard dog who will be glad to work for his chow."

Seeing Olivia's determined expression, Jamie picked up a menu with a sigh and gave it her earnest attention. "So... what looks good to you? Grilled Veal Shoulder Steak with Truffle-scented White Bean Ragout? Pesto-crusted Salmon with Wilted Field Greens and Shaved Parmesan? Lobster and Avocado Club Sandwich with Chipotle Mayonnaise?"

Olivia chose the veal, which was slippery and heavy on the garlic. She took away the leftovers wrapped up in a Styrofoam "doggie bag." Might come in handy while making friends with her new life's companion. She'd have the week to train him. Her assignment at the law firm of Crowe, Crabbe, and Savage didn't begin until Monday next, a big job that would last several weeks. C C & S had a dinosaur filing system that kept biting off its own tail.

Although she was a specialist who might have worked full-time as Records Manager at any bank or insurance company, Olivia preferred her temp status as a consultant, even at the sacrifice of benefits. She'd seen enough of corporate inner workings to know that, soon after signing on, petty office politics and the reigning corporate culture would begin to make her crazy. With self-limiting consulting assignments, there was always a choice, always a way out. Olivia always liked to know where the exits were.

A longish stint with a brokerage firm, however, had introduced Olivia to a game she was born to win, stock trading. Her meticulous research habits, her analytical mind, and even her caution, had paid off in a most satisfying way—so well, in fact, that despite Hank's wild wheeling and dealing, recently she was able to pay off the second mortgage on the pleasant little three-bedroom Cape Cod cottage in Scituate, now hers alone, with a garage and a half-acre of neatly fenced yard.

Peace at last, Olivia sometimes thought. Other times, the phrase *lonely splendor* came to mind. Perhaps a companion dog with a low tolerance for intruders was just want she needed. The patter of little paws was better than no patter at all.

MARCH 27
Things to Do Today

Buy dog food, treats, bones, pooper scooper etc.
Read up on choosing breed, 1ˢᵗ impress etc.
Shawmutt, bring veal doggie bag
Make list of spring projects:tulip beds, lawn furniture etc. boyfriend
Record affirmations

As soon as Olivia parked her Chevy van in the lot, her ears were assaulted by a cacophony of yaps and howls rising from the yellow cinder-block building. The Shawmutt Dog Pound was new and cheerless. *It must take nerves of titanium to work here all day,* she thought, but the attendant who greeted her looked more stupefied than high-strung. "I'm looking for a dog," Olivia said.

"We got 'em." The ruddy, stocky man gazed everywhere except at her face as he gestured vaguely toward the cages where indignant dogs were protesting their incarceration, resigned dogs had flopped down in attitudes of depression, and puppies were curled together in disconsolate heaps. Beneath the odor of urine, feces, and disinfectant, Olivia's fine nose detected the reek of misery. A horror shop. Olivia was sensitive to atmospheres, a drawback for someone who had to cope with new offices season after season. She'd better get out of this gloomy prison fast.

"Okay if I have a quick look?"

"Suit yourself."

"I'd like to adopt a good guard dog."

"We got those, too. Big bad fellas toward the back."

Clutching the Styrofoam container from yesterday's lunch and averting her gaze from needy spaniels, woeful retrievers, and pitiful mutts of dubious lineage, Olivia walked straight back to the cages farthest from the front desk. According to the index card taped to the left side cage, Bruno was the name of an oversize shepherd mix, who eyed her suspiciously, then lunged at the cage door and barked repeatedly, exposing an excellent set of teeth. On the right, Sadie, an elderly American pit bull terrier, hunkered down on her haunches against the back wall, growling deep in her throat without moving a muscle.

"Good boy! Good girl!" Olivia said in her most confident tone, breaking out the leftovers. Determination alone was keeping this enterprise alive. Congratulating herself for true grit, she tore the slippery veal remnant into several chunks, inched one between Sadie's bars and tossed another to Bruno, buying about two seconds of détente before the barking, snarling, and growling recommenced.

Olivia seated herself cross-legged on the cold concrete floor between the two dogs and waited. Having read about the canine take on confrontation, she didn't look directly at either animal. After a while, Sadie ceased growling, got up stiffly, and strolled over to the bars. She retrieved the chunk of meat with surprising delicacy, devoured it in one gulp, and sat up looking expectantly at Olivia. Alert to Sadie's change of mood, Bruno stopped his menacing noises and wandered nearer to his cage door. Olivia held out the remaining morsel flat on her palm near the bars of his cage. The dog lapped it up in a flash, leaving Olivia all five of her fingers. *Yes!* she said to herself.

"Do you have any leashes? Would you help me to take Bruno and Sadie into that little fenced-in area I saw outside?" Olivia asked the attendant, who was nodding over a newspaper spread across his desk. "If they don't kill each other, or me, I'll take them both—is that okay?"

"Okay with me. They've been here too long as it is." He got up heavily on feet that seemed to be paining him or had gone to sleep. "Dogs pouring in here every day. Those two gotta make room. If you want the leashes, that's extra, after the regular donation. Sadie's fixed, so you won't need to have that done." The exertion of such a long speech reddened his face even more.

"Are they housebroken?"

"No idea. Probably. They both came from homes not kennels. Bruno got sacked for growling at his owner's grandson," the attendant reported with relish. "And Sadie was petitioned out of an apartment complex for menacing some old lady in the elevator."

"Oh, swell," said Olivia. Still, she hesitated to back down in front of this man's mocking grin.

The attendant took two flimsy braided leads off a hook on the wall and walked the gauntlet to the back, expertly leashing each dog without opening the cages. "Okay, go to it," he said. "Out that side door." No more help with the two dogs would be forthcoming.

Cautiously, Olivia released Sadie from her cage and grabbed the end of her lead. Surprisingly strong for her size, Sadie sprinted joyfully for freedom, but Olivia tugged and hauled her out the side door. Closed in the small fenced yard, the pit bull began barking crossly. Olivia went back for Bruno.

Nose to the concrete floor, Bruno followed Sadie's trail with enthusiastic snuffles and was excited to find her peeing on the one tiny grass plot in the otherwise gravel-covered yard. Both dogs sniffed the wet spot with interest. Then Bruno made an attempt to check out Sadie herself, but the pit bull growled and snapped. The shepherd wisely backed off, and Olivia was heartened to see that neither dog attempted to kill the other on the spot.

I know this is a mistake, so why am I doing it? Olivia asked herself, as she signed two sets of papers and made out a double "donation" check. *Because once I'd fed them, I couldn't choose between them. One to take home, the other to die in some antiquated gas chamber. What a ninny I am!*

The March sun was just setting in a cool pink haze when Olivia arrived home with her new housemates. After a mad dash around the fenced yard, they explored the house inhaling every conceivable scent. *They need to run about after being cooped up in those cages,* Olivia decided

She found two old stoneware casseroles in the pantry, and spooned in cupfuls of dry dog food. Opening a large can of *Natural Nibbles Gourmet Lamb, Duck, and Pasta Dinner,* she divided it between the two dishes. It certainly has a strong smell, something like lamb liverwurst, but the two dogs seemed to relish the aroma. Soon they were eating blissfully in the separate places that Olivia had designated. It occurred to her that a number of the mystery packages in the freezer might be recycled into some pretty decent dog food.

"Welcome to the good life, you mutts," Olivia said. "All you have to do is to scare off all intruders. It's the job you were born for!"

MARCH 30
Things to Do Today

Strong let to Scituate Times re: dog pound
Libr, rent video dog training
Also yoga, easy stuff
L L Bean – order dog beds
Call C C & S. Half-days okay if nec?

Olivia woke up from her dream and realized that she was not smashing bumper cars at an amusement park—there was a real noise in the house. After a moment, she identified the sound as one of the dogs, probably Bruno, steadily bumping his body against the door of the laundry room, the dogs' temporary sleeping quarters until they proved themselves to be truly housebroken. She glanced at the clock: ten minutes past three. But why wasn't Sadie barking? Sadie barked at everything that moved in the street. Bruno was slower to start but usually followed her lead. Maybe Bruno was having a gastro-intestinal emergency. New brands of dog food could do that, she'd read. Maybe the canned stuff with duck in it. Best to let him out for a few minutes.

With a sigh, she stuck her feet into slippers and shrugged on her robe. As guardians of home and hearth, these dogs might prove to be more work than they were worth. Perhaps she should have listened to Jamie. But she will never admit that to her friend.

Once freed from the laundry room, Bruno and Sadie burst through the hall and headed straight for the kitchen door. Olivia hurried to let them out, shivering as she watched the two silent streaks in the faint light of the moon, now directly overhead. Why were the dogs racing toward the back? For the past two days, whenever she'd let them out into her fenced yard, they'd checked out the street first. At least they weren't waking up the neighbors with a frenzy of barking. Daytimes were noisy enough. Any time now, Olivia was expecting a patrolman to knock on her door with a complaint in hand.

Ten minutes later they have returned, tongues lolling, tails wagging. "Mission accomplished?" she asked, resisting the impulse to hand out dog biscuits for behavior she didn't want to encourage. "Okay, back to bed you two."

By now it was twenty to four, the worst time of the night to fall back to sleep. Fears crouched in the dark corners of her imagination. Loneliness chilled the sheets. For some reason, the unknown woman in the heavy silver frame came into her mind and wouldn't leave. The room felt icy. Reaching out with one goose-pimpled arm, Olivia pulled up the quilt folded at the foot of the bed and snuggled under it. Downstairs, Sadie howled three times, then all was silent for a few minutes. But just as she was drifting off, Olivia heard a series of crashes coming from her office.

"Oh, for Christ's sake," she said aloud, struggling up and into her robe for the second time. Both dogs began barking in high worried yelps, muffled slightly by the laundry room walls. A thrill of terror, cold as a snake, slipped down Olivia's back. She grabbed the flashlight she kept in the drawer of her night-table and, holding it like a club, crept down the hall to her office. The door was open; light from the hall shone into the room. Olivia's family photos were lying on the floor in a jumble of glass and silver, tipped over one another like a row of dominos. She put down the flashlight and snapped on the overhead light.

Earth tremor? she wondered, approaching the mess with caution. Animals were supposed to be especially sensitive to such things. Not wanting the dogs to tread through broken glass, Olivia checked out the rest of the house by herself, aware of a certain irony in protecting her protectors. Could someone have been searching her office, accidentally knocked over the frames, and fled before she reached the scene?

Nothing else looked disturbed, every plate, saucer, and cup still on the shelf, every spice jar in place. Unaccountably, though, the scent of some perfume which Olivia could not quite identify wafted over the wreckage. Floral, but much too exotic for Olivia's taste.

Sleep now seemed impossible. Olivia got a paper bag, dustpan, and brush and set to work on the mess in her office. The glass had broken in several frames, but the frames themselves and photos were undamaged. The fallen family could be restored to their rightful places for the time being.

"Oh, for Christ's sake," Olivia said again, this time a whispered prayer. The auction woman's picture was upside down in its frame but otherwise unharmed. Collapsing into her desk chair, Olivia studied the photo to be sure she wasn't imagining this. No, it was not a fantasy. When she set the frame on the desk, the photo was reversed, as if the woman were standing on her head. Olivia looked at the back of the frame. The tiny screws were tight and the backing intact as if they'd never been moved. Olivia broke two nails getting the frame open. Underneath the photo she discovered a smaller snapshot. It showed two men, arms around each other's shoulders, grinning, holding up a large fish between them. One of the men looked somewhat familiar, but she couldn't quite place him. She turned the photo over, looking for a note such as "Me and Henry at Loon Lake" but found instead a number and letter sequence printed in tiny letters at the bottom and a small key held in place with yellowed tape. Etched into its surface was the manufacturer's name, Deibolt, Inc. Canton, Ohio. A bank safe deposit key, Olivia knew instantly, but without its little plastic case there was no way of telling which bank. After gazing off into space for a few mindless moments, she added three more reminders to the March 31 list.

Call auction house. Name?
USv99-1899? refers to?
Which bank?

Olivia put the snapshot and key back as she'd found them, righted the woman's photo, and reassembled the frame. She set it in on her desk and wished she had a hot cup of cocoa that was too much trouble to make at this hour.

If I'm afraid of a break-in, why don't I let these two feisty dogs really guard this place? Olivia wondered. She padded downstairs, freed the dogs a second time, picked up the folded blankets from the laundry room floor and moved them to the hall floor.

Olivia got two dog biscuits from the kitchen, and put them on the blankets. In the blink of any eye, Sadie gobbled up both biscuits. Olivia had to get a third biscuit and hand it to the sad-eyed German shepherd. "Stay!" she said in her low, forceful dog-training voice. "You guys can sleep in the hall tonight. Just don't mess on the rugs!"

With ears down in fake-submissive posture, Sadie sidled after Olivia up the stairs and Bruno soon followed.

By now it was four forty-five and Olivia was too bushed to assert her dominant place in the pack. "All right, just for tonight," she said, and crawled under the blankets and quilt, feeling sure she'd never get back to sleep. Bruno slumped down at the foot of the bed with a satisfied sigh. Without a moment's hesitation, Sadie jumped up beside Olivia. The old pit bull didn't try to cuddle up to her new companion, just found a comfortable place in the queen-size bed and curled herself into a furry lump. After a few minutes, Bruno got up, strode around restlessly, then put his front paws on the bed, but Sadie curled her lip at him with a meaningful snarl, making it quite evident that she wasn't in a sharing mood. Bruno accepted the inevitable. So in a way did Olivia. Bruno snored, but if the shepherd was snoring away, all must be well with the night, no intruders or other dangers in the blackness outside.

For some reason she couldn't fathom, the company of the two dogs evoked in Olivia melancholy thoughts of her two miscarriages, how there were no little gravestones to mark the year that those almost-children were never born. Even now they seemed as real to Olivia as if she'd been able to hold them in her arms before they died; she'd even given them names: David—the beloved one—and Patricia—of noble birth. If she wanted to get pregnant again, she'd have to find someone to love. The road of her future loomed ahead like a narrow pass through treacherous mountains. Just before dawn, Olivia heard a light rain, like a scattering of tears, and then at last she slept.

The next morning, Olivia realized that her pantry window and the screen were wide open. She might have left the pantry window ajar yesterday but never the screen. An inexplicable occurrence, but then, how could she explain a picture that turned itself upside down in its frame? Olivia felt as if the floor was tilting under her feet; she staggered to one side, hanging on to slipping walls, desperately trying to keep herself upright. Nausea overcame her, and she rushed into the bathroom to sit on the floor in front of the toilet, waiting to toss up her toast and juice. The tile was cool and somehow reassuring. Breakfast did not reappear after all.

Later, when Olivia was outdoors cleaning up dog messes, as she vowed to do every day—this was her backyard, too— Bruno and Sadie seemed unusually interested in something bright yellow near the bare forsythia bush. She went over to check and found a spanking new flashlight lantern lying on the ground at the far side of the yard. *He must have bolted over that fence in one big hurry,* she thought.

"Good work, you two mutts! Let's go inside and find a treat." Handing out biscuits and pats, Olivia called the Plymouth County Detective Division. "Please tell Detective Sergeant Lowenstein that someone tried to break in my house *again*," she instructed the disinterested woman on the switchboard. "But this time my guard dogs chased him away. The intruder dropped his flashlight when he jumped over the fence."

LILY

Another thing about being a ghost, it's not true that you're led by The Light into some Great Family Reunion in the sky. Good thing, too, because I never was on swell terms with my relatives, living or dead.

By the way, there's nothing wrong with the word Dead. Let's not shilly-shally, Hon. "Dearly Departed" or "Gone Before" only make me think the train has left the station, and "Passed Away" sounds like a hunk of meat with an old sell-by date.

Bits and Pieces, that's all I've got to go on. One thing's for sure, though. There's something I have to take care of before I can, like, move along to Another Place, a real nice place they've been telling me about. And I have a pretty good idea that this, like, Mission Impossible is connected to Frankie. Whatever he was into in a Real Heavy Way before the accident.

The thing is, I haven't even seen Frankie once since I got here. Maybe later, I've been promised. So I can't grill him about why I got stuck with his Flaming Crusade. I just know something went wrong for us, and it's up to me to make it right. We weren't supposed to die when we did. We had plans—sweet secret plans to get out of town and, like, Start Over in a new place, Monaco or Brazil. Well, I suppose you might say we're doing that, but not the way we imagined, damn it.

But it's lifting a little, finally—that Pea Soup Fog I've been in since I found myself here. I'm remembering things that were blurry at first. And one thing I do know now—I'm hanging around in this Andreas gal's house because she was sympatico, *as they say, at that lousy auction arranged by my greedy cousins. And I got her to buy that Special Photo of me where Frankie hid some stuff. So maybe I can nudge her into helping us finish whatever it was that Frankie started.*

They tell me the first step is to try to Catch Her Attention. But no one here has provided, like, a Manual of Instructions, so I don't quite know how to get through to the Other Side. The slightest tap on the wall seems to be more of a sweat than it ever took me to high kick my way across a stage. But we Off-Earth Entities are persistent, Hon. You have to give us that.

It was sweet of Olivia to keep my photo intact, but actually I was hoping she'd open that frame and see what was there for herself. So I had to fiddle with it. One of my favorite photos, by the way. Made me look like one of those Cool Hitchcock Blondes, Tippi Hedron or Grace Kelly.

I just about had that photo fixed when I got the Danger Buzz. Suddenly I knew that there was Big Trouble downstairs. So I floated downstairs (it's one of the perks of being a "ghost") and spotted two wiseguys trying to climb in the window, up to no good. Where were those so-called guard dogs? Sleeping off their big meal, the ungrateful mutts.

It didn't take more than a little rap-rap at their door, though, to get those two dogs banging to be let out of the laundry room. Animals don't dig us ghosts much. I hope that isn't going to be a problem.

But Olivia let the dogs out to pee and never even noticed the break-in. That made me so frustrated, I just Thrashed Out and knocked over the whole damned lot of pictures.

Made a mess, but woke her up. Then when she spotted my upside-down photo, she did take off the back of the frame and find the snapshot and key. I learned something there. A little Lesson in the Afterlife, Hon. Getting emotional helps us ghosts make contact.

So I'm getting stronger now. Strong enough to leave another message for Olivia. Frankie's name. Gotta to be careful, though, (so I hear) not to get Too Real and be trapped in that world again.

MARCH 31
Things to Do Today

Reorganize clothes closet—not worn 1 yr, dump!
Dog licenses
Appt groomer
Call auction house. Name?
USv99-1899? refers to?
Which bank?

Spring hadn't exactly arrived but seemed poised to sail in, like Botticelli's Venus on the scallop shell. Olivia began to look with distaste at the scratchy wool suits in her closet, but as a provisional New Englander, she knew it was still too early to pack them in herbal *Moth A-way*. Just to get a start on the coming season's fresh colors, she paged through her spring suits hanging in plastic shrouds in the smaller guest room's closet. She could perhaps take out the cool colors. She might meet some terrific Mr. Right at C C & S. Olivia admitted to herself that she was truly finished with Hank (no more casseroles in absentia) and ready to begin again. It wouldn't do to look like someone's maiden aunt in sensible woolens.

The complementary scarves were neatly folded in the guest bureau drawer. She'd make a start on her spring wardrobe by airing the navy and green linen suits and moving the scarves to the Italian chest she'd bought at auction.

And that's how Olivia discovered the wrinkled white envelope lying on the green silk lining of the chest. *Incredible... am I going nuts, or what?* She'd examined the inside of the chest during the auction preview, and she was willing to swear it was absolutely empty. Would someone at the cashier's desk have discarded the envelope, tossed it into the nearest receptacle? Why, when there was a perfectly good wastebasket under the registration table?

Removing the envelope with two fingers as if it were a dead bug, she looked it over. A name and address were written on it with what looked like a ballpoint pen, but it appeared to have been dragged through muddy water, because the writing was faded and blotched. Olivia could, however, just make out the name. *Frank Rossi.*

Later, when Olivia had finished freshening up her work wardrobe, she sat down at the laptop in her office to read e-mails, which proved to be worthless stock tips, questionable dating services, misdirected penis enlargement schemes, and threatening chain letters to which she would never respond no matter how much bad luck or lost miracles might result.

Wishing for a real note from a real person, she idly keyed the name Frank Rossi into the Google search link. There were 140,000 replies in 39 seconds. Then she narrowed the search to Frank Rossi Boston Massachusetts, knocking off nearly 40,000 hits. Her eye ran down the first page entries, 1 to 10, and, for some reason, fixed on number 7.

Olivia clicked on the heading and brought up the *Boston Globe* home page. In order to read the entire article, she had to register her personal information and pay a small fee. Still, she proceeded. The article appeared on her screen, dated the previous April.

FEDERAL WITNESS KILLED IN HIT-AND-RUN. Frank Rossi, CPA with the firm of Paolucci & Desanto, Inc., subpoenaed to appear before the Grand Jury investigating an alleged tax fraud perpetrated by Angelo Benedetto, Jr., was struck and killed in a hit-and-run accident yesterday morning as he attempted to cross the parking lot in the custody of two police officers, Sergeants Nathan O'Leary and Tom McCrudden, on their way to Boston Courthouse. O'Leary, suffered a broken leg, the other officer was unharmed.

Witnesses to the accident said a black van with tinted windows "roared out of nowhere," plowed into the victims, and raced off. Officer McCrudden took down the license number of the vehicle, which was found later that day abandoned in New Jersey. A homicide investigation is underway.

The Benedetto hearing has been postponed until Federal prosecutors can reconstruct their case after the loss of a witness whose testimony was considered crucial.

The news item was illustrated by a grainy photo of the victim, who seemed vaguely familiar. Where had she seen him before? Olivia peered at the picture more closely but nothing came to her mind, which was almost completely absorbed in the problem of what the envelope was doing in her Italian chest in the first place and what made her think this might be the same Frank Rossi when there were over 100,000 such hits in Google. If Olivia believed in intuition, she would have admitted to a strong hunch that there was a connection between the mystery envelope and the dead witness.

Olivia shook her head, as if to rid herself of these troubling thoughts. Many a puzzle could be solved if one went about investigating it in a methodical manner. The first step, she thought, was to find out the name of the restless woman in the Art Deco frame, who was, after all, the former owner of the Italian chest with the oddly appearing envelope. Yes, that would be a good start.

☙

"Bill Byatt's Auction," said the voice of an older woman answering Olivia's call.

"Hi. This is Olivia Andreas. I think you'll find my name on your mailing list, or it might be under Olivia A. Robb. I often receive your brochures in the mail. I bought a few things at your auction on March 13."

"Everything was sold 'as is,' dearie," the woman said crisply. "Except gold, sterling silver, and precious stones. Those we guarantee."

"This isn't a complaint," Olivia hastened to reassure her. "All the items that particular night seemed to be the possessions of one person. I thought I recognized her from one of the photos. She might be someone I went to school with, and I was just curious. I wonder if you'd tell me her name."

"Wait a minute." The woman sighed. Olivia could hear the phone being put down, the squeak of a file drawer, a rattle of papers. "Lily Lamoureaux, it says here. But I think that might have been a stage name. The sellers were heirs—cousins, I believe. Plunkett."

"Oh yes, of course. Lily Plunkett." Olivia feigned recognition. "Do you have their address? I'd like to get in touch with the family, express my condolences and all."

"Just the firm that handled the sale. Crowe, Crabbe, and Savage. I think they're on Court Street in Plymouth. Do you need the phone number?"

Olivia smiled to herself. The South Shore was a small world indeed. Next week she'd have unlimited access to the firm's records, to those mercenary Plunkett cousins, and to Lily—*who was Lily and why was she turning upside down in her frame?* Olivia, a Virgo and a fact-checker, didn't believe in an afterlife, reincarnation, ghosts, and other paranormal gibberish, but a number of enigmas had insinuated themselves into her orderly life, like an infestation of some rare beetle that must be tracked to its lair and exterminated—before it marched out of control through everything that was hers.

APRIL 1
Things to Do Today

List for Lowenstein
Watch video again, start leash training
USv99 Foreign zip? license plate? safe combination? bank acc.?
Check garden tools in garage—new weed whip?
Work on personal improvement list—tighten abs or learn French

On Wednesday Detective Lowenstein got around to returning her call and made an appointment to view the place where she'd found the flashlight on the ground, and other details of the foiled break-in. Olivia didn't think she needed to dress up for this interview. Dave Lowenstein probably didn't fit the twelve criteria for Mr. Right that she'd jotted in her personal control journal. He was reasonably attractive in a rough way, true, and maybe intelligent, possibly with a sense of humor. But there was no way of knowing on short acquaintance about the rest of the criteria: *single, monogamous, fiscally prudent, robustly healthy, no family idiots, not a fan of Country & Western, acid rock, or polkas, good with children and animals, et cetera.* Jeans with a blue silk shirt, she decided. Casual but not dowdy.

The detective got no farther than a foot on the front door step before Olivia's new early warning system alerted her with vociferous barking. It took some persuading to get Bruno and especially Sadie into the fenced backyard so that Olivia could open the front door.

Appearing without his partner this time, Dave Lowenstein grinned at her in such a foolish manner that it made her wonder for an instant about that potential for idiot genes. Still, he *was* rather good-looking, with soft, kind brown eyes, a generous mouth, and dark hair unsuccessfully slicked out of its natural curliness. Almost the same height as Olivia, maybe one or two inches taller, with a sturdy muscular build.

"That's quite a crime deterrent system you've got there," he said, following her into the living room where the April sun shone through the windows with a false show of warmth. "Where were those canine characters when we interviewed you the first time?"

"Bruno and Sadie. They're new here," Olivia explained over her shoulder. "I adopted them from Shawmutt Pound. We're going to watch out for each other, and judging by what happened the other night, they know their job." As the detective sat comfortably on the sofa, she noticed with annoyance that some strange white things seemed to be scattered across its flower-patterned fabric. What have the dogs torn up now? Their trip to the groomer's had left them in a rather excitable state. For that matter, the groomer, a burly fellow with *Semper Fi* tattooed on his forearm, had not been in a very good humor either.

"Probably a very sound idea, if you don't mind the mess, noise, and being tied to their schedule," Lowenstein said.

"Dogs can be trained not to be pests. Don't you like animals?" She felt stupid for asking, but this was one of her important criteria.

"If they like me," he replied noncommittally, taking his notebook and pen from an inner pocket in his tweed jacket. "So, now ... what happened here this time? And did you ever figure out why someone would want to make off with your photo album? When we were here before, you hadn't missed anything." He turned a page back in his notebook. "But you called in later to report the theft. Anything else turn up stolen since?"

"No, nothing. And I haven't a clue as to why that album of all things. But it wasn't your ordinary, run-of-the-mill photo album. I only paid twenty dollars for it at the auction, but it was a beautiful specimen of Victorian workmanship with wonderful old photos inside. Red-velvet cover. *Our Family* embossed in gold on the cover. I was going to display it on my coffee table."

"That's a romantic notion," the detective commented.

"Is it?" Olivia was annoyed. "More aesthetic than romantic, I would say."

"Well, they weren't your relatives, were they?"

"No, of course not. But such interesting faces. Some of the groupings had an immigrant look. I never did get to see if anything was written on the backs of the pictures, like when and where they were taken."

"What ethnicity, then?"

"Oh, possibly European. We'll never know, though. Unless you recover the album, that is. Not much chance of *that*, is there?"

Olivia thought this remark made the detective uncomfortable. Probably all too true. So she changed the subject to the matter of the most recent break-in, the one the dogs had foiled.

Not wanting to omit any vital evidence, Olivia had made a list of the events of two nights ago, and now she read them aloud in the order in which they occurred. During her recitation, Olivia noticed that Lowenstein only jotted down two or three lines. He had nice hands, long fingers, no rings. She imagined their grasp was warm and firm. Shaking her head to clear her brain of such stray thoughts, she began to wonder why he didn't make more notes. *Perhaps he has a prodigious memory*, she thought. *Or maybe he's just a lazy oaf who relies on informers to solve his cases.* Olivia enjoyed crime news, as well as detective fiction and film noir, and she'd concluded from her reading of the daily papers that most felons, and even spies, are caught by some chance occurrence rather than by true detective work.

"I'm impressed with your thoroughness, Miss Andreas." Lowenstein closed his notebook and stuffed it back in his jacket.

"Actually, it's Mrs. Robb. Or it was. But I'm thinking of going back to my maiden name. Perhaps with a Ms. rather than Miss. But that's neither here nor there, is it?"

Lowenstein looked at her steadily. "Yes, you informed us of the divorce after the first break-in. We spoke to Mr. Robb at that time. Sometimes it's just the husband looking for his favorite fishing rod or some CDs he forgot to pack. But Mr. Robb was at work all day, as verified by his co-workers and supervisor. Big day selling homes and all."

After this lame conversation petered out, Olivia took Lowenstein to view the pantry window, then upstairs to see the frames whose glass had been broken. She did not, however, reveal the second snapshot hidden behind Lily Plunkett's smiling visage. If she told him that the woman's photo had turned itself upside-down, he would think she was batty. By now she had nearly convinced herself that she'd imagined the strange occurrence anyway. Weird things like that just didn't happen in the real world. The envelope was genuine enough, though. *Frank Rossi.* Olivia was tempted to ask Lowenstein if he knew about the hit-and-run, but she decided *not yet.*

Lowenstein accepted her tentative offer of coffee, which Olivia, who left little to chance, had already brewed and was keeping hot in the kitchen beside a tray with creamer and sugar at the ready. But Lowenstein drank his coffee black, as she did. When Olivia filled his cup, she noticed a rather pleasant outdoorsy scent hovering around the detective— something like new mown grass. While he sipped, she asked him if any of the other people who bought items at the Plunkett auction had reported break-ins. Although his expression was skeptical, the detective promised he'd get a list of their names and addresses from Byatt and cross-check against reports of recent B & Es.

After coffee, Olivia grabbed Bruno and Sadie (whose antipathy toward Lowenstein's intrusion was unswerving) and closed them into the garage so that the detective could survey the back fence where the flashlight had been found. He seemed surprised when she suggested that he have the flashlight dusted for fingerprints. Apparently he wasn't prepared with proper plastic evidence bags either, so holding the flashlight gingerly, she dropped it into a gallon food storage bag and presented it to him.

Lowenstein smiled his thanks, gazing at her intensely, which to her annoyance, made Olivia flush. He *did* have sympathetic eyes. Probably made it easier for him to extort confessions from criminals. "Take good care of yourself," he said, handing Olivia his card. "And give me a call right away if anything else strange happens. My pager and home numbers are on the back."

Home number? Might that mean he's single? Olivia wondered.

When she let Sadie and Bruno back into the house, they ran around wildly, sniffing every footprint Lowenstein had made, the sofa where he'd sat, the cup he'd drunk from. She picked up the cup and the white things on the sofa that she'd noticed earlier. Not tissues or pieces of paper as she had thought. They were soft and bruised. They were white petals, actually. Tentatively, Olivia smelled them. Lily petals. "This is crazy," Olivia said.

That night Olivia dreamed she was still married to Hank, and they were out together at some boozy club. There was a girl at the table with them, someone Olivia knew but couldn't quite remember. When Hank spoke to the girl, he leaned forward and put his hand on her knee, then up her skirt between her legs, all the while conversing as if it was nothing out of the ordinary. In the dream, Olivia was not so much furious as embarrassed. When she woke up, however, she felt a genuine flare of anger dampened by a lingering sense of loneliness. But there was, at least, something companionable about Sadie's curled-up figure and Bruno's snores, and they smelled a lot better since their baths. Disinfected rather than doggy. Reassuringly flealess. Olivia dozed off for an hour, but at five-thirty was suddenly so wide awake she knew she might as well get out of bed and clean something.

While the coffee was making, Olivia started in on the pantry, deciding to clear one whole shelf to store canned dog food, biscuits, treats, vitamins, and canine medicines. The two dogs, who had stirred reluctantly when she padded downstairs, were now sitting side by side on their haunches in the kitchen and looking at her with mute hope in their eyes. *They're beginning to look like mismatched siblings*, Olivia mused. *I suppose it wouldn't hurt to feed them a little breakfast.*

"You guys like scrambled eggs?" she asked.

APRIL 6
Things to Do Today

How to identify men in snapshot?
Investigate Plunkett estate—and Lily!
Lily petals—consult parapsychologist?
Rake out borders for perennials etc.

"Aren't you going to invite me over to meet your new puppies?" Jamie's voice sounded raspy, as if she'd had one too many martinis at lunch. Olivia, who'd munched a sandwich in her car after dashing home to let Bruno and Sadie out for a few minutes, was now back at her new post, delving deeply into the problems of the antiquated C C & S filing system.

"Not quite yet," she advised Jamie. "They're just getting used to things, strangers at the door and all. They'll bark at you." Actually, during Olivia's lunch break, they chased away the UPS man, who'd hurled her spring order from the Burpee gardening catalog right over the fence before he sprinted back into the safety of his truck. He had a good aim, too. The package of seed envelopes and tiny perennials had landed upright and square in the middle of the front steps. Maybe lobbing packages so that they fell upright was a regular part of UPS driver training, Olivia had thought as she'd hollered an apology at the departing truck.

"Nonsense. Anyone who knows dogs expects a little barking. Besides, I want to hear all about that cute detective," Jamie said.

"How do you know he's cute? You've never seen him," Olivia parried.

"I could tell by the way you blushed when I asked you about him before."

"I don't think he's very methodical—for a detective, that is. But he does exude a pleasant scent, like a freshly cut lawn."

"That's a sex scent, Liv. Male musk. So, watch yourself." Jamie laughed raucously. Olivia was not amused. "Anyway, by your standards, no one ever could be methodical enough. So... are you inviting me over for a drink after work, or not?"

"Okay," Olivia said without enthusiasm. She'd been planning on raking borders until dark. Brooding about those perennials awaiting planting made Olivia think about the petals. "Maybe you can help me with a little problem I'm having."

"Sure. What?"

"Lily petals. I keep finding lily petals around the house. If I believed in ghosts, which I don't, I might think that Lily Lamoureaux—or Plunkett—was trying to contact me. But that's nonsense. You remember Lily—the woman with that stunning white mink coat whose portrait I bought at the auction? You bought her watches. I'll be home by five-thirty. Give me a chance to get the dogs into the yard, so let's say six. Oh, and plan on dinner, too. I still have a lot of mystery casseroles that I need to thaw and use up. I've been feeding them to Bruno and Sadie, but there are still so many of them packed in the freezer after my last cooking binge."

"Gee—casserole roulette and the ghost of lilies past. I can hardly wait. See you at six."

Before she went home that afternoon, Olivia managed to find the Plunkett file, photocopy most of it, and tuck it into her briefcase for later study. *What a spy I would have made*, she thought as she drove home for the second time that day, a little smile hovering over her lips.

Pleased to see her but not effusive about it, Bruno and Sadie headed right for the back door and got shunted into the fenced yard to relieve themselves while Olivia consulted her list of the cellar freezer's contents, which was somewhat academic since the labels had peeled off. Peeking under a foil corner, she took out something pinky-brown that might be the chicken stew and a brick-shaped package that could be one of several meat loaves the list itemized. Time and a 300-degree oven would tell what was what. Buttered noodles went with anything, and, of course, a salad. Maybe that chocolate cake, too, if she could find it.

Depositing assorted foil packages on the kitchen counter, Olivia went into the dining room where French doors overlooked a newly blossoming magnolia and two gamboling dogs in the backyard. Sadie had taken hold of a long slender branch fallen from the river birch tree and was teasing Bruno into a tug-of-war. Smiling, Olivia opened the china cabinet to take out wine glasses.

She heard herself screaming in a shrill piercing wail. Surprise, like a giant hand, pushed her abruptly into the nearest dining room chair. Right there in front of her wide eyes, set neatly on the shelf between rows of glasses, was the framed portrait of Lily! *How did it get downstairs?* Olivia's heart fluttered like a seabird trapped in ice as she tried to make sense out of this scary new phenomenon. Maybe she walked in her sleep carrying Lily's portrait? Had someone else been in the house since yesterday? Not likely, with Bruno and Sadie on guard duty. Becoming aware of her own short, shallow gasps, she forced herself to breathe more quietly and deeply. Breathing slowly from the diaphragm, the Zen masters taught, dissipated feelings of fear.

With her attention turned inward as she struggled for control, Olivia hardly noticed the time until a fearful barking outdoors alerted her to Jamie's arrival. Opening the front door, Olivia found her friend sitting on the hood of the old white Volvo she drove, clutching a bottle of wine under each arm, with a small tote bag dangling from her fingers, while Bruno and Sadie, were leaping at the 5-foot picket fence that bordered the front walk.

"Down! Down, you bad, bad dogs!" said Olivia faintly. She was still too shocked by Lily's traveling photo to assume her assertive dog-training stance. "It's okay, Jamie. They're not going to jump over."

"Thanks, but I think I'll wait for you to escort me."

"Don't say I didn't warn you. But I think you'll find they're really very gentle when you get to know them." Olivia put an arm around Jamie and walked her into the house, which seemed to make Sadie even more suspicious. The smaller dog snarled and jumped higher than before, her head and shoulders appearing over the fence like a jack-in-the-box. Between ill-behaved dogs and unexplained phenomena, Olivia felt as if the comforting routines of her life were slipping away, leaving her mired in chaos. Problems were supposed to have solutions, step-by-step procedures leading to the restoration of order. But perhaps this was Step One—enlisting Jamie's help.

Jamie had brought Olivia a gift, two videos to add to her collection of prized oldies—*The Ghost and Mrs. Muir* and *The Uninvited*. "I know you usually prefer crime *noir*, but maybe these will give you some pointers on how to exorcise Lily," she said.

"Speaking of Lily, listen to this—something else happened. So uncanny, it really took my breath away." While opening Jamie's wine, Olivia told her friend about the eerie photo that turned itself upside down in its frame and then moved from her office to the dining room downstairs. As she had with the detective, Olivia omitted the detail about the snapshot and key hiding behind Lily's picture.

They carried the bottle into the dining room, where Jamie viewed the traveling photo skeptically. "Are you sure you didn't put this here and then forget you did it? You have been a little preoccupied lately. And no wonder, with break-ins and whatnot."

Olivia took two glasses out of the cabinet, carefully avoiding the framed woman who now appeared to be leering. She poured the Merlot, and handed one glass to Jamie. "Yes, I am absolutely sure. Well, here's to solving mysteries! Now let's take these into the living room, and you sit down while I let in the dogs. That way they'll know you're an invited guest."

"Oh, yeah? What if they want to see my invitation? Listen, why don't you give me a few munchies I can throw their way while I'm making friends."

Bruno was easily mollified by the dog treats, but Sadie kept barking, moving closer and closer to Jamie in an effort to scare away the intruder. Olivia had to be quite assertive and strict before Sadie gave up her intimidation and crouched at Jamie's feet. The dog remained alert to her quivering ear tips. Jamie tossed her a treat from time to time, which she snapped up instantly.

"Would you please refill my glass. I'm afraid to get up," said Jamie. "Listen, there's a woman I know of who might be able to help you with this Lily thing—the teleporting portrait, ectoplasmic lily petals, and all. She's an American Indian shaman channeler. Wampanoag. Florrie Mitchell, but her professional name is Moon Deer."

"Oh, *please*," Olivia protested, pouring more wine for them both. "I'm not quite that desperate. Anyway, I've brought home all the C C & S papers on the Plunketts. After dinner, we can go over them together, maybe find a clue to what's going on here."

"For a psychic mystery you need a psychic detective not a bunch of legal papers," Jamie said.

"But I don't believe in psychic mumbo-jumbo," Olivia objected. A bell in the kitchen rang. "Oh, that's dinner. Come on, you can help me bring the dishes into the dining room."

"Well, this mumbo-jumbo happens to have jumped into your lap—like a cat always jumps on the one person who doesn't fancy felines. Do you think it's safe for me to move?"

Olivia glanced at the dogs. They were flopped over and appeared to be sleeping. Sadie's ears were still perky, but her eyes were shut and her hips relaxed. "Safe as houses," Olivia said. Sadie opened one eye and rolled it toward Jamie but didn't stir when the visitor got up to help carry dishes. Only the fragrance of meat loaf wafting out of the kitchen brought the two dogs to life. They trotted into the dining room to position themselves near the new person, in case Jamie might prove careless about dropping food to the floor.

After dinner, having taken a tray of coffee and chocolate cake into the living room, the two women read through the papers in Olivia's briefcase, which revealed that Lily Lamoureaux (a. k. a. Plunkett), who died without writing a will, was a distant cousin indeed from the several inheriting family members, not all of whom were named Plunkett. Besides her Boston apartment and its contents, her estate had included a bank account of over $75,000, certificates of deposit amounting to another $9,000, and a safe deposit box in the Boston Private Bank and Trust that contained, $50,000 in cash, several pieces of jewelry appraised for another $15,000, personal letters, a passport, some keys, and a Smith & Wesson .38.

"I wonder if that gun was registered," Olivia said. "Possibly not." She also wondered if the key she'd found in Lily's photo related to the safe deposit box in the Boston Private Bank and Trust. Why go to such lengths to hide a key that might be in frequent use? Olivia kept her own safe deposit box key in her jewelry box. The suspicion arose in her mind that this might be a second safe deposit box unknown to the heirs. Wouldn't that be a hoot!

Jamie was more interested in the jewelry than the gun, unregistered or not. "An 18-inch strand of matched pearls! A diamond tennis bracelet. *Those* never made it to the auction," she exclaimed. "Probably sold directly to a dealer in estate jewelry. Quite a haul for those third cousins twice removed! What do you supposed Lily died of?" She finished the last bite of chocolate cake with a sigh of satisfaction. Olivia felt a twinge of envy that her well-rounded friend never seemed to fret over fattening food.

"I figured you would be able to find that out for me," suggested Olivia.

"I'll see what I can do," Jamie promised. "But just being a nurse doesn't entitle me to access patient records indiscriminately."

"Don't you have any friends in the coroner's office?"

"Not exactly. But I do have one contact who might ..."

"I *knew* I could count on you."

∾

Dave Lowenstein called twice to inquire if there had been any more worrying incidents. The second time he seemed quite chatty, asking about her job at C C & S, and if the dogs are settling in okay to their new life. "Pit bulls can be a problem," he warned. "Some neighborhoods don't want them around."

"I'm fairly certain that Sadie wasn't bred for fighting. She's quite friendly with Bruno. And I'm careful that they never roam free."

"So, how about you? Do you get a chance to roam free from time to time?"

Olivia laughed without answering. She suspected he was attracted to her and might soon ask her out. It could be a blessing right now to have a detective taking a personal interest in her life. Also, she'd had very few dates since her divorce became final. Actually, one occasion had nearly been a date-*rape*, but Olivia's strong muscular build and quick knee action had saved her. That asshole had got off easy with a little cramping.

But Olivia was lonely, and Lowenstein was a really appealing man. If not *Mr. Right*, at least he might prove to be a pleasing *Mr. Right Now*.

THE LISTENER

Lee Washington was listening to hour after hour of tapes recorded from wiretaps in the walls of the Benedetto Fruit Company office. It was Washington's job to analyze what he heard and decide whether it had any relevance to ongoing racketeering investigations or might be the basis of an entirely new line of inquiry. This he would summarize in a report to his boss, Randall Glumm, who basically didn't want to know anything that would stir the pot too much. Washington was more than half convinced a climate of racial prejudice at the Bureau was to blame for his getting stuck with this boring-as-shit assignment.

Day after day, he heard little that was meaningful or promising. It had become obvious to Washington that the subject had got wise to the wiretaps. Every time the conversation became remotely incriminating, Rosario Benedetto went for a walk. As he left the Fruit Company, The Rose often waved at the third floor windows of the building across the street where he knew that FBI agents were manning a camera aimed at the building in hopes of photographing Benedetto's criminal associates. Washington was aware of this little game of Benedetto's, and so was his boss Glumm.

Still, there was something curious about the incident Washington was now writing up in his report. A younger man's voice that Washington identified as belonging to Junior Benedetto had said, "Here's the other box of frames, boss." From the sounds that followed, The Rose must have been smashing whatever those frames were—artwork? photos?— while foully swearing, apparently not finding what he was after. Then he complained that two of his men had "missed something." Missed what? Where?

Junior had let drop something about an auction where one of the men had been sent to buy the frames. And he'd mentioned the name of the auction house. Byatt.

The Rose was looking for something, not finding it, and he was angry. Washington thought this might point to missing evidence that might be damning to the Benedettos. Wild guesses like that, however, were frowned on at the Bureau, and Washington's speculations were routinely buried by Randall Glumm. Okay, then, he'd report this possibility anyway, and let Glumm stick his head up his ass again.

Maybe Washington would just make a few calls on his own. Check out what auctions this Byatt had been running lately. He punched a few keys on his computer, ignoring the little voice in his head that warned him against taking initiative. A sure way to end up assigned to Nome or Tijuana. "Remember, LeRoy, curiosity lights the wick in the devil's candle," his straight-laced Mama often warned him when even as a youngster he would pry into local affairs best left alone.

Google turned up only one Byatt Auction House with a home page. The most recent Byatt auction was still listed under *Past Auctions*, and nothing about it rang a bell. Washington made a note of the Milton phone number.

The woman who answered his phone call was weary but obliging. She didn't even ask why he was interested in the winter schedule of auctions. Apparently, odd requests didn't faze her one bit. She recited the auctions' titles: January 30, Collectible Toys. February 13, The Franklin Reed Estate with Additions from Several Other Notable Local Estates. February 27, Fine Art and Important Prints. March 13, The Lily Lamoureaux Estate.

Lily Lamoureaux! Frank Rossi's girlfriend.

Bingo!

APRIL 8
Things to Do Today

Check out Florrie Mitchell
Lily's keys and letters—C C & S?
Who's in pic? Key to what?
Plant perennials, annual seeds
Review 5-year plan—add husb?

A few days later, Jamie called with notes from the coroner's report on Lily Plunkett. "The classic sudden death of a ghost," she declared. "Fell down the stairwell in her apartment building, four flights—died instantly, massive brain damage."

"Why ?"

"Why what?"

"Why did she fall down the stairwell?"

"Drunk probably. Cardiovascular system was normal. Her liver wasn't in great shape, but she probably didn't know that yet. Lily'd had a couple or three drinks. Sloe Gin Fizzes. The coroner guesses it could have been enough to impair her balance."

"What time? Did her neighbors hear anything?"

"Wait a minute." Olivia could hear Jamie rustling some papers. "Ah...about 2:30 AM No, but the guy next door complained about loud music coming from Lily's apartment. Thinks he may have heard her cry out. The body was found at the bottom of the stairs in a pool of blood. No one else in sight. Listen, Liv … it sounds legit to me. Let's not make a mystery out of a perfectly ordinary accident."

"Did they check for drugs?"

"Yes, of course. No controlled substance in her system."

"She may not have fallen. Someone may have beaten her to death at the foot of the stairs," Olivia said.

"The report said most of her injuries were consistent with a fall. A few facial bruises were questionable, but the bottom line verdict was accidental death. Liv, you've definitely been watching too many crime shows. Wild speculation is not like you. Who would do such a thing?"

"I don't know. But why is that photo drawing attention to itself? All right, I'll say no more."

That night, some stubborn streak induced Olivia to move Lily's photo back to the upstairs office where she'd first made a place for it. She lay awake for a while, listening for whatever weird thing might happen next, but the only sounds were Bruno's snores and occasional traffic. Sadie sighed and rolled over, her nose on the other pillow. Somehow Olivia felt comforted—it was almost like having a family.

She fell deeply asleep and dreamed of climbing a ladder into the sky where the clouds had formed a village peopled with giants. Spying a stranger in their midst, one giant began to bang a warning drum to alert the others. Frightened by the noise, Olivia forced herself to wake but the beat of the drum continued. The dogs woke, too, barking and running through the upstairs rooms. Olivia struggled out of bed and into her office, where she was jolted by the sight of Lily's photo hitting itself against the wall again and again. This was absolutely unbelievable. Olivia felt imprisoned inside some kind of waking nightmare. Her heart was a trapped bird fluttering in her throat. The terror she felt could stop her breath at any moment.

"Stop that! Stop that!" she yelled, her icy fingers pressed against her chest. Like a penny arcade machine running down, the portrait slowed its steady *whack, whack, whack,* finally coming to a dead stop and falling facedown on the shelf. It was as if the portrait could hear and react to Olivia's words, the most unsettling thing of all. This ghost was no illusion. The dead woman was coming to life while Olivia's world view was falling apart.

"In heaven's name, what do you want of me!" Olivia cried, fleeing from her office to the bedroom, pulling the coverlet over her head. But she knew sleep was impossible now. It was four in the morning, the hour of despair. The dogs were snuffling and whimpering, so she got up again and went downstairs to let them out for a few minutes. Everything looked so normal on the first floor, it made Olivia feel nearly herself as well. *Maybe a cup of cocoa*, she thought. She mixed up the powdered chocolate, sugar, and milk; it only took a minute to brew in the microwave. Carrying the steaming mug into the living room, she paused at the dark doorway. By the light from the hall, it seemed as if a figure was sitting in the wing chair facing the fireplace. In that one chilling vision, Olivia saw the gleam of blonde hair smoothly coiled, a shoulder wearing some white silky garment, a hand on the arm of the chair, a diamond tennis bracelet sparkling on the wrist, a suggestion of rings, at least two, on the pale fingers.

"Why me?" wailed Olivia.

She thought she heard a reply. *"Yoooou ... yoooou"* ... before the figure dematerialized, slowly, part by part—diamonds first, blonde chignon last.

In the midst of her glacial fear, Olivia glanced down to find that the mug had turned over in her hand pouring the cocoa over her slippers and staining the pale green carpet. Quickly, she kicked off the slippers. "Shit! I must be losing my mind," she exclaimed. Just then the dogs began clamoring at the kitchen door. Olivia hurried to let them in before they woke up the neighborhood. They rushed into the living room, right past the delicious puddle of cocoa to confront the wing chair. Only they didn't bark exactly. With their ears down, they crouched as they approached the place where the figure had appeared. They crept forward, scenting and yelping. Sadie reached the chair first. Suddenly she started up and threw back her head for an odd sort of pit bull howl that crackled through Olivia's nerves like a jolt of electricity. *If the dogs sense that Lily is here,* Olivia thought, *I'm not so crazy after all. I guess I've got myself two ghost detectors. Sort of like miners' canaries.*

By morning, a shimmering April dawn that shone gently and sensibly on the new grass and on a few tulips not yet trampled by the dogs, Olivia had nearly convinced herself that the photo thumping in the night and the wing chair apparition were dream-inspired illusions. Or maybe too much Merlot. But for a few days afterward, neither Sadie nor Bruno could be enticed into the living room, even with proffered liver tidbits. And despite all Olivia's scrubbing, a trace of the cocoa stubbornly remained in the rug, looking like dried blood.

LILY

I did it! I did it! Damned if I didn't appear right in Olivia's living room. ("Living room"—that's a laugh.) And you know what it felt like, Hon? Like Walking Blind through a bunch of wet sheets hanging on a clothesline. But I just kept pushing through, and by Christ, I did it.

I wish everyone weren't so scared of those of us who have Passed Over. Olivia spilled her cocoa, and the puppies went Ga-Ga. I mean, I know I'm no angel but I'm not a monster either. Really, My Kind are harmless, Hon.

But that's okay. I made my point. I'm going to be Hanging Around until my death and Frankie's are avenged. Yeah, I remember now that Frankie got run down so he wouldn't testify against that punk Junior. I told Frankie we should get out of town before the Grand Jury convened, but he said "out of town" wasn't far enough. He wanted to vamoose with me to a New Country and start a New Life. But first, he was going to take care of the Benedettos in his own way.

Well, we're in a New Country, now. It's Never Too Late, as we say here in the Timeless Zone. But I'll be surprised if it's not too late for Olivia's wall-to-wall. She'll never get that cocoa stain out.

APRIL 9
Things to Do Today

Library for? historic ghosts?
Carpet stain remover
Re-check L.P. files
Look up cousins in phone book, Google etc.
Practice leash training before 1ˢᵗ obed. cl.
Call Lowenstein—other break-ins?

Bringing C C & S's records into the 21ˢᵗ century was an assignment made-to-order for Olivia's talents, and incidentally for her investigation of Lily, which she hoped was not bordering on the obsessive. As soon as she had a few unsupervised minutes at C C & S, Olivia went through the Plunkett file again. Having copied all the papers relevant to Lily's estate, she now wanted to make certain she hadn't overlooked anything. The contents of the safe deposit box had been turned over to the Plunketts, of course—the letters, the keys, the .38 (legal or illegal?) and more significantly to the heirs, the $50,000 in cash. Why does a woman keep so much cash earning no interest? Unreported income? Hush payments? Getaway money? And what about those heirs? Shouldn't Olivia look into their backgrounds, too?

All that remained in Lily's file that Olivia hadn't copied were the dead woman's personal papers: driver's license; Brockton High School transcript; birth certificate of Bernice Lily Plunkett 1973; death certificate, "massive head injuries;" and an invoice from the funeral parlor for a cremation service. *Poor Lily! Not a glamorous academic career, not a grieving family, not a beautiful funeral. I wonder where they dumped her ashes.* With all the goodies those Plunkett relatives inherited, Lily should be enshrined in an alabaster jar on some cousin's mantelpiece. Olivia remembered a gold-washed jar at the auction, brimming with matchbooks from exotic restaurants and clubs. She peered more closely at the high school transcript, a shiny, nearly illegible reduction with a postage-stamp photo of Lily in the upper right corner—long straight brown hair and that smile, not yet the practiced allure of the later Lily, but definitely seductive for a teen-ager. *Class of '91—I should be able to find a yearbook. But why? Why am I being haunted by this complete stranger?* Olivia considered letting the whole matter drop—forget Lily, throw out the photo and the snapshot and key behind it, return to her rational, predictable life, and think about taking a cruise, maybe meeting someone who would fit her twelve criteria for *Perfect Husband*.

But later that morning, while members of the office staff were milling around the coffee station, Olivia found herself searching through the computer's yellow pages for the phone number and location of Florrie Mitchell. The woman's name was listed, not as an American Indian shaman channeler, but as the proprietor of a gift shop called the Moon Deer in Plymouth Center. Although Olivia was certain she'd never call on Florrie to channel Lily or any such nonsense, Olivia decided just to stop in during her lunch break anyway and have a look at this shaman character.

The Moon Deer was only a few blocks away from C C & S, just around the corner on a charming little lane within sight of the ocean. Swinging in the breeze, the painted sign was of a glowing white deer. The shop's windows sparkled; the inviting displays featured a man's feathered war bonnet and a woman's white doeskin dress. Arranged around these were beaded belts, turquoise and silver jewelry, handmade baskets, decorated pottery, and other artifacts. Nothing in the window was priced. *Classy!* Olivia went inside.

A broad-faced older woman with fine high cheekbones and black hair pulled back into a bun sat behind the register reading *The Wall Street Journal.* She looked up at Olivia with shrewd dark eyes and a faint smile. "Is there something special I can show you?" she asked.

The shop was pleasantly fragrant, like the scent of a soft wind riffling over a grassy meadow. The cool, shadowy interior combined indirect lighting and muted spotlights to show off displays of jewelry, baskets, handbags, quillwork and beadwork. A rhythmic chanting music played softly in the background.

"Are you Florrie Mitchell?"

"Yes, I am. Ah ... are you here to arrange a craft demonstration? No, I see you have something more serious on your mind."

These fortune-teller types are masters at guessing, Olivia thought. Although she was not given to intuitive first impressions, Olivia rather liked the look of the Mitchell woman. She reminded Olivia of a retired character actress; someone who still retained a confident stage presence, perfect diction, and a significant bank account.

"A friend suggested that you might help me with a problem I'm having. As a shaman, that is. Of course, I may be just the victim of an over-active imagination," Olivia began.

"Somehow I doubt that." The woman's gaze was direct, interested, but not avidly so. "What your friend's name?"

"Jamie Andrews. Or you may know her by her married name, Jamie Finch, but she's gone back to Andrews now." Olivia knew she was babbling but went right on doing it anyway. "I don't believe in an afterlife, you see, and certainly not in ghosts. Yet recently I've had some strange occurrences in my home. They seem to be centered around a photo I bought at auction. Well, I didn't actually buy the photo. I bought the silver frame." Olivia waited for a question that didn't come, then answered it anyway. "I felt sorry for the woman in it. So many of her personal photos were being dumped at that auction, no one to value them, selling all those smiles for their frames. I thought I'd keep the woman's picture on a shelf with my own family photos. I suppose that was a whimsical thing to do—especially for me, since I've never gone in much for whimsy." Olivia paused for breath.

"Jamie Andrews...oh, yes," Florrie Mitchell said. "She nursed my mother in her last days at home. A caring, thoughtful person. Full of fun, too." Mrs. Mitchell put away the newspaper and picked up a half-finished basket. She began to thread a plait of sweet grass through its spokes. "So, then what happened? Photo began to bang around, did it?"

Is she still guessing? Olivia wondered. "Yes, and that's not all. Once it turned itself upside down in the frame. Then it traveled downstairs to the china cabinet in the dining room. And there are all those lily petals. I keep finding lily petals scattered around the house."

"Lily petals?"

"The woman in the photo was named Lily. Lily Plunkett. I happened to come across some information about her. She died from a fall in her apartment building. And then, too, I had this break-in, someone searching through my things. But he only took one thing—a red velvet Victorian photo album. Lily's album."

"That's something different, now." Mrs. Mitchell looked up from her work with a glint of curiosity. "Talk to the police, did you? But didn't mention the photo and the lily petals?"

"Yes. To both," Olivia admitted.

"And there's something more. Something you haven't told anyone."

"Yes."

"I don't need to know what it is. It may be important for you to keep silent on that matter. At least, for now. How exactly may I help you?"

"Could you...do you...*communicate?*"

"You mean with the ghost you don't believe in?"

Embarrassed and a little annoyed, Olivia felt herself flush. "I really need some help here. I'm beginning to see the ghost woman. At least, I did see her once. And the dogs saw something, too. Sadie and Bruno. That's how I know I'm not crazy."

Mrs. Mitchell looked down at her basket, weaving the sweet grass in and out, in and out. Finally she said, "Let me check my appointment calendar."

Putting the basket aside, she opened a leather-bound book on the desk and ran a thin dark finger over the entries. She was wearing a very fine turquoise ring on her right hand, and on the other an impressive diamond in a platinum setting. Olivia began to worry about money. Will she charge by the hour like a lawyer? "May I ask about your fee, Mrs. Mitchell?"

The woman didn't suggest that Olivia call her Florrie or Moon Deer. "It depends on what I find is going on with Lily, and what I may have to do. It's not a good thing for the dead to haunt the living. It creates an emptiness like antimatter, a black hole in the fabric of life. The dead have to travel the Sunset Path." Florrie Mitchell said "path" with a long "a" like one of the Kennedys. "If Lily doesn't go to the West Wind on her own, I might have to give her a little uplift. But I'll need to evaluate the situation before I can give you an estimate."

An estimate indeed! It sounded to Olivia as if Florrie Mitchell were being asked to fix the plumbing or paint the living room. Still, the woman's business-like approach was commendable. Olivia's suspicious nature felt sufficiently mollified. She wasn't going to be made the victim of some psychic confidence game.

"And if we need a sweat lodge, that will be extra, of course," Florrie Mitchell said.

༄

Back at C C & S, Olivia worked diligently and guiltily on her recommendation for reorganizing the firm's records: warehousing the reams of paper generated by old court cases and converting current redundancies to a clean, viable system in perfect retrievable order. Perhaps she should stay a few extra weeks to oversee the changeover beyond her present commitment. Maybe even coast a little. With all the anxieties at home, there was no need to take on the challenge of a new job right now.

Being a consultant had its perks. Olivia left at four that afternoon. After a flying trip to the hardware store, she visited the library, where she literally grabbed off the shelf *Haunted Houses, U.S.A.* and a number of other books about ghost-hunting, hoping one of them might hold a nugget of valuable insight. She signed them out—fortunately the subjects were varied enough not to run afoul of the library's three-book rule—and hurried out the door to the van. As she tossed in her tote bag of books, it occurred to Olivia that her life seemed to have picked up speed, like a DVD film on fast forward.

Her answering machine was blinking, a promising little red pulse. She pushed the button and listened to Dave Lowenstein asking her to call him at the station between twelve and two tomorrow for an update on the Plunkett business. His deep, pleasant voice gave nothing away, not a flicker of excitement or disappointment or warmth. She played it again to make sure.

"I really appreciate your giving me an update. I realize you're not obligated to tell me anything, but I am *so* curious," Olivia confessed. Although it had taken several phone calls to track down Detective Sergeant Lowenstein, now that she had him on the line, he sounded happy to hear from her. Perhaps that was just the agreeable manner of a disarming interviewer. Olivia cautioned herself not to get her hopes up just because she sensed a flicker of attraction. She knew how a man was— he'd give you a big rush today, and tomorrow his attention would turn to someone else.

"So, how are the pups?" Lowenstein asked. "What are their names, now—Bonnie and Clyde?"

"Sadie and Bruno. Glad to be off death row. Hungry and feisty. Eager to protect the premises. But I didn't call to talk about my crime control unit."

"You want to know if anyone else from the auction reported a break-in or a robbery?

"Of course. You probably think I'm crazy to believe there's a link with the auction. I think so myself. I'm not used to operating on hunches, and it's making me uneasy," Olivia said.

The detective laughed, his chuckle so rich and warm that Olivia couldn't help smiling along. He said: "Don't quote me on this, but without hunches, few crimes would ever get solved. As a matter of fact, I did cross-check the auction's purchase records for March 13 with police reports, and there were two coincidences. A woman who purchased two sterling frames reported a burglary. She already owned a number of silver frames displayed on her fireplace mantle and on some tables. All were stolen, the Byatt buys and the older ones, along with some jewelry from her bedroom. And another report from the couple who bought the entertainment center for their Quincy apartment. Curious, isn't it?"

"Did the Quincy couple say anything was taken?" Olivia asked.

"The only thing the thieves took was some cash in the desk and a home video. Apparently it was stuck in back of one of the cabinets. The couple had already watched it, though. Probably thought it was hot stuff, some kind of turn-on. They described it as 'just a vacation video of some guys playing cards in a log cabin.' Taken through the porch window. They figured it was a fishing lodge because there was fishing gear leaning against the porch wall. They didn't recognize anyone in the video."

An image of the snapshot behind Lily's photo flickered through Olivia's mind. Would she mention it? *Maybe later.* She felt the power of information withheld, like cash under the mattress. "Yes, curious," she echoed, just to keep the conversation going.

"How much do you know about Lily Plunkett?" His tone was easy and conversational.

He's after something.

"Not too much," she hedged "I drew some conclusions, I guess, based on her collections and other belongings. All spread out there for the auction, you know."

"Still, you *are* working for Crowe, Crabbe, and Savage, the same law firm that handled the Plunkett estate," he commented, making his point with a deft needle.

Olivia was glad he couldn't see her face. She wasn't a really good liar. Lying was like quicksand—once you made that first misstep, no matter how valiantly you struggled to free yourself, you just sank deeper and deeper. She reminded herself there was no way he could know she'd read and copied everything in that file, unless she gave it away. "No kidding," she said. "How did you know I was at C C & S?"

"You told me. At our first interview. You explained that you are a consultant, and that you would start working at C C & S in a week or so. And you left the firm's phone number, which connects to a receptionist who announces the name of the firm."

"Oh, yes, I guess I did. So then, is there anything special I should know about Lily? Lily Plunkett?"

"A. k. a. Lily Lamoureaux, former Las Vegas showgirl. A. k. a. Lily Lamour, girlfriend of Frank Rossi, among other guys. Frankie was a CPA with the firm Paolucci & Desanto, Inc. They handle the financial affairs of the Benedetto family.

The boyfriend died in a suspicious hit-and-run just prior to being called to appear before the Grand Jury investigating an alleged tax fraud perpetrated by Angelo Benedetto, Jr."

"Benedetto? The name sounds familiar," Olivia said, just as if she weren't a major news hound, with a minor in crime and racketeering. "Rather a coincidence that Lily died not long after Frank, also by accident, don't you think?"

"You checked on her date of death?"

"Someone said it. At the auction."

"Well, don't make too much of it. There are such things as coincidences in the real world," Lowenstein said. *A little condescending.*

"I sure hope those gangsters have found what they were looking for." Thoughts of the hidden snapshot were like a tiny festering splinter. Could Lily's secret cache be the objective of these break-ins?

"We'll see. If the break-ins stop. You know what I'd like to do? I'd like to have another look at what else you bought at auction. Didn't you say there was a silver picture frame, too?"

Instantly, Olivia was of two minds. She really would like to see this attractive man again. On the other hand, what was he up to? "Sure," she said. "That would be fine. Sadie and Bruno are always looking for a little action." Why was she throwing these roadblocks in his way?

"What time do you get home?" He was unfazed by the pups—good!

"Around five or five-thirty. I don't punch a time clock. And sometimes I bring work home," she said. After all, she wasn't a file clerk.

"I'll be there at six, then. Give you a chance to feed the beasts first. If that's convenient. I promise I won't stay long."

His tone was coaxing. He really wanted to see her again. And it *was* personal.

The staff was coming back from lunch, laughing and chatting, checking e-mails. "Okay. See you later." She hung up fast and dove back into the ancient case records she was analyzing, all of which should be retired to a storage facility. She imagined how tidy, current, and functional C. C. & S's records were going to be when she got through, and it made her feel pleased with herself. She liked to leave everything in good order. So what was she doing with a ghost, a burglar, two dogs with attitudes, and a visiting detective who might be on the make?

ဢ

"Tonight you're going to make a new friend," Olivia explained to Sadie and Bruno, scooping chow into the new stainless steel dog dishes. "You can't just bark and jump at every visitor, or you'll be spending half your lives in the laundry room," she explained, splitting a can of Organic Sliced Turkey and Brown Rice between the two. She'd come home at four-thirty again, to give herself time to change into something casual and devastating—but lost her nerve on "devastating" and settled for beige linen slacks and a black silk blouse. Sadie and Bruno were throwing themselves into their dinners with ecstatic abandon.

Moving behind the counter in the hope that they wouldn't leap on her affectionately while their chins were dripping turkey gravy, she glanced into the dining room. Blood drained away from her head leaving her feeling faint and cold. She was looking at the silhouette of a woman gazing through the French doors into the backyard. An instant later the specter was gone, dissolved into the slanting rays of the sun. Olivia's limbs felt frozen; she couldn't have made a move right then if her life depended on it.

It took a few minutes to regain the use of her hands and feet so that she could put Sadie and Bruno outdoors. She had to coax them past the dining room door. Olivia felt reassured to know that the dogs, too, had sensed something weird in there. They seemed glad to bolt through the kitchen door into the backyard.

She was still moving in slow motion when the dogs fell into a frenzied barking that clued her to the arrival of Dave Lowenstein. She might never need a doorbell again. When she opened the door, he was standing outside his car, a dark red Bronco, grinning at her in a way that warmed her right through, like a fireplace on a snowy evening. He was carrying a box of biscuits for large dogs with the picture of a smiling collie on it. Lowenstein tossed a handful of biscuits over the fence, possibly thinking this would buy him several moments of quiet crunching while he sidled into the house.

It didn't. Sadie wouldn't touch them and growled at Bruno when he tried to take advantage of the largesse. Meanwhile, Olivia escorted Lowenstein down her front walk and into the living room, where she invited him with a gesture to sit down. At first he headed for the wing chair where she'd seen Lily's apparition, then unaccountably swerved and chose the black rocker that was too short for his long legs. Olivia was not surprised. There was an iciness still hovering around that wing chair.

"Would you like a beer, a glass of white wine, Perrier?" At six, the cocktail hour had begun all over the South Shore, while in its kitchens, seafood suppers were being poached, fried, baked or boiled alive. In Olivia's Frigidaire, a plate of sole fillets on ice awaited their sauté in butter and lemon; Olivia was planning to share tidbits from this humble feast with Bruno and Sadie, who were lying at ease now, their bellies sprawling on the cool evening grass.

Lowenstein accepted a Perrier, waved away the glass. He was looking at her again, drinking her in as thirstily as he guzzled the bubbling water. Poised on the edge of the sofa, Olivia took small sips of her wine. If her shining black hair were longer, she'd have been fussing with it now, but it was so short it never flew about or stuck out like a cowlick. Instead, she grabbed her no-nonsense round glasses, which she hardly needed anymore, put them on, and peered at the detective inquiringly. "It's your meeting," she reminded him briskly.

"Oh, sorry. Yes. I do want to see that framed photo again. But I have to confess, that's not all I want. I was wondering if you'd like to … if we could … do you like lobster? … how about sailing? There's a beach party Saturday—or if it rains, Sunday—a few other guys from our division, four or five couples, and me. Nothing too late or too wild."

Olivia smiled, hardly aware of how much that smile lit up her whole being so that even her olive skin took on a golden sheen. At last she knew where she was, her feet on a familiar path. The more Lowenstein stumbled about in asking her to go out with him, the more in control of the situation she felt. There was only the question of deciding what her answer would be.

LILY

Remember that song, "Love is lovelier the second time around"? Same with materializing, Hon. It was much easier this time. I simply wafted into Olivia's dining room on a surge of anger, thinking of Frankie's and my interrupted lives. Yeah, I suppose if he hadn't got the bright idea of copying those financial records for what he called "insurance," none of this would have happened. I don't know how the Benedettos found out, though. Another Friggin' Mystery. When I get my head on straight, maybe I'll remember who else was in my apartment, who might have heard or seen something.

They say Revenge is a Dish Best Served Cold. Well, I'm cold enough—ha ha—to carry on even without Frankie, if I can get this gal Olivia to give me a hand. Have to admit it, Hon ... there are some things only the living can do. So now Olivia should take that key and snapshot out of the frame and hide them before those bastards come after my photo again. But I doubt she'll think of it. I'm just going to have to keep an eye on that situation, maybe give Olivia a spectral nudge or two. Not that I aspire to be one of the Guardians or anything like that. Perish the Thought. No designer dress could possibly hang right over wings.

Which reminds me ... I've been told I'm going to get my white mink back in the Fullness of Time—whatever that means.

At least Olivia's on track with that key. Gotta give her a little hint, though. Otherwise she'll be looking for a bank in a haystack, so to speak.

They tell me I'd better hurry because I can't stick around here too long, if I ever want to Move Along and maybe see Frankie again. And where exactly is he, I'd like to know. Talk about being a Stranger in a Strange Land, that's me.

APRIL 12
Things to Do Today

Mail tax returns
Clean house, food shop, Perrier
Compare DL to husb priorities
List 10 fun things to do on dates
Internet search Benedettos, snapshot
Key, poss. banks?

Her beach date with Dave Lowenstein had been perfect in its imperfections of fizzled fires, half-cooked burgers, spilled wine, missed Frisbees and a tentative kiss tasting of sand and salt in the shadow of scraggy beach pines. If April hadn't chosen that very moment to live up to its reputation as the cruelest month with a sudden intense shower, who knows what might have happened, the way that kiss cut right through her sensible resolutions like lightning dazzling its way through a wall of clouds. It's a good thing that the storm ended their soggy beach party so abruptly or all her first date rules might have gone sailing off with the tide.

Driving home in Dave's Bronco, they'd been chaperoned by a chubby red-haired detective and his giggling wife who delighted in her husband's inexhaustible fund of anecdotes.

Ned and Ellen Parks, neighbors of Dave's needing a ride home to Marshfield, had been blissfully oblivious of intruding on a romantic interlude.

"How's it going at home—same old madhouse?" Parks had asked, leaning over to address his jovial question to Dave. The reply was a mute shrug as Olivia's date concentrated on the twists and turns of the dark, winding road.

"This is one brave man you got here," Ellen had tittered at Olivia, who wondered what they were talking about. It couldn't be a wife. Her internet research hadn't turned up a wife, present or ex.

Hearing Dave and Olivia at the front door, Bruno and Sadie had yelped, jumped, and frantically scratched at the wood panels on the other side of it. Still, he'd kissed her again, not at all tentative this time—a thorough, insistent, promising kiss—before letting her go just as she felt her body was dissolving into his.

It was his good-night kiss tasting of longing and discovery that Olivia had savored as she fell asleep after midnight in her big bed with Sadie curled up on the other pillow and Bruno snuffling into his blanket on the floor. And all the next day, finishing her regular weekend chores, dusting and mopping fluffy balls of dog hair, stocking up at the supermarket on canine goodies and fresh produce for the week, tenderly washing asparagus and strawberries, Olivia felt herself in a delicious daze, reliving that rain-swept embrace on her front doorstep.

On Sunday, she cleaned house with a frenzy worthy of a troop of Valkyries. No call from Dave only caused her to scrub with more vigor.

A full day at work on Monday spent in the morass of C C & S's filing system brought Olivia back somewhat from her turbulent state. After work there would be laundry to finish and dinner for her and the dogs to prepare, more mystery packages from the freezer.

Chores should always be completed before one is allowed to play around, Olivia believed, and internet searches definitely were a dessert to be enjoyed after one's plate was clean. So it was past seven-thirty in the evening before she got upstairs to her office and began her perusal of the Benedetto family saga as reported by the various media. What she was looking for now were photos, and she found them here and there among assorted alleged criminal acts and various dubious plea-agreements or outright acquittals. She printed out every photo from her color printer and filled a file folder with the Benedettos in camel's hair topcoats or black leather jackets, smiling benignly on court house steps or waving from Mercedes windows.

Gingerly picking up restless Lily in the silver frame from her office shelf, Olivia unscrewed the backing, and removed the little picture hidden there. It wasn't really a very clear likeness of the two grinning men with the fish hanging between them. It was only a small, wrinkled, faded black-and-white snapshot.

As she continued to click on one news article after another, Olivia did register one surprising hit. But it wasn't the picture of a Benedetto mobster that electrified her. It was U. S. District Court Judge Norman Millhouse's dignified, aquiline profile. Questioned by newsmen in yet another dismissal of charges against Junior Benedetto, he was quoted as declaring, "Yes, I do believe justice has been served. When the district attorney's office fails to supply sufficient evidence, a case cannot proceed to trial." The headline read, "Benedetto Freed, Judge Blames D.A."

Olivia studied the print-out of Millhouse, then the guy to the left of the fish, using her desk magnifying glass, going back and forth between the snapshot and the news photo, and yes, it *was* the same man, maybe fifteen years younger, when Millhouse was only an up-and-coming junior prosecutor. Serendipity! Who was vacationing with Millhouse, Olivia wanted to know, and why did Lily hide a picture of their big catch?

Olivia thought she'd show the snapshot to Dave as soon as she identified the second person, Millhouse's fishing chum. Not to forget the number inked in tiny numerals on the back of the snapshot. And the key, definitely to a safe deposit box, the bank as yet undetermined. Still, these were mysteries she'd really like to solve herself. She wasn't about to turn everything over into Dave Lowenstein just because he was a man, a detective, and a great kisser. Or maybe a great kisser-*off*, because she was still waiting for him to call.

Meanwhile, for some unaccountable reason, she decided not to return the snapshot and key to their original hiding place. Instead, she clipped the key onto her own key ring, and slipped the photo of a younger Millhouse into her wallet where she'd once kept a photo of Hank.

Dave did call, finally, at ten-fifteen that Monday night. Having just turned off the laptop, Olivia was in her bedroom getting undressed to take a bath. The minute she heard his voice, she reached for her bathrobe. Feeling silly, she put it on anyway and sat on the edge of the bed.

Dave said he was sorry for not calling earlier, he hoped he didn't wake her, but even though it was late, he just couldn't wait until tomorrow to tell her how much he'd enjoyed their date. Sunday he'd spent working all day and into the night, he said—a missing eleven-year-old whom they'd found soliciting in Provincetown. Monday there was an early morning convenience store hold-up in Marshfield, might be the same guy who hit a liquor store in Pembroke. Then a car-jacking at the Independence Mall, a Lexus. The owner had jumped out when the car-jacker slowed at a red light. Broke her arm but that was better than being shot or stuffed in the trunk. Dave sounded so weary, Olivia felt guilty for having shallow romantic misgivings while the detective was out grappling with an invasion of big city crime into the South Shore.

"I want to see you again soon." His tone was husky, as intimate and thrilling as his mouth on hers; she shivered. She saw his kind brown eyes, so clear and expressive that she was sure he'd never told a lie in his entire life; his dark hair falling out of its slick combing into easy, innocent curls. She felt his warm, solid arms, a safe place to let go of herself. It had been so long since she'd responded to anyone this way. She remembered how she'd felt about Hank in the beginning, enthralled, besotted, eager to drown in his embrace. She ought to put on the brakes right now and evaluate her situation realistically—make a list, pro and con. But she knew she was already in trouble, about to say a few inviting words in the low sexy voice she hadn't used for a while.

But before she could murmur even one word, Olivia noticed something that took her breath away. The bedspread suddenly formed an impression, as if someone had just sat down beside her. *Someone who happened to be invisible.* And it was not a cold presence this time. It was as warm as the heat of a body close to hers. Soft fingers seemed to lightly brush her shoulder. The fragrance of a sweet, heavy lily perfume invaded the room.

The two dogs, who'd been lounging in the bedroom, waiting for bedtime biscuits, immediately yelped and ran out the door. Olivia dropped the phone and screamed. Not really a big scream, the way a person might holler if a rhinoceros came crashing in the window. Just the little squeal of someone too terrified to breathe correctly from the diaphragm.

All Dave heard was the crash in his ear when the phone hit the floor, and he was wondering what he'd said that would have made her hang up on him. Only he didn't hear a dial tone, so he kept listening.

Olivia watched wide-eyed as the bedspread smoothed out again. She thought she heard soft footsteps move away from her toward the dark hallway, squeaking a little as they tiptoed across the bare floor between two braided rugs. Then silence. Her heart was beating like a trapped bird. "Lily," she wailed aloud. "What do you want of me?" But there was no answer, only the fading scent of lily perfume.

"Olivia? Liv?"

A tinny voice seemed to be coming from the floor. Olivia collected herself, and picked up the phone. "Hi, Dave?" She took a big gulp of air and continued. "I'm so sorry. What a fright! Something sat down beside me. That damned ghost again."

It took quite a while to sort out what she meant by that. Olivia didn't quite tell Dave the whole story, and he only believed part of what she said anyway. Although her sexy mood had dissipated like champagne gone flat, when Dave asked her to have supper with him after work on Wednesday, Olivia was delighted that he didn't think her too crazy to date. They could "talk through" these mysterious events, he said. She agreed there must be a reasonable explanation. Even weird events had their logic, if only one knew the whole story.

So it was only sensible to contact Mrs. Mitchell, in the interest of gaining a deeper understanding of what the hell was happening with Lily. Olivia made arrangements for the woman to have a look around and do whatever it was she did. The channeler agreed to come to the house on Tuesday evening, tomorrow, at seven. They would discuss what was needed to get Lily to take the Sunset Path, as Mrs. Mitchell called it, and her fee for any services she recommended. Olivia hoped to get a handle on all these strange events before she discussed them with Dave.

"I have dogs," Olivia said. "They'll bark, but I'll put them into the laundry room."

"That won't be necessary," Mrs. Mitchell said.

KING STREET

As Rosario Benedetto passed the crates of fruit on the loading platform, he helped himself to a big red apple—Roma, his favorite—and polished it against the old brown leather coat he wore to the office. "Take an apple, Junior," The Rose insisted. "Good for your teeth, your heart, your digestion. Fruit—you can't beat it. That's what makes the family so healthy, we got fruit."

They went out the door munching and walked around the building to King Street. "An apple a day keeps the G-men away," the older man laughed quietly and gave his usual genial salute to the top windows of the dilapidated building across the street.

Continuing in the same avuncular tone, The Rose said, "When a disease begins, it's difficult to diagnose and easy to treat. When a disease takes hold, it's a cinch to diagnose but impossible to cure. You know who said that, Junior?"

"Some doctor?" Junior guessed, hardly listening, his attention being taken by the two young women walking ahead of them, laughing and swinging their slim hips like a couple of models.

"No, *ignorante*. Niccolo Machiavelli, a very smart guy. You gotta read his book The Prince. A classic among classics.

Learn something. The idea Machiavelli was trying to get across is that if a ruler doesn't recognize a problem when it's small and lets it get out of hand—like a boil, say—it may get big enough to do some real damage, maybe even poison the whole fucking system. You get it? Now I'm counting on you, Junior, but you still haven't come up with the goods."

"Hey, Uncle, we been working on that one. Everything's going to be A-okay, count on it." The two women turned into a coffee shop, still laughing. One of them looked back at Junior, checking him out. He gave her his slow, sexy smile.

"Okay, Junior. Never mind the *ragazze*. Let's review. We know that whore's son Rossi copied some financial accounts pertaining to the family business. Maybe he thought he'd hold us up one of these days. Well, that's okay, he got paid all right. And we know from the girlfriend's nephew, what's his name? Bobby Rat? that she and Rossi hid a bank key behind one of those photos in her apartment. Only those brainless brothers you sent to deal with this matter killed her before they found out which one. Still, a simple problem to solve. Get the photo, get the key, and find the fucking records Rossi stole from us. I want to destroy them with my own hands."

"Only there's a fucking million of those photos, Uncle. That fucking whore was in love with herself. But not to worry. Didn't we get that video that motherfucker Rossi took up at the lodge?"

"Now you see, Junior? This is where that little boil starts to swell and fester. You got the video, that was the easy part. But the key to the whole business is still out there. What about the broad who bought the Rossi album. She got a frame, too. It's right there on the auction manifest. Why didn't your two prize morons get that frame when they got the album?"

"They didn't find it, Uncle. And they've searched her place twice. All they found was a bunch of photos of the gal's own family. And a couple of attack dogs."

"Photos of her family? Did you ever hear of the idea, hide it in plain sight, Junior?"

"Is that the Machiavelli guy again?"

"No, *idiota*. I got more than one book, you know. This one was written by a guy who was really smart but fucked-up in his head—weird, you know.

"You mean, like Capone?"

"Yeah, sure. Tell me, Junior, are you or are you not a graduate of St. Jude?"

Angelo Benedetto, Jr., looked down at his fine Italian loafers with a sheepish expression. "Hey, Uncle. You know you put a word in with Bishop Bertone on that one."

"Never mind." The Rose reached up to pat Junior on the cheek but turned it into a pinch. "Concentrate on what you have to do now, which is to get your *stupidos* to find every fucking frame that slipped through their fingers at the fucking auction. Got it? And have another look around that bitch's house, the one bought the album. I got a gut feeling, she's the one."

"Hey, Uncle. Not to worry. We're on it."

"And for Christ's sake, poison those damned dogs if you have to."

Mikey D'Amico stepped out of his deli with the usual fragrant, oily bag of sandwiches and was graciously thanked by Benedetto.

"Right. Poison. Got it," Junior mumbled.

Benedetto shrugged at D'Amico and threw up his hands in despair. "Kids! They'll drive you *pazzo*, eh?"

The deli owner smiled nervously and scurried away.

APRIL 14
Things to Do Today

Lunchtime: Pick up herb teas, candles
Mrs. M at 7 pm Where is Bible?
Research numb sequence
Make list Dave pro & con
Outfit for Wed dinner?

Olivia made it a point to be on time—neither eagerly early nor carelessly late. When planning a commute, she took into consideration the prevailing weather, road conditions, highway reconstruction, and the vagaries of traffic. So fine had her inner timetable been tuned, she could count on arriving anywhere for any event with just enough time for a glance in the vanity mirror in her Chevy van to check her short-cropped hair and minimal make-up. Mrs. Mitchell, on the other hand, Olivia noted with disapproval, had no such guiding principle.

When the black Lincoln Town Car drew up to the curb at quarter to eight, Sadie and Bruno immediately went into their customary barking fury. Olivia had been keeping herself occupied by searching for some reference to identify the mysterious number sequence. By the time she turned off her laptop and ran downstairs, an unusual silence prevailed. She threw open the front door, not knowing what she expected to see.

Mrs. Mitchell was crouched down on the front walk, talking in a low, musical tone to the two surprised dogs, pressing her hands flat against the fence. Sadie was sniffing Mrs. Mitchell's palm. When she saw Olivia, the woman rose to her feet with no apparent effort and smiled pleasantly.

"Those two tough guys have been through some troubled times," Mrs. Mitchell said as she sailed past Olivia into the house. "How happy they are to have found such a responsible, caring companion. They'll take good care of you, too. The white bitch especially is a canny old girl. Nothing much gets by her. And that big fellow—I'm guessing a shepherd-chow mix? Plenty of muscle there."

The channeler was wearing a turquoise shawl over a long slim black dress, the perfect background for her elaborate silver and turquoise necklace. Her shining black hair was coiled into a heavy knot at the nape of her neck. She might have been in her late fifties, or even sixty, still a handsome woman.

"Would you like a cup of tea?" Olivia asked. "I have ginger, chamomile, kava..."

"A pot of the kava might be calming," Mrs. Mitchell said. "And it's okay to let in your dogs. In fact, it might help, if they're sensitives. Most animals are."

"I don't know if they're 'sensitives,' but they certainly make themselves scarce when one of those crazy incidents occurs." Olivia went into the kitchen where she'd left a kettle on Low. She spooned kava tea into the pot, poured in the water, now sputtering and splashing out of the spout, and placed it on a tray ready with tea things. Adding a few dog treats, she opened the back door for Sadie and Bruno, then picked up the tray. "You'd better be good, you two," she muttered as they rushed past her.

Mrs. Mitchell stood silently, not even looking at the two dogs, and casually held out her hands, palms up, low against her body. Sadie edged in boldly and licked the tips of her fingers. Bruno sat by the door, waiting. "This is Sadie, and that's Bruno," Olivia introduced them formally.

"Bruno, the bear," Mrs. Mitchell said. "He'll come around when he's ready." She accepted a cup of tea and stirred in some honey. They sipped in silence for a few moments, Olivia collecting her thoughts, again wondering about the channeler's fee.

"Why don't you recount those what-you-call 'crazy incidents' for me now, right from the beginning," Mrs. Mitchell suggested.

Olivia sighed, began with the story of buying Lily's photo at the auction, how it turned itself upside down, and then traveled downstairs to the dining room. She went on to relate the tale of the scattered petals, the apparitions, the fragrances, the voices, the impression beside her on the bed, shivering as she mentioned the fingers brushing her shoulder. By the time Olivia had finished her recital, the pot of tea had been consumed, along with several lemon wafers. Bruno had crept forward to accept his treats alongside Sadie at the visitor's feet. The dogs' mannerly behavior really impressed Olivia. She thought that maybe Mrs. Mitchell really was a shaman and wondered if she would teach Olivia her animal magic.

"Why didn't you simply toss the troublesome photograph out with the trash?" Mrs. Mitchell asked. "You could have kept the frame—silver art deco, I believe you said?"

"Yes, and unusually heavy, probably valuable. That makes sense, and as a rule, I'm sensible. But there is something about the woman's smile—Lily's smile. This is *so* hard to explain. I'd feel as if I were turning my back on a friend asking for help. Even though I never knew Lily. And, from all I've learned about her, we wouldn't have been at all simpatico. So I'm at a loss to explain this sense of responsibility I feel toward her. But you're right, that's what I should have done. Chucked the damned thing into the trash."

Studying her hostess intently for a few quiet moments, Mrs. Mitchell said, "I think you're a person with whom I can have a meaningful séance. What do you say we give it a try?"

"Oh, you're wrong about that. I've never done anything in the séance line. I don't even believe in the supernatural. At least, I never have." Olivia disapproved of her own whiny tone. Of course she had to assist Mrs. Mitchell to solve the mystery of Lily in any way she could, however bizarre.

"But some extraordinary things have happened here, according to your own account" Mrs. Mitchell said. "So as a reasonable woman, you have to revise your life-view to include this new data, isn't that true?"

Olivia was struck dumb by this logical approach.

"I think we can use that little side table over there." Mrs. Mitchell pointed out a small table of spare Shaker design. "Let's move it into the center of the room and put straight chairs on either side. And we must have Lily's photograph, too."

A few minutes later, everything was arranged as the shaman had requested, including dousing the electric lights in favor of five lit candles in various parts of the room "for the four directions of the world, and the spirit above," Mrs. Mitchell explained. Olivia felt a slight physical uneasiness, as if she'd eaten something indigestible that was just making itself known in the pit of her stomach. Sadie and Bruno settled on the floor in front of the sofa, noses on paws, ears pricked up alertly, watching the proceedings with apparent interest.

"Now what?" Olivia said.

"Now we put our hands on the table, like this." Mrs. Mitchell touched the table with her long elegant fingers, wrists high, as if she were playing a piano. Olivia did the same. "And we wait."

It seemed a long time, just sitting there staring at their hands, Olivia fixing on Mrs. Mitchell's fiery diamond, but it was in fact only a few minutes before things began to happen. First there was a sharp rap on the wall over the fireplace, causing the candle flames to tremble. *That's just the house settling*, Olivia thought. Bruno sat up uneasily. Then there was another louder rap on the opposite wall. Sadie whined and crept out of the living room as if scuttling through tall grass. Bruno bounded after her.

By the time the little table began to tremble and bang one of its legs rhythmically, the dogs had run up the stairs at full gallop. Olivia pictured them hiding under the bed, paws over their ears. "What's going on?" she whispered.

"Spirit in this house, spirit in this room," Mrs. Mitchell chanted in her musical voice, "tell us what you want, tell us what you need so that you may fly away into the sky, fly with the west wind."

It felt to Olivia as if the west wind, or some wind, had indeed entered the room. All the candles suddenly flickered wildly. Two of them guttered out entirely leaving the sharp odor of burnt wick. A soft moaning breeze circled the table.

Help me, the stairs, I'm falling, I'm falling … breathed a voice. Olivia barely heard the words, which seemed to be little puffs of air escaping from between her own lips.

"That must be Lily," Mrs. Mitchell said. "She's speaking through you."

"I can't take this," Olivia whispered. "What is it, Lily. What are they after?"

A soft exhalation trailed away from Olivia into the corners of the room and seemed to whisper from all of them. *The key, the keeeey. Watch out ... they're coming, they're coming here.*

Then there was a perfect stillness, the most ringing emptiness of sound that Olivia had ever heard, as if a large bell had just stopped pealing.

After a few long minutes of unearthly quiet, Mrs. Mitchell said, "She won't come back this evening. That's all we'll get from her this time. I fear she'll not fly away until we settle this business. I've seen this many times. They won't let go, especially those who've been murdered. They want their killers punished. It makes them frantic. But that's not the most surprising thing."

"It isn't?"

"No. The most surprising thing is that she spoke through you not me. You must be a natural, what used to be called a 'medium' ... now, 'channeler.' We shamans have a different word, same idea. Normally, evidence of the spirit world terrifies our people, especially the Western Indians, makes them so nervous and frightened that they run away from anything to do with the dead, but I happened to be born with a knack for communicating with the other side. And so, apparently, were you."

"It's all so incredible," Olivia murmured. Suddenly she felt exhausted, as if all her energy had been sucked away. "What is a ghost, anyway?"

"Energy," Mrs. Mitchell said, resettling her turquoise shawl around her perfectly poised shoulders. "An invisible part of the physical world that can never be destroyed. That's just Physics 101, my dear. When someone goes to the West Wind, their life energy goes with them, perhaps to dissipate into the energy of all life. But when there's been a serious emotional event connected to a passing, that person's spirit may get stuck in the groove of some material desire— thwarted love or revenge—something like that. Then you have a haunting. Most of the time, a ghost haunts a particular location, like a house or a battlefield—but occasionally a person, a portrait, or some meaningful possession—a musical instrument, for instance."

"*Un*real."

"It will seem more real when you get my invoice," Mrs. Mitchell said.

LILY

Hey, I went to a séance once. Before I came here ... while I was still one of Them. So I know the Dearly Departed routine, if you take my meaning, Hon. What a lark to give that Indian dame just what she was expecting, knocks on the wall, levitating table, spooky voice—the works! But Holy Shit, how surprising to find I actually did have a voice that Olivia and her Madame Pocahontas could hear! Got a bit tongue-tied right there and could only think of how I struggled with those killers at the stairwell. Why didn't anyone in the building come to help me? Or at least call 911. Bet they were all hiding under their beds, hoping not to get involved with the cops and the "show girl" in 4C.

Olivia's okay, though. She seems to know what to do. Already she's hidden that key, sort of. Anyway, it's in her handbag, safe from those goons when they come for my photo. And they will. But it will be Too Late, ha ha.

But you know what, Hon? I want that photo of me to stay in Olivia's possession, anyway. I mean, she's like a Real Friend now. And she did actually feel my touch on her shoulder when I sat down beside her that night in her bedroom. Made me feel sort of warm for the first time in a long time. So she should have something to remember me by, even when I move along to Another Place. The

Sunset Path the Indian woman called it. What does she think this is, the Mohegan Sun?

Anyway, the Murky Mist is clearing, which is not turning out to be such a great thing. Like, I remembered who was hanging around my place that time when Frankie hid his stuff and tried to get me to concentrate on what and where. It was dear third cousin Bobby Ray who'd dropped in to butter me up and incidentally hit me up for a few hundred, that punk.

So, Knowledge Is Power but Information Is Money, as Frankie always liked to say. Could it be that Bobby Ray sold what he knew about his Favorite Aunt so that he could score? Next thing I knew, I ended up a splotch of blood on a black and white marble floor. And to think that whole Motley Crew of relatives inherited all my Beautiful Things. Bobby Ray must have had a bird, though, when his mom tossed in that special frame with all the others going to auction. I doubt the little turd could tell Art Deco from Art Carney, anyway.

I'd like to get that little creep good and proper, but I'm not sure how that would look on my Curriculum Vitae, ha ha. The Guardians we got here tell me it's far better to rely on a Higher Justice rather than to Pursue Revenge. I wonder how they'd feel if some greedy kid with a big mouth got one of them dropped down four flights of marble stairs.

APRIL 15
Things to Do Today

shop noon shoes, lipstick match red dr
pros & cons Dave poss. Mr. Right Now
research C. Benedetto

Doodling at her desk the next afternoon, Olivia started to make a list of reasons why she should or shouldn't get involved with Dave Lowenstein, but at first she couldn't think of any negatives. Finally, in letters so carefully formed and supremely legible they looked as if they'd been written by a first grade teacher or a computer, under *Cons* she wrote: *Hazardous profession,* then added under *Pros: Danger is exciting*, something she didn't even know she believed. One negative led to others: *Possibly will leave young widow* and *Men change—remember Hank.* Hasty affirmatives followed: *Intelligent, Brave,* and *Life is change.*

The bottom line—there were several more *Pros* than *Cons*. If it were the other way around, it still wouldn't make any difference because the lead-off item was *Great kisser.* She was definitely going to pursue this relationship. Not only that, she was going to wear her killer red dress with the revealing neckline and short skirt for their dinner date, which was just a few short hours away. She got a fresh cup of the excellent coffee that this law firm had in ample supply, then glanced at her watch again. *Time to get some work done,* she admonished herself but found her hand reaching for her cell phone instead.

Jamie answered immediately. She was in her old Volvo, which sounded as if it were gasping its last. "I'm just on my way to meet a new patient in Quincy. My regular shift will be noon to eight; the housekeeper and body man cope with the rest," her friend explained. "Rich old guy, but this one's already got a young fiancée."

Olivia laughed to hear the note of regret in Jamie's voice.

"Name's Cesare Benedetto. Maybe C C & S is his law firm. His pre-nup could be right there in your files," Jamie said.

"If it is, professional ethics forbid my telling you so. Benedetto? Don't you know who they are?"

"Not this one. C. B. made his money legitimately in real estate. The black sheep of the family, you might say. The housekeeper is very defensive about his reputation. Well, there was one little escrow mix-up years ago, but that was thrown out of court. And don't give me that professional ethics bull. After *you* copied everything in Lily's file, you could at least have a peek at Cesare Benedetto. But never mind that, what's up with *you*?"

Olivia made a careful note to research this new Benedetto on her To Do list while replying, "Dave Lowenstein—you know, the detective—is taking me out to dinner tonight. I'm having a difficult time concentrating on records retrieval, so I thought I'd give you a call for a pep talk."

"Any guy who gets you out of your shell must be something special. How's he getting along with those two unfriendly mutts?"

"It's a sort of détente. But they *love* Mrs. Mitchell. Remember you suggested she might help me? Last night we had a séance at my house—can you imagine that?"

"Oh, my Gawd—no shit. That is *so* unlike you. Did Lily show up?"

"Seems so. Apparently she's obsessed with getting even for past injuries."

"Good for her. Some rotten man, I suppose?" said Jamie. "So ... what are you wearing tonight?"

"That little red dress you talked me into buying. This will be the first time I've worn it. Well, this is the first date I've had since then. Oh, and I bought a matching lipstick this noon. Also some new shoes to go with my little Gucci evening bag. Black patent, killer heels."

"He won't have a chance. Which is good, because the way your life has been going lately, a chivalrous cop could come in handy."

"Any words of advice to impart?"

"How much time have you got? Oh, never mind ... just one rule. You're not obligated to tell the truth on a first date. Save any skeletons in your closet until the night he proposes. Or better yet, after the ceremony."

"Not to worry. He'll probably talk about himself anyway."

"Call me tomorrow. I'll want *all* the details!"

Still thinking about getting down to work, Olivia had a quick look to see if C C & S ever had a file on Cesare Benedetto. She was not surprised to find that no Benedetto was ever a client of this Yankee firm which is too uptight and upright even to take a case on contingency. Idly, she typed Jamie's patient's name into the blank space provided by the company's internet search provider, and clicked Go. Several news articles on real estate were cited. They looked rather dull, but still resisting getting back to her own work, Olivia clicked on *Cesare Benedetto Named to Massachusetts Real Estate Board.* The article included a thumbnail photo of the new appointee. Olivia peered at it closely, then made a printout, which she put away in her briefcase. *Later,* she thought.

But "later" was much taken up with Dave. He was wearing a navy blazer with muted brass buttons, creamy silk turtleneck, tan chinos—*South Shore casual, very handsome on him. We're going to one of those classy but busy seafood places,* Olivia guessed. Although Olivia was feeling rather more showy in her sexy dress than was comfortable for her, Dave's response of quiet appreciation was just right. She thought he might have kissed her then and there if the dogs hadn't been milling about, growling darkly until he stepped away from her. It was a good thing that Sadie and Bruno were learning to tolerate him.

Even though he handed her up, stepping into the Bronco wasn't easily managed in her short dress and new shoes. Just as Olivia was tugging the skirt back into place, Dave swung into the driver's seat and pulled her into his arms. *There's goes all my careful make-up,* she worried, but abandoned herself to the moment anyway, a delicious plunge into the unknown. His kiss was easy and subtle, a teaser that left her wanting more and deeper kisses. "You look wonderful," he said, letting her go too soon. He turned the key and started the motor. "I've made a reservation at a little French place I think you'll like—serene atmosphere, rather like yourself. The chef is an unpretentious sort of genius."

"I think that may be a contradiction in terms," Olivia said, but it proved to be true. She especially enjoyed having been surprised by Dave's veering away from the ubiquitous South Shore baked stuffed lobster into French Provençal. The place was small and intimate, with crisp linens, tiny pink-shaded lamps, and a single pink rose in a crystal vase on each table.

She didn't imagine this was the usual hangout of the law enforcement gang. She asked Dave if any of his buddies were regulars at *La Bella Campagne*. "No," he said. "And that's just as well. I wouldn't want to bump into any of them and have to talk shop. I'd much rather spend this time learning more about you. I know you're some kind of records expert, you're divorced, and that's about it. Oh, and you must be a dog lover. Did you have pets as a kid? Are your parents …?"

Remembering Jamie's advice, Olivia decided against revealing the story of her father's disappearance with dormant trust funds. She implied a tragic early demise instead, which may have happened for all she knew. Glossing over her mother's habitual disapproval, she merely said that they were "not close, but not estranged." She was never allowed to have pets. "Dirty things," her mother insisted. Always longing for a dog of her own, she had worked after school for a local boarding kennel, helping to exercise the long-term boarders. Then she married Hank, who never met an animal he wasn't allergic to. She hoped she wasn't coming off as too negative about family life. He probably grew up in a clone of the Brady Bunch.

But Dave's family ties, or lack of them, were something like her own. His parents were retired school teachers. Their home in the Silver Streak Senior Community of St. Augustine was more like a launching pad for the series of Elder Hostel and other tours that kept them busy all year. Their disappointment at Dave's choice of career—they were hoping for a college professor—although civilly restrained, had cast a damper on their relationship that had not been improved by their constantly roving off on instructive holidays.

"Now what's all this about a ghost sitting down on your bed," Dave asked in such a neutral tone that Olivia couldn't detect even one note of derision. So she went over the details again of the story she had lightly sketched for him on the phone, about the auction and the apparitions and other phenomena that followed. But she didn't tell him about the hidden snapshot and key, nor did she mention participating in a séance with an American Indian shaman.

"Maybe you should get rid of the haunted photograph," Dave said. "And the chest and the strange crumpled paper with Rossi's name on it. Maybe you need a rest from these unsettling experiences."

"Maybe," she agreed. "On the other hand, I do like to get at the root of things. Call it an intellectual pursuit or plain old curiosity, my interest has definitely been aroused." Then Olivia heard her own words played back in her head, and she blushed.

They drank quite a lot of Pouilly Fuissé with their Sole Veronique, and were giddily mesmerized by a tableside preparation of Crepes Suzette. They leaned over the small table to talk more intimately, both inhaling the sweet fragrance of the pink rose. She confessed that she was addicted to auctions, film noir, and culinary excesses. She learned that he enjoyed bicycling on country roads and working with metal. She couldn't abide household clutter and unpaid bills. He despised office politics and child abusers. Exchanging the minutia of their likes and dislikes was somehow endlessly fascinating. *Who are you, really?* her soft gaze was asking. *How did you get to be so wonderful?* he silently responded. Sipping their after-dinner Galliano would have been a perfect moment, perhaps leading to a perfect night, if Dave hadn't ruined it.

"I want to see a lot more of you," he murmured over the rose petals, his knees pressing against hers, "so there's something I ought to tell you before you sweep me off my feet entirely." He smiled a smile of such great charm and warmth, Olivia felt the hard stone of her heart melting like candle wax. "I'm unattached, no girlfriend, not even an ex-wife—but there's a catch."

Olivia was startled. At first she thought he was saying, "... *I'm* a catch." But then his exact words registered on her wine-and-sex-fevered brain. "What's the catch?" she asked. Her voice sounded different to her own ears, like the voice of a woman trying to speak normally after watching the last fifteen minutes of *Casablanca*.

"I have children. Three children."

Drawing back ever so slightly from the rose between them, Olivia said, "Gosh, you hardly seem old enough to have *three* children. And if you've never been married ..." Olivia loved children, specifically the two she lost to miscarriages. After that, she loved the children she might yet have, if she were lucky. And she was very fond of Jamie's son, Mike. But *other* children, strange children—Dave may as well have said, *several aliens from a planet far, far away.* Her face must have been revealing her startled reaction to this news, because Dave, too, leaned back in his chair.

"I should say, I have three *foster* children. But I'm hoping to adopt them. They're a family. They should stay together and not get parceled out all over the country."

"What happened to their parents?" Suddenly cold-sober, Olivia didn't even consider asking for another Galliano.

"They're the kids of my first partner, Tom O'Hara, who was shot dead in front of his home a few years ago. You may have read about it. Got in the way of a local crime boss, so we think. One of those Teflon bastards. We never could make anything stick to him."

Who could that "local crime boss" be but one of the Benedetto gang? Olivia speculated silently. *No wonder he's been so interested in Lily Lamoureaux and her photo. And what about me? Did he ask me out merely to further his investigations into his partner's murder?* Olivia knew at some deep level that Dave's interest in her was genuine and sexual, but the unhappy discovery of his being tied to three unknown youngsters was making her thoughts unreasonable.

Aloud she said, "What about their mother?"

"She's in jail—and will be for the next eight to fifteen years. It's a long, long story."

"It must be a rather unusual one." This patch of emotional quicksand that Olivia had unwittingly stepped into was sucking her down into sure trouble. She imagined telling Dave's story to Jamie, her friend's predictable cries of horror and warning.

"Once upon a time, Alice belonged to an urban terrorist gang that got involved in some armed bank robberies. She was barely sixteen. She got out, changed her name— formerly Teresa —altered her appearance, started a new life. Eventually—inevitably—the FBI caught up with her. Tried her as an adult, of course."

"Good Lord! Wasn't marrying a police officer a rather dangerous move for a fugitive?"

"Apparently they fell in love. Alice put herself through nursing school, with the aid of some forged papers, and became a trauma nurse. Tom kept bringing victims of street fights into the ER where she was working the night shift. There was rather a run on turf disputes that summer. He fell for her hard, and she didn't resist. They got married and started having kids right off."

The waiter, who had removed the dessert dishes, the coffee cups, and the cordial glasses and replaced them with a leather booklet containing the check, was hovering nearby. Dave laid a credit card on the check, and it was whisked away. Olivia's earlier hopes for this night and this relationship were whisked away as well. Still, she asked, "How old are the children now?"

"Kevin is fourteen, Moira thirteen, and Danny ten."

Teen-agers! thought Olivia. *For my sins.* This was definitely going on the *Con* side of Dave's list—as three separate items, not one. Still, she couldn't help but admire him. He must be a very loving person. That was one for the *Pro* side.

"They're a good lot, really," he was saying. "But dealing with their family's double tragedy has left its mark. Once a month, I take them to see their mother in Danbury, but usually Kevin won't go, and Alice has mixed feelings about having her kids see her in that environment. She wants to give up parental rights for their sake. So that I can adopt them, and they won't have to enter the foster care system. And with me as their legal father, she knows she'll always be welcome in their lives. At least as far as I'm concerned. We don't know how Kevin will feel about that as he matures. Kevin's my chief babysitter now, and Moira pitches in with cooking. Amazing girl. Danny and his pals are into computer games— he's a whiz. Well, they're all amazing, each in a different way. I don't mean to go on about them. I just thought you should know what you're getting into—if you are."

"So...do they call you Uncle Dave?"

"Danny and Moira do. Kevin's a bit too savvy for that stuff. Maybe you'd like to meet them sometime."

"Sounds like fun," Olivia lied. She guessed he wouldn't be inviting her back to his place in Marshfield for a nightcap. Sadie and Bruno could be closed into the laundry room, she supposed, but Dave's revelation of a ready-made family in the midst of their terrible teens has had a chilling effect on Olivia's libido.

Her prudent resolve not to fall in love—or in bed—on their first date was somewhat weakened by Dave's I-hope-it's-not-a-good-night kiss and his big warm hands gently holding her arms. But in a flash of resolve or cowardice, she jumped out of the Bronco and ran up the walk before he could escort her to the door. Turning on the front stairs, she hollered her thanks and "I had a wonderful time" but her voice was nearly lost amid the welcoming barks within the house. Olivia thought Dave might be laughing at her, and she wouldn't blame him.

It took a long time to fall asleep that night, her mind befuddled with conflicting emotions and her body vexed by desire, but just as she was finally drifting off into blissful unconsciousness, she thought that tomorrow she would research the O'Hara saga on the Internet.

The next morning, after breakfast and a romp with the dogs, Olivia dashed into her office for her briefcase, an uncharacteristic extravagance, soft Italian leather in a reddish umber that went well with anything. She carried this emblem of her professional status every day to wherever she was working, even if it only held an extra pair of pantyhose. As she hastily stuffed in some current paperwork, Olivia glanced at her desk and saw that Lily's picture had moved out of its place on the photo shelf again and was sitting near her laptop keyboard. Olivia wasn't even surprised and only a little chilled.

"Okay, okay," she said. "We'll have another go at the Benedettos tonight. And the O'Haras, too." Then she thought, since it was her last week at C C & S, she'd just take a long lunch break to mosey over to Plymouth Court House for some research, if she could find an obliging clerk. She wondered if the number penned on the back of that mysterious snapshot might refer to a Federal trial. USv99-1899 might stand for United States versus somebody or other

THE AGENT

Lee Washington couldn't help himself. He was like a terrier with a fresh marrow bone. No way was he going to let it go.

After Glumm had read Washington's report on the possible connection between the Benedettos and the Lamoureaux-Plunkett auction, he'd stamped the cover No Further Action. His nasty smirk had spoken volumes. Not only was Glumm cool toward tenuous conclusions or, worse, hunches, he wasn't about to let an inferior come up with a winning interpretation for which he might want to take credit later.

The only question for Washington now was how to bypass Glumm. Well, he'd jump off that bridge when he came to it. Whatever he discovered would be put to good use. The important thing was to nail the blood-sucking Benedettos who preyed on the desperation of the poor. It was the same in New Orleans where Washington grew up. Gangsters fattening on drugs, sex, gambling.

The problem of Glumm did give Washington a few nostalgic thoughts about his great-aunt Marie Josie, though. All those powders, incenses, drums, and white cocks. "LeRoy," she would say, "sometimes you just got to do a little bad to make things come out good."

Lee laughed. He had a rich, baritone laugh. No way was he going to wring some poor chicken's neck to get Glumm off his back. But he was going to protect his own special project from Mr. No Further Action.

At the Byatt Auction House, he decided on a low profile, no flashing of his FBI identification. That might just get the receptionist's back up. Instead, he smiled winningly at the distracted, disheveled, middle-aged gal who was not too careworn to respond to that mega-watt grin. Washington explained that he was looking for a special family heirloom, a Bible that had been sold at the Lamoureaux auction, and if he could just see those auction records, he might be able to contact the buyer and possibly coax a resale.

She looked him up and down. "Hey, Honey, you're not saying you were a member of the family, are you?" He wanted to reply that even Thomas Jefferson's family had its darkies, but he stifled that remark. "No, M'am," he improvised. "Mz. Lamoureaux got that Bible from my great-aunt Marie Josie who was a little senile at the time. It's a family Bible with great sentimental value."

The receptionist mumbled that she didn't remember any Bibles in the Lamoureaux woman's collections but he was welcome to look through the print-out of final sales. She suggested he pay particular attention to box lots where a stray item like that might get consigned. She even printed out a copy for him so she wouldn't have to dig into her file.

Out of sight in his old black Pontiac, Washington checked through the sales. A box lot described as "asst. pict. frames" and several single "silv. frames" were sold to one buyer, M. Klein. The other four "silv. frames" were purchased by O. Andreas, E. Williams, R. Manaici and K. Hagen respectively. Washington made notes in the small leather book he carried in his inside jacket pocket. Then he locked the printout in his briefcase. Of particular interest was M. Klein with the King Street address, who left the auction with one hell of a bunch of "pict. frames." Lee's intuition told him that could be Moses Klein, Moe the Monkey, if memory served. One of the wannabes who hung around Benedetto's office. He and his brother, Benny Klein, Ben the Butcher.

APRIL 20
Things to Do Today

Lunch with Jamie, bring L's evid.
Research O'Hara family
S & B specimens to vet
Dog-safe ant traps!!
Last invoice C C & S

"I can't believe the things that have happened to me in just a few short weeks. My life has changed completely. I hardly know myself anymore," Olivia complained with an air of satisfaction that did not escape her observant friend Jamie.

They were having lunch at The Scallop Shell, a three-story, gray-shingled seafood restaurant with several porches that would be open to the ocean breezes in another month. Their table on one of these porches, now enclosed in glass, was still a chilly place, despite the deceptively sunny view of bright waves and mild blue sky. Olivia was glad to be wearing a turtleneck sweater under her suit coat. They had both ordered salads and bowls of "our award-winning clam chowder" in which the potato chunks remained as hot as live coals. Olivia wrapped her hands around the bowl. Jamie wrapped hers around a double martini straight up with three olives.

"If you ask me, Liv, your fail-safe life style was in need of a little loosening up. But three teen-agers? And he wants to adopt the lot?" Jamie seemed bemused by information that did not compute. "You may think your life has changed since the auction, but if you take on this guy, you'll never have another peaceful moment in the foreseeable future. Not to mention, you'll be enduring abject poverty while you two pay for their college tuitions, and they lark about at frat parties. And I thought you were crazy to bring home those two unsociable dogs! *This is far worse.*"

"Bruno and Sadie are okay. They're good company, always interested in what I have to say, never critical, and they have no interest in taking degrees at expensive colleges. They're dependent on me for their well-being, which keeps me from being too self-centered. And they're protective, too, which is their real job. I got them, remember, because of that break-in. And they did foil a second attempt." Olivia took a sip from her glass of Pinot Grigio. "Are you still nursing Cesare Benedetto?"

Jamie pushed some escaped strands of red hair into place and narrowed her gray eyes warily. "Yes, I am. Why do you ask?"

"Friendly curiosity. What's wrong with him?"

"Rheumatoid arthritis, advanced and painful. I supervise his medication, his physical therapy, oversee his diet, check his vitals—that sort of thing. There's a burly bodyguard-type who takes care of Mr. B's personal needs, thank Gawd, and that determined little fiancée Yvonne hanging over his wheel chair. An Asian executive assistant handles the real estate business, comes and goes 'on little cat feet.' There's a sniveling secretary—I mean literally, allergic to every known allergen. A good-looking blond accountant, a bit young for me, but apparently not for the fiancée. A formidable housekeeper, Mrs. Gunner. It's quite a menagerie. I know this sudden interest you're taking—you want something from me."

"Yeah," said Olivia, spooning up the last of her chowder. She wiped her hands carefully on her napkin and opened her leather handbag. Glancing around the room, she took out a small zippered notebook and passed it to Jamie. With raised eyebrows, Jamie unzipped the notebook and examined the loose contents hidden within. She looked disappointed to find only a faded snapshot, a small key, and a crumpled envelope with the name Frank Rossi written on it.

Jamie was the first person to whom Olivia had revealed these secrets—Lily's hidden evidence—and she felt nervous about it for reasons not entirely clear. "Have a good look," she said. "I need to identify the man on the left. I thought you might find that face among the Benedetto family photos."

"Who's the guy on the right?" Jamie peered at the snapshot closely. "He looks familiar."

"His Honor, U. S. District Court Judge Millhouse, much younger. Appointed by the President for life. Presides over Federal criminal trials in the Boston area—drug trafficking, kidnapping, money laundering, racketeering. Next in line to be top judge among the thirteen districts when Judge Wiskoski reaches age 65."

"My Gawd, I think you're right. And you want me to find out if he's been, like, buddy-buddy with some member of a big-time crime family? Where the hell did you get this old photo?"

"It's a long story, and you wouldn't believe it anyway."

"Does this have something to do with all the weird stuff that's been going on at your house—like, the break-ins and the ghost on the castle ramparts? Say, what's this little number? A Swiss bank account, I presume."

"That's what I thought, too, but no. The number is a Federal Appeals number." Olivia took a folded print-out from her handbag and read in a low voice: "The United States Court of Appeals, August Term 1995, United States of America *Appellant* v. Angelo Salvatore Benedetto, also known as the Angel, also known a Goombah Sal, also known as Tore; Louis Benedetto, also known as Louie the Bull, also known as Crazy Cook, *Cuoco Pazzo* ; Rosario Benedetto, also known as the Rose; Dominick Benedetto, also known as Dapper Dom, *Defendants*."

"Nice nicknames. You'll note that Cesare Benedetto is not among them. So what was the appeal about?"

"The right of the US to seize certain disputed assets under RICO. The Racketeer Influenced and Corrupt Oganizations Act. Angelo had been found guilty of racketeering. His solely owned assets had been forfeited, but the rest of the Benedettos, although indicted, had not been convicted. Their assets, including the Fruit Company on King Street, either singly or mutually owned, were also in question. According to this synopsis, there had been two previous appeals whose verdicts had not agreed, and this was the third appeal. It was decided in the Benedetto family's favor. Before three judges of whom the Chief Judge was *guess who*."

"My Gawd, Millhouse." Jamie put her elbows on the table and leaned forward, chin in cupped hands. "I'll bet he got a nice big basket of fruit when the dust settled."

Olivia, too, leaned forward, although no one was lunching nearby. "I suspect that the Benedettos wouldn't want this matter of their assets to be revisited as it surely would be if anyone could prove that Millhouse and the Benedettos hung out together in earlier years."

"And wouldn't the Feds *love* to see that snapshot you've been hiding. Why don't you give it to your nice detective then? Let him have the glory. Think of the points you'll score." Jamie sat back, grinned, and polished off the last of her martini. "Just because he may not be marriage material doesn't mean you can't have a lovely fling."

"Yes, I will show this to Dave eventually. But first I want to know who the other guy is. And that's where you come in.'

"Sure, sure. The resident snoop. And what about the key then. More dynamite?"

"The guys who broke into my house may have been looking for something Lily Plunkett or Frank Rossi was saving for a rainy day. The key and this photo could fill the bill. It's a bank safe deposit box key, from the looks of it, but who knows what bank? No clues—yet. Do I need to tell you never, *never* to breathe a word of this?" Olivia picked up the key and snapshot that had been lying on the table between them.

"Hey, my lips are sealed." Jamie did the zipper motion across her mouth but her eyes sparkled with mischief.

"Yeah, well, just remember all the dirt I've got on you," Olivia warned. "Listen, you know what else? I even made a trip to the Federal courthouse to inquire about other trials involving the Benedettos at which Judge Millhouse presided."

"Is that your idea of keeping a low profile? Find anything?"

"A nasty clerk. Could have doubled for Mr. Clean, same shaved head, golden earring, and rippling muscles."

"Women are supposed to love Mr. Clean," Jamie said.

"So I'm a-typical. First he wanted to know my name and business. So I gave him my card. Then he brought some records up on his computer screen and apparently didn't like what he saw because he said information was not available to the public on unspecified trials. Behaved as if I'd asked him to steal government secrets or something. Federal trials are a matter of public record. If I'd had the numbers, I could have looked them up myself. I demanded to see his supervisor. The guardian genie was pissed, told me his supervisor left early on Fridays, to come back this week."

"Gawd, Liv. Don't you think you're asking for trouble digging around in the open like that? Think about it. That resident ghost of yours is getting you into some deep waters. Maybe with cement shoes."

"As for my resident ghost, Mrs. Mitchell says I'm a natural channeler, and that's why I'm being haunted. Can you beat that?"

"You're right. You're not the same old Liv you used to be. I'll have a look around at Mr. B's family photos, but that's as far as I go. I have no wish to end up as land fill in New Jersey, you know what I'm saying?"

"I don't think you'll be in any danger simply for peeking into Cesare's beloved family."

"Sez you," Jamie muttered, picking up the envelope. "And what's this little memento? Frank?"

"I found it in that Italian chest I bought at the Lamoureaux auction. Frank Rossi was Lily's boyfriend, killed in a suspicious hit-and-run just before he could testify at a grand jury hearing." Olivia suddenly realized that this interesting anecdote would do nothing to dispel Jamie's fears, so she babbled on. "The damned envelope thing simply appeared out of nowhere, like ectoplasm or something."

Jamie held the envelope up to the light. "Is that a tiny slip of paper stuck in the corner?" Jamie asked.

Olivia was surprised that Jamie would notice a detail she herself had not. "Here, let me see that."

But Jamie was already prying out the prize discovery using two pink-painted fingernails as pincers. "It's got something printed on it, see?"

"Oh, wow. *Oak Street Branch.* I wonder if ..."

When the waiter strolled over, Olivia turned the snapshot upside down. They both wanted hot black coffee. Jamie ordered a slice of chocolate cherry cheesecake, but Olivia refrained. "Bring two forks," she told the waiter. After he was well out of earshot, Jamie asked, "I supposed you've dug around in the O'Hara family's history as well. Find out anything juicy?"

"I didn't have time to go into the news accounts in depth, but I intend to have another go," Olivia admitted. She was still studying the slip of paper. Was it part of a bank address? "But from what I've gleaned so far, what a tragic mess for those poor kids."

"Watch that sympathy," Jamie warned. "Sympathy is hazardous to a woman's emotional health."

"Sometimes I find it hard to believe that you're a nurse," Olivia said. The coffee and cheesecake arrived. She used the second fork to chop off a large bite of Jamie's dessert for herself.

છ૭

When Olivia got home around 2:30, there were three messages blinking on her answering machine. With a vestige of her old self-discipline, before she sat down to listen to them, she let out Bruno and Sadie (who ran through the back door already barking in case there might be a stranger in the street), then made a cup of hot, strong tea. As she pressed the Play button, she found herself brooding over Dave Lowenstein—did she want him to call her? *Pro and con*, thrilling kisses versus dysfunctional family scene.

The first message, however, was from the local head hunter with whom Olivia was listed, Slobokin's Executive Placement Agency. An opening for a records consultant at Mattakeesett Town Hall. The project was to begin in May, was fully funded, did not require competitive bids, and was expected to take three months. Olivia was far and away the most qualified candidate for the position. Call back if interested. Olivia could just imagine what kind of chaos awaited her in the Town of Mattakeesett files. Perhaps she needed a challenge to take her mind off Lily and the Benedettos. And Dave, of course.

Dave Lowenstein's deep, sexy voice emerged from the little black box next, enveloping her in warmth, sending a pleasant shiver from the back of her neck down her arms. "If you haven't given up on me entirely—which I sure hope you haven't—how about coming over for a very informal cook-out at my place on Sunday. You'll get a chance to meet my gang. Before you say no, remember how I toughed it out with Sadie and Bruno. At least my kids won't growl and threaten to bite you." There was a slight pause. Dave seemed to clear his throat a bit. "Please say you'll come. It means a lot to me."

Olivia's mind was beclouded with vague desires. She barely listened to the final message, a reminder from her dentist's office that a cleaning was scheduled on Thursday. The appointment was already noted on her To Do list. While she was sitting there, still wrapped in the rosy glow of Dave's words, the phone rang.

It must be Dave—what would she tell him?

Totally unprepared to be jarred out of her romantic mood, Olivia was struck dumb as a guttural voice rasped out its message. "Miss Olivia Andreas. Just call me Big Brother, because I got my eye on you. Whatever you're looking for, all you're gonna find is a mess of trouble. So knock it off. Take this as a friendly warning." There was an abrupt click.

Olivia felt as if all the blood was draining out of her body, leaving her weak and chilled. She sat a long time in stunned silence, finally getting up to let her dogs back into the house. They milled around her—it was not too early to tease for their dinners—and she welcomed the warmth they exuded, their doggie smell, which wasn't too bad now that she'd had them groomed.

Olivia reasoned it was unlikely that someone had hacked into her computer and perused her search records. So what had she done to get herself noticed? Calling the auction house for Lily's name? Ordering the full text of articles on the Benedettos from the Boston Globe? Asking that unhelpful clerk for information on Federal trials involving the Benedettos and their old chum Millhouse?

One simple action, Olivia reflected, can change your whole life. Just going to an auction and buying a framed photo could be a dangerous move. If only she hadn't been so curious. *Curiosity killed the cat.* Proverbs, after all, were the sum of common wisdom, like common law.

Had the time come to tell Dave Lowenstein about the secret snapshot? If she did, wouldn't the detective try to stop Olivia from continuing her search for Millhouse's fishing buddy? Olivia had come to believe that this was something

Lily wanted her personally to do, as if Lily were still alive in some spectral way and she'd chosen Olivia as her champion. Perhaps there were matters in Lily's past life—and death—that must be cleared if she were ever going to rest in peace. If Olivia gave up now, she'd never feel right about it. She'd always wonder if Lily's accident was really staged, and the murderers got away Scot-free. Without witnesses or informants, the law wasn't really all that swift at catching criminals. Olivia believed in justice, if not in the Justice System.

Well, she might as well wait to see what Jamie turned up. Then she might tell Dave all about her Benedetto research. Maybe.

Meanwhile, the wisest move would be to stay away from him until she had some real evidence instead of just a mess of incoherent suspicions. And she was definitely not in the mood to get involved with Dave's troubled teens. Sure, she got along with Jamie's Mike well enough, for the five or ten minutes of his attention that he could spare from computer games and soccer meets. Nice manners, appealing freckles— Mike could have modeled for the All-American boy. He seemed well-adjusted, too, with two caring parents, even if they were divorced, who had agreed to divide custody in a civilized fashion. Mike's father had remarried, so Mike lived with him through the week, then spent weekends and most holidays with Jamie, providing she was not in some live-in nursing situation.

But Olivia's guess was that the O'Hara kids were not Norman Rockwell poster children. A mother in jail, a father shot down in the streets—not their fault, poor tykes, but not Olivia's idea of a future family. She was not, after all, Mother Teresa.

LILY

If there's one thing I've learned in this place, Hon, it's that a ghost with a message is easily messed up. I keep trying to get through to Olivia, nudge her in the right direction to bring down the Benedettos. I know I'm scaring her, but what's a ghost to do? I have to see justice done before I can Move Along Elsewhere.

And I'm not alone, wandering around in this miasma. There are others here who can't leave their old haunts either. What worries me most, though, is when I encounter those guys in tattered uniforms from wars of yore, still trying to Make Things Right. Sure, I know time has no meaning here, but those Civil War boys really ought to give it up and march along to Tipperary or some other Better Place. Which I wouldn't mind doing myself.

One good thing, Olivia's got the key in a safer place now. Only she has no idea what to do with it. She got the snapshot, too, so I hope she realizes that it's Big Trouble waving evidence like that around under the wrong noses. Those gangsters have their fingers into so many pies you wouldn't dream. Playing against them is a dangerous game. Hey, just look where Frankie ended up. And me.

Anyway, all I could manifest this time was an envelope with Frankie's name on it. The Guardian said I wasn't emoting strongly and deeply enough. So I brooded on how I used to be a Featured Show Girl at some swell clubs, Making Good Money, cut off in my prime. And I forced myself to remember falling down that stairwell, trying to scream Help Help while the words strangled in my throat. Hitting the marble floor—well, I really don't remember that, but I can imagine what a mess it made of me. I'd just had my hair done, too, a slightly more platinum shade. Fabulous. And there I was with no Frankie to gaze at me adoringly. No wonder I was singing along with Bessie Smith (Baby Won't You Please Come Home, one of my favorites) and drowning myself in Sloe Gin Fizzes when those goons broke in.

Thinking about that night somehow gave me a surprising lift of angry energy so's I could tuck another little message in the envelope. Whew! Hard Work. If I could sweat, I would be drenched from all that effort.

Still, I feel encouraged. I think we're Getting Somewhere, Olivia and me. That detective she's got her eye on could be mighty useful, too. I wonder if I could pull a few metaphysical strings to bring them closer. I do love a Real Romance.

Hang in there, Frankie. Think of Romeo and Juliet. A little sleep for each of us, and then we'll be together forever.

APRIL 22
Things to Do Today

Dr. K cleaning 9:00 am
Interview Mattakeesett 11:00 am
Call Dave, beg off
Libr,, Exorcism for Beginners, Husband Hunting Handbook,
Understanding Your Teen
Check summer goals based on 5-year plan

It was harder than Olivia had imagined, putting off Dave Lowenstein. Her excuses sounded lame even to her own ears, and his good-natured acceptance, his implicit understanding left her feeling rotten but relieved. *He's such a decent man*, she thought. *But not so decent that he isn't exciting, too. Maybe later, if he doesn't give up on me.*

After the dental technician got through polishing Olivia's teeth, she smiled bravely at herself in the Chevy's vanity mirror, then rushed home to let the dogs out before leaving for her Mattakeesett appointment. Her schedule was a tight one, but she prided herself on being on time for appointments. While Sadie and Bruno enjoyed their twenty minutes romp, Olivia heated up a cup of coffee in the microwave and stood at the French doors in her dining room, sipping and watching her dogs lose a race with a bold squirrel. They barked and jumped ineffectually at the magnolia tree in whose top branches the squirrel had taken refuge. She glanced at her watch.

At that moment Olivia's smile froze as she felt rather than saw some motion on the wall beside her. She whirled to confront whatever it was and saw the wall, papered in pale blue, stretch as if it were rubber, molding itself into the form of a woman's torso made of the same floral design. Olivia could see the distinct outline of a head and bust emerging from the wall as if from a grave. The mouth was working, trying to speak through the wall of blue fronds burying and suffocating the woman. Olivia heard a high-pitched note come out of her own mouth.

Her scream brought the two dogs bolting toward the French doors. They hurled themselves at the glass. Olivia started away from the figurehead in the wall, moving without thought to throw open the French doors before the dogs could shatter them. Sadie and Bruno plunged through. They stopped short, sniffing the air wildly, ears pricked, their paws scraping the rug. If dogs could look startled, these two were registering surprise and alarm, noses pointed at the wall that had now returned to its normal flat surface. All trace of the blue woman had disappeared.

By the time Olivia collected her wits and left the house again, she was already behind schedule. If traffic didn't favor her, she would be late for that interview—a first in her professional career. Usually she made a practice of driving in the middle lane, but today she moved her van into the passing lane and zipped past everyone. Still, her mind kept jumping back to this latest apparition, remembering a woman's mouth stretched wide on the wall. Olivia believed the soundless word trying to emerge from the apparition's mouth was *Help*.

It was Lily as she must have cried out when she hurtled down those stairs, that agonizing split second when she knew her bones were about to shatter.

Olivia was driving now on some kind of automatic pilot. Her foot pressed down on the gas pedal without her fully realizing it. Possessed by the vision of Lily's body hitting the floor of the entry, perhaps marble tiles, her neck snapping, her skull crushing, blood and splinters of bone oozing across the floor, Olivia wasn't looking at the mileage needle passing seventy ... seventy-two ... seventy-five ... eighty. Dimly, Olivia felt that a strange waking dream was holding her in a tight grip. She needed to shake it off before ...

It was the siren that broke the spell just as she was zipping across four lanes of traffic to take the Mattakeesett exit. Whatever had she been thinking? Suddenly she was conscious of her van rattling like a demolition car—*after* the derby. The state police cruiser raced to catch up, motioning her to pull over onto the exit ramp she was aiming for anyway. Panic gripped her. Should she explain that she was terribly late for an interview at the town hall on J. F. Kennedy Avenue? Probably she *shouldn't* say, "The ghost made me do it." As the grim-faced officer strode toward her Chevy, she wondered if it would be too nervy, after turning down Dave's cook-out, to ask him to fix the ticket she knew she was going to get. Yes, maybe it would be.

❦

The Mattakeesett Town Hall was a handsome brick building with four white columns and neat awnings on the long windows. Her interview, when it finally happened, was as weird as the commute, although in a different way. The

Assistant Town Administrator for whom she'd been crafting a careful apology—sincere but not craven—hadn't, in fact, come in yet. It was ten of twelve before he strolled in, and Olivia was getting downright impatient, tapping the toe of her navy pumps. He was a pear-shaped man in an ill-fitting brown suit that didn't complement his bushy gray fizz of hair. His smile was amiable; he seemed completely unaware of the time—not only the hour but perhaps the decade or the century. How could people in positions of authority be so unprofessional? *Your real estate tax dollars at work*, Olivia reflected.

Alfred Bortz wasn't completely clear himself on what the Administrator was hiring Olivia to do, only that the town documents needed to be scanned and other records computerized for easier access, a system that Olivia would set up, with recommendations on hiring the right person to follow through and complete the transition. Olivia would have to learn the present filing system from the Town Clerk, Emma Ridley. Ms. Ridley was described as an elderly woman, something of an autocratic fixture at the town hall, presently out on sick leave and due to retire the moment she stepped foot back in her office. Olivia wondered how she was supposed to work with an absent clerk—perhaps with her newly developed skill as a channeler? But it might be just as well not to be tripping over the old dame's pet systems at every turn. The job was vaguely outlined as implementing their new computer system and "smartening up" the older records—births, deaths, deeds, and what-have-you. "Damn dusty in that files room," Bortz warned. "Don't wear any good clothes like you have on. Pretty suit though."

What an unsettling day, Olivia said to herself as she drove home, aware that this was a massive understatement. The grim-faced officer had claimed she was hurtling along at ninety miles an hour, something she could hardly believe. A speeding ticket on her spotless driving record! At the moment, Olivia was keeping to a cautious fifty-five in the middle lane, maintained by Cruise Control. The Mattakeesett project would be a horror show. After all, she was supposed to be a consultant not a housecleaner. She'd need to talk Al Bortz into additional hires—minimum wage, but would the budget stretch that far? Then there was the matter of facing two spooked dogs—again—and that creepy wall sculpture, like something out of a Vincent Price film. Worst of all, lurking in her mental list of woes, was the threatening voice on the phone. How did they—whoever they were—find out about her amateur investigation?

She was almost ready to lay all her troubles on Dave Lowenstein's broad shoulders. Just as soon as she heard from Jamie about the Benedetto family photos. How wonderful it was, Olivia thought, to have a good friend who would help her through the vicissitudes of life with a bit of illicit sleuthing.

When she turned into her driveway, she knew in a heartbeat that something was terribly wrong. Olivia never left the dogs out in the yard while she was away from home, yet there they were, barking frantically, Bruno running back and forth, Sadie taking a defensive stance by the fence. With shaking hands, she hurried from the garage into the backyard enclosure, the dogs jumping up on her with an urgent canine warning as she took out her key to unlock the kitchen door. Only she didn't have to unlock it, because the door swung in easily, hinges loose and lock broken.

She was afraid to go in, but not Bruno. The fur on the shepherd's back was standing straight up, and there was a low growl in his throat as he pushed past Olivia into the kitchen. Close behind him was Sadie, turning her big head from side to side as if to prevent any hidden danger from getting the jump on them. *It's like having my own personal SWAT team,* Olivia thought as she followed cautiously. "How did anyone get into the house with you two guys on duty," she asked. They didn't answer. Bruno and Sadie were busy checking out the house. Sadie dashed up the stairs. Her paw nails could be heard clicking between the scatter rugs as she trotted from room to room. Bruno rushed into the living room and then bravely put his nose into the recently haunted dining room and sniffed the air.

Olivia began her own wary inspection. Thanks to her crime control team, at least she knew no one was still in the house. Nothing seemed to have been disturbed by the intruder anywhere downstairs. Sadie began barking in a distressed fashion from the study. Racing upstairs with Bruno, Olivia found the pit bull snuffling back and forth over the study rug. The first thing that registered in Olivia's mind was an unaccustomed emptiness. Then she saw what it was: although the monitor was still there, the laptop was missing. Olivia's mind froze, blank except for the thought that she really must give that desk a good polishing. Then she remembered to check out the shelf of framed photographs. Twice. Yes, Lily was missing as well. Well, they didn't get the key and snapshot, at least. A good thing that she had tucked those two hot items in her handbag. But she had to admit that she'd miss Lily's smiling face, trouble though it had been. She wondered if the ghost would depart from her life with her photograph.

No help for it, she'd have to call Dave Lowenstein after all. Whoever the intruder was, he must have smashed into the kitchen and simply held the door open when Bruno and Sadie rushed at him, letting the dogs run right on by into the yard, then closing the broken door on them. That's the only way he could have got away with it. Picked up the laptop and the photo of Lily, and walked calmly out through the front door. *Where were the neighbors?*

Dave would be justifiably angry with her for not informing him sooner about the photo's hidden treasures. Still, the photo and its aftermath—her own pursuit of the Benedettos and the phone threat—were the only things that made sense of the break-in and the stolen laptop. Olivia sighed. She wished she could go back and start this day over. Nothing good ever came of a day that began at the dentist's. She smiled to re-examine her newly-cleaned teeth in the hall mirror, then went downstairs to pour herself a large glass of wine and call Dave.

When she walked into the dining room to take a wine glass out of the china cabinet, she noticed that the glasses were out of alignment. As she reached in to straighten the rows, her hand touched a familiar object: silver frame, art deco with a spray of leaves. *It's Lily!* Hiding face-down behind the wine glasses! Olivia sat smack down on the Hareke rug and laughed until she cried. Bruno sneaked in uncertainly and licked her ear. Sadie burrowed under her arm.

It wasn't good form to frighten the animals. Olivia pulled herself together, got up, and took Lily and a wine glass into the kitchen. She gave each of the dogs a biscuit and poured wine for herself from an open bottle in the refrigerator. Clutching the photo to her breast, she called Jamie first.

"Stop babbling," Jamie said. "Some druggie, probably. Computers are easy to turn into cash. And anyway, it gives you one more chance to mix it up with that cute detective, the would-be Father of the Year."

"So ... did you look around at Benedetto's?"

"Yes, but don't you ever tell anyone. I even took a sneak peak at the family albums. There's a whole passel of Benedettos, you know."

"*And?*"

"Looks to me as if the guy Millhouse was buddy-buddy with in that old snapshot could well have been Louis Benedetto, Cesare's first cousin. I found a few pages of fishing photos in one album with cute captions, like *Me and Goombah land a big one* and *Crazy Cook Lou grills the catch*. No Millhouse, of course, but plenty of Benedettos. This Louis looks like the goodfella in your photo. Same heavy-lidded eyes and eyebrows that meet in the middle. Same crooked nose, thin mouth, and heavy shoulders. But what does that prove, really?"

"It proves that Millhouse is an old pal of the Benedettos, obviously," Olivia said. "Something Lily knew or planned to use, for leverage or money. And that number, remember it pertained to a Federal court case? I think now it was the unhelpful court clerk tipped off the Benedettos that I was sniffing around similar cases involving Millhouse, and they're wondering what I have on them. It's a damn good thing they don't know about that little key."

"You ought to get out of this and stay out," her friend advised. "Give what you've got to the Law and let them handle it. Do you want to end up like Lily, neck broken in some specious accident? And there's a good chance she was knocked around first. Remember how the autopsy showed that some of the facial damage did not seem to be consistent with the fall?"

"Yes, but her death was ruled accidental anyway. No, I'm not especially keen on martyring myself," Olivia admitted.

After they hung up, Olivia removed the snapshot from her wallet and put it between the leaves of *Gourmet* on the living room coffee table. She checked the key still clipped to her key chain and returned it to her handbag. Then she called Dave. Wonder of wonders, he was right there at his desk. "There's been another break-in," she said.

"Good God, Liv! Are *you* all right?" He sounded worried in a reassuringly protective way.

"Yes, we're fine. I was at a job interview. He kicked in the door, let Sadie and Bruno race into the backyard, and made off with my laptop. But I'd like you to come over here— alone, if that's feasible. I have something to confess, and it'll be easier if you don't bring your partner."

"Confess, eh? You certainly know how to be intriguing," Dave said. "Yes, I think I can swing that, if we don't make this an official report just yet. I'll be there in about twenty minutes."

Olivia placed Lily's framed photo on the coffee table. Sitting in one of the big easy chairs, she put her feet up on the hassock. She studied Lily's face. Same untroubled glamorous smile. "I should never have taken you home from the auction," she said aloud. "I know it's usually a mistake, giving in to a whim. But the truth is, I rather liked your style. There's no rhyme or reason to it. I'm sure we have, or had, nothing in common."

Olivia once read about a haunted portrait of a woman in Virginia that banged on the attic floor until the family took her out of storage and hung her in a place of honor. Aunt Pratt was her name. Olivia hadn't believed a word of it. Nevertheless, she was now in possession of a photo that moved from room to room, and even hid from danger. Was it her imagination, or right this minute was she seeing the frame slide an inch or so on the gleaming surface of the table? And was there a trace of lily fragrance in the air? Sadie sprang up restlessly and trotted to the kitchen door, followed anxiously by Bruno. Olivia let them out into the backyard and refilled her glass. If these emergencies kept piling up, she was going to end up being a drunk. A nice, refined drunk, of course. The kind who kept her skirt down when she passed out.

The dogs announced Dave's arrival more stridently than usual and dashed inside with him, as if to make up for being hoodwinked by an intruder earlier in the day. It was nearly three in the afternoon, and Olivia, who'd had no lunch, was halfway through her second glass of wine. Immediately Dave took her into his arms, her wine glass waving behind his back. His comforting hug soon turned into a lingering kiss that wasn't entirely about soothing her fears. Her hands moved appreciatively over those broad shoulders onto which she planned to lay her problems. Subtly muscular. How would they feel if he weren't wearing that form-fitting polo shirt? Olivia shook away the seductive fantasy that was moving through her body with a rush of heat.

"You poor kid," he murmured. "Do you feel up to showing me exactly what happened this time?" Reluctantly pulling away, she took him by the hand for a short tour of the broken door lock and the rifled office, whisking him past the open bedroom door and her own desire to pull him inside and fall on that soft rose comforter.

Downstairs again, Olivia couldn't help postponing her confession a while longer. Dave would only accept a cup of black coffee. Olivia waited until it was ready before she began to spill her story. Filling a mug for him, and one for herself, she fleshed out the bare bones of what he knew with the relevant facts she'd been concealing. When she got to the part about the threatening phone call, perhaps the result of her courthouse queries, she took the snapshot out of *Gourmet* and handed it to the detective. Dave studied this new evidence carefully. A strange expression came over his face, a combination of recognition and apprehension. Turning the snapshot over, he inspected the small number sequence.

"I think I've identified both men," Olivia said.

"Yes?" Dave cocked an eyebrow and waited.

"I think that's Judge Millhouse on the right—long before he got on the District Court bench, of course. The other guy might be Louis Benedetto. And that little number on the back? That's a Federal Appeals trial held in the August Term 1995 and presided over by Judge Millhouse. Assets of the Benedetto family seized under RICO got restored to most of them, all except Angelo. I haven't had a chance to track down any trials involving the judge and the family. Well, I tried at the Federal Court House but I ran into that brick wall I mentioned. But looking at that snapshot and the trial number, I'm thinking that Lily Plunkett may have got herself into a little blackmailing scheme that went sour."

"Good God," Dave said angrily. "So, they know you've been poking around in this?"

"Yeah. After I got that scary phone call, I guessed it was probably a mistake to inquire about those court records from that skinhead clerk."

"*You think?*" Dave said.

Olivia wished he wouldn't sound quite so sarcastic. After all, when you got right down to it, she'd been doing some darned good police work here.

Dave made her repeat again every word that the rasping voice had uttered, its insinuating "advice." He ran his hand through his hair in a disturbed fashion, leaving a few strands sticking up in a humorous way. Olivia had the good sense not to laugh. "Listen up," he said. "You're to keep out of this entirely. These people don't fool around."

Olivia didn't tell Dave that she'd already made a copy of both the snapshot and the number just in case she ran across any new leads herself. She thought about giving him the key, but hesitated. As a bank records expert, wasn't she the ideal person to locate the bank in question? Time enough then to present him with the key.

Nevertheless, she advised him insincerely, "You're going to have to tell someone. A break-in happened, and I guess you have to report that, don't you?"

"Okay, okay." Dave got up and walked back and forth in an agitated fashion. "We have to report the break-in, yes. I'll come back with my partner and a crime scene team and really go over your office for prints. But the Millhouse photo, now—once this can of worms gets opened, God only knows where it'll end up. I'd like to check out the men and the USv number rather quietly on my own before I take it to the Chief of Detectives."

"Better check out Lily's death, too. There's a reason why she's haunting me—because it wasn't an accident at all. The Benedettos had her murdered."

"God, this could be really big." Dave looked off through the living room windows at some horizon of his own imagining, like Byrd contemplating the vastness of

Antarctic, a mix of desire and desperation. Then she saw something else cross his face and tighten the line of his mouth, a bitter enmity she wouldn't have thought him capable of. "How I'd like to nail the Benedettos—those sons of bitches! I'd better get back and organize things. Mendez and I will return to take a formal statement from you—when he gets back. You remember my partner Hector Mendez? Had to take his wife to the hospital—Gloria's having a baby. Two girls so far, cute little things, but Hec's praying for a boy this time. They'll find out soon." The bitter line dissolved into a smile for his partner's macho concerns. "Anyway, the crime scene investigators will come with us to look for fingerprints. I have to take this, too." He waved the snapshot in his hand. "You can keep Lily, though...for now."

Before he left, Dave borrowed her tool kit and managed to repair the kitchen door sufficiently for her to be able to close and lock it, but he made her promise to have a locksmith in to fit it with a new lock and a proper deadbolt.

Despite all her worry and fear over the break-in and the possibility that it might happen again, Olivia felt lighter at heart since she'd told Dave almost everything she knew and suspected. She was so grateful—and attracted—she could hardly keep her hands off him. She almost asked if the cook-out invitation was still on. Maybe she could just meet the kids and see how it went.

But something stopped her. *Good sense*, she called it. If he was looking for a Mama to look after his brood, she wasn't the right gal. Right now her life was complicated enough without taking on a sexual adventure and a ready-made family. When he kissed her good-bye, she stepped back immediately, out of his arms, out of trouble.

Alone with her churning emotions, Olivia took the dogs outdoors to clear her head of lingering lustful thoughts. Bruno ran straight for the front fence, trying to nose something on the ground. Whatever the prize was, Sadie was determined to guard it, snarling in a meaningful way to keep Bruno at bay. He ran back and forth, barking excitedly. Olivia realized the two dogs had been behaving the same strange way when she'd arrived home earlier and found them loose in the yard. She strolled over to the fence wondering at this dog-in-the-manger behavior, suspecting an injured or dead bird. Instead, the source of canine argument was a piece of butcher's paper lying on the ground; it cradled what looked like a half pound of hamburger turning gray. Olivia leaned over, picked it up, and smelled the meat suspiciously.

"You are some smart girl, Sadie," she whispered, feeling a red rage begin in the pit of her stomach and rise to her head, a gush of hot blood darkening her vision. "Good thing Bruno has you to look out for him." Shaking, she wrapped up the meat and took it straight into the house, sequestering it in a plastic container in the freezer. After washing her hands thoroughly in the hottest water, she called Dave again.

"I think those guys who broke in here tried to poison my dogs, the bastards," she said as soon as he came on the line. "I hope you catch them and put their asses away in some miserable penitentiary forever."

"Me, too," Dave said.

THE RESTAURANT

"You gotta turn the screws on that pair of losers you got working for you, Junior. If I understand you correctly, they've broken into that dame's house three times now and still haven't found the photo of Rossi's broad that you were supposed to get for me." The Rose sighed heavily and dipped a piece of bread into the dish of olive oil and crushed red pepper on the table.

"Hey, Uncle. That fucking photo is nowhere to be found. And remember, my boys did have the smarts to pick up her computer this time. A real fucking inspiration, that was." Looking over his uncle's shoulder, Junior was watching for that curvy blonde waitress. He was definitely going to need something stronger than the wine his uncle had ordered to accompany their meal at Patsy's, a cozy King Street trattoria.

"So, tell me, Junior. Who'd you get to read her computer files?"

"I got Georgie, Dapper Dom's grandson. That kid really knows his way around computers. You oughta put him on the payroll, Uncle, keep in step with the times."

The Rose was annoyed. Georgie would brag to his Papa about what a smartass he was with computers, and Papa might put two and two together, figure out that his Uncle Rosario was still dealing with the fallout from the Rossi screw-up. "Yeah? What do you know about keeping in step, *stupido?* Computers been running our family business since you were still in soggy diapers. So, what did the little genius find?"

"You're not going to like it, Uncle. That Andreas broad has got some bee in her panties about the Plunkett dame. Thinks she's got evidence, too. Internet searches into the family. I also got a tip from a friend at the courthouse that she's been over there looking for Federal trials involving us and our friend the judge. She thinks she's some kind of fucking investigative reporter."

The Rose took a sip of wine, a half-decent Perricone that Patsy supplied him with, gratis. Today, though, it tasted a little too sharp, and he feared it would give him *agita*. "Listen, Junior f it's time you gave her a serious warning to mind her own business," he said.

"Already did that, uncle."

"Yeah? Well, make it stronger. Skin one of her pets and hang it on her front door. Something like that makes the right impression on a broad.

Junior made a face. This was not the kind of assignment he liked to handle. He didn't mind a good clean hit, just whacking a guy who was maybe screwing with the profits. Business was business. But poisoning a dog, skinning a dog ... Junior thought about his own mutt, Brutus, a Rottweiller with a big slavering smile. He supposed he could delegate the job. Ben the Butcher wouldn't give a fuck who he flayed, dead or alive, but it shouldn't be necessary. Junior believed that his insinuated threat uttered in the menacing tone he'd perfected should have put the fear of God into that dame. Signaling the waitress who was chatting seductively with some guy in the corner booth, he called loudly, "Hey, could we have a little service over here?"

The Rose sighed again. It was hard when a family member turned out to be soft and stupid. "You know, Junior, if you don't have the balls for effective persuasion, you can quit the business, no hard feelings. I could see you set up in trash collection. Or gaming management, that's a good field. But I don't need no sob sisters working for me. It's like Machiavelli said, a prince can't let a reputation for cruelty disturb him, if it's the price of keeping his subjects united and obedient."

The waitress hurried over. Junior ran his hand over her ass while he ordered a double Bushmills straight up, and she didn't move away, which put him in a slightly better humor. But if there was one guy he'd really enjoy whacking, Junior reflected, it was that Machiavelli dude. "No problem, uncle. I'll see that she gets the message all right." Junior was congratulating himself on thinking up a less disgusting way to follow his uncle's advice and still put the fear of God into that stupid Andreas woman. Where the Christ was his whiskey?

The Rose saw Junior looking for the waitress to come back with his drink, but the older man had already canceled that order with a discreet gesture the kid never saw. "You shouldn't be drinking that Irish swill with a good dish of *osso bucco*. Dulls your palate," his uncle said. "Here, have a glass of Sicilian red. Good with gravy, good for your heart, too." The Rose reached over to fill his nephew's glass. "*Salute! Per cent anni!*"

APRIL 24
Things to Do Today

Canine obedience school 7:00 pm
Summer goals:
Meet eligible single no fam
Develop mind and body Yoga? Strength training
Great Books course? Learn Greek?
Stop baking!!

Olivia didn't know if Sadie and Bruno learned anything in their first session at the Chuck Borgia's Canine Obedience School, but she herself learned plenty. She learned that Bruno had an issue with poodles. She learned that Chuck Borgia was something of a sadist who thought a good clip across the nose or being hung by the collar was acceptable dog training. And she learned that her friend Jamie knew how to stamp a high heeled boot into a guy's foot hard enough to make him scream, "Shit. Shit. Shit."

"Oh, I'm so terribly sorry." Jamie had given the trainer her 1000-watt smile. "I must have been thrown off-balance when you grabbed the leash to strangle Bruno."

"Way to go, Mom," Jamie's son Mike had mouthed softly. Sitting on the sidelines leafing through *NASCAR News,* he was the image of Jamie, with his freckles, snub nose, and ever so slightly chubby body, except that his tousled curls were dark gold rather than flaming red. Residing on schooldays with his father Mitchell Moody, Jamie's first husband, Mike seemed unperturbed by the gypsy life of shared custody. He'd learned to travel light with whatever he needed or treasured stashed in a sturdy backpack. For one so young, he exuded an unflappable, philosophical air.

A few minutes before the Borgia class was officially over, Olivia pushed Jamie and Mike out the door ahead of her. "We'd better cut out before the poodles break," she explained. "Here, you take Sadie. I'll keep a firm grip on Bruno, in case."

Sadie, who'd behaved like a perfect lady, was swaggering and bumping against Bruno disparagingly.

"Oh my good Gawd, lead me to the gin bottle," Jamie moaned. "How many more sessions to this course? I may have to deck that Fascist."

"You just attended our final one, my dear," Olivia assured her. "But don't breathe a sigh of relief just yet. I think I'll try that school over in Kingston—Carrie's Courteous Canines, where choke collars aren't even allowed, never mind required."

"I think you broke Mr. Borgia's toe, Ma." Mike glanced back into the hall, then beamed up at his mother. "He's taking off his Nikes to have a look."

After the martinis and the braised apricot chicken, Olivia kept on learning. From a casual conversation with Mike, who was enrolled in the same middle school as the younger O'Haras, Olivia learned that Kevin O'Hara, Dave's oldest ward, was constantly in trouble for smoking, fighting, and skipping and that Moira his sister was so bossy no one would hang with her. "She tried to kiss me once at recess," Mike said. "Eck!"

Olivia passed around dessert, a platter of almond cookies and pumpkin bars from her freezer stash.

"Danny's got these real big ears. He can even wiggle them. And he takes fits." Mike continued to be a gold mine of information. "I didn't see it myself, but I heard. Mr. Grubb had to put a ruler between his teeth so's he wouldn't bite off his own tongue. Wet his pants, too, I think." Mike loaded up a dessert plate and headed into the living room to watch the sports news. Bruno and Sadie, who were surprisingly subdued after their evening's adventure, followed Mike, sniffing the spicy wake of his dessert plate.

Jamie raised an eyebrow, "So what did you expect? The Stepford Children? Epilepsy can be controlled with drugs, you know. I wonder if those kids are getting proper medical treatment."

"Oh, I think they must be," Olivia protested, pouring coffee for them both. "Dave seems to be a fairly responsible dad-type. But say, Jamie, weren't you the one warning me off the teen scene?"

"As the song goes, *a good man is hard to find.* And besides, we've been friends a long time. So I can tell that you've really got the hots for this guy."

"Maybe. But I find his situation a little daunting. Anyway, after unloading that Benedetto-Millhouse association on him, not to mention the ghost of Lily, he may want to distance himself from a bad-news gal like me."

"Yeah? Did he kiss you good-bye? Was it like, a real deep kiss?"

Olivia's face answered for her.

"So, then," Jamie said. "He's still plenty interested. Poor guy."

༻

Al Bortz called and, in his rambling way, invited Olivia to start the Mattakeesett job on Monday. In her remaining free time, Olivia spent several hours at the Hawthorne Library. Most of the computers were lined up in two back-to-back rows in the main room, but a few were in separate "quiet study" rooms. Olivia opted for privacy. Searching the internet, she read all the newspaper accounts she could access about the O'Haras. She found that she couldn't get two news pictures out of her mind. A grainy photo of Alice being brought out of her home by the Feds, a cardigan half-hiding her face, while neighbors stood in a cluster; a small boy's face at the living room window screamed silently. And a glossy colored one dated a few months later, Tom's body sprawled in front of that same house, the ground soaked in his blood, someone trying to block the photographer's camera. Was that Dave's hand? Phrases leapt out at her. "Drive-by shooting," "possibly drug-related," "witness in the Benedetto trial."

The Benedetto trial! That was a real Eureka experience for Olivia, everything clicking together. *Dave might have clued me in about this,* she thought. *After I bared my soul to him, too. Well, except for the key.* Olivia followed the links to read accounts of all past Benedetto trials. There were many trials, but few convictions. They made such fascinating reading, she felt herself bogged down in loan-sharking, bribery, pornography, prostitution, illegal gambling, and frequently, murder. Finally, she located the link to Tom O'Hara.

Four years ago, Dave's murdered partner had been scheduled to be a witness in *The United States versus Angelo "The Angel" Benedetto* on a charge of operating an online child pornography ring called KiddyFlicks. Instrumental in discovering the ring, O'Hara had used his own informants to follow a money trail that led from porn customers charged with possession to distributors, manufacturers, molesters, accountants, and various payoffs, then finally to Angelo B., alleged to be the end of the trail, the brains of the operation. All this he handed over to the Justice Department, who brought the indictment. Defense lawyers claimed evidence had been manufactured to frame their client. O'Hara would testify to the chain of evidence, how it had been collected and preserved, because he himself had handled most of it. Olivia wondered how that could be so. Where was his partner Dave Lowenstein during this investigation? Maybe she would ask.

When the time came to testify, however, Tom O'Hara was dead. A regrettable loss, some drug case gone wrong. Then the scandal, and the big question. Bags of heroin were found in the cabin of O'Hara's little speedboat moored at the Quincy Marina. Why? Was he a dirty cop, after all? Could he have been a drug dealer trying to put a frame on The Angel?

Still under a cloud of suspicion, Angelo Benedetto was nonetheless acquitted, for as the jury foreman told reporters later, "the evidence of a pornography ring was there, but under the circumstances, we couldn't be absolutely confident of its tie to Mr. Benedetto."

These people are so ruthless, Olivia thought. *Wasn't it obvious that they planted that heroin to discredit O'Hara? If I were on that jury, The Angel would never have got off so easily. But I'd better be really careful now. I don't want to end up like Lily, another victim.* She packed up her briefcase, put on her jacket, and squared her shoulders.

When she'd entered the welcoming gray stone library, it had been a mild April morning of cherry blossoms and bustling birds. But now as she left two hours later, threatening dark clouds were massing on the horizon. Bone-chilling winds cut right through her spring jacket. A wild shaft of lightning zigzagged in the eastern sky, and the following ear-splitting crack of thunder sounded much too close. Olivia hurried to the safety of her van, quickly locking the doors as if the sudden squall were deliberately coming after her. Another flash cut through the sky; this time the thunder was right over her head. Olivia didn't believe in omens, otherwise, she would have counted this storm to be a portent of evil.

MAY 6
Things to Do Today

Washable work outfits & apron
Remem use cruise control
Summer goals 2
Get rid of ghosts and gangsters
Train S & B better manners
Try be patient w Ridley

It was fortunate, Olivia thought, that the Town of Mattakeesett had agreed to fund one other person at minimum wage to work in the file room. But with only one assistant, there was no way she could clean up the Mattakeesett records without getting her own hands dirty. She would need to review storage standards for 100 years of town archives, transactions, and deeds, then introduce a program of document imaging. Still, her professional standards must not waver. She insisted on wearing suits, spring weight and washable, her only concession being a voluminous canvas apron for the real muck-outs.

Despite having been cornered into retirement with a luncheon and the parting gift of a sterling silver Paul Revere bowl (small, but nice for nuts), Emma Ridley lumbered in and out, sneering at every change of procedure and attempting to intimidate the new records manager. Emma was a heavy-set woman with pendulous breasts barely confined in a khaki T-shirt. Her long full skirt seemed to have been made out of a wool blanket embroidered in odd places, as if around moth holes. With Ridley at the helm, it was easy to see how the town records ended up in such a mess. Olivia shuddered at the stacks of unfiled permits, deeds, liens, birth and death certificates, and assorted correspondence she found on desks and bookcases, stuffed into drawers in the Town Clerk's office, or stashed in boxes in the cleaning closet.

The new assistant clerk, Ray Chance, was baby-faced but swaggering, with a slim strength that shrugged off the likes of Emma. Olivia chose him because he was the only applicant who appeared to be both literate and able-bodied. Now she thought she might have made a mistake. She didn't care for the way he frequently presented his tightly jean-clad body to her gaze, as if he were a life model with something special he thought she should sketch. She tired of having to look elsewhere. And besides that, he reeked of cigar smoke; there were always one or two cigars protruding from his shirt pocket. She assumed he lit up during his lunch break, after which the odor was particularly offensive.

Struggling to make sense of the indexing system by which some of the more recent documents had been scanned and computerized á la Ridley, Olivia got Ray out of her sight and scent by giving him a broad outline of record-keeping theory and a great deal of latitude in rearranging and cross-indexing the dusty Mattakeesett town archives. When Olivia was finished here, she assured herself, the new Town Clerk would be able to access any deed, certificate or permit in this entire place according to a system of fail-proof logic. Since she'd also been commissioned to interview applicants for that permanent position, Olivia would make certain it was someone who could follow in her own neat footsteps.

With the prospect of a homeowner's insurance payout to pick up part of the tab, Olivia splurged on a top-of-the-line laptop for her own office, something she had missed desperately since the last break-in. She was thankful that she'd copied her stock market buys and sells onto a travel drive that she carried in her handbag, so that now she could restore her data to the new laptop and get back into action. And she was also thankful that she'd made a habit of permanently deleting e-mails, except for the last few days before the old computer was stolen. *What careless remarks about the Benedettos had she written to Jamie?* She hadn't bothered to keep hard copies of those e-mails, because that went against all modern record management theory. The paperless office was the true ideal, for those with complete confidence in the inviolability of Nstar Electric.

It felt good to be up and running again. She began to access information about the companies in whose stock she was interested, wondering if this wasn't a bit like studying racing forms.

◌

A few days after the crime scene investigators got through tracking dirt through her house and making a mess of her office, a breezy but sunny Saturday, Olivia found a basket of flowers from Dave on her front doorknob. The card, not in his handwriting, said: *Springtime or anytime is a good time to spend together. Dave.* The flowers looked a little frazzled as if the delivery person may have flung them at the door, made a lucky hit, and hastily run for the truck. She remembered an earlier ruckus in the backyard while she was down in the cellar folding laundry. Having a fenced area alongside the front walk was not a great idea. Perhaps she should have it moved back a few yards. On the other hand, the present arrangement might cut down on purveyors of Avon products, Watchtower magazines, and neighborhood petitions.

Calling Dave to thank him for the lovely thought, Olivia hoped to get his answering machine but instead got the real, warm voice of the man himself. For some reason, it conjured up a mental image of the hollow of his throat showing above that open-necked polo shirt, its cool gray against his warm tan skin. Imagining laying her lips right there, she felt a little frisson of excitement that settled deliciously in her lower torso. But just then she heard the kind of background noise that stiffened her determination not to get involved—a combination of rap music, whining voices, and maybe even some kind of ball bouncing in the house. *Very sorry* that she was going to be tied up all weekend, she explained to Dave, without specifying with what. *And that should be that*, she told herself.

What happened later that day tossed all Olivia's good resolutions up in the air. She had just come home from a grueling trip to the vet's to test the dogs for heart worm, which had involved taking blood samples. After that ordeal, it was a little boost to her morale finding yet another delivery on her doorstop, a lovely oval tin box tied with a velvet ribbon. *Maybe chocolates*, she thought. *No, too deep. Perhaps a special chocolate cake?* She brought the box into the kitchen and laid it on the table. *This guy is really determined to sweeten me up.* Sadie sniffed the box and barked a sharp warning. But Olivia pulled the ribbon, which slid easily out of its bow, and lifted the cover, smiling with anticipation.

Ugh! A dog's head, Jesus! Hacked off. Bloody. Who would do such a thing? Olivia gagged and barely managed not to vomit. The involuntary collapse of her legs sat her down hard in a kitchen chair facing the horror. The dead animal's head was lying in a nest of some kind of plush red lining. There was a folded piece of paper tucked between its teeth.

After a while Olivia stopped screaming. Then she had to comfort the frantic dogs who'd been jumping on her and the table's edge. Putting on the rubber gloves normally used for dishwashing, she steeled herself to reach gingerly into the box and remove the paper. Unfolded it. One typed line, all caps. It read: "THIS COULD BE YOUR DOG. DON'T LOSE YOUR HEAD."

Olivia threw the gloves into the trash and washed her hands until her skin was bright red and raw. Afraid to let Sadie and Bruno out alone in the yard, she called Dave on her mobile land line. This time she did get his recorded message. She left a weepy, cryptic story of her discovery. Desperate for reassurance, if not rescue, she called Jamie's cell phone and got her at home, getting ready to work her shift with Cesare B. Olivia described the whole picture, dog's head with shut eyes propped in the red lining of a tin box, *billet-doux* shoved between its jaws.

What were good friends for? Immediately she got Jamie's "I told you so," in almost those words.

"Hey, I need a little comfort here," Olivia complained. "I already know I'm in trouble, thank you very much. But if I can't get comfort, I'll settle for information. Some of my last e-mails to you may still have been in my computer when it got stolen. Could you look and see what exactly I wrote to you in, say, a week or so before the break-in?"

"Oh my good Gawd," Jamie squealed. "Don't tell me you've got *me* involved now! Wait. Let me boot up and see."

While she was waiting, Olivia got herself a glass of wine. It was only just past one—was she becoming an alcoholic? The organized life she'd desired and worked for was looking more and more like a thin skim of ice over the deep dark lake of chaos. And worse than that, she might be running out of wine. The open bottle in the refrigerator yielded only a half glass. Were there any more bottles in the pantry? It tasted wonderful. She tried to sip it slowly, but it was gone before Jamie came back to the phone.

"Thank heavens we didn't mention the Benedettos," Jamie said. "In fact, during the two weeks before you got raided, there was only one thing that might've raised a red flag. I don't know if you remember, but you wrote this." Jamie read her e-mail aloud. "*I know it's crazy, but I have this gut feeling that Lily Plunkett's accident was not an accident at all, that she's counting on me to find the people who arranged it, you know who. And I have some evidence to go on. I'll bring it with me to The Scallop Shell tomorrow.* Oh my good Gawd, Liv ... doesn't that make it sound as if *I* know something, too? But maybe this message wasn't in your computer for the thief to read. Didn't you once tell me you deleted all your e-mails permanently as a matter of good record-keeping?"

"Yeah. But I do keep them for a few days, in case I want to refer back. I guess I won't do *that* anymore."

"What about your phone? Are you using your land line? Suppose someone is listening in to our conversation."

"Cell phones can be tapped as well. And you're the one who mentioned the Bs, Jamie," Olivia said. "Yes, there's that possibility. Well, let's just say good-bye then, and I'll ask Dave to check it out."

"Listen," said Jamie. "Don't call me. I'll call you."

"I'm hanging up right now. I have a call waiting. Dave, I hope."

His voice came through urgent and concerned. "Are you all right? What happened? Who's the dog you were crying about?" he demanded to know. Now that she was suspicious of the phone, she tried to explain her wild disjointed message in the most circumspect terms. She even called the dead dog's head "part of a deceased canine." But she couldn't control a tiny sob creeping into her voice when she got to the hate mail, which she called "the gift card."

"Listen, I'll be right over. You don't sound like yourself, Liv. You don't have someone holding a gun on you, do you?"

"No, but it sure feels that way."

While she waited, Olivia checked the wine supply in the pantry. To her relief, there was at least a half case of the inexpensive but pleasant Chardonnay she favored. Giving the kitchen table with its ghastly package a wide berth, she put a couple of bottles into the refrigerator to chill, a bulwark against *the slings and arrows of outrageous fortune.*

As soon as Dave arrived, Olivia flung herself into his arms and babbled the whole story, including the e-mail to Jamie, and the possibility of their phones being bugged. His arms were sturdy and reassuring. Olivia would be content to stay there for a long time, but he let her go in order to check out the premises. What a relief that the first thing he did was to remove the bloody box from her kitchen! It had filled the whole room with a revolting putrid odor. That dog had been lying around somewhere dead for a while. Olivia opened the window and sprayed the room with Citrus Magic.

After Dave had stashed that nauseating tin container in the trunk of his car, he examined the phones, the lights, the heating ducts, the closets, the windows, the doors, and everything else his detective training had taught him to suspect. Dave even inspected the cellar, and her car in the garage, with Bruno and Sadie following him every step of the way, enjoying this new game and snuffling for danger with their sensitive noses.

Olivia trailed in their wake, admiring Dave's thoroughness, his slicked dark curls, his trim muscular body—wide shoulders and neat seat. She remembered with rising warmth the security of being held in his embrace.

"No evidence of bugging or tampering. Do you want to file a complaint?" he asked.

"I don't know. What do you think?"

"I have two thoughts, honey. On the one hand, a disturbing incident like this—a lousy, puerile scare tactic—should be on record in case you need to make a complaint on another matter later. But I can't help thinking you'd feel safer keeping a low profile for a while."

"I think I'll opt for the low profile while you round up the bad guys. Want a glass of wine, a cup of coffee?"

"Coffee."

While she was measuring the coffee, Dave came up behind her and put his arms around her waist. She turned toward him, yearning, giving in to it. He kissed her mouth, her neck, her throat, murmuring in her ear, his gentle hands moving all over her. She pushed herself against him eagerly, her body taking heat from his hardness. Never taking his mouth from hers, he caressed her breasts, her thighs. She was beginning to feel faint when Sadie and Bruno came rushing in from the living room where they'd been resting after their last patrol of the premises. Before they could take alarm from what Dave was doing to her, Olivia pulled away to lead him up the stairs.

Moments later, she and Dave were wrapped in their own world of discovery and abandon. He smelled of new mown grass, leather, laundry soap and something else that was entirely himself. Tender and insistent, he eased away the awkwardness she feared, intent on her pleasure as well as his own. She lost herself entirely in the pulse of their shared climax. Lovemaking was so natural and inevitable, she could hardly believe that she'd put off this wonderful lover for so long.

Much later, when Dave was lying beside her, one hand resting on her breast possessively while his breathing said that he was nearly asleep, Olivia heard a sound like a woman laughing. A soft sound, barely audible through the closed door, seemed to be coming from somewhere down the hall. A fragrance drifted into the room, an exotic perfume with an intense bouquet of lilies. Not at all like the light fragrance Olivia favored: *White Linen,* or something floral from Estee Lauder.

Dave stirred. "Mmmm, you're delicious," he said, his tongue tasting her skin. "Were you laughing?"

"No, that's Lily," she said, waiting for that bit of intelligence, like a flick of cold water, to bring him fully awake. "I think she's haunting my office today."

Dave sat bolt upright in bed, looking dazed. "Haunting? Are you sure? Maybe I'd better ..." Just then the cell phone hooked to his belt, which at this moment was on the floor with his trousers, began to ring with startling urgency.

Olivia stretched lazily, listening to Dave try to explain to his partner why he'd been gone for three hours on a call he said would take forty-five minutes. By now, she thought, his car must smell like an abattoir. It was difficult to summon up any real concern over recent terrors when at that moment every muscle in her body was so tranquil and relaxed, *rather like a zen state*, she mused.

There'd been another liquor store robbery, in Hanson this time. Dave said he'd meet Mendez there in twenty minutes.

"That's rather optimistic timing, isn't it? And by the way, that *was* Lily we heard all right. If it were a living person, the dogs would have made a ruckus. But this ghost stuff spooks them." She giggled at her own pun, while she watched him get dressed with practiced quickness, strapping on the shoulder holster, shrugging into his jacket. Getting out of bed, she put on the sensible terrycloth robe hanging behind the door, wishing it were something silky and seductive from Victoria's Secret. It was definitely time to rethink her intimate apparel.

"With the red bubble on top of my car and the siren going, I turn into a regular Dale Earnhardt, Jr. Will you be all right alone here—except for Lily and the Dynamic Duo, of course."

"I think so," she said with wavering conviction.

"Listen, I'll be back as soon as I can get away, honey. I want to get that dog head over to the ME in Pocasset, for what I don't know. Maybe a print, if we're real lucky. But first there's this liquor store incident, and maybe some leads we'll need to follow up. After that, I'll have to make sure my crew at home is okay. Say, about seven. I want to investigate this ghost of yours for myself. And that's not all I want."

As if he had all the time in the world, Dave took her in his arms for a long ardent farewell. Then he stuck the bright knob of flashing light on top of his car but didn't turn the siren on until he reached the end of her street. Watching him drive off, she wondered how the medical examiner could examine such an item without gagging. Probably they were desensitized after years of dealing with such horrors. Experiences like this must have toughened Dave as well. Still, he was a really caring, gentle person. Thinking about the tenderness of his touch, she shivered with anticipation of this evening.

After he'd gone, she wandered down the hall to her office, amazed that she was feeling so calm about everything—the disgusting carrion, the persistent ghost, the breathtaking lover. The dogs followed her to the doorway, sniffed the air with apprehension, then skittered back through the hall and ran downstairs. The alluring fragrance of lilies was even stronger inside this room, overpowering, like being closed in an elevator with a heavily-perfumed woman. All the photographs on the shelf were lying face down, except for Lily, who was looking out from her Art Deco frame with every blonde curl in place and her glamorous show-girl smile. Was that smile subtly changed, Olivia wondered—was it more of a knowing grin, now?

"Give it a rest, Lily," Olivia said aloud to whatever invisible force might be there. "Things are moving forward. Dave's on the case now." She wondered what it would be like if she could have a real conversation with Lily, what she might find out that would help Dave nail one of the Benedettos, maybe even the very person who had ordered Tom O'Hara's death and subsequent disgrace. *Oh, sure...chat with the "passed" just like John Edward,* she admonished herself. *What* is *happening to you?*

Instantly, the thought of Mrs. Mitchell came to mind. A kind, wise woman, a little pricey, but worth it. Maybe

Mrs. M. would have an idea of how to learn what Lily knows
… *knew*, rather. That key, for instance. When she found out
which bank had an Oak Street branch and, possibly, the name
the box holder used, she'd turn the key right over to Dave.
Faintly, from the corners of the room a woman's low laugh
rose again, then faded slowly away. As Olivia made a note
on her To Do list to consult Mrs. M., the scent, too, slowly
diminished, leaving the room empty in a strange new way.
Like her crumpled, cooling bed, now that Dave had left it.

THE INVESTIGATOR

Stake-outs were not Lee Washington's style. Rather than sipping rank coffee and being bored out of his skull, he preferred cruising the fascinating links of the Internet to find out what he wanted to know about suspects and victims. But the Internet could only carry him so far. Having learned that Olivia Andreas of 223 Edgewood Road, Scituate, had reported two recent break-ins, the same Olivia Andreas who was listed on Byatt's March 13 records as the buyer of an Art Deco, silver-framed photograph at the Lamoureaux auction, Washington felt the peculiar sensation on the back of his neck that so often in the past had alerted him to a breakthrough in the case he was working on. Exactly what his great-aunt Marie Josie would call "Vodou intuition, LeRoy, and don't you never deny it!" Washington shook his head to rid himself of those memories. He wasn't interested in pursuing his roots. His sights were set on becoming a special agent in charge of important investigations, not a flunky at a cellar listening post.

But that prickle wouldn't let him alone, which was why he found himself squandering his free time staking out Andreas. This was the second week-end he'd spent sitting across the street from her house, neatly parked on a side street in a spot half-hidden by a forsythia border but with a full view of his target. And this time, it looked as if his efforts would pay off after all. A dark Jeep Commander with tinted windows pulled up far down the street. A guy in a dark gray sweat suit got out. Carrying a beribboned oval tin, he jogged down the street and, looking around in a furtive manner, delivered it to Andreas's front door. Washington took a photo with his cell phone, but the man's face was shadowed by a black baseball cap. While he waited for whatever would happen next, Washington called in the Jeep's plate and was not surprised by the name on the registration. He began to talk into his voice memo.

He observed Andreas return home with her dogs, pick up the tin with a smile, and take it inside her house. Not long after, he noted the arrival of the plain-clothes cop in his obvious cop vehicle. Only a few minutes later, the detective carried the tin gingerly to his car and locked it in the trunk. Washington didn't know what was inside, but he knew the delivery guy, Ben the Butcher, so it didn't take a genius to figure out the gift was not a box of chocolates.

Then a surprising thing happened, or rather didn't happen. The detective never left the house. Over two hours went by; it felt more like twenty to Washington, who finally gave up, drove off to a Front Street pub, used the facilities, and got himself a sandwich and a coke. But curiosity grabbed him again, and he drove back, just in time to see the detective clapping a signal light on the roof of his car as one who was now in a tearing rush. Well, yes then, a matinee with the dark-haired, handsome young woman? But what was in that tin? Washington tailed the detective's car at a discreet distance to a crime scene, a Hanson liquor store, where apparently the subject met his partner, a Latino. Less than a half hour later, the subject drove off, again tailed by Washington. It was a longish drive; Washington was just beginning to curse himself for a fool when the subject turned into the medical examiner's office in Pocasset, took the tin out of his trunk, and brought it inside. Well, now! That confirmed Washington's guess about the tin's contents. It was too small to be a horse's head, but it sure must be dead meat.

It had been a profitable Saturday after all, and a good change from listening to the guarded conversations at the Benedetto Fruit Company's office. But in an unsanctioned project like this, how could Washington proceed without risking his own career?

Find out the name of that Detective Romeo, Washington decided. Maybe he could work through him. At the FBI's computer, he learned the identities of the two detectives investigating the Hanson liquor store hold-up, David Lowenstein and Hector Mendez. The guy who spent three hours with Andreas sure as hell didn't look like a Mendez; must have been his partner, Lowenstein.

Washington thought he might have a quiet word with Lowenstein, take his measure, see if he could be trusted. Eventually, though, it would be necessary to find a way around Glumm if any good was to come of this rogue operation.

MAY 11
Things to Do Today

Call Mrs. M —communicate with Lily?
Victoria's Secret online
Poss new perfume, Filene's South Shore Mall
Also new linens for bedroom—silk too much?
*   Summer goals 2B*
Keep at it with Sadie and Bruno—you can do it!
Great Books, one volume per week, start Marcus Aurelius
Tell Dave, meet the kids (before in too deep.)

On Monday afternoon at the town hall, Ray Chance seemed particularly offensive, practically sniffing the air around her as if he sensed her altered status as a woman starting a hot new love affair. Or maybe it was the effulgence of perfumes she'd tried on at the mall during lunchtime before finally settling on *Obsession* (recommended for day wear) and *Opium* (recommended for evenings).

In the midst of fine-tuning the computer's document retrieval program, a work that required absolute concentration, her mind kept straying to the creamy white silk sheets and pillowcases she'd also purchased in a moment of madness during her long lunch break—the first time in memory that she actually took the entire hour. And then to be subjected to the unwelcome sight of Ray parading back and forth in his tight jeans and black T-shirt with two cigars sticking out of its pocket like dark fingers—insupportable!

There was not only the memory of Saturday afternoon to revel in, but also that same evening. After a rushed trip to check on the kids, it was almost eight when Dave had returned with an armful of roses and a bottle of champagne. They'd made love like two famished, lonely people, which they were, until just plain exhaustion had felled them. Some time past three in the morning, Dave had crawled away to catch a couple of hours sleep at home before seeing his charges off to school.

Just thinking of Dave's touch—his hands, his mouth— made her skin feel sunburned in places that normally never saw the light of the day. She hoped she wasn't blushing, but if she was, that Ray didn't notice and take credit.

She gave herself a mental shake and tried to turn her attention back to Births, Marriages, Deaths. *Marriages. Mrs. Dave Lowenstein. Olivia Lowenstein. Oh, cut that out!*

The next time Ray wandered by, she assigned him a time-consuming dusty project in the files room so that she could call Mrs. M. in privacy. "Moon Deer Native American Gifts and Artifacts," Mrs. M. answered in her low musical voice.

"Hi, Mrs. Mitchell. It's Olivia Andreas. Perhaps you recall helping me earlier with a little problem—a kind of household phenomenon I couldn't explain?" Olivia said.

"Oh yes, of course I remember you—and the revenant show girl you brought home from the auction. Is she still there?"

"I'm afraid so—*the ghost who came to dinner*, you might say—and she's shown herself in several new guises that may interest you. I've become quite used to having her around, but I can't say the same for my canine companions."

"Animals have special sensitivities," Mrs. Mitchell murmured. "So ... how can I help you now?"

"It's become quite a complicated story, Mrs. Mitchell, and I do indeed require some additional assistance. I need to communicate with the Other Side, or wherever the hell she is coming from. Oh, sorry. I probably shouldn't say *hell*. Apparently my girl ghost had some mob connections and may hold the key to important information wanted by the police. Do you have any idea how I might make contact?" This kind of request, if made to a psychiatrist, Olivia realized, might land her in a mental institution. Also, she regretted using the words *mob* and *key*.

"Yes, I see," Mrs. Mitchell said in her soothing voice. "I did try to channel your ghostly friend, but she seems to prefer to communicate through you. Ouija comes to mind. Do you know what that is? An old-fashioned tool but still very effective. Or automatic writing, but I really don't think you'd enjoy giving over your consciousness to another's persona."

"Doesn't sound like my cup of Earl Grey," Olivia agreed. They made a date for the following evening. Mrs. Mitchell would arrive at six with her ouija board. Just before Olivia hung up, she thought she heard a soft click on the phone. A prickle of apprehension like an icy spider ran up the back of her neck. Could it be that Ray Chance had been listening to her conversation from an extension? Trying to be calm, Olivia thought for a minute about the extensions. She remembered a connection between the Town Clerk's office and the front desk. Racing out to see if she could catch her assistant at the front desk, if indeed he was the listener, the only motion she saw was the swing of the Men's

Room door closing. No one else at the front desk. Where was everybody? Two of the girls from other offices were supposed to take turns at that desk.

She hung around for a minute. One of the front desk girls did show up—a blonde with a sailor's tan, wearing inappropriate Capri pants and a striped jersey. Feeling foolish to be keeping a vigil outside the Men's Room, Olivia went back to her computer in the Town Clerk's office. She picked up the phone and called the files room. It rang six times before Ray answered. *Gotcha!* she thought. *Or should that be the other way around?* She decided on the direct approach. "Ray, was that you on the front desk phone just now?"

"Doing what?"

"Listening, actually. Listening in on my personal conversation."

"Nope. As I recall, you said no personal calls are allowed in the Town Hall."

"Don't get smart with me."

"You need a cup of coffee or a Midol or something, Ms. Andreas? I been doing nothing but toting around those crappy old books." Ray's tone sounded both solicitous and offended.

"I see," *you lying piece of trash.* "Carry on." Olivia ran her fingers through her short black hair. Her attempt at confrontation had not gone well. Why, she asked herself, would Ray spy on her? Or was she just becoming terribly paranoid? Soon she'll be seeing a conspiracy around every corner, the Grassy Knoll Gang meets Mrs. Muir.

She was spared continuing on this line of disparaging self-analysis by the arrival of Emma Ridley. It was rather like having a rusty battle cruiser sail into the office with half-cocked guns blazing. "What the hell is that creep doing in there, messing up my deeds and transactions?" Emma demanded, basso profondo.

Olivia sighed. "As I explained before, Emma, we're initiating a different system of record management. Our emphasis will be on efficient retrieval as well as safe storage. But I wouldn't want you to waste a moment of your valuable thought on our work here. Just continue enjoying your retirement, and rest assured that we will always be grateful that you have left the Mattakeesett town records ... eh ... stamped with your own unique imprint." Olivia has made a version of this speech on a dozen other occasions. It was mannerly but didn't seem to mollify the old battle-ax.

Emma Ridley leaned over her shoulder to peer at the computer screen. "Well, you're welcome to that beast," she said, poking a few keys experimentally. "If I had my way, we'd have never installed this Imp of Satan in the first place. Original documents were good enough for our forefathers, and they're good enough for me."

"Please don't do that," Olivia cried as Emma fingered the delete key. From the smell of the woman's breath, Olivia thought she must have lunched on the Mattakeesett Deli's specialty—chopped liver and sliced onion.

Emma grinned and straightened, leaning on the keyboard. An error message flickered across the screen. "I suppose you got to look like you're earning that big fat fee somehow. Try not to make a complete dog's breakfast of my land deed books, will you? I'll be downstairs in Licenses if you need me. They're a bit short-handed today." She swayed toward the door, her blanket skirt swirling around her L. L. Bean work boots. At the threshold, she paused and looked back over her shoulder. "If I were you, I'd keep an eye on that cheeky assistant of yours. Sneaky bastard. Caught him when I came through the hall earlier, lifting up the phone on the reception desk and having a quiet listen. That phone connects with yours, you know."

"I knew it! This whole phone system is so antiquated," Olivia complained. She was on the verge of hysteria wondering what Ray Chance was up to, and how much Emma had screwed up her program by pressing several keys at once with her ample bosom. The monitor appeared to have frozen.

"When I was Town Clerk, I made it my business to know what was going on out front. I had the phones connected so's I could keep an ear on who was calling in and what the reception girls were up to. Very little got by me, I can tell you that, Missy." Emma was in the hall now. The blonde at the front desk looked up from her magazine with a startled expression. Emma steamed away still muttering. "None of those fancy-dancy phones with a bunch of buttons for me."

∾

Mrs. Mitchell showed up twenty-five minutes late for their six o'clock appointment. Olivia was hoping to have Mrs. M. out of the way before eight, when Dave planned to drop in for a late supper if all was quiet at his house. She'd been hovering between the front door, the tray she was setting up for tea with Mrs. M., and the beef *bourguignon* braising in the oven. Sadie and Bruno, outdoors on patrol, barely woofed at the channeler's arrival. As soon as they caught Mrs. M's scent, they sat back down on their haunches with attentive ears while she praised them and continued on her way to the front door.

Mrs. M. was wearing a graceful black jersey dress and a hand-woven brick red and beige shawl of Navaho design.

She carried an artist's portfolio, which when opened on the dining room table, revealed a lettered and numbered board and a tear-shaped pointer she called a "planchette." "My, something smells delicious," she said. "Beefy, with onion and thyme. You must be expecting a gentleman caller." She studied Olivia's face and laughed softly. "I'll send you one of my dream-catchers. Very useful for giving fate a little push."

Pouring tea for them both, Olivia let this psychic reading (*or shrewd guess*) pass by without comment. She explained that some recent phenomena had happened in this dining room— the traveling photo and the woman-in-the-wall apparition. Mrs. Mitchell claimed to feel Lily's vibrations very strongly indeed and approved of their working in the "hot spot."

"Wrap your fingers around that tea cup," Mrs. Mitchell suggested. "It's important not to handle the planchette with cold hands."

After they'd sipped their scalding tea, Olivia copied Mrs. Mitchell in placing the fingertips of her right hand on the pointer with her palm lifted as if she were about to play the first notes of a piano piece. Mrs. M. slid the pointer around in slow circles, still "warming up," she explained. Then she paused for a moment. "Let the planchette move on its own now, Olivia," she instructed. A cloud of barely discernible doubts like gnats assailed Olivia.

She felt a tremor under her fingers and glanced swiftly at Mrs. M. "I'm not moving the planchette," the woman told her. "We are asking Lily to come to us. Lily, come to us now. Are you here, Lily?"

Instantly the planchette zoomed to the *YES* printed on the board. It moved so fast, Olivia had to lean forward to keep her fingers in position. "Wow, look at that," she said. "Are you sure that isn't you—unconsciously, of course?"

"Nothing is sure in this game. But try this—ask a question to which only you and Lily know the answer," Mrs. M. suggested.

Olivia thought for a moment. "Lily, what letters were written on the back of that snapshot of the guys fishing?" she asked.

Before she even finished the question, the pointer was rushing to spell out the letters *USv.*

"Wow," Olivia said again. "That's amazing."

"I take it that Lily has passed the test, then." Mrs. M. appeared amused. Her smile said that she'd dealt with skeptics before and won every skirmish.

"Unless you're a mind reader. You could be simply divining my thoughts." Although mind-reading might be considered equally incredible, Olivia was loathe to give up her stance as a skeptic. "I've never really believed in ghosts, but Lily is something else. The other night I heard her laugh and then there was this exotic fragrance wafting around me, rather overwhelming."

"What were you doing at the time?" Mrs. M. asked.

Olivia blushed. "I think the perfume may have been lilies and musk." Anything to change the subject. "I've never had a resident ghost before."

"Speaking of perfume, isn't that a new scent you're wearing this evening?" Mrs. M. tapped the board with her left hand, the one with the significant diamond ring. "The older you get, the more deaths surround you, the more ghosts you may encounter. Shall we continue then?"

Feeling a little foolish, Olivia addressed Lily directly. "Lily, I know you've been appearing in my life for a reason. There's a mystery connected to your death that you want me to solve ..."

Olivia hadn't finished her question, when the pointer pulled their hands toward *YES*.

"I may not be able to investigate myself, but rest easy, Lily. I've turned the matter over to people who are much more qualified than I am to find the answers. But it's not easy."

Carrying the light touch of their fingers, the planchette began scurrying around the board again. It spelled out *I* ... *K* ... *N* ... *O* ... *W* ... *W* ... *H* ...*O* ... and paused.

Olivia said, "A detective named Dave Lowenstein is on the case. Apparently you made some powerful enemies, so Dave will need all the help you can give him. Is there something, anything you know that will point him in the right direction?" All the time Olivia was speaking, the planchette jiggled back and forth like a nervous person swinging a foot. But once the question had been posed, it hurriedly spelled out a long string of letters. As they were chosen, Mrs. M. spoke each one aloud. When the planchette paused again, Olivia wrote the message on a pad of paper.

B ... *A* ... *N* ... *K* ... *F* ... *R* ... *A* ... *N* ... *K* ... *I* ... *E* ... *S* ... *F* ... *I* ... *L* ... *E*

"Bank Frankie's file," Olivia defined the message. "But which bank, Lily? And what name is on the safety deposit box?"

There was a *DON'T KNOW* lettered on the board. And now, to Olivia's great frustration, the planchette skittered in that direction. She kept asking the question, trying to phrase it differently each time, but the answer was always the same. "Is Lily getting tired or something?" Olivia asked.

"Don't Know is a kind of safety valve," Mrs. M. explained. "If a spirit loses energy or gets confused for any reason, it will insist on Don't Know. It's the equivalent of taking the fifth when being cross-examined in court. On the other hand,

Don't Know may be a simple statement of fact. Lily does not know which bank. Or she may have trouble remembering in her present state. I am supposing, of course, the first message made sense to you?"

There was a sound like two sharp cracks somewhere in the vicinity of the wall over the fireplace. "Wait, don't quit now," Mrs. M. declared to a startled Olivia. "Lily wants to tell us something more. Instantly, the planchette began to move purposefully again.

W ... A ... T ... C ... H ... O ...U ...T ... B ... O ...B ...B ...Y

"Who in the world is Bobby?" Olivia wondered aloud. "Don't you want to tell us anything else?"

G ... I ... R ... L ... G ... O ... T ... S ... H ... A ... M ... R ... O ... C ... K ...F ... R ... A ... M ... E.

Olivia thought about this for a moment. *Of course.* "Lily had many collections," she explained to Mrs.M., "including a number of silver frames with photographs of herself, some casual but most of them glamorous, show girl stuff. Everything was sold at that auction I told you about. Some guy bought a box lot of less valuable frames and a couple of the silver ones, but after he left four other frames came up. I bought the Art Deco frame with Lily's photo, and the rest went to other women. If one had a shamrock pattern, I didn't notice it."

"You bought Lily on a whim?"

"It seemed wrong that no one wanted her anymore."

"Ahhh," said Mrs. Mitchell. "Just so. You stepped into her circle. You offered yourself as her friend."

"I've never given such things any credence. Communicating with the dead is beyond my belief, even though I seem to be doing just that."

"That was the old Olivia's belief system," Mrs. M. said. "The new Olivia is open to unexplored worlds of experience.

Emotionally as well as spiritually." She glanced at her watch and began to pack up her ouija board, as if she knew exactly when Dave was expected. "I trust you have what you need now. I'll mail you my invoice. Oh, and Sadie seems to be bothered by something. Have a look at her back right paw."

❧

Sadie was discovered to be limping a bit. Olivia had to lie prone on the floor, murmuring soothing words, to convince the pit bull to surrender her paw for examination. The wad of gum wedged between the dog's toes must have been as uncomfortable as a plantar wart. Removing the sticky mess, Olivia inadvertently tore a bit of Sadie's paw pad, which although it was a small wound, bled profusely; she cleaned it with hydrogen peroxide. When Dave arrived carrying a bottle of Beaujolais, Olivia greeted him with her new white linen sheath spotted all the way down the front with fresh blood. He was already calling 911 while she hastened to explain that it was the dog not she who was injured, and that only slightly.

Oh well, he soon had the ruined dress off her! Nothing seemed to go the way Olivia planned anymore. Not that it wasn't thrilling to be swept away into ardent love-making. Dave, that most wonderful kisser, kissed her everywhere, even in places she'd never been kissed before. Meanwhile, the beef *bourguignon* disintegrated into shreds that resemble Mighty Dog more than French haute cuisine.

In the afterglow of sex, they polished off the Beaujolais before ever lifting a forkful of the dinner which it was meant to complement. Still, her standard Chardonnay filled in nicely when they finally dined at ten-thirty. Beaming at each other, they were barely hungry but still thirsty. As she admired Dave's sensuous mouth and soft brown eyes glowing in the candlelight, Olivia made a mental note to stock a few bottles of red wine in future.

There was no avoiding her promise to meet Dave's "family" on Sunday. Again, he was planning a cook-out. She supposed it would be charred chicken raw at the bone, petrified sausages, and potato salad with egg that has been sitting too long in the sun. Olivia prayed it wouldn't be as deadly a picnic as she imagined.

A visit to a man's home revealed much about his inner being, and Olivia was in favor of *knowledge is power* on principle. Beside that, she was feeling a bit uncomfortable about falling into bed with this guy at every opportunity when she knew so little about him, except for how marvelously his body was made, the firm muscular curves, the soft brown hair on his arms and legs that faded to blond on his thighs.

But what if all she found in his bookcase were volumes of Reader's Digest's abridged novels and ashtrays stolen from strip clubs? And how about his CD's? Heavy metal? Bagpipes? Straus waltzes? Hip hop? Madonna?

She decided to bring a Devil's Food cake to the dreaded event. It seemed appropriate somehow.

Her wits must have melted away as soon as his lips brushed her neck. It was much later in the evening, as they nestled together on the living room sofa drinking cups of strong black coffee that Olivia's brain came back to life. Finally she remembered to tell Dave about Lily communicating with the ouija, Frankie's file, the shamrock frame, and the unknown Bobby.

"It sounds as if there may be some information hidden in that other frame, too," Olivia concluded. "Maybe even the file itself. You once told me that Lily's CPA boyfriend, Frank Rossi, worked for the firm of Paolucci & Desanto, accountants for the Benedetto family, that Rossi had been subpoenaed to appear before a Grand Jury on the matter of Angelo Benedetto Junior's back taxes. Rossi never testified, though, because of his fatal car accident, and then Lily fell down the stairs, a supposed accident, a short time later. So, I figure you might want to investigate the silver frames at the Plunkett auction that were sold to other women. One of those frames might hold an important clue."

"Let's see," Dave said, his fingers turning around a curl in her hair. She'd just begun to let it grow longer than her usual Joan of Arc buzz cut, thus revealing its natural wave. "I could subpoena the auction records, check to see what females bought the other silver frames. I'll just tell the judge that my girlfriend got the idea to investigate silver frames while she was conversing with her resident ghost through a ouija board. That should do it."

"If you're going to make fun of me, we'll never get anywhere," Olivia said. "And I'll sic Bruno and Sadie on you."

Dave looked at the dogs and smiled. Bruno was lying on his foot, snoring, and Sadie was curled up on the well-cushioned windowseat that overlooked the front yard, her sock-bandaged paw dangling over the edge. Both dogs continued to stay clear of the wing back chairs in front of the fireplace since Lily had appeared in one of them. "It's too late. They've learned to love and trust me."

Olivia wondered if it was too late for her, as well. It was well past midnight; she was half asleep, drowsing on Dave's shoulder. She didn't want to say good-night, but Dave had responsibilities and must leave soon, she knew. *Two sleepy people by dawn's early light,* she was singing to herself when something big and metallic crashed in the kitchen with an awful clatter.

Bruno's head came up off Dave's foot in a flash, and he threw back his head and howled. Ignoring her injured paw, Sadie leapt off the windowseat and stood poised, a statuette of canine indecision—should she rush to investigate a dangerous, spooky sound or hightail it upstairs?

Dave jumped up from the sofa, unsettling Olivia so that she just caught her balance before flopping onto the cushions like a discarded rag doll. "What the hell was that?" He snatched a poker from the fireplace and marched toward the kitchen. Bruno and Sadie slunk after him, dogging his footsteps. "This is really weird," he called back to Olivia. "Come and see."

Olivia had to push through the dogs, who were transfixed in the doorway. Two stainless steel skillets that normally dangled from a cast-iron pot hanger had fallen off their hooks and landed on the stove. Dave touched them tentatively with the poker clutched in his hand. Nothing happened.

"I think there's a message from Lily here," Olivia said. "And it might be, 'Out of the frying pan into the fire.'"

"I don't know how much more of this craziness you can take, honey. Are you going to be all right after I leave?" Dave's tone was anxious and exhausted. *Did he really mean, he couldn't take much more?* "Do you want to come home with me?"

Little did he know that she'd rather be dragged away by flesh-eating zombies than spend the night in his menagerie. "Thanks for the sweet thought," she said. "But I'll be fine. I'm getting used to these bizarre happenings, and I have the dogs to keep me company."

Dave looked around. The doorway was empty now. "Some great guard dogs. They seem to have vamoosed. Where are they, hiding under the bed upstairs?"

"Probably. They'd fight any intruder to the death, but ghoulies and ghosties are another matter. Poor babies. I'll comfort them, and they'll comfort me. And you … you'd better get going while you can still drive without falling asleep. Don't forget to get those auction records tomorrow!"

"Yes, m'am." He saluted her, touching the poker to his forehead. Farewell kisses took a while longer, but finally he said good-night. "Until Sunday, then. Moira's already studying her recipe book. Her mother's legacy. Alice— Teresa—was quite a cook. The kids are really looking forward to meeting you."

"How nice of them," Olivia said. She wondered if Moira was getting an early start on the ptomaine potato salad.

LILY

I guess you could call this thing I do in the blink of an eye Astral Travel. Believe me, it's a whole new Learning Experience, Hon, whizzing around the Benedettos and their goons. We'll be doing the world a favor to put those heartless bastards out of business. But that Liv sure is getting herself in a whole passel of trouble. I hope she doesn't end up a bloody mess on a marble floor like I did. I guess I should feel guilty about involving her, but any emotion really strains and drains me. I'm still working on getting angry. I need the energy from a good fit of fury to help me manifest.

Some big surprise to find Bobby setting himself up as a full-fledged wannabe, gofer, and hanger-on with the Benedettos. I suppose it seems to him like a fast route to Big Bucks and Easy Drugs. Bobby always was a kid who liked to press his nose against a candy store window. I've warned Liv to watch out for him, but I don't think she gets it. What else can I do? Popping out of the wallpaper or rattling frying pans just doesn't seem to get the message across. The ouija board was the best, but the Indian woman took the damned thing home with her.

To think I had to get to this side of things to play with a ouija board. It just never came to my attention Before. I wish Liv had more faith in me. Even though I couldn't for the life of me—ha ha—

remember the name of the frigging bank. I'm still struggling with that Swiss cheese memory I got now.

Probably it's a good thing Liv's got herself mixed up with that hot detective. She's going to need her wits, her intuition, and her muscle from now on, and getting laid always sharpens a gal.

So I'm counting on Liv to catch on to Bobby. Because my lousy nephew sure got a lot to answer for. I'm gonna see that the little sonofabitch gets his if it's the last thing I do before I have to move along to a Higher Plane.

MAY 17
Things to Do Today

Beaujolais, devil's food for cook-out
Gifts for kids—what? Consult Mike
Gift for Dave—plant??
Ask Dave check out Ray
Be cool. Emulate Marcus Aurelius: "The universe is transformation ..."

As they did every morning when Olivia left home, the two dogs hopped up on the windowseat in the living room to press forlorn noses against the glass. She saw them in her peripheral vision as she carefully placed on the van floor a picnic hamper containing her triple-layer, chocolate-filled-and-frosted Devil's Food masterpiece garnished with fresh cherries. Did they purposely try to make her feel she was deserting them? Beside the hamper, she stashed a hanging geranium whose blossoms were an unusual shade of deep cerise. Next, some games that Jamie's boy Mike suggested for the O'Hara children and a straw tote containing two bottles of Beaujolais for Dave. Possibly there was no point in waving good-bye to dogs, but she did so anyway. Returning later to feed them should provide an excellent excuse for an early escape from the family scene.

This perfect weather certainly wouldn't curtail the festivities, Olivia noted as she drove along familiar roads winding between Scituate and Marshfield. She was wearing a yellow-flowered sundress with a matching jacket and white espadrilles with yellow trim—instead of de rigueur jeans and sneakers—and she was bringing a white shawl, a white rain jacket, and a flowered umbrella. Olivia's outfits were planned for all eventualities. Nevertheless, it was the kind of spring day that May ought always to bring and so seldom does. Gentle sunshine, azure skies with a scattering of fluffy clouds like swans on a lake, and just enough of a breeze to tease the skin with blissful ideas.

Olivia was off somewhere on a ninth cloud when she had to brake abruptly for a reckless squirrel. The wine slammed into the hamper, the hamper collided with the hanging plant. *Perfection belongs to the gods*, she reminded herself later when she arrived at Dave's and peeked at her lop-sided cake and crushed geraniums.

Dave's home was a Colonial-red, L-shaped farmhouse not far from the center of town. A dogwood in the front yard was just past its prime, still clinging to a few flat, faded pink blossoms. On the other side of the front walk, a magnolia had gone to green leaves entirely. The lawn was neatly mowed, but there had been no attempt at anything that might be described as landscaping, just a few small evergreen foundation plants. The front porch held two old cane rocking chairs, and a row of four bicycles. There was a basketball hoop on the garage door, and beside it, a wooden box overflowing with sports equipment. Carrying the hamper and the plant, she walked around to the back where music was playing—Celtic folk tunes, she realized as she got closer. *Shades of Riverdance!*

"Here she is, here's Liv," Dave exclaimed, hurrying over to relieve her of the bundles and deliver a chaste kiss on the cheek. So that's the way it was going to be—*not in front of the children*. "Gosh, you brought us red geraniums, really pretty." He hung the plant on the limb of a maple tree that shaded a redwood picnic table. One of the blossoms fell off.

"There's another package in the car for all of you, and some wine for Dave," Olivia said, smiling her best job-interview smile at the youngsters who were studying her as if she were some alien species that might or might not be friendly to humans. "And I brought you a chocolate cake." She took the hamper from Dave and handed it to Moira, who was standing in the kitchen door, wearing a chef's apron that came down to her ankles. The girl had a halo of frizzy carroty curls through which the skin of her scalp shone pale and vulnerable. A scattering of freckles, light blue eyes.

"Oh, that's okay," Moira said, not reaching for the proffered hamper.

"Chocolate, my favorite!" Dave rushed in, lifting the hamper out of her hands, brushing past Moira to carry it into the kitchen. "Isn't this nice of Liv!"

After he emerged, there were proper introductions, enthusiastic on Dave's part, while Kevin, Moira, and Danny, exuded a studied indifference. It was going just about as Olivia feared. Why couldn't children be more like adults and display a little civilized hypocrisy when the occasion called for it? She was certainly setting them a good example with her glow of general approval and exclamations of pleasure. When, oh when, would she get a drink?

The backyard was large and had a lived-in look that Olivia found pleasant. Besides the long table and benches, she noted a sturdy gas grill, a double rope hammock slung between two trees, a glider, and several redwood folding chairs, some open, some leaning against the house. There's was a trellised rose bush bursting with buds beside the back door, but no flower beds. Several well-placed shade trees gave the yard a roof.

A metal wind chime—stars and crescent moons—hanging from a nearby branch trilled in the breeze. "What a pretty sound that has!" she said. Looking around, she saw that the backyard was decorated with several metal sculptures as well— a bemused Don Quixote on horseback, a seductive mermaid on a dolphin's back, a sly Peter Rabbit popping out of a watering can. Each of them had a whimsical touch of magic and humor, designed with a unique artistry. "Oh, these figures are so wonderful," she exclaimed. "Where did you get them?"

"I made them. It's what I do." Dave's tone was neither shy nor boastful, simply matter-of-fact. "I told you I like to work with metal—at *La Bella Campagna*—do you remember?"

"Yes, but I never dreamed you meant works of art. I pictured something else entirely—oh, I don't know—fenders and planters, things like that. These are superb."

Olivia was rewarded with a modest grin and a hug.

"Dave can do fenders, all right," Danny declared loyally. "He put a new one on my bicycle last week. And he gave me this compass so I won't get lost when I ride it somewhere I don't know."

"Maybe I can give Moira a hand in the kitchen," Olivia offered after admiring the compass, "while you boys look over those games and Dave opens the wine."

"Shall we let it breathe, honey?"

"I'm sure it's breathed enough for me. I'd love a glass right now."

Moira had already ducked into the kitchen. Olivia followed her, momentarily blinded as she stepped out of the dazzling sunshine. As her vision returned, she saw that it was a large, homey kitchen with many wall cabinets painted a cheery shade of green that had never been a favorite of hers. A kitchen should be pure white and starkly efficient, with shining chrome machines lined up at the ready, like an operating room. "Is that dill I smell?" she asked brightly

"I've made a dill mustard sauce to go with the poached salmon," Moira said, warming just a little, like a small iceberg softening at the edges. "Maybe you don't like salmon," she continued hopefully. "Dave is probably going to cremate something on the grill anyway. T-bones, I think. That red wine will be okay with those."

"It's a light red that will work with your salmon, too. I love salmon."

Moira looked disappointed but bore up bravely. She busied herself brushing partly sliced loaves of French bread with a savory herb butter whose fragrance reminded Olivia that she hadn't had much breakfast. On the round oak kitchen table was a pretty bowl of macaroni salad studded with artichoke hearts, chunks of cheese, and olives. "Wow, did you make that? Dave told me you're a whiz in the kitchen. I'm really impressed. Where did you learn to cook like this? Not Home Ec, I bet."

"Home Ec. is for nerds," Moira said, licking the butter off her fingers. She took a large roll of heavy-duty foil out of a drawer and proceeded to wrap the loaves expertly. "I learned to cook from my mom. She's the best cooker in the world. Especially fish. Where she is now, she works in a really big kitchen." The loaves went into the oven. Moira fussed with the dial and, without turning, said, "I made a pineapple upside down cake for dessert, but I guess we can have that other thing, too." The hamper was still on the chair where Dave placed it.

"Whatever you say. You're the hostess. And if there's anything I can do to help, please let me know." Olivia opened the hamper and removed her cake. "This got a bit dented when I slammed on my brake for a squirrel. Could I borrow a knife to smooth out the frosting on this side?"

Moria handed her a metal spatula. "It works better if you run it under hot water," she said. "If you really want to help, you could go outside and make sure Dave's got the coals going right. They should be gray with winking red embers. Tell him twenty minutes, start the steaks."

When she finished fussing over her Tower of Pisa cake, Olivia went outside to deliver the cook's orders. She was glad to see that Dave had done his part just right. The coals were perfect, and the wine was poured. He put a glass into her hand and lifted his in a toast. "Here's to families," he said, grinning at her with foolish delight.

For some obscure reason, Olivia thought of her two miscarriages. "All right," she said. "Here's to families." She was thirsty and the wine went down too easily. There didn't seem to be anything for her to do. Kevin was setting the table with plastic dishes and stainless steel flatware. He was also studying her out of the corner of his eye, his gaze wandering from her bare legs to her breasts. *Fourteen*, Olivia thought, studying him back. Everything about him was darker than Moira. Dark brown hair, gray-blue eyes. But the three children shared similar features—snub noses, small mouths, and narrow faun-like chins.

Danny flipped through the games—a South Shore version of Monopoly, Sports Trivia Fun for the Whole Family, and a video game called Dimension of the Dinosaurs II. "Cool," Danny said. His fair hair was cut almost long enough to hide his outstanding ears, and he wore an unguarded expression that gave Olivia hope.

Kevin glanced over. "We have that already," he said.

"It's the sequel, Kev. Dinosaurs II." Danny's voice had an undercurrent of whining that sounded as if it was characteristic. "We don't have Dinosaurs II."

"Whatever it is, I'm still going to beat you at it. You'll be dead meat for the dinosaurs, O Danny Boy."

"Hey, I won last time. And the time before. Don't you remember, Kev?" Danny insisted on his rights, his tone getting bolder.

Kevin rapped him smartly on the head. "That's because your pals taught you how to cheat, you punk."

"Yeah, well Vinny knows more about Dinosaurs than you do," Danny said, moving away and rubbing his head. "I gotta go tell him I got D II."

"You two geeks ought to quit with the stupid hourly e-mails," Kevin said scornfully. "That computer is for all of us, you know."

There was a delicious sizzle going on at the grill. Olivia noticed that she was getting hungry as well as thirsty. And she was tired of standing but wasn't sure if she ought to be helping in some way. She felt her hands hanging off her arms like useless appendages.

"Hey, Kev, come over here and watch the steaks, will you please?" Dave said. Leaving Kevin in charge of the grill, he refilled her glass, put an arm around her waist.

"Great games, great wine, great gal," he whispered. "Now, this isn't as bad as you thought, is it? Aren't they extraordinary!" His merest breath on her ear caused a shiver to run down her neck to her spine like a sensuous feather touch.

"I'm having a wonderful time," she lied.

ᐧᗡᑎ

Whatever their feelings about the strange woman in their midst, around whom their uncle was hovering attentively, the children were polite enough to observe the conventions and treat the guest decently. Moira gave her a copy of the macaroni salad recipe written out in her sub-teen scrawl. Kevin showed her his Celtic drum, called a bodhran, and played a few riffs. And Danny taught her to whistle a loud piercing two-finger screech that he had perfected. "You can use this to call your dogs," he told her, his fair face shining with enthusiasm. "Uncle Dave says you have lots of dogs. Next time, maybe you can bring them with you. I'd love to have a dog but Uncle Dave says not now, maybe later."

"Just two dogs, Danny. That's all I have, and they're enough. Sadie and Bruno. I'm sure you'll meet them sometime." Olivia's whistle came out more like a squeak. Danny said she should keep practicing.

"You bet I will. Thanks for the lesson. Now much as I hate to leave," Olivia said at seven on the dot, "I do have to get home and give the dogs a run. A long afternoon is about as much as they can be expected to endure." She'd drunk several glasses of wine, just enough to take the edge off her nerves. Fortunately, she'd also eaten a fairly large meal—the food was truly good, not at all what she feared it would be— that Moira! She admitted to a bit of admiration at the girl's cool skill, as well as her insistence that her brothers help with the clean-up and her refusal to play a game that would bore

her silly. Olivia, therefore, had allowed herself to be severely
trounced in the Sports Trivia game from hell, Kevin's choice,
while Danny whined and fussed because he wasn't winning
and it was everyone else's fault.

While Dave walked her to the van, carrying the empty
hamper and straw tote, she asked him to check out her
assistant Ray Chance, to see if he had any kind of record. He
looked at her with a quick frown of worry. "What's he done
to make you suspicious of him? Why don't you just fire the
bastard?"

"No, no … it's not that easy to fill a minimum wage
position that's temporary by its very nature, and I need
some real help. But I caught him listening in on my phone
conversation with Mrs. Mitchell, that's all. So I just wondered.
I'm afraid I didn't check his references as thoroughly as I
should have."

"Why don't you ask the former Town Clerk to come back
for a few weeks, and give you a hand?" Dave asked.

Olivia laughed, imagining Emma Ridley in an assistant's
role, obliged to follow her directions. "Not on your life!
That woman is totally impossible. You have no idea what an
impenetrable chaos she's created in Mattakeesett. And she's
both proud and protective of it!"

"Okay, but you can always hire someone else, maybe a young
person with a degree in the humanities and no job prospects
for the summer. I'll run Ray Chance though the computer first
thing. And if he's dirty, you'll get rid of him, no matter what."
He slid into the front seat with her, and kissed her until she
was breathless, slipping away into a fever of desire.

"Hey, Dave," said Danny, coming around the corner of
the house, "Moira says hurry up, the garbage disposal is stuck
again."

"Damn," Dave muttered against her mouth. He let her go still looking at her longingly. "Hey, honey, this was wonderful. The kids loved you, I could tell. You'll be all right driving home, won't you?"

She put her hand against his rough, warm face. How could someone so smart and talented be so ingenuous? If he was looking for a mother-figure to help him raise that brood of urchins, he was looking in the wrong direction. But she couldn't deny a deep rush of feeling for him that was beyond passion, a kind of aching tenderness that flowed into her bones like water. "I'll be careful." A simple statement that has always been her credo. But now she has somehow been swept off-course into uncharted seas. "Careful" did not describe the present direction of her life.

ᑲᐧᓇ

It was very early on Monday morning. Olivia was still lingering over a second cup of coffee and the *Boston Globe*— *Middle-East Peace Talks Fail. Night Club Brawl Ends in Stabbing. Miss America Rides Swan Boat with Mayor*—when Dave called. "Get rid of him, honey," he said at once.

"Good morning, Dave. I had a great time yesterday. Why, what's Ray done?"

"Me, too, honey. Robert Ray Chance, parents used to run a farm stand up in Harvard, Al's Apples. Your typical young suburban wastrel. Petty stuff. Juvenile detention for a joy ride on a stolen motorcycle. Did a short stint for aggravated assault. Associates with some sleazy characters— drug pushers, gamblers, loan sharks. It's conceivable that he might be connected."

"Connected?"

"To the Benedettos."

"Oh. *Damn it*. I'll have to think how I can manage this. Call me tonight and I'll let you know how it went, okay?"

"If you have any trouble at all, give me a buzz earlier, honey. I know how to handle these small-time hoods."

"What about your own job? You can't keep taking time off to rescue me. Doesn't the South Shore have any big-ticket crimes to solve these days?"

"Sure, but you're more important. Also, through no fault of your own, you're mixed up with the Benedettos now. I admit to a kind of obsession where they're concerned. They killed my partner."

Olivia resisted quoting from *The Maltese Falcon,* "When a man's partner is killed, he's supposed to do something about it." In the first months of her separation from Hank, when she couldn't get to sleep until early morning, Olivia had become conversant with every old classic, especially film noir, on DVD. She wondered if there was a Movie Trivia Fun for the Whole Family she might bring to Dave's—insist on a rematch she could win. If she ever goes back there, that is. "I've fired employees before. I don't think I'll have a problem, but if I do …"

"Oh, God … sorry, honey, I have to go *right now*. There's been an appalling incident at Norwell Junior High. Apparently, some deranged parent sprayed the teachers' cars with buckshot. Jesus!" A click, and Dave was gone. Oh well, he'd promised to call her tonight. And she'd be seeing him on Wednesday—he was taking her out to dinner at *La Bella Campagna* again.

Olivia felt a frisson of anxiety about firing Ray Chance, but she brushed it aside and called him into her office at ten that morning. He arrived still wiping dusty hands on his jeans and grinning in that knowing way of his. "What's your pleasure, Ms. Andreas?"

"I'm sorry, Ray. I find that I have neither the funding nor the need for an assistant that I had anticipated when I first began this project. I have to let you go, but I'm adding two week's severance to your last paycheck. You can pick it up on Friday at the front desk."

He stared at her, caught off guard for once, incredulous. "You want me to leave *today*?"

"Yes. Right now, if you don't mind. Just clear up the stuff in your locker. You'll be paid for the day and the rest of this week, plus another week's severance. Again, I'm really sorry about this."

"The hell you are." His gaze raked over her in a way that was calculated to be insulting. Taking his time, he turned toward the door, casually trailing his hand across her desk so that her bud vase, pencil jar, phone, and desk calendar crashed to the floor. "Frigid bitch," he muttered, sauntering toward the door.

Olivia felt weak all over but thankful that she would finally be seeing the last of this insolent young man. But then, halfway to the door, Ray stopped abruptly, changed direction, and came back toward her. His face appeared choleric with rage. His fists were clenched at his sides. She gripped the edge of her desk to keep from ducking away from him. She knew there were no guards, no security in this entire building. Her phone was still lying on the floor.

"I know what *you* need." His tone was mocking. He smirked and raised one fist.

"What do you think you're doing, you little weasel," boomed a voice from the doorway. Emma Ridley loomed into view, almost as if she'd been listening to the whole exchange and

waiting for just the right moment to intervene. She was holding a cell phone in one hand and punching in numbers with the other. "The lady told you to haul ass, didn't she? And you'd better get your scrawny carcass out of here in a hurry because I'm calling 911 right this minute."

Giddy with relief, Olivia nearly giggled. *Emma with a cell phone?* Never had she imagined that Emma Ridley's appearance could be so welcome. Ray lowered his fist and slunk toward the door. Emma moved her bulk to let him pass, lifting her blanket skirt to one side so that no part of Ray would touch it.

"Good riddance to bad rubbish," Emma said, not waiting for Ray to be out of earshot. "Messing around with my land deed books. Making notes, too. Probably working up some scam in that pea-brain of his. You want to hire a nice little girl next time, someone who'll listen to what you tell her to do. You never know with a man. Most of them can't be trusted farther than you can throw a computer. You need me, I'll be in the Justice of the Peace's office today. Secretary has the trots." With that, Emma lumbered off down the hall.

Olivia fell back into her desk chair. *Breathe slowly and deeply*, she told herself. *Emulate Marcus Aurelius—impervious to villains, immune to threats* After a while, she set about picking up her desk paraphernalia. She speculated that Emperor Marcus Aurelius merely called in the slaves to clean up when the rabble rose against him and trashed the imperial villa.

The phone began to ring. Picking it up from the floor, she wearily lifted the receiver to her ear. "Mattakeesett Town Hall. Records. Olivia Andreas speaking," she whispered.

"O my Gawd," Jamie said. "I know Monday mornings can be rough, but you sound like death warmed over. What's going on? Too much weekend?"

"No, nothing like that. A little problem at work, that's all. It's straightened out now. What's up?"

"I called for two reasons. First, to see how you liked Dave's family, *ha ha*! And second, to ask if you want to take in that auction at the Grange Hall tomorrow night. We haven't been to an auction in *ages,* and the brochure shows some intriguing jewelry—unusual cameos and antique lockets—a very pretty Winthrop desk, some Roseville pottery, collectible kitchen pieces. Viewing is five to six-thirty, you'd have to get out of work early, but then you're more or less your own boss, aren't you?"

"Sounds like fun," Olivia said, her voice still weak. "I don't know if I'd dare to buy anything, though. I wouldn't want to bring home another ghost."

"Just don't bid on anything of a personal nature this time. No portraits of Aunt Pratt, no braided-hair bracelets, no Civil War diaries or ectoplasmic photographs. And speaking of ghosts, what do you hear from Lily these days?"

"You won't believe this. Mrs. Mitchell and I communicated with her by ouija board, and she gave me some hints to pass along to Dave. I'll tell you all about that at the auction."

"*A ouija board!* You're right, I don't believe it. Shouldn't that Mrs. Mitchell be doing a Navaho Blessing Way or smudging or something like that? But what about Sunday? How did that go?"

"Don't ask," Olivia said. "Dave and I may still be an item, but there's little chance of our becoming one big happy family with the O'Hara kids. The games were okay, though. Tell Mike I said thanks. And Mrs. M. is Wampanoag not Navaho."

"That Dave must be a real optimist if he believes you'll take over the Donna Reed role. I'll be at your place at five sharp tomorrow—that way we'll have plenty of time to browse through the lots."

"We'd better take my van, in case. Although I probably won't buy anything."

"Sure, sure ..." Jamie said. "Auctions are like love affairs. Surprising, exciting, and full of unsuspected pitfalls. Caution flies out the window, and you end up getting feverish over winning some impossible piece of trash."

Olivia laughed and felt better. Ray Chance was gone forever, and there were good times ahead.

JUNIOR

Junior leaned back in his hot tub, sipping a glass of Bushmills straight up. This was his sanctuary, this luxury townhouse with harbor views. It had been leased to him for a song by a real estate dealer for whom Junior had done a quiet favor in a custody dispute. Immersed in heat and whiskey, Junior felt himself begin to relax after yet another bad news day, and no end in sight. Not only had he lost a useful contact he'd had in place, all he could deliver to Uncle was more frustration. He'd have to try to put a good face on it.

What the hell was this ghost crap the Andreas broad had been talking about on the phone? And why was she mouthing off about a "mob connection"? He'd thought the dog's head he got at Shawmutt Pound would have warned off this persistent bitch for good, but she was still sniffing around. It would be simple enough to make her disappear, but she had something or knew something they needed. Uncle was convinced of it. Junior would like to take her long white neck between his hands right now. He'd shake the truth out of her in no time. Maybe fuck her till she passed out. She wasn't really his type, though. He liked them small, curvy, and compliant. Still, a fuck was a fuck.

Not a chance of that, though, now that she'd hooked up with that Plymouth detective. If she'd been alone, it was one thing, but with Lowenstein in the picture, Junior would have to be careful of how he went about leaning on her.

Uncle had been after him night and day to find whatever it was Rossi had hidden with Lily. Junior had never trusted that little motherfucker money man, always sitting quiet as a mouse in the corner, filling his face with pastry while everyone forgot he was there and spilled the family business. Uncle thought he was so smart, him and that Machiavelli, but he'd never seen that one coming.

What would happen, Junior wondered, if he told the *capo de capo* of the Benedetto family about Uncle's screw-up? Might cause a ripple effect in the chain of command. Maybe then Junior could get out from under the fruit man's thumb and into something a little smoother and more lucrative. What he'd really like was to run a classy club or an elite escort service—or both. Yeah!

Not yet, though. When the right time came, he'd have a confidential talk with the real head of the Benedetto family. He'd express affection for Uncle, concern for his carrying too much on his shoulders alone, worry about how the family might be affected by an unstable situation getting worse. Junior would exude maturity and confidence. He would get rid of the old bull, and he would move up. Junior drained the Bushmills and smiled.

MAY 19
Things to Do Today

Don't forget magnet, magnifying glass, notebook, checkbook, sandwiches
Leave Mattakeesett early—S & B feed, run
Ask Dave—Plunkett auction records?
Wed morn—dry mop, dust, change bed, silk sheets
Cut flowers for bedroom

Olivia enjoyed making her own hours. *Flex time is the new wave,* she told herself, as she rushed home early on Tuesday afternoon, vowing that she would work extra hours later in the week. She was ready to go out the door when Jamie showed up, impatiently and proudly honking the horn of her new torch-red convertible. After admiring the Thunderbird extravagantly, Olivia insisted that her friend park the gleaming car in her garage for safe-keeping. They took off in Olivia's van right on schedule, prepared to transport any mad purchase to which they might succumb.

As the auction progressed, Jamie bought two cameos and a sweet little maple desk with matching chair. Olivia sat on her hands for most of the evening but finally fell for a large stoneware crock, only thirty-five dollars, perfect for storing dog chow. By nine, they decided they'd had enough. After loading their purchases into the van, they headed for home. Olivia wanted to make it an early night, so she'd be rested for her dinner with Dave the next evening. They stopped at Jamie's to drop off the desk and chair, which didn't seem so dainty—rock maple, after all—when they had to haul it from their parking place into the townhouse. Then they headed back to Olivia's place so that Jamie could pick up her car.

It was such a pleasant May night of blossom-scented breezes, they drove with the windows open. As they rounded the corner onto Edgewood Road, Olivia's street, the first thing they encountered was the sickening smell of smoke, then the garish flickering lights of fire trucks and police cars, loud speakers blaring. Imagining her dogs trapped in a burning house, Olivia screamed and slammed on her brake. Jumping out of the van, they raced toward the house. Olivia breathed a deep sigh of relief to find her home untouched, the dogs barking loudly.

It was the garage that was smoking and steaming.

"Oh my good Gawd, *why didn't I leave it in the driveway* ... or even in the street?" Jamie wailed, viewing the scorched remains of her sporty Thunderbird. "I'm sorry to say this, Liv, but I think you're becoming a jinx—a real jinx. Did Lily do this?"

"Not Lily," Olivia was quite sure. "Someone all too human, I'd say. Listen, I'm really awfully sorry about this, Jamie. What a terrible thing to have happen to that lovely car." She felt quite composed but chilled to the bone, surveying her wrecked yard. The garage was a charred skeleton, the lilac bushes that grew beside it now a web of black lace, all her carefully planted flower borders trampled into mud.

"Oh, that's all right," Jamie said, tears spilling out of her eyes. "I wasn't even used to driving it yet. It only had 68 miles on the odometer. I suppose my insurance company will pay up and then dump me."

Olivia empathized deeply with her friend's grief and couldn't escape feelings of guilt and responsibility. A brand new car paid for with her own hard-earned money was a precious possession to a single woman. That Thunderbird represented a whole lot of shots in the rump and bed pans.

"I guess I'd better give you a ride home." Olivia was trying hard to make her brain function normally.

"*No way, Jose,*" Jamie protested. "You're still in shock."

"You aren't afraid to be with me, are you?"

"Nonsense. I admit Lily gives me a twinge or two, but I have every faith in you. After all, we've been friends practically forever. And it's your garage that got wrecked, as well as my cute car." Jamie's voice broke, just avoiding a sob.

After they identified themselves to the officers in charge and explained about the Thunderbird, Jamie insisted on fixing a cup of strong sweet tea for Olivia and gave her half a Xanax to "take the edge off." Then Jamie hitched a lift in a patrol car. But first, she gave Olivia a big hug and whispered, "Thank Gawd it wasn't the house! I'm so sorry that you have to face this mess. Call Dave! Men are really useful in emergencies like this, especially cops."

༄

Jamie was right about that, Olivia discovered. Dave was a tower of strength throughout the ordeal of investigation that followed, and he was a great hand with the clean-up as well. Jamie's insurance covered towing the wrecked roadster out of her garage, but it was Dave who found an outfit willing to remove the ruined garage, and a landscaper who would clean up and partially restore the backyard.

Meanwhile, *La Bella Campagna* got scrapped. Instead, on the night after the fire, they ordered in Chinese, which had the advantage of being ready to nuke in the microwave whenever they were ready to eat it, which was much later in the evening. First they talked, worried, planned, drank wine, and made love.

"I'll find out who did this, honey," Dave vowed, helping himself to more spicy beef with broccoli. "Even the preliminary investigation is suggestive of an explosive, they tell me."

"Amateur or professional? I imagine Jamie's insurance company will want answers, too." Olivia passed him the hot mustard sauce in a tiny cut-glass bowl. Despite everything that had occurred, she was serving the food in serving dishes at the dining room table, not cardboard containers in the kitchen.

"Can't be sure, yet. They're thinking dynamite with a detonation cord, not the usual Plastique. And I haven't ruled out that guy you fired Monday. If he's been in the service, he may have handled explosives."

"I haven't ruled him out either. We almost had a rather nasty scene. Ray actually raised his fist at me, but Emma Ridley turned up as my rescuer. Rats! I guess I owe her one now."

"That son-of-a-bitch!" Two angry red spots flushed Dave's cheeks, and his eyes narrowed. "Why didn't you tell me right away that he threatened you?"

For the first time, Olivia could imagine Dave aiming a gun, firing a gun. It suddenly occurred to her that this quiet guy might be rather dangerous under certain circumstances. "I was going to, but then we ... "The vision of a fearsome Dave faded, and she smiled, remembering their trembling rush to get into bed. It wasn't easy to stay as angry as she should at Ray or whoever set fire to her garage when she was looking at Dave's mouth and thinking libidinous thoughts. Not even fear for her own safety had penetrated the sensual fog. Her brain must be dancing to an overload of serotonin. Her priorities seemed to be seriously screwed up. Were these symptoms of real love or merely the pheromones of sexual chemistry?

"By the way, you haven't told me how you made out with the auction people," she asked, letting her bare foot glide toward his under the table.

"I persuaded them to give me a copy of their sales from the Plunkett estate. Every item is described, including silver frames, plus addresses for buyers who'd registered to bid and been assigned a number. But I really don't have enough evidence to proceed. That is, to confiscate all the suspect frames. Ouija boards don't cut it with judges."

"But you have to! I promised Lily." She pulled her foot back just as it was snaking its way up his shin.

"Liv, my love...get a grip. Lily is dead and gone. You owe her nothing, nothing at all. Remember that I want to find out if, how, and why she was murdered by the Benedettos as much, even more than you do. I'll do everything I can ... legally." To soften his words, Dave took her hand across the pork fried rice, caressing the inside of her arm.

Exhaustion set in right after dinner and all the wine they drank before, during, and after. Dave thought he would just shut his eyes for a few moments before he had to drive home. He looked so sweet and vulnerable sleeping on her couch, she had to resist the desire to squeeze in beside him. Instead, she set about brewing a pot of strong coffee to see him safely on the road. Then she picked up his jacket from the stairs, smoothed it out, and hung it on the chair beside him.

Maybe this isn't quite fair, but I'm going to do it, Olivia thought, as she felt the folded auction records in his inside breast pocket. She lifted out the pages and ran them through the printer-copier in her office. Dave's hands might be tied, but hers were not.

The three women who bought single frames would be easy enough to find, but none of the listings noted the design, so the owner of the shamrock frame was still in question. Before Rossi the CPA was killed, he'd tucked away proof of illegal financial dealings by the Benedettos. They got Al Capone on tax evasion, didn't they? Olivia would simply go around to each of those women and offer to buy back her frame. No harm in that.

It was well after midnight when Olivia woke Dave. He drank two cups of very strong black coffee and, after many reluctant kisses, took off for home. Although every bone in her body was weary and aching, Olivia went into her office to have another peek at the Byatt papers. The two sheets were just where she left them, face down beside the printer-copier. But on top of them was a new paperweight. Lily's framed photograph had moved off its shelf again and was pinning down the list of buyers.

"Relax, Lily. I'm going to find Frank Rossi's little book, if it exists," Olivia said. "Oh, there I go, talking to myself again."

The photo thumped twice. It was a heart-stopping sight—a frame that hopped up all by itself, then came back down without falling over. But somehow, weird events were more acceptable in the small hours of the morning.

"All right, so I'm not talking to myself. I'm talking to you, Lily. And you know what I'm saying? *Good night.*"

With barely strength to go through her bedtime ritual of teeth-brushing and face-cleaning, at last Olivia collapsed into a heap under the comforter. Bruno was already snoring. Sadie lifted her head an inch, then let it fall back on the other pillow. From the window, open just two inches, the acrid smell of burned wood drifted in over the three unmoving forms.

Olivia's world was growing even crazier. Her brand new love life was inexpressibly sweet but complicated by Dave's house-full of children. Her work, once viewed as a challenge and a commitment, had become more like a constant interruption to things she'd rather be doing. Plus there was the hassle of hiring a new assistant and the unsettling knowledge that she owed one to Emma Ridley. At home, overseeing the clean-up crew and the landscaper, who only showed up when the spirit moved them, was a continuing problem. And she felt driven to find Lily's frames, at least the one with the prize in it. Again, *The Maltese Falcon* came to mind. If she believed in mystic symbolism, she'd be trying to figure out why. But time to ruminate was a luxury she couldn't afford. She rose earlier and got to bed later. Her lists and timetables became somewhat scrambled.

Unfortunately, her first attempt to buy back a frame was not very successful. In fact, she was nearly thrown out of the charming rose-covered cottage in Cohasset where her first contact lived, Rosa Manaici, a formidable woman with the build of a Sumi wrestler. Olivia remembered seeing her spread out in the front row at the Plunkett auction.

Manaici immediately fixated on the idea that her silver frame must be worth much more than she paid if Olivia has turned up on her doorstep wanting to buy it. "I'm wise to you smarmy antique dealers, bunch of thieves, that's what you are," she muttered, giving Olivia a muscular push off the front step and closing the door in her face before she could ask about the shamrocks.

The next night she tried the Hingham address. Kristie Hagen, South Street, second floor. Taking a tip from telemarketers, Olivia decided the dinner hour was a good time to catch people at home. Ms. Hagen answered her bell promptly, encircled by the aroma of frying chicken. She was a rosy-cheeked young woman wearing a brilliantly striped dirndl skirt and a slightly daffy smile. Olivia went into her spiel: *family heirloom sold at auction through a dreadful mistake must be returned so that dying aunt can expire in peace.* A bit fanciful, but plausible. With a puzzled look, but still smiling, the woman invited Olivia to step into the living room.

She gestured toward the etagere where a collection of photographs was displayed. "The one I bought at auction is on the middle shelf."

No shamrocks. "Oh, I see," Olivia says. "Golly, I'm so sorry to have bothered you. That is definitely not the frame Aunt Lily is crying over."

"You know, you're the second person this week who's asked me about a frame bought at Byatt's. I told him I didn't have such an item. I didn't like his looks, so I thought maybe he was going to try to rob me. What's going on, anyway?"

That's exactly what Olivia was wondering. She made her excuses and got out of the apartment house fast. Something new to worry about as she drove home. Had some member of the Benedetto clan fingered the shamrock frame as a hiding place? Perhaps she should tell Dave that someone had been making inquiries—but how could she do that without admitting that she copied the list and was pursuing the buyers herself? She wouldn't blame him for being furious with her.

With all these questions bouncing back and forth in her brain like a tennis match, she was home before she knew it, with no sense of how the traffic was or what she'd passed on her way. Two men were in her backyard, picking up charred timbers and tossing them onto a truck. She was glad to see they were just finishing. As soon as they drove off, she let the dogs out for a good run and poured a glass of cold chardonnay for herself. Carrying her cell phone and an old towel so that she could flop onto one of the still sooty lawn chairs, she followed them into the backyard.

First she walked around the yard, observing that not much was left of the garage except its cement floor, like a blackened patio. The insurance would pay for a new garage, but no recompense for the headache of getting it built. The landscaper had dug out the borders, not yet replanted.

Dave called right at the time he said he would, six-thirty. He told her that Ray Chance didn't have an Army service record. No longer living at the Harvard address on his employment records, he'd sold the motorcycle he was driving, which was now in a used car lot. Probably he was slinking back into Boston's alleys like one of the city's wily invisible rats.

Olivia listened with fascination but did not fill him in on her adventures. Maybe when he came over on Wednesday evening—which was fast becoming one of their regular date nights—she'd confess. And maybe not.

"I did turn up one other piece of information about Mr. Chance that may interest you. The last time he was arrested on an assault charge, the lawyer who bailed him out and subsequently got him off was a junior member of the same firm that handles the Benedettos' legal affairs."

"Small world," Olivia said. "With too many coincidences. I'm getting paranoid."

"Being sensibly paranoid is a survival skill," Dave said.

"I'm afraid I'm being rather a lot of trouble."

"I don't mind a reasonable amount of trouble." Didn't Dave realize that he's quoting Sam Spade's line straight out of *The Maltese Falcon*. Another coincidence? Olivia had the chilling feeling that she's supposed to understand all these signs and portents. But then he added, "And besides, you're worth it" which was not in the film noir script at all.

After they'd said good-bye, Olivia sat in one of the towel-draped chairs, sipping her wine, a dog perched upright on each side of her. Perhaps they were paranoid, too. "What have I got you guys into? Maybe you were safer at the dog pound." Bruno gazed at her with his tragic shepherd eyes, silently reminding her that he hadn't yet been fed, and Sadie nuzzled her hand for a pat. Olivia thought she'd cut up that leftover lamb chop into their chow tonight. There was so little you can do to thank dogs for their devotion, except to love them back and feed them well.

の

Wednesday again ... in Olivia's mind, *our night*. The two lovers found themselves in her bedroom with no actual memory of how they got there, a trail of clothing being the only clue to their actual passage up the stairs. They made rough, quick, thrilling love as if they'd been separated for months instead of days. Then, later, they explored each other more gently and deeply. Olivia was surprised by urges and desires that she'd never experienced in her marriage.

After such rapturous sex, it was difficult to move or even to think. Olivia felt as if she'd discovered a short-cut to the transcendental state that long practice in meditation may or may not achieve. It was like wandering in a beautiful mist of non-being, a preview to nirvana.

Again they dined late by the light of many candles arranged on the dining room table and around the room. Barber's concerto for violin was soaring through the CD player. A low vase held a few early roses, pink and yellow buds. Olivia had cooked the never-fail, never-dries-out-from-overcooking, all-in-one-pan chicken casserole she saved for uncertain times, which is all the time lately. Everything tasted wonderful. *The best sauce is hunger,* as the French said— and Olivia and Dave were very hungry.

Over the chocolate mousse that came after the reliable chicken, Dave admitted, with a rueful and endearing grin, that he was no closer to solving the mystery of the conflagration in her garage or to obtaining permission to collect the Plunkett frames from their present owners. A little snake of guilt slithered into Olivia's Eden. Should she confess what she'd been up to? The craving to clear her conscience proved nearly irresistible, but it was stifled by the fear that Dave might become enraged. Wouldn't he shout and rant and threaten the way Hank used to do over her smallest deceptions?

Seizing upon any distraction from this moral dilemma, she said the first thing that came into her panicked brain. She heard herself inviting Dave and *his whole family* for Sunday dinner.

He was delighted, of course. *Perfect timing*, he declared, because it would be a week *before* the children's monthly visit to their mother. Sometimes, Dave confessed, they were a little edgy and unreasonable after they came back from visiting hours at Danbury Federal Correctional Institution where Alice O'Hara was serving not less that 15 nor more than 25 years for armed robbery. If he went with them at all, Kenny would be in a fighting mood at school the next day. Moira closed herself in her room for hours on end, and Danny wet the bed. The younger boy would often have a seizure around that time, but Dave saw to it that Danny took the medicine that controlled epileptic episodes.

Olivia studied Dave with pity and admiration, as she might ponder the painting of a martyred saint. "I don't know how you do it, or even why you do it," she said.

"It's me or the foster care system, honey. And I'm not about to let Tom O'Hara's kids get split up and dumped in sub-standard homes with people who may be abusive or sexual predators. Social services doesn't have enough personnel, time, or money to keep on top of those cases. Sometimes you have to take on responsibilities just because they turn up at your door, and there's no one else. And besides, I really like the little devils. Most always. That Kevin, though, he's a handful. Don't be surprised if he comes up with some excuse to duck out of your beautiful invitation. But Moira and Danny go where I go, no problem."

"That's okay. We'll play it by ear. My real worry is how Sadie and Bruno will behave with the children."

"Most dogs love children," Dave said. "Don't give it another thought."

THE CONTACT

Picking up a black coffee at the Dunkin' Donuts booth in Stop & Shop, Lee Washington studied the man and girl in the produce aisle. It appeared that the girl—Lowenstein had called her "Moira"—was the brains of the expedition. She carefully examined every item she selected and checked it against her list before dropping it in the cart her companion was pushing. Lowenstein appeared slightly bored but good-humored. Looks reasonable enough, Washington thought.

"Hi, there," Washington said. "Could we have a word, do you think?" He held his identification low so that only Lowenstein could see it.

Dave read the card and looked up at the man, startled. The stranger had a long thin face with Egyptian features and the tall lithe build of a Watusi warrior. Although he was wearing traditional FBI garb—a good basic dark two-button suit that might have come right off the rack at Louie's, conservative tie, and button-down pale blue shirt—this was not an agent who would blend in anywhere. Dave glanced at Moira, still absorbed in choosing tomatoes, and nodded briefly. "This had better be good."

"I'm going outside for a minute, honey," Dave told the girl. "I'll be back before you reach check-out."

"Who's your friend?" she asked, still comparing the merits of Roma to Hot House.

"It's a work thing," Dave said.

"Okay," Moira said, snapping off a plastic bag. As she filled it with Roma tomatoes, she was thinking that there was something about this guy that reminded her of the stone-faced suits who had taken away her mother. "If it walks like a duck, quacks like a duck ..." she muttered to herself. Uncle Dave was no fool, but Moira thought she'd alert Kevin anyway.

Outside the store, the two men sat on a bench provided for smokers and customers waiting for rides. Dave had a closer look at the FBI man's credentials, focusing on the number, trying to memorize it, while the stranger sipped his coffee, unperturbed. The identification appeared to be authentic. "What's up?" Dave asked.

"I think I can help you." Washington looked straight out at the parking lot as he talked, and Dave did the same.

"With what?" Dave thought there was something incredibly unorthodox and suspicious about this contact, but you never could tell.

"Frames," Washington said. "Silver frames like the one your girl bought at the Lamoureax auction."

Dave sat up straighter, suddenly very interested and very angry. The hands at his sides balled themselves into two fists. "Son of a bitch, did you ..."

"It wasn't us," Washington interrupted coolly. "But I know who did break in and what they were after. You must be aware that this isn't going to stop. Andreas is going to be in danger until they find what they're looking for."

"Yeah? Who's 'they?' And what kind of help are you offering exactly?"

"You and I both know who they are. As for my help, I'm in a position to gather some information that I'm willing to pass on to you. Information that may help to protect Andreas and, down the road, lead to an arrest of those involved."

Dave laughed. "You can't be FBI, man. The FBI doesn't play well with others."

"They don't, but sometimes I do. Listen, I'm trusting you here. If I could go through channels, I would never have contacted you. But there's an obstacle to my taking anything upstairs. And I sure would like to see that family go down. Are you interested or not?"

"Agent Washington, I'm the most interested cop you'll ever waylay in a supermarket. What've you got for me?"

"Drop the 'Agent,' please. Call me Lee. And I'll call you Dave, if I may. Dave, if you report our conversation to anyone, I'll learn about it, I'll deny it, and I'll get you demoted to traffic cop and audited way back to your first pay check."

Dave smiled. "And what about you? Disbarred and dismissed in disgrace?"

Ignoring the counter-threat, Washington said, "First, maybe you'll satisfy my curiosity. What the hell was in that fancy tin box that Benny Klein delivered to your girlfriend's front door?"

Dave recoiled, stretched back, hit a fist into the palm of his other hand. Benny Klein! He'd once seen a rap sheet on that creep. "A dead dog's head."

Washington barely stifled a laugh. The poor man's Godfather threat, he thought.

"You didn't know it was the Klein boys, did you? Will that serve as my bona fides?"

"Damn straight," Dave said. "What else you got?"

"I think they're looking for Rossi's little black book."

"I figured. Who else? I mean, who are those two goons working for?"

"That I know also. Angelo Benedetto, Jr. Or Junior, as he is known affectionately in the family. Acting on the orders of Rosario Benedetto. The Rose."

"Of course, the head of the family," Dave said.

"Maybe he is," Without moving his head, Washington's peripheral vision took in every motion in the parking lot around him. A quiet suburban scene. He finished his coffee, crushed the cup, and threw it expertly into the tall wastebasket several feet away. "And maybe he isn't. I've got a notion. But I'll save that one for later. Meanwhile, I'll see if I can find out where the Klein boys are hanging out these days."

How Dave would like to break those two bastards! "I think we can do business, Lee. What do you want in return?"

"Later, when you bring in the Bureau—and you will have to do that—if I can figure a way to get around that cement ceiling I keep hitting my head on. Then, I'd like to step in."

Thinking about his own "cement ceiling," Detective Lieutenant Badger, Dave felt he understood where this FBI guy was coming from. All he wanted was to get the job done, and some power-hungry turkey stood in his way. No wonder Lee was forced to skulk around corners, just as Dave himself had done.

"Deal," said Dave. "I'd better get back now. Kids have to get dinner. How can I get in touch?"

Agent Lee Washington took out a business card and wrote a number on the back. "My private cell," he said. "But it's better if you don't call me, I'll call you."

The two men stood up and shook hands. Dave liked what he saw in the other man's eyes, and the trust was mutual.

I hope I don't regret this, Lee said to himself as he drove away. And I hope Glumm does.

Back in Stop & Shop with Moira, Dave was thinking, Shit! I should have asked him about Ray Chance. Could it be that creep ...?

"Earth to Uncle Dave. Earth to Uncle Dave," Moira said crisply. "Could we pul-eeze get a move on? I don't want to miss American Idol. Who was that guy, anyway?"

"Forget that guy," Dave said. "He's no one you need to know, honey."

Yeah, right, Moira thought. Bet this has something to do with that new squeeze of Dave's. She was trouble for sure.

MAY 22
Things to Do Today

Hit another buyer It's got to be somewhere!
Vet – tranqu for B & S?
Libr for Your Troubled Teen etc.
Great Books: crack Emerson, Self-reliance

On Friday, Olivia finished early at Mattakeesett with a clear conscience. She finally had the new records program up and running smoothly, and that had surely earned her a break. There was the dreaded dinner party to get ready for; she hoped Saturday morning grocery shopping would inspire a menu that so far had eluded her. Never mind trying to upstage a thirteen-year-old cook, she'd settle for simply pleasing everyone, which was impossible enough. Her ad for an assistant would run on Sunday, so the beginning of next week would have to be devoted to interviews. This afternoon off, therefore, was a well-deserved respite. And since it was a mark of an efficient manager to make full use of any little island of time that came her way, she seized the opportunity to pursue the last frame on her list.

Norwell. On her way home anyway, practically next door to her place in Scituate. It was a gorgeous spring day of blissful sunshine and newly leafed trees; those twisted country roads would be shaded and pleasant.

Stony Acres Farm was easy enough to find, just off Bridge Street, which crossed the North River. Williams was the name on the rural mailbox outside the neat gray farmhouse. Olivia had found her quarry—Emily Williams, the woman who took the last silver frame home from the March auction.

Olivia knocked for quite a long time before she heard a crash against the door. It flew open with a fierce bang against the interior wall. Two boys, who might have been eight or nine, were jostling with each other, giggling and smirking, both apparently intending to get to the door first. The winner of this skirmish had pushed himself into position with the aid of a skateboard scooting over the polished wide-planked hall floor.

"Oh, hell!" said the skateboard boy, with a disappointed scowl. "It's not Fed-Ex, it's some woman. *Ma!*" he shouted. *"Some woman is here."*

"How many times have I told you *not* to use that thing in the house!" Rushing into the front hall, a sandy-haired woman in a long flowered cotton dress gave both boys a cross look and pushed them right out the door past Olivia, who jumped quickly to one side of the stone step. "Oh, sorry," the young mother said. "The boys are expecting a package from their Dad. Fed-Ex shows up around this time. What can I do for you? If you're selling something, I'm afraid I probably don't want any."

Olivia explained that she was inquiring about a silver frame that Mrs. Williams had bought at a Byatt auction.

Emily Williams looked confused for a moment. "Oh, yes. I remember now. I don't know why I bought that thing. I still haven't found the right photo for that odd size. But that's auctions for you—I always end up with something useless, know what I mean? Don't tell me it's antique sterling after all!" She brightened at the thought. "Okay, then, I suppose you should come in and explain."

Olivia was grateful for the invitation; her story didn't play so well on a doorstep. It played very well, however, in the pretty little front parlor with sprigged violet wallpaper where Emily Williams brought Olivia. In fact, the other woman seemed almost in tears over the loss of the family's beloved photo portrait. Encouraged, Olivia brought up her buy-back offer. The receipt said the frame went for $35.00. Olivia would pay $45.00 to return the portrait to her ailing Aunt Lily.

Emily Williams looked thoughtful. "$45.00? For a cherished family heirloom, possibly sterling silver, with those lovely engraved shamrocks? Surely you can do better than that."

So much for that homespun Laura Ashley look, Olivia thought. She offered fifty. Emily Williams remained unconvinced. By the time Olivia finally got her hands on the shamrock frame, she had spent $125.00. No time to take the photo's backing off now. She laid the newspaper-wrapped framed photo of Lily (riding on a float in the Boston St. Patrick's Day parade, year unknown) on the seat beside her and headed home, smiling as she contemplated her first success in gathering evidence that Dave couldn't get his hands on.

"It just needed a woman's touch," Olivia explained to Sadie and Bruno as she unwrapped the frame and placed it on the kitchen table. She found a tiny screwdriver in her tool kit, and proceeded to remove the elaborate backing. Obligingly, it fell off into her hands, with two pieces of filler corrugated cardboard and Lily in her Irish colleen outfit, smiling brilliantly and waving at onlookers.

Whoa! Was that all? Olivia separated the cardboards from each other, shook them, turned them upside down.

There it was, a small slit at the bottom of each corrugated sheet. From one she pried out an unmarked computer disc. From the other, a business card.

"Compliments of the First Federal Bank of America, Brockton, Massachusetts, Oak Street Branch." Brockton was Lily's home town!

"Eureka!"

She turned the card over. On the back, in tiny letters, Bernice L. Plunkett.

Meanwhile, the dogs had begun whining to go outside. Needing a few peaceful moments to concentrate on what she should do next, Olivia opened the back door and let them race into the yard. Immediately, a frenzy of barking commenced. Olivia realized that she would have to see what was going on. She hoped it wasn't another meter reader up in her maple tree.

It was a Tweedledum person, and he wasn't climbing anything. He was sparring with Sadie using a clipboard as a jousting lance and his briefcase as a shield, while an excited Bruno barked and ran around them in circles.

"Sadie! Bruno! Come at once!" Olivia used her most commanding dog trainer voice. The dogs, determined to protect their too-trusting companion, continued to hassle the chubby intruder. Olivia put two fingers in her mouth and whistled the way Danny had taught her. She was surprised by the piercing loudness of the sound, and even more surprised when Bruno trotted over and sat in front of her, tongue lolling, and Sadie backed off from the rotund man's knees.

"You'd better get yourself an extra umbrella policy with these vicious beasts." His voice squeaked a little. "But you'll have to pay extra. These are considered dangerous breeds, you know."

Olivia grabbed each dog by its collar and hauled them into the kitchen, meanwhile talking over her shoulder to the indignant man. "Sadie is a trained companion, not an attack dog. And she's never allowed to run wild. Either she's on leash or in her own fenced yard." She slammed the kitchen door on the two bewildered dogs, and caught her breath, making a mental note to buy *Beware of the Dog* signs. "Ordinarily, she's very gentle. It's just that you startled her, walking in like that. We've had break-ins here and an arson, so she's naturally wary."

"Ms. Andreas? I'm Jim Broadbent, your insurance adjuster. I'd check into that policy anyway, if I were you. A future homeowner's claim could be denied if you haven't specified that you own two guard dogs." The adjuster had an earnest expression and a shiny face. He hugged his clipboard and briefcase to his chest. "I'll just have a look at that garage site now, if you don't mind. Those dogs can't get out, can they?"

"No, no. Sorry about that." Olivia accompanied the man on his tour, wondering how much Sadie's spirited defense was going to cost her. Broadbent walked around the blackened slab of concrete, pursing his lips and making tiny notes on his clipboard. Olivia didn't imagine that he was planning a lavish restitution for her loss. Well, it might have been worse. He could have been the real estate assessor.

Olivia was glad when he left so that she could return to the shamrock frame and its contents. What great evidence might be on that disc, or secreted in that safety deposit box?

How clever and distrustful of Frank Rossi to hide the name of the bank in one frame and the key to the safety deposit box in another. She put the disc in her desk drawer with similar ones, then returned the business card to its cardboard hiding place. Reassembling the frame, she stood the new photo of Lily on her desk and waved back at the waving colleen. "We're on our way now, Lily."

She was not in the least surprised when the essence of exotic lily perfume wafted into the room.

Still fussed over her encounter with the adjuster, Olivia was feeling grimy and in need of a hot bath, closely followed by a refreshing glass of cold chardonnay. After that, she would plan her next move.

MAY 24

Things to Do Today

Menu:
Crudités with cheese, tortilla chips and salsa etc.
Lemon, Garlic & Herb Chicken
New Potatoes with Chives
Asparagus Bundles with Prosciutto
Tossed Baby Greens Salad
Strawberry Shortcakes

Olivia had never been a relaxed hostess, and the prospect of this dinner party riddled her with even more anxiety than usual. She'd decided to invite Jamie and her son Mike, who was just about Kevin's age. Pushing aside the fact that Moira had once tried to kiss Mike, which he'd reported with great disgust when asked about the O'Hara youngsters, Olivia hoped Jamie's son would be a buffer with Dave's wards. And Jamie herself, witty and jolly and full of stories about the idiosyncrasies of recuperating rich old duffers, added a note of cheer to any occasion, especially after a martini or two. She had always been, and still was, a dependable antidote for Olivia's perfectionist jitters. Besides, it was time her best friend met her new love interest, if only to deliver the usual warnings.

With the backyard still such a mess, Olivia decided against a cook-out. Dinner would be served in the dining room, which overlooked the best part of the backyard, not the burned platform where the garage used to be. Still, a dining room could seem a bit daunting to youngsters. Not to mention, it had been the scene of some pretty scary paranormal phenomena, leaving an aura that even the dogs found intimidating. But with the French doors wide open to the May sunshine and the birds trilling their mating calls, it was pleasantly airy and informal. Olivia filled tall vases with Shasta daisies and placed them on the sideboard. She set the table with her kitchen set, colorful Fiesta ware, and arranged a fruit bowl centerpiece. *There! Cheerful and not intimidating!*

As predicted, Kevin opted out of a grown-up dinner party, the bane of teenagers, but Dave, Moira, and Danny arrived promptly at one. Dave was looking rugged and handsome in a navy blazer, woven plaid linen shirt, and twill jeans. Danny's fair hair was slicked down with great determination except for a single stubborn cowlick on the crown of his head; he was wearing faded cut-offs, an oversize Matrix V T-shirt, and beat-up Nikes. Moira's shocking pink shirt, at war with her carrot-top hair, ended two inches above the waist of her aqua Capri pants, thus exposing her vulnerable navel. Olivia concluded that Dave allowed his charges to choose their own outfits. She hoped their school required uniforms but realized that the dress code probably consisted of barring out-and-out Nazi gear and full nudity. So much for preparing youngsters for the business world.

Besides worrying about the menu and the youngsters, Olivia was also uneasy about explaining to Dave how she happened to have found the prize that several determined housebreakers were searching for, the unmarked disc holding who-knew-what kind of evidence, plus the name of a bank where Lily had an undisclosed safety deposit box. After all her conniving, would the disc be any use to Dave? Of course she'd had a look at its contents. It wouldn't be easily decipherable. Names or mere initials, dates, amounts, sometimes places. Secrets that Rossi must have mistakenly believed were his insurance policy.

But wasn't it a tactical error on the part of interested mobsters to murder Rossi and Lily before getting their hands on the disc and the name of the bank where they had a secret safe deposit box? Olivia shuddered to imagine what means might have been employed in questioning the couple. So maybe they didn't know Rossi had made a disc—then. Possibly they found that out later. And that's why Lily's face was banged up in a manner "not consistent" with her fall.

Olivia was tempted to keep the disc to herself a little while longer. After all, with her expertise in record-keeping, she might yet figure out Rossi's system of recording data. Perhaps she would present Dave with an interpreted version, something he could use before the Feds grabbed that hot evidence away from him, as they surely would. Perhaps the disc would prove to hold details of drug deals or pay-offs or— Olivia's heart did a quick-step just thinking about it—a kind of Murder, Inc. hit list.

Letting go of this disturbing train of thought, Olivia resolved to give her full attention to her guests. Dave greeted her with a kiss that would have been nearly chaste if it hadn't gone on a shade too long. Maybe her fault; he had a most seductive mouth.

Danny sighed heavily and tugged on Dave's sleeve. "Where are the doggies?" he demanded. "You promised."

Dave's kind brown eyes look down on the boy affectionately. "And a promise is a promise, Danny boy."

"They'll be along later," Olivia assured the youngster. "They're taking a little nap in the laundry room right now."

Moira was balancing a plate of deviled eggs on one hand and a peach cobbler on the other. Each egg was garnished with an olive, anchovy, or pickle slice. "Here," she said, thrusting them forward toward Olivia. "You can probably use these."

"Oh, how lovely." Olivia took the two dishes awkwardly. "You made these yourself? They'll go wonderfully with my asparagus bundles."

"Any fool can boil eggs," Moira said. "And the peach thing is Dave's favorite. You didn't make potato salad, did you?"

"No. I thought new potatoes would be nice."

"Good. When potato salad stands out it can give you the runs for days. Where's the kitchen? I'd better put those eggs in the fridge."

"Sure. It's right through here."

The crudités were laid out on the coffee table in the living room. She poured chilled chardonnay for herself and Dave, offered Danny and Moira a choice of soft drinks. In the laundry room, Bruno and Sadie were taking turns woofing mournfully. She'd let them out later when the coffee table was clear of irresistible nibbles. Moira sat stiffly in one of the wing chairs, sipping orange soda. Danny grabbed a handful of chips, trailed them through the salsa, and wandered out of the room. Olivia heard him heading up the stairs. Dave looked ready to spring after him, but Olivia laid a hand on his wrist. "That's okay," she said. "He's just exploring."

Just then Jamie zoomed into the driveway and honked at the wheel of her new Thunderbird. This one was ice blue metallic, replacing her former torch red model that had burned up in Olivia's garage. After the new car was properly admired, Jamie said, "I'm leaving this one in the street, dearie. Don't let Lily near it, please."

"Who's Lily?" Mike asked. With his vulnerable round face and slightly chubby frame, he didn't look like the kind of kid who would get along well with the wiry, cynical O'Hara tribe.

"Don't ask," said his mother. "Here, honey, take this platter of deviled eggs into the kitchen for me." Jamie's eggs were plain jane, with a sprinkle of paprika.

Moira examined them scornfully. "You'd better give those to me," she told Mike. "There's not much room left in the fridge, but I think I can wedge them in." She grabbed the platter out of Mike's hands, and sashayed away into the house, wiggling her aqua-clad butt.

Mike rolled his eyes at his mother and looked around the living room. "Where's Kev?"

"Kevin had some urgent kind of skateboarding meet," Dave explained. "These days he always seems to be busy with friends. He's not big on family parties."

Mike's expression registered disappointment and weary acceptance. Now he'd be stuck with the younger kids all afternoon.

"I remember being the same at Kev's age." While making a 6 to 1 martini with two olives for Jamie, Olivia was mulling over that word *family*. Maybe she will give the disc to Dave today, along with the convoluted story of how she obtained it. She excused herself to refill the chips basket and find a bottle of soda water to clean the salsa that's been dribbled onto her pale green living room rug.

"Our kitchen is about twice the size of this one," remarked Moira, who had followed Olivia and was lifting lids from pots to peer inside. She sniffed the chicken. "Garlic, lemon, and thyme?"

"Yes, and rosemary plus a little fresh sage. You're so talented in the food line, Moira—are you thinking of becoming a chef when you grow up?"

"Naw. I'd rather be a nightclub singer or a soccer coach or a jet pilot. They let women be jet pilots now, you know."

Before Olivia could comment on this eclectic life plan, Danny came clattering down the stairs. She'd forgotten all about him. What could he have been doing all this time?

"Who's the weirdo lady up there in the office?" Olivia could hear him asking Dave. She hurried back into the living room.

"What lady? There's no one in this house but us, Danny." Dave looked over Danny's head at Olivia and raised one eyebrow. Olivia shrugged tiredly.

"There is, too! She's blonde like an actress or Madonna or somebody, and she's sitting by the window in the office room, you know where the computer is? Looking out at the driveway. And it's cold, really cold in there. *And I can see right through her!*" Danny's voice began to hit a whine pitch.

"Well, that's a load and a half of crap!" declared Moira, putting a fist on each small hip and glaring at her brother. "And you haven't even said a proper hello to Mike and his mother."

"Hi, Mike. Hi, Mrs. Finch. There's a frigging ghost-lady upstairs."

"It's Ms. Andrews now" Jamie corrected Danny absently. "Mike is Moody. Uh-oh. I wonder if I should move my car down the street. Out of Lily's way."

"I know what," said Olivia brightly. "Let's meet the doggies now, shall we?" She picked up the appetizers and put them on the mantle. No matter how bad Bruno and Sadie behaved, at least it would be a distraction from Lily's apparition, if that's what Danny had encountered. And dinner! She'd serve dinner right away before her party fell apart completely. *Frightening the children! Thanks a lot, Lily!*

Distraction was right. Sadie rushed around the room, her big head swiveling from side to side, not neglecting to raise up on her back paws to sniff the mantle, then back again to race in another wild circle. Moira pulled her legs up and stood in the chair. "What's she *doing?* I never saw such a crazy dog. Is that a pit bull? Some people say pit bulls should be outlawed."

Meanwhile, Bruno rushed toward the stairs, then pulled his ears in flat to his head, and cowered on the floor, whimpering.

"See, I told you so," Danny said, leaning on Dave's side. "That big dog knows there's a weirdo up there, just like I said. Hey, Moira, I double dare you to go upstairs and see! I bet you'll be peeing your pants."

"No one has any business going upstairs in Liv's house without her invitation. So knock it off, you two. Probably just a trick of the light. Now go wash your hands for dinner," Dave ordered.

At least Sadie and Bruno seemed to have accepted the O'Haras without incident. *Maybe they're getting socialized at last*, Olivia congratulated herself. It helped, of course, that the dogs were already buddies with Mike, since their evening at Chuck Borgia's training school. Sadie gave Jamie's boy a wet nose nudge, then continued her dash around the living room. Olivia grabbed her by the collar, firmly insisted on a Sit-Stay, and was agreeably surprised when Sadie obeyed.

"Shall I have a look around upstairs?" Dave asked in a low tone.

"Brave boy!" Jamie said, munching an olive. "You wouldn't catch me going up those stairs for a million bucks."

"I'm sure it's nothing. But just to put the boy's mind at rest, I'll go," Olivia said, conscious that she was still using her dog-training, brook-no-contradiction voice. She ran up the stairs, glancing in her bedroom, then went straight on to her office. Olivia, who always knew where she left everything, saw that papers had been disturbed on her desk but the new photo in the shamrock frame was still where she'd left it. The unmarked disc, however, had been taken out of the middle drawer and left on top of some pamphlets. The new computer, bought to replace the one that had been stolen, was turned on, the screen saver trolling its transcendental question, "Where am I?" in various colors.

Lily caught Danny playing around up here, Olivia thought. A slight chill in the air and the now familiar fragrance of lily perfume suggested the spirit's recent presence. The traveling Art Deco frame, so often the channel for Lily's energy, had moved slightly away from where Olivia had placed it among her family portraits and was teetering on the shelf's edge. Lily's smile had a rakish air, almost as if she might wink at any moment. *If that smile is not actually different from day to day*, Olivia thought, *I am indeed going bonkers*.

Ignoring Lily's tricks, Olivia looked around for another place to hide the disc. Clearly the desk drawer wouldn't do. She found a temporary place for it in the guest room, inside a zippered throw pillow, white lace with embroidered daisies, that decorated the bed. *There!*

"No one is upstairs now, Danny," she assured the boy when she came down. She smiled ruefully at Dave and Jamie. Jamie took the opportunity to signal her approval of Dave with a favorable nod to Olivia. *What have Dave and my Rubensque friend been talking about?* Olivia wondered. Jamie could be quite a flirt, she recalled.

As if in answer, Jamie said, "I've been telling Dave about my adventures as Cesare Benedetto's nurse. Quite a menagerie, that household. Dave says with my observant eyes and ears, I'd make a good undercover informer. Could be a whole new career for me!"

"Hey, way cool, Ma," Mike approved.

"Sure you could—*Sue Barton meets 007*," Olivia agreed. "And I remember how you love the thrill of physical danger!"

"You're being a bit sarcastic there, dearie. Only a fool goes hang-gliding. But actually nursing is fraught with dangers—drugged-up street people, violent nutcases, Aids patients bleeding on you. That's one of the reasons I went into private nursing. No trauma units for me!"

"Okay, scratch the undercover idea," Dave chuckled.

"Not necessarily. What's the rate of combat pay?"

Olivia's menu was a great success, even with a surfeit of deviled eggs and Moira, who tasted each dish cautiously, like a wary tourist at an aborigine feast. The girl had seated herself beside Mike, who kept pushing his chair as far as possible in the other direction, toward Jamie. Jamie pushed him back with a hardly discernible pinch of his upper arm.

After the strawberry shortcakes and peach cobbler, they collapsed outdoors on lawn chairs in a satisfied stupor, especially Mike and Moira who had consumed numerous fizzy drinks for the ultimate in burping distress.

Danny was lying on the grass with Bruno beside him, while Sadie busied herself digging a new hole behind the site of the burned garage. "How come you don't have any real computer games?" the boy asked Olivia. "There was a disc in the desk drawer, but that was just a bunch of names, numbers and stuff, all jumbled up. Anyway, that's when the creepy lady showed up, and I got out of there in a hurry."

There's no hiding secret stuff from a kid, Olivia thought, a chill running from her neck to her arms. "Hey, Danny, I think you were looking at my work. That's what I do, you know, organize records."

"Uncle Dave won't let me watch *The Sopranos,*" Danny said.

"What made you think of that all of a sudden, Danny Boy?" Dave asked.

"I dunno. The names sounded like a bunch of Wops."

Jamie glanced sharply at Olivia, who shrugged.

"We don't use that word, Danny. We say Italians. And people's desks are off-limits, you know that." Dave's voice was stern, almost his cop-voice. He looked over at Olivia with a questioning expression.

"Eye-talians," Danny repeated dutifully. "I just wanted to see if she had any good games."

"Olivia, not *she,*" Dave continued his deportment lesson. Olivia felt relieved that civilizing this family wasn't her responsibility.

"*Boys!*" Moira said with utter scorn. Mike had begun playing with the dogs, throwing tennis ball after tennis ball against the back fence, ignoring Moira completely.

"I know just what you mean," Jamie agreed.

෮ඌ

Olivia was not sorry that the necessity of getting ready for Monday morning motivated her guests to leave by early evening. Dave was the last, sweeping her half into the coat closet for a fervent but brief embrace. After he'd gone, leaving the body that he'd pressed against so hotly feeling bereft and her world empty and silent, Olivia had time to congratulate herself that the afternoon had gone surprisingly well. That was if you didn't count the appearance of Lily, probably trying to protect her treasure, that incriminating disc. Wouldn't Dave be thrilled if it implicated the Benedettos in some indictable way!

But Olivia had decided, after all, to hang onto the disc for a while longer just to see what she could make out of it herself. All those "Eye-talian" names. What if she tried matching them up on the internet with news stories about disappearances and murders? *Yes!*

The thought of murder—not just a fictional murder or a newspaper story, but the real deal—gave Olivia an uneasy stomach. She thought about the disc in its present location, and all the crime films she'd seen in which pillows are slashed and scattered. Surely she could come up with a better hiding place.

She removed the disc from the guest room and stood in the doorway, waiting for an inspiration. "Hide it in plain sight," was a vastly overrated notion, she felt—no offense to Poe. Her first idea was to wrap the disc in foil, label it "Sliced bologna," and stash it in her refrigerator under the package of liverwurst. But it occurred to her that some of the data might suffer at temperatures below 50 degrees F. Instead, she walked down the hall to her office, where she simply slipped the disc into the Art Deco frame between Lily's photo and the heavy silver backing. Let Lily guard her own secrets!

Just a few more days to carry out her research. Olivia continued to believe that she would be the one to unlock the Rossi mystery.

LILY

*Hey, no trouble making myself known to that blond kid with the big
ears! Too bad being able to step through to the Other World gets lost
along the way to growing up. My Kind would have a much easier
time if there were more kids like Danny in the world.*

*Of course, I did scare the bejesus out of the little rascal when
he started playing with Rossi's disc. Serves him right, too! Did the
whole White Lady in the Rocking Chair by the Window tableau,
and my audience of one was absolutely transfixed, if I do say so
myself. Haven't had so much fun since I used to do burlesque skits.
Anyway, it will be a long cold day in hell before that kid Danny
fools around with my stuff again.*

*That's just a figure of speech, of course. Hell isn't hot at all, it
isn't anything. Nothing with a capital N. Anyone with a spark of
enlightenment wouldn't be caught dead there, ha ha.*

*Myself, I'm what you might call semi-enlightened. Not exactly
Guardian Angel material. Still, I am watching over someone who
needs it, and that's Liv. You see, the thing is, I'm really responsible
for getting her into danger with those Neanderthal mobsters. If I
could only get her to toss that hot potato of Rossi's into the hands of
her cute detective, but she's one stubborn gal. Wants to run the whole
show herself.*

Take it from Sad Experience, Hon, when you cross the Benedettos, it's time to run for cover. Guess Liv is going to have to find that out the hard way. But don't worry, I'll be keeping an eye on her, so to speak.

MAY 25
Things to Do Today

Research names, who is Needlenose?
Disc and key to Dave?????
Brown bag deviled eggs
Work on rug stains

Olivia wished she had never taken on the Mattakeesett Town Hall project. Work was seriously interfering with her sleuthing. Still, she took a little time at lunch (she had to admit that Moira's deviled eggs were something special) to Google the names she'd jotted in the small notebook she always carried in her handbag. Most of the appellations were merely initials, but there were names or nicknames scattered among them. Needlenose, Papa P., Pinhead, Calvino, L. Hogg, Santos. What she got were thousands and thousands of hits. Santos alone brought up 2, 600, 000 possibilities in 10 seconds. Very well, then, she tried another gambit. Assuming that murder may have been involved (no, there was no J. Hoffa on the disc), she typed into the search line "Massachusetts murders," the year, and the word "mob." Only 3, 890 entries. She tried the same again with "L. Hogg" added.

Bingo, Baby! "Prominent South Shore businessman Lancelot Hogg found shot to death in his car," a mob-style execution that was the subject of several newspaper articles. Nothing about an arrest or trial. Sounded as if the case was never cleared. Hogg was a real estate magnate, same as Cesare B., the one adult male of the Benedetto family with no criminal record. A business conflict, perhaps? Turn to the brothers for help? Olivia made a few notes.

How had Rossi found out all he'd known? How much privileged information would a Mafia-type share with his CPA? Maybe Rossi was like the classic butler, invisible to his employers who felt free to discuss family business in his presence, whether tax shelters or mob hits. Olivia's head was beginning to hurt. She swallowed a couple of buffered aspirin with bottled spring water and went back to her Mattakeesett job to clear her brain, happily bringing order to Emma's chaos. Tonight, definitely, she would call Dave and deliver the goods.

When Olivia was through browsing the Internet, she tore out the page of notes, folded it into quarters, and slid it into her credit card folder, between Macy's and Sears. She couldn't have said why she did this; was she finally giving way to irrational fears?

Driving home at four-thirty (consultant's hours!) she continued to consider the hand-over, *pro* and *con.* For the first time, *pro* got top billing.

Since the demise of her garage, Olivia had been parking in the street. The moment she eased her Chevy van to the curb in front of her house, a dog ran up, barking lustily. Olivia leaned out the passenger side, saw the familiar big head and slobbering smile. *It's Sadie! What is Sadie doing out on the street? And where's Bruno?* As she grabbed Sadie's collar and rushed her into the fenced backyard, Olivia's left eye registered an instant migraine. She clutched her cell phone, thinking she ought to call for help, *but later*. Right now she was too worried about Bruno.

With trembling fingers, she put her key into the new kitchen door lock, found it already unlocked. Sadie surged past her and headed for the living room in a frenzy of barking. The television was on. Olivia could hear pop psychologist Dr. Phil exhorting someone to release her anger. A swarthy stranger was sitting on the sofa, his feet propped on the coffee table watching the show. As he swung around and stood up, she saw that he was built like a fire hydrant, short and square with powerful shoulders.

Sadie confronted the man, snarling low and mean, while Olivia punched 911 in her cell phone. With a smile that never reached his steely eyes, the square man pulled a pistol from under his loose-fitting jacket and held it in a business-like grip.

Before the emergency operator could answer, the intruder said "Drop the phone or I'll kill your dog. And hang onto that bitch's collar." His tone was conversational but somehow very convincing. Olivia was a head taller than this man, and she had an Olympic swimmer's shoulders, but she recognized an "equalizer" when she saw it. She dropped the phone onto a nearby chair and lunged forward to restrain Sadie, easing back toward the door.

"Stay right where you are," the thickset thug ordered.

"Where's Bruno? Where's my other dog?"

"The fucking shepherd mutt? I kicked him down cellar. That one got away out the door. I should have ..."

Olivia went cold all over, which somehow cleared her brain of fog and fear. "You son-of-a-bitch. He'd better not be hurt." Although she was against capital punishment on principle, Olivia made an exception for animal abusers, whom she felt should be taken out back of the police station and shot. And if anyone harmed her two animal companions, she herself would volunteer to be part of the firing squad.

"Olivia Andreas. You are not in a position to be making threats. You have something that belongs to us. Let me have that purse. No, don't come any closer. Toss it to me. And stand away from that cell phone or the dog's dead."

Olivia did as she was told, struggling to keep Sadie from leaping on the intruder. He dumped her handbag onto to the floor and pawed through it with the toe of his shoe. Make-up case, tampon case, glasses case, tissues. He picked up the notebook and flipped through its pages. Olivia was thankful she's torn out the notes. Next the wallet, which he opened and rifled through, tossing away photos, license, medical and AAA cards, and credit card folder.

"Okay, that's enough of this shit. Now you're going to tell me where that fucking disc is or you're going to need a new fucking knee."

"Let the healing process begin between you and your mother, and let it begin with you," Dr. Phil intoned.

"What crap!" said the intruder; he wheeled around and shot at the power button on the TV, which effectively ended the show. The sound of the shot coupled with the TV splintering was incredibly loud. The rank odor of gunpowder and fried wires enveloped the room. Sadie howled and Olivia's heart began to beat wildly, the only part of her body that wasn't made of ice. "I don't know what you're talking about."

He moved the pistol so that it was aiming straight at Olivia's left knee. As she winced in painful anticipation, Olivia's grip on Sadie's collar involuntarily loosened. Instantly the dog wrenched free, jumping in a perfect arc to bring down the enemy. The man lifted his pistol to shoot the dog in midair. Just as his finger closed on the trigger, there was a fearful clatter upstairs, as if a china cabinet had tumbled to the floor. Distracted, the intruder missed the dog and drove a bullet into the coffee table instead.

Sadie continued her leap to grab his right arm between wrist and elbow. Man and dog snarled at one another. In one quick motion, he flipped the pistol into his left hand, where it became a steel club. He wrapped the dog's head sharply twice. Sadie's jaws released his arm, and she fell to the floor, motionless.

Olivia screamed. The man raised the pistol butt to quiet her, too, but then seemed to think better of it. Unless he stood on a chair, he was not going to be able to bop her on the head as he had Sadie. Glancing wildly up the stairs, he flipped his pistol back into firing position.

"Shut the fuck up. What the hell was that crash?" His stance suggested he was ready to shoot whoever might appear at the head of the stairs.

"I have no idea." Actually, Olivia did have one idea, but she was not going to risk sharing it with this trigger-happy mobster. "If you've killed my dog, you bastard, you're in big trouble."

"*You … You …* I don't believe you. Get up those stairs ahead of me and let's see what's going on. Got an office up there, have you? Maybe bought yourself a new computer?" The man laughed evilly. "Is that where the disc is? *Move!*"

So this was the bastard who'd stolen her laptop!

Olivia saw that Sadie's flank was rising and falling, *thank God.* The dog seemed to be breathing, although rasping. Better if this brute didn't notice she was still alive. Her brain

raced through a lifetime of crime dramas searching for her
next move, how to turn the tables on this squat little man
who was obviously going to kill her as soon as he got the
disc. Half looking backward, she started upstairs followed
by the pistol and the man who was aiming it at her. On
trembling legs, Olivia reached the landing and turned
toward her office. Whatever was going on, it was happening
in that room.

Yes, indeed. Once again the photographs in their frames
were strewn all over the floor, but not in a neat domino row
like the last time. Adding to the chaos, a bookcase that had
stood on the wall opposite the desk was now toppled over,
the books tumbled among the disarray of broken glass and
bent, twisted picture frames. The window was open, the
drape drifting inward on a pleasant May breeze. The desk
was untouched, however, and sitting on top of the computer,
grinning at Olivia and the thug behind her, was Lily in the
Art Deco frame.

"Jesus Fucking Christ," the man said, looking at the mess
on the floor and then at the photo. "Hey, I know that broad.
That's Rossi's girl, Lily Longlegs." The photo did a little
pirouette into the air and tapped on the computer twice as
if speaking in ghost code: *two taps for yes.*" His eyes bugging
out of his head, the man was drawn forward as if by invisible
threads toward Lily. He pulled a cell phone out of his pocket
and hit a speed dial. "Hey, Moe, you'd better get in here.
Yeah, you asshole, I could've handled one little cunt, if that
was all. But there's someone or something else in this house.
Knocked over the fucking bookcase. And there's this fucking
photo of Rossi's girl banging itself."

Olivia didn't hesitate. There would be no second chances
here. As the man sputtered at the shouted abuse he was

hearing on the cell phone, Olivia picked up a heavy little brass lamp that had stood on the bookcase, and in one fluid motion, bashed him on the head with it. A satisfying *thunk.*

The man grunted and dropped the pistol, went down on his knees, then bounded up again just as Olivia flung herself toward the weapon. With his hefty shoulder, the man bulldozed her out of the way, but she grabbed his arm, staggering toward the toppled bookcase. They fell together. Olivia was on top, but not for long, as the man reached up with thick, strong fingers and began to throttle her, cursing and spitting in her face. The blackness closed in on Olivia. Just before she felt herself tumbling off the man onto the floor, she heard a second intruder crashing into the house.

Suddenly the hand released her throat, and Olivia's vision cleared.

Sadie had rushed into the room, full throttle, as if she'd never been knocked out. Thrusting herself between Olivia and her attacker, she growled low, drooling, and went for his jugular. The man threw his arm across his neck to guard it and screamed, "get her off, get her off." Olivia hoped Sadie would not take out the guy's throat but she didn't look back to see. She grabbed the pistol off the floor and, holding it in her shaking right hand, reached over with her left for the desk phone, punching in 911.

A second man, squat and dark, a dead ringer for the first, lunged in the door with a drawn pistol. Seeing his partner under attack, he aimed at Sadie, waiting for a clear shot that wouldn't take out his partner. A lightning jolt of fear caused Olivia to squeeze the trigger of the weapon in her hand. The newcomer screamed, clutched his stomach, and fell to the floor. Olivia stepped on his right wrist just as the operator answered. The pistol fell uselessly from the injured man's fingers. Nevertheless, she shoved it under the desk with her other foot.

"Two men with guns have broken into my house, 223 Edgewood Road," Olivia said to the responding operator, desperately trying to marshal facts in a calm, logical manner. "One of them got shot. In the stomach, I think. My dog is holding the other. Yes, my dog. By the throat, sort of. No, she's not killing him. Hurry, will you *please* hurry. Yes, we need an ambulance. This guy who got shot is bleeding all over the place. And a vet. *Yes, a vet*, like an animal doctor. No, not Animal Control." She began to lose her grip, hearing herself screech into the phone. *"Do you mean to tell me you don't have a vet on call?"*

With a loud cry, like Bruce Lee in mid-chop, the first man suddenly pushed Sadie off her menacing position on his chest. Olivia dropped the phone, which missed its cradle and fell to the floor.

Kicking the exhausted Sadie out of his way, the man hurled himself across the room and through the open window, pushing out the screen. He dashed across the porch roof and jumped, missing the fence and landing on soft grass. Rolling over, he sprinted for a nondescript black car parked across the street. Too far away for Olivia to read the license plate.

She braced her arms on the windowsill and aimed at the man. Sadie was beside her, big head out the window, barking like a deranged animal.

A voice in Olivia's ear whispered in a sultry tone, "You got one of them, good for you! Now, shoot the other bastard! Do it now!"

Was that a real voice she heard? At the last moment, with Sadie deafening her and her finger closing on the trigger, it occurred to Olivia that it was hard to claim self-defense if you shoot a guy in the back. Instead, she fired up in the air, hoping the sound at least would give that son-of-a-bitch a heart attack.

Already she could hear sirens on the next street. *Too late! They'll never catch him now.* The black car had hurtled away and disappeared around the corner.

Half-dragging and cajoling Sadie back from the sill, Olivia slammed the window shut. The injured man had stopped moaning and was utterly silent, she hoped unconscious and not dead, but she had no time for him now. She picked up the pistol under the desk and looked around for a place to leave the two weapons. Pulling open her desk's file drawer, she dropped them inside.

Racing downstairs, she flung open the cellar door and saw Bruno in a whimpering heap at the foot of the stairs. He could get up and did, to greet her and complain, but he couldn't put full weight on his front right leg. Olivia had two vets, both numbers beside the kitchen phone. She rang the second one, a gal who ran Vets-in-a-Van, a practice conducted solely via house calls, then hurried down cellar to keep Bruno immobile.

A few minutes later, Olivia heard the cops running into the house. Bedlam ensued, as Sadie, embarrassed by her earlier defeats, attempted to defend her territory even more ferociously. Olivia took the cellar stairs two at a time, shouting, "Don't shoot the dog! Don't shoot the dog!" But it was too late.

One of the cops fired at the canine attacker but wily Sadie leaped away and was now sensibly cowering behind the kitchen rocker. Another room reeked of gunpowder. The dog was shaking her big head as if deafened.

"That dog is bravely defending her home," Olivia shouted in a withering tone. "How dare you shoot at her for doing her job, the same as you are, although you took long enough to get here." The chastened cops backed up slightly. The shooter holstered his weapon, but there was a smoking hole in her kitchen table. *Time for new furniture*, she thought wildly. *This whole place is a disaster.*

She forced herself to calm down. There were things to be done here. "One intruder took off in a black sedan. I didn't get the license number. The other one is upstairs on the floor, shot, bleeding a lot. Better get the paramedics upstairs as soon as they arrive."

"Where's the gun he was shot with? Is it yours?" the older officer asked sternly.

"Two intruders, two pistols, neither of them mine. But I had to take them away from those maniacs. You understand. Before someone got hurt. So I shot the second man, the one who came running up the stairs. Then the first one jumped out the window. I put the two weapons in the file drawer of my desk. Not filed or anything. Just loose in back."

"Geeze, Ms."

The vet was just coming in the kitchen door, black bag in hand and a fearful expression on her face. She was a tiny thing, about five feet two and vastly pregnant, seven or eight months. Olivia wondered who would help her lift Bruno up the cellar stairs. "Dr. Barbie Barker," the vet said. "What on earth is happening here?"

Olivia thought she'd better go through her encounter with two gunmen again. The officers, a florid-faced, gray-haired man and his trigger-happy younger partner who looked about sixteen, still appeared to be dumbfounded. She nodded to the vet to include her in an account of the last half hour. "A small square man in a black car—Chevy maybe—broke in here while I was at work and assaulted my dogs.

When I came home, he threatened me with a gun which I later managed to take away from him. Then a second man came in waving another gun, and I shot him. The first guy ran out over the roof not ten minutes ago. Don't you want to call that in or whatever it is you do when you're not taking pot shots at dogs?"

Dr. Barker was leaning down behind the rocker to examine Sadie. "That's Sadie," Olivia said. "She'll be okay when she gets over the shock of being shot at by our rescuers. It's my other dog, Bruno, who's in trouble." She offered her hand to help haul up the pregnant woman. "Just a minute while I put Sadie in a safe place." Then, giving the two policemen the most killing look her dark eyes could muster, Olivia dragged Sadie off, cooing sweet nothings in her ear about how brave and wonderful she'd been but now it was time for a pleasant rest on a folded blanket in the laundry room. She slammed the laundry door and ran back to the kitchen.

"I didn't get the license plate number, and I don't know what the gunman was after," she announced to the officers. "But you'll see there's quite a mess upstairs. I suggest you contact Detective Dave Lowenstein. He investigated my other break-ins. But right now, I have to see a vet about a dog."

Olivia took Dr, Barker's hand and pulled her toward the cellar. "That bastard who broke in here kicked Bruno downstairs. His right leg is hurt, maybe a sprain, I hope not broken."

As the doctor gently examined Bruno, Olivia could hear paramedics rushing in and more officers wandering through the house talking to each other. "I'll get one of the uniformed idiots to help bring Bruno upstairs. Hang on a minute." She trotted upstairs. The injured man had been removed, and some officers were making notes while standing in the center of her living room with the shattered television and demolished coffee table. She grabbed a small rug off the floor in the hall and enlisted the younger of the two men to help her carry Bruno to the laundry room on the improvised stretcher. Bruno never so much as lifted his head.

"He don't look too good, M'am," the cop said.

"The vet gave him something to ease the pain."

"I guess it did that, all right. My partner called Lowenstein. The detective said to tell you he's on his way, but he's still in Middleboro so it will be a half hour or so."

"Okay. Good." A feeling of relief surged through Olivia.

"He sort of vouched for you, M'am, about the shooting. Said you'd been harassed, and it must have been self-defense."

"Well, of course it was self-defense. I already explained all that to you."

"Yes, but there will have to be a report. You'll have to sign a statement."

Sadie's muzzle was sniffing at the bottom of the door when Olivia eased it open. "It's all right, now, Sadie. The nice officer is just going to help me with Bruno."

Sadie stiffened, snarled, and tried to scrabble her way out the door. The officer dropped his end of the rug and backed away. Somehow Olivia managed to slide Bruno into the laundry room without letting Sadie squeeze out.

With a perfunctory "thanks" to the officer, Olivia raced back to the kitchen to pay the vet, who seemed glad enough to waddle away from the ruined house to her neat little white van decorated with cute dogs.

"What a mess," Olivia moaned softly to herself. "Boy, could I use a drink." Would the policemen think her a lush if she poured herself a medicinal brandy? *Oh, what the hell!*

She sloshed a double into a tea cup and sank tiredly into an armchair in the dining room, one of the few unwrecked places in the house. Sipping gratefully, she punched in Jamie's cell phone.

"Help," she said when Jamie picked up.

"Now what have you done!"

Olivia told her.

"I'll be right over," Jamie said. "Well, half hour, tops. I just got off shift. Where's the gallant detective?"

"They've contacted him. He's coming from Middleboro. You have no idea what a mess I'm in here."

"For Gawd's sake, sit someplace. Have a shot of liquor. Better yet, a double. Then have a hot cup of tea with lots of honey. There's no mess so horrifying that I can't cope with it, after what I went through with Finch."

෴

Curvy Jamie with her cloud of red hair had no trouble getting the cops to help her set the heavy bookcase back in its proper place against the wall. She pushed the books onto the shelves, intent on simply getting them off the floor. Then she began roughly shoveling up the broken glass and twisted frames.

The older officer came into the room with two evidence bags and removed the weapons from Olivia's file drawer. Jamie stopped sweeping and watched him in amazement. "Wow. That Liv! You never know about people, do you? What were those filed under, G for Guns?"

Olivia lay in her room with a cold cloth on her forehead. Cops were still coming and going. The older officer leaned in the door. "M'am, you're going to have to speak with a detective about what happened here, the wounded man and all."

"Fine, I'll speak to Detective Lowenstein and no one else," Olivia said. "Is that man who got himself shot still alive?"

"Paramedics said he's stabilized, but you never can tell with stomach wounds."

"Okay, thanks." *Where was Dave?* With a throb of guilt, Olivia heard the vacuum cleaner buzzing away in her office. She should get up and help. Jamie would put things every-which-way.

But when Olivia tried to sit up and swing her legs over the side of the bed, the terrible shakes began again. "Adrenaline surge," Jamie had explained. "Pumps you up for extreme action, then after the danger has passed, it courses around your system giving you a mammoth case of the jitters." Olivia gave in and flopped back on the bedspread she should have asked Jamie to fold down.

A few minutes later, Dave came bursting in like a thundercloud to a house that reeked of gun smoke. Olivia could hear him cursing the cops when they explained about shooting at the aggressive dog and accidentally shattering the kitchen table. "All dogs are protective," he shouted. "When you're called to a crime scene, give the animal's owner a chance to leash her dog before you go shooting up the house."

Olivia smiled, warmed by his defense of Sadie. Soon he bounded up the stairs, his face tender and anxious, and took Olivia gently into his arms, a haven of comfort. "Are you all right? Did they hurt you? Shall I call the paramedics? If those were the Klein brothers, you're lucky ... they're an ugly pair. For God's sake, tell me what happened." Olivia moved away far enough to see his concerned face and settled herself against the headboard, still holding both his hands. She was thinking about how gratifying it was to have a caring man looking out for her and which of his questions she should answer first. Soon enough, she feared, he would be as angry with her as he was with the officers downstairs.

Olivia told him about coming home, finding Sadie roaming free, and her confrontation with the threatening mobster. Although she was feeling slightly nauseated—probably another affect of adrenaline overload—she was relieved that her mind still functioned in its orderly way and she could present the facts of the story in logical sequence—sort of. The part where she was being throttled, and later, when she shot the second mobster, were still a little hazy.

Lily had probably saved her life by toppling the bookcase and addling her adversary's brain with a thumping photograph, but Olivia stuck to the facts. She went straight to the tricky part, determined now to admit the details of her private investigation. She confessed to copying Dave's list of names and addresses so that she could pursue the matter of Lily's silver frames. She told Dave where she hid the disc and bank address. She watched his face get flushed and incredulous. *Oh, well. This relationship was sweet while it lasted.*

Hearing voices, Jamie rushed in with the vacuum cleaner wand in her hand, ready to use as a weapon. "Oh, it's you, Dave. Glad you're here. See that Liv rests a while, okay?" Putting the wand down, Jamie leaned on it like a weary crusader on his sword. She reached over to take Olivia's pulse. "Liv, I've put all the books in the bookcase. You can rearrange them later. I'm cleaning the floor now. Gawd, you must have had quite a struggle with that bastard! And you know, I could swear that photo turned to watch me. I'm getting as balmy as you."

"You're a good friend. Thanks," Olivia said. She felt her eyes getting teary.

"Feeling better? Your pulse is almost normal."

"Much, much better." Dave moved to sit next to her and put an arm around her shoulders. She nestled back against him.

Jamie grinned. "I'm impressed with your powers of recuperation. I'd be a basket case at the thought of confronting two armed gangsters like that." She rushed back to her clean-up campaign.

"Not true!" Olivia called after her. "Remember how you stomped Borgia's foot!"

Now Olivia was alone again with Dave and her sins. She told him about the key, which was the hardest to admit, because she'd had it all along.

"It's a safe deposit box key," she explained, "and possibly Lily felt more secure using a bank in her own home town. Apparently no one knew about the box, or its contents would have been part of the Plunkett estate. The cousins would have rifled through it and probably tossed the disc in the trash. Anyway, I think the Benedettos knew or suspected that Rossi was compiling evidence against them—I doubt it was for blackmail. More likely it was for a deal with the Feds in case Rossi got accused of aiding racketeers. Then there was the matter of his being subpoenaed to testify. So the Benedettos disposed of him in a hit-run incident. Then they went after Lily, in case she knew what Rossi had been up to—and they tried to beat it out of her. They probably made her tell them about the disc—and that video in the entertainment center, remember that? Then maybe she got away and ran for the stairs, they struggled, and she fell. Otherwise they would have kept beating on her until they knew everything."

Dave moved away to face her. Olivia couldn't quite read his expression. It seemed to be halfway between admiration and aggravation. With a little hurt at the corner of his mouth. She reached up to touch his cheek. "I'm really sorry," she said. "I know I should have told you all this sooner."

He was silent for a long time. Then he leaned over and kissed her softly. "Well, I probably wouldn't have got my hands on that shamrock frame as neatly as you did. What made the Benedettos fix on frames, do you think?"

"I don't know. When they were working over Lily, she might have given them that much."

"And you, my foolhardy girl—they must have caught on to your interest in Lily's death and your attempts to gather evidence."

"Possibly I shouldn't have followed the frames on my own," Olivia admitted.

"Not only am I disappointed that you didn't trust me more, I'm really worried about your safety," Dave scolded. "I'll see about police protection, at least close supervision by the local cruiser." He shook his head ruefully and stood up, anxious now to retrieve Lily's deadly treasures.

It wasn't a matter of trust, Olivia thought as he went down the hall. She was aware of her own competitive streak. Making her way in a "man's world" with its slights and inequities, it was always so important to get in first with the best stuff—to prove herself. Even now she was not content to let him root around in her private office by himself. With a sudden spurt of renewed energy, she got up from the bed, slipped on her shoes, and hurried after him.

Jamie, who was putting the brass lamp back on the bookcase, looked up at them with surprise. "What's the matter?"

"I'm giving Lily's things to Dave."

"Ah. So he got you to come clean at last. Good show." Jamie picked up the vacuum cleaner. "I'll go downstairs and see about that television set. And the rest of the wreckage. Those idiot cops!"

After her friend left, Olivia picked up the wandering Art Deco, which was now standing quietly in the middle of her desk next to the shamrock frame, the only two frames unbroken in the earlier melee. She took off the backing, removed the disc and business card, handing them to Dave. Then she put the frame back together and placed it carefully back on her desk.

"The stuff from my handbag," she said. "He kicked that around on the living room floor. The safety deposit key should be on the ring with my other keys. The bank info is hidden between my credit cards." She sighed, feeling completely exhausted and chilled to the bone.

A silk shawl hanging on the back of the rocking chair had slipped away unnoticed during her struggles with the armed men. Olivia saw the corner of it sticking out from under the desk, picked it up, and put it around her shoulders. The scarf felt warm, as if it had just been worn, and it smelled of lily perfume. Olivia wondered if she was imagining things, if she has been doing that all along.

The photo thumped once on her desk. *One thump for "no,"* Olivia thought. These phenomena have all been real; Olivia's orderly life now resembled a deck of cards thrown into the air. No wonder she felt as if she weren't playing with a full deck anymore.

Dave had turned on her new laptop and was studying the obscure material on the disc. Suddenly he yelled "Jesus Christ" and stood up so quickly the desk chair fell over.

"What is it? What's the matter?"

"671 is what's the matter!" He banged the desk with his fist. His eyes were moist and his mouth twisted in pain. "That's Tom's badge number."

"Horrible—those monsters! I've suspected that Rossi was keeping some kind of a record of mob hits on that disc," Olivia said. "But I don't think that's real evidence, do you? I mean, evidence that would stand up in a court trial."

"God damn it!" Dave banged the desk again, rattling everything on it. Lily's photo shimmied to one side but Dave didn't even notice. Olivia realized that the realistic world view—which up until recently had always been her view, too—caused a person to ignore certain provocative events. It was like being color blind, she supposed.

THE HANDOVER

Washington was surprised when Lowenstein actually contacted him on his private cell phone with "something of interest." They arranged to meet at the Kingston Stop & Shop this time. There was a light rain; they leaned against the building near the outdoor display of annuals. Washington sipped a latte.

Dave thought that J. Edgar Hoover never would have hired this impressive black man who stood out among an ordinary crowd more than he himself probably realized. Tall and memorable. People glanced at Washington covertly, wondering if he were a basketball star they should recognize. No wonder the Bureau might be leery of his presence and abilities.

"My boss, Lieutenant Badger, is an asshole with a giant ego," Dave said, guessing that Washington would relate to the situation. "I got him this computer disc with some tenuous evidence gathered by Frank Rossi on Benedetto mob hits, and he can't even get the Federal Prosecutor to return his phone calls. So I said to him, how'd you like to bypass that SOB and go directly to the Bureau. That makes this a sanctioned handover. I hope you can crash through that cement ceiling with it."

"Got it from Olivia Andreas?"

"Yeah."

"If you don't mind my commenting, that's an amazing young woman," Washington said. "When word got out that one of the Klein brothers had been shot in the stomach, forgive me, but knowing they'd been hassling Andreas, I naturally looked into the police report. I learned that the two of them came at her armed, and somehow it ended up with Ben the Butcher fleeing for his life, and his brother Moses in the hospital with a cop outside the door."

"Right. It's quite a story. It was Liv who recovered the disc, too. Bought it back from the woman who took it home from that Byatt auction, hidden in a silver frame."

"Jesus. Rosario Benedetto will be shitting nails. He's been trying to get his hands on every one of those Lamoureaux frames."

"How'd he get a hardon for frames, anyway," Dave asked.

"How does anything happen in his world or in ours? There was an informer. A young punk cousin of Lily's, a wannabe soldier, spied on Rossi hiding the stuff at her apartment, telling her what he was doing. But the punk couldn't see which frames, and that dame had a hundred or more glamour portraits following her so-called show biz career as an exotic dancer."

"Rossi put away some other stuff, too," Dave said.

"Well now, and what would that be?"

"I don't know yet. Lily had a safe deposit box not recorded with the firm handling her estate. My girl got her hands on the key and found out the name on the box and the bank branch. We're getting a warrant. It'll be a day or two, I'd guess."

"Damn ... we ought to recruit that Andreas gal for the Bureau. Maybe she's just too good, though. Tell her to try the NSA. So ... you'll get into the box, then, what?"

"Badger's nose is out of joint," Dave said. "He's going to sit on whatever evidence he turns up from that bank until he can figure out how to maximize his glory. I don't know whether I'll get to pass more stuff along to you or not. I've got some ideas, though. If there's another disc, that is. And I figure there must be another disc, because Rossi was the mob CPA, and what we don't have yet are their financial accounts."

Washington whistled. "You let me know, you hear?"

"Yeah. Now you may be wondering why I'm being so kind to you?"

"I can guess."

"You can? What makes you so sure?"

Ignoring Dave's intimidating expression, Washington waded right in. "Your partner Tom O'Hara was shot dead and subsequently disgraced. His wife is incarcerated on a Federal charge. And you're the guardian of their three kids. Doesn't take a genius to figure you've got issues, and what they might be."

"You're doing good, so far, my friend." Dave was beginning to feel transparent and more than a little resentful. But he could put his own feelings aside if he got results for the O'Haras.

"I can't do anything about reducing Mom's sentence, that's a whole other story, but if your partner wasn't dirty and the Benedettos set him up ... Well, with the right evidence, we might be able to clear his name as well as put away whoever ordered the hit."

"Good enough," Dave said, handing him a folded newspaper containing a small, plain manila envelope. "Nice working with you, Lee. Just be sure that Lieutenant Badger of the Plymouth County Detective Force gets an impressive commendation out of this, even if you have to fake it. I'll be in touch."

MAY 30
Things to Do Today

Chk courses in self-defense
What about join gun club?
Groomer S & B

"Now, don't you guys embarrass me," Olivia warned Sadie and Bruno, as they hopped out of her Chevy van to sniff these strange new environs with interest. She had brought them to visit Dave and his family, their first social outing since being adopted. At first, Olivia had taken a dim view of this idea—after all, the dogs had no formal behavior training—but Dave seemed to cherish the notion of their two households mingling as one happy family. *For a police detective who has seen all kinds of human and animal misbehavior,* Olivia thought, *this man is some optimist.* She's insisted on dropping in for a short time *after* dinner on Saturday as the most reasonable and stress-free meeting she could devise. Dave's backyard was almost fenced, partly picket and partly privet hedge. At seven, it was still light out, the kind of perfect evening that only happened in spring, sensuously warm, but with a hint of breeze that brushed bare skin like a caress. Olivia was wearing black jeans and a short-sleeved black T-shirt, an outfit that showed off her wide shoulders and narrow waist. She'd tied sporty bandanas around the dogs' necks, much to their disgust. It was bad enough having that big guy douse them in soapy water and clip their claws.

Kevin and Danny were shooting baskets in the front yard. Danny greeted the two dogs like old friends, and they responded agreeably. Olivia led them into the backyard so that she could unclip their leashes. Slouching along behind them, Kevin wore his usual bored expression but she could feel his eyes watching her every move.

"Ah, here you are!" Dave said with ingenuous pleasure, giving her a big hug so soul-nourishing that it almost made this enterprise seem worthwhile. "Moira, Liv is here!" he called in the kitchen door.

Moira appeared, scowling at her brothers. She was wearing very brief denim shorts with a short orange top that made the frizzy halo of her hair appear all the more carroty. "Oh, hi, Liv," she said without enthusiasm. "Kev, you get in here now and carry out this tray for me. Danny, you'd better wash your hands. They must be covered in dog drool."

With Moira to organize the party, they were soon sitting around the picnic table having iced tea, cokes, and a dense, spicy gingerbread that the girl had made herself. Olivia thought longingly of a glass of chilled wine but the tea was real brewed tea with plenty of lemon slices and not bad at that.

Kevin was wearing earphones so that he could march to his different drummer, which in his case happened to be a folk music drummer from what Olivia could overhear. Sadie and Bruno's antics with Danny and a basket of tennis balls, however, created a relaxing focus for the rest of the party.

Dave had an easy way of drawing out the O'Hara youngsters, so that soon they were all chatting comfortably.

Kevin admitted to playing in a band with two of his friends. "Celtic rock, if you can believe that," Dave said proudly. Two of Moira's paintings had been entered in a school art show. With an arm flung around each dog's neck, Danny declared that when he grew up and joined the Boston police force like his dad and Uncle Dave maybe he'd work in the K-9 corps.

"We should have stayed in Boston instead of moving to this morgue," Kevin muttered, kicking the leg of the picnic table which made their aluminum drink glasses dance. Moira sighed with exasperation.

"Sorry, Kev. I decided we'd all be better off in Marshfield. It's a great place for kids to grow up, and my hours are much more predictable," Dave said.

"No one knows much about our family business here," Moira said. "Anyway, they don't say mean stuff. And I like that."

"But if they do ever say mean stuff, you'll punch them out, right, Sis?" Danny said admiringly.

"You bet your ass," Moira said, showing off a quick one-two rabbit punch. "You want to see my room, Liv?"

Surprisingly, the girl's room was almost frilly, a white canopy bed heaped with assorted dolls and stuffed animals. Moira's softer side was showing here. There were ruffled white Cape Cod curtains in the two windows, and a framed photograph of her parents on the bureau. Tom and Alice (a.k.a.Teresa) on the beach—Revere perhaps—hugging and laughing. *The good old days*, thought Olivia. *Before her mother went to jail and her father was murdered.* It was a wonder these kids weren't more screwed up than they appeared to be. But then, Olivia had survived her own father's absconding with trust funds and becoming a wanted felon. If caught, he'd be in jail, too. *Life is tough, kids. Lucky for you that you have Uncle Dave.*

Olivia sensed that the youngsters had especially cleaned up for this "state visit," and she was properly impressed. She looked around with interest, searching for clues to improve her relationship with the three O'Haras. The second floor of this L-shaped farmhouse was larger than it appeared, big enough so that the boys had separate rooms, although Danny's was small and crowded with two fish tanks. Kevin's room was surprisingly austere, like a monk's cell except for the stark poster on the wall. Some performer Olivia didn't know whose expression was a total sneer; he clutched his microphone as if about to take a bite out of it. Standing in the corner was Kevin's bodhran, a frame drum covered by some kind of animal skin.

Moira didn't invite Olivia to see Dave's room, but she figured out which one it was by the process of elimination. "Oh, this one must have a nice view of the magnolia," Olivia exclaimed, opening the door slightly and peeking in. Neat as a pin, she was happy to see. Almost military, which was surprising. There were photographs on Dave's bureau, too, but they were at the wrong angle for her to see from the doorway, and she felt she'd been nosy enough for now. *Another time!*

Later, the O'Hara youngsters went off on their various pursuits. In the kitchen, Moira paged through a notebook of her mother's recipes. Kevin was upstairs practicing his drumming. And Danny took the dogs indoors to have a look around, leaving Dave and Olivia alone in the backyard. They sat together on the old canvas glider, swinging idly, his arm around her as they watched the stars come out through the new leaves of the maples. That's when Dave told Olivia that the computer disc Rossi had hidden in Lily's shamrock frame was, as they had deduced, a provocative list of possible mob hits, probably including Tom O'Hara's shooting, but without Rossi as a witness, not conclusive evidence.

As the moon, a slim crescent, rose over the maples, Dave went on to explain that his superior, Lieutenant Badger, had thought he'd get special credit for passing this hot potato disc on to the Feds. Let their staff toss it around, Badger had said. But his subsequent call to the Federal Prosecutor's office went unreturned. And so did his second one. And the third. "Those son-of-bitches in Boston," he raved, "probably think we're a bunch of hicks down here."

Dave had said he knew a guy in the Bureau who would act as courier, and Badger had agreed.

"Do you really have a friend in the Bureau?" Olivia asked.

"Sort of. A contact anyway." Dave decided not to mention that his "friend" had been keeping an eye on Liv, something he had mixed feelings about. "So we'll see what comes of that. And more good news, honey, we got the warrant we needed to open the safety deposit box of Bernice L. Plunkett."

"You didn't tell me that!"

"I wanted to tell you in person." He gave her shoulders a squeeze in the balmy spring darkness. "Opening that box was like the opposite of opening Al Capone's safe. Better than our wildest dreams. That Rossi was a ballsy guy. Or maybe a worried guy, covering his ass. Anyway, he'd stored a clear, readable copy of the Benedetto financial accounts—stuff he must have worked on—on that disc. Had his girl Lily sock it away in a safe place in case he ever needed some leverage. Well, that idea didn't work out too well for him. But from what I can make out, a good forensic accountant will find sufficient money laundering, tax evasion, and assorted racketeering evidence to put away the Benedettos for a good long stretch."

"You'll get the credit, I hope," Olivia said, thinking she deserved some praise as well.

"I hope *not*. And I don't want your name involved, either. It's better that way, honey. These guys are not going to go down gently. With evidence of this caliber, the Boston Police Department will insist on taking over the investigation, but so will the FBI who've had the Benedettos under surveillance all along. State and Federal Prosecutors will wrangle over jurisdiction. Most likely, my name will be lost in the shuffle."

"You might have got a promotion, or a medal, or something," Olivia insisted.

"Promotion to what? where? Well, I wouldn't mind making detective lieutenant, but other than that, I'm a guy who's learned to keep a low profile. I like it where I am and what I'm doing now. Small time, small town. It's good for the kids, and it suits me."

"So ... have you at least made a copy of this new disc, in case you'd ever need it?" Olivia's whole record-keeping style was geared toward the elimination of unnecessary duplication, but this was a special case.

Dave's face reddened. "How did you know?"

Olivia shrugged. "It's what I would have done. This business has had a lot of curious twists and turns. You never know what might happen next. But, it's explosive stuff. So where are you keeping it?"

"Maybe better if you don't know."

She gave him a long look. A look that said as clearly as words, that he was an ungrateful bastard.

"Okay, okay—I know I have you to thank for everything." He leaned over and whispered in her ear, "It's in the lock-box where I keep my gun when I'm off duty. And that's in a locked cabinet in my bedroom. With kids, you know, you can't be too careful."

"And the original disc?"

"Lieutenant. Badger's had it locked up in our evidence room while he decides how to proceed. My guess is, he's trying to figure how to get the most personal credit out of this deal before he passes it along to the higher-ups."

"Unlike you," said Olivia.

"Unlike me. Because I've seen what happens when you go up against the Benedettos. I think that's why Tom O'Hara played a lone hand. He knew how dangerous they are, and he wanted to keep me out of it." Anger and sadness played over Dave's face. Olivia beside him on the glider turned to reach up and kiss him when Danny came bursting into the backyard with Bruno trotting after him.

"Hey, Uncle Dave ... is Sadie with you?"

"Oh, God ... what did you do?"

"Hey, it wasn't my fault. We were watching TV, and I got sleepy. Then Bruno here nosed me, and when I looked, Sadie had vamoosed. Must have pushed open the screen door."

"But we didn't even see her!" Olivia exclaimed.

"Aw, you were probably smooching," Danny said.

Dave and Olivia were on their feet now, looking around anxiously. "The hedge is fairly impenetrable," Dave said as he ran toward the front of the house. "Except for the hole near the garage. She may have wormed her way out into the driveway."

Olivia clipped Bruno's leash onto his collar and, with the dog racing ahead, rushed after Dave. Danny gamely tried to follow but he couldn't quite keep up. "Wait for me," he cried. "I want to help find Sadie, too. You need my compass, Uncle Dave?" Just then they heard Sadie in the street, barking, and they ran out after her. She was about a hundred yards down the road, but her white coat shone in the darkness so they could see as well as hear her. The pit bull seemed to be attacking a black car parked under a huge old maple that loomed over the street.

"Dave, that car—it looks like the car the Kleins ..." Olivia didn't finish this urgent intelligence because just then the car roared to life and surged forward. Sadie's bark became even more frenzied as she leapt at the front tire. Olivia screamed, sure the pit bull would be hit, and Bruno strained forward, adding his voice to the fracas. The car jumped toward Sadie. She sprang away—an impossible leap, like a dog twisting in midair after a Frisbee—a nanosecond before the car could hit her. It zoomed ahead down the road and out of sight with Sadie running recklessly after it. She didn't stop until she was so exhausted she fell on the road's shoulder. She was panting as if these were her last breaths.

When Olivia caught up, she crouched down beside Sadie, stroking her gently, while Bruno leaned over them both, making little worried sounds. "Sadie, you dope. Are you trying to kill yourself? There's no way you can ever catch a speeding car." Was it crazy to reason with a dog, Olivia wondered.

"Shit!" Dave said. "I tried to get that guy's license number, but he got out of here so fast. And no lights. That's the giveaway."

"If that mobster is watching your house, you're already in big trouble," said Olivia, who spoke from recent experience. "What's he want with you now? Does he know about us then? Or worse, does he know you've been to Lily's bank?"

"Shit!" Dave repeated. "All I got were the last two numbers. Z2."

"What make? I never did find that out, but it sure looks like the same car that bastard got away in." Olivia wondered if Sadie had recognized the car. Who knows how the extraordinary canine senses work? There were dogs who could smell cancer and dogs who could feel the vibrations of their human companion's oncoming seizure.

"It's a Chevy, about two years old I guess. Shit!"

"Let's get Sadie into my van. That was a terrific run for a dog her age, but it must have been very tiring. I think I should take her home to rest now. Unless you want me to stay and talk this through?"

"No, I think you both need some rest from all this. But I'm worried about you." Dave's concerned expression confirmed his words in a satisfying way. Olivia wanted to reach up and kiss that soft, generous mouth right that minute, but it wouldn't do to interrupt a serious discussion of dangers with a sexy digression. "I'll have a patrol car follow you home and hang around. Make sure that guy doesn't turn up at your door again."

"I think it's your door that's most in need of watching now," Olivia said. Discussion over. Time for that kiss.

∾

"I hope you're satisfied, Lily," Olivia said. She'd taken to talking to the dead woman's photo wherever it ended up. Tonight, Lily's smiling face was back on the upstairs office shelf with the remains of Olivia's family photographs, standing exactly where she'd placed it after the auction. The blonde's expression seemed almost demure. "Sure, butter wouldn't melt in your mouth."

Suppose she hadn't gone to that auction and bought the photo, Olivia mused. Everything would be different, or rather, the same as it used to be B.L, *Before Lily*. She wouldn't have had a break-in, so she wouldn't have met Dave Lowenstein, and she would have missed out on some memorable kisses and amazing sex. She wouldn't have adopted Sadie and Bruno who had become inexpressibly dear to her. But her head would be screwed on straight, so her stock market research wouldn't be going to hell from sheer neglect. She'd never have participated in a séance, heard a ghost knocking on the wall, or questioned her own sanity. She wouldn't be talking to a ghost right now, this evening, or to herself, whichever the case might be.

Olivia realized that she was making another mental list of pros and cons but decided not to write it down. Some things simply didn't equate. There might be more items on the "cons" side of the list, but Dave, Sadie, and Bruno outweighed them all. It was the first time Olivia had ever questioned the efficacy of intellectual analysis. *Maybe real life defies analysis,* she said to herself, remembering with a throb of desire the last time she lay in bed pressed against Dave's naked body. *On the other hand, it's not an outstanding idea to replace reason with runaway libido.* Olivia thought about where the initial rapture with Hank Robb had led—right down the garden path to emotional and fiscal insecurity. But Dave was different— caring, stable, and all those other criteria important to Olivia: *single, monogamous, fiscally prudent, robustly healthy, no family idiots, not a fan of Country & Western, hard rock, or polkas, good with children and animals, et cetera.*

She thought about the martial arts course idea she'd jotted among her *To Do* notes. *Kung Fu Kicks for Chicks* might be just the ticket. Learn some protective moves in case she had to confront another enforcer like the hydrant guy (as she thinks of him, remembering his short, square build.) Or would it make more sense to buy a gun and learn to use it, sign up for some ladylike instruction with the NRA or similar?

"What do you think, Lily? Kung Fu or a little handgun? You had that unregistered Smith & Wesson .38. Much good it did you." The photograph, of course, was maddeningly silent and motionless. *Ghosts exist on their own wave length and are never predictable—or cooperative,* Olivia concluded.

Before going upstairs to bed, she made herself a hot cup of cocoa, comforting treat of her youth. *Lovely!* Olivia sipped the thick fragrant drink.

I prefer a sloe gin fizz. A woman's voice, raspy, like the voice of a jazz singer who's had too much booze, seemed to be coming from the living room. Carefully, Olivia carried her mug in both hands (she'd never been able to get the old cocoa stain completely out of that rug) and cautiously entered the living room. As before, the room was in shadow, lit only by the hall light. The figure of a woman with smoothly coiled blonde hair was again barely visible in the wing chair facing the fireplace. It looked as if she were wearing the same soft green as Olivia's living room wallpaper, or the color was reflecting off ... what? *An airy nothing?* Her hand on the arm of the chair wore the suggestion of an emerald ring.

"Lily, is that you?" asked Olivia. *Okay. Now I'm having another conversation with a ghost,* she thought. She stood frozen in the middle of the room.

Yes. Warn you ... warn you. The heavy scent of a musky lily perfume filled Olivia's nostrils. *It's Bobby Ray you have to watch out for. He's going to ...* and then the voice and the figure began to fade.

Olivia couldn't make out the last few words. Bravely, she inched forward toward the fireplace. The wing chair was empty.

"Bobby Ray," she said aloud. "Is that the hydrant man's name? Or some other hoodlum?" No response. Olivia sat in the *other* wing chair, opposite Lily's, gazing at the fireplace she'd filled with white birch logs and a basket of potted ivy. She hadn't turned on the lamps; the light from the hall was enough. Olivia waited in silence for what seemed an endless time, then shook herself and tasted the cocoa. What had seemed a long while hadn't even been long enough to cool her hot drink.

"Lily, it would help tremendously if you'd stay around to specify exactly what danger I should fear? And who the hell is Bobby Ray?" She sipped her cocoa and waited.

After a while, in the shadowed room, Olivia saw, or imagined she saw, Lily's form materializing again in the matching chair—but not quite. Olivia's hands began to shake. Slowly, she placed her mug on the end table and clutched the arms of her chair. She heard the ghost's voice now, quite clearly. *The disc. They want it destroyed. They're coming after ...*

Again the form dematerialized, and there was nothing more to be seen or heard.

Finally Olivia went upstairs. What to do? Should she tell Dave about Lily's warning? Still in a quandary, she started getting ready for bed. It would be perfectly natural to give him a call anyway—just to reassure him after their evening's hectic ending.

"Dave, I'm all right," she said hastily as soon as he answered. "I just called to say good night, and ... and that I'm a little worried about you and that stuff. How secure is it?"

"Why? Has something happened? Is anyone threatening you?" His concern flared up instantly. Olivia liked feeling cared about, protected—that lovely illusion.

"Well, you know how I explained to you that I get these vibrations that seem to be coming from Lily? Believe me, I know just how crazy this sounds, but I feel she's been warning me to safeguard ... *you-know*. As if there's anything *I* can do."

"As far as I know, honey, that *thing* is locked up securely in the evidence room. It shouldn't take the lieutenant more than a day or two to figure out how he's going to handle it. He won't dare sit still much longer. Then the matter will be out of our hands for good. So although I appreciate Lily's concern, I think we've got the situation under control."

"Okay. I'm going to sleep now," Olivia yawned.

"Wish I were there," Dave said.

His voice seemed to reach right though the phone and caress her skin. She shivered. "I wish you were, too."

LILY

I feel as if I'm getting stretched a bit thin. Transparent, like the Invisible Woman. Well, that's not exactly it either. It's more like becoming less myself and more part of Everything Else, if you know what I mean, Hon. But even as I feel myself being drawn away from my Good Old Days, I struggle to hang on even tighter. Like I wish I'd hung on to that railing when those two goons were beating me up on the stairwell. The clock may be striking midnight, but I don't feel it's My Time to Go just yet. I'm sticking around to see Justice Triumph. Those Benedettos gotta get what they deserve before I'm swept away and dispersed like a breeze over the ocean.

I mean, right now I've finally got things perking. Liv has let go of the evidence that her hot new boyfriend needs to wrap up indictments. And now there's another guy in the picture, this LeRoy. Comes from good stock down in New Orleans. I've met his Auntie up here, Marie-Josie, and she's keeping an eye on him like I'm watching over Liv.

I wish I could get through to Liv, though, make her realize how dangerous that rotten Bobby Ray Chance can be. I know in my bones (ha ha) that he'll be bad news for her and her guy, just like he was for Frankie and me. I tried to tell her, really vocalize, which is about the toughest thing for My Kind to do, even tougher than materializing. Much easier to bang the shutters or do the Footsteps-

on-the-Stairs thing. But I thought about how that little turd turned us in to the Benedettos just so's he might get on their payroll and score some easy drugs. That made me so damned mad, the energy just flowed out of me. Strong Emotion ... that's the ticket, just like the Guardians told me.

Still, I wonder what's going to happen to me next. Actually I get quite excited thinking about Moving On. It's not scary like you might think, being absorbed into the Great Unknown. Because of this indescribable Loving Light. I would tell you about it, Hon, but like I said, it's indescribable.

JUNE 1
Things to Do Today

Call J. Any info?
Rev. affirmations. Freedom fr anxiety, strength thru detachment
Pro & con wedd?
Who is Bobby?

Even on Sunday, any decent person should be out of bed by nine, ready to take on Life, Olivia believed. She punched in Jamie's number.

She herself had been up since seven, giving the house a quick run-through, moving with extra speed as she vacuumed and dusted around the wing chairs in the living room so as not to encounter any remaining ghostly vibes in the sensible light of day. In the dining room, she flung open the glass doors, admiring her garden, inhaling deeply. Being in love, or at least in romance, gave a touch of magic to every mundane task, just as it made every color of this June morning more vivid, the scent of the first roses floating on the breeze more intoxicating. Light-footed and light-hearted—that's the way Olivia felt.

"Oh my gawd, Liv. Don't you ever sleep in? What's up?" Jamie, who had caller I.D., didn't disguise the yawn in her voice.

"I was just wondering if you've turned up any interesting tidbits at Cesare B.'s this week."

"What, no 'Good morning, dear friend! How are you today?'"

"Good morning. How are you, Jamie, dear friend?"

"How can you be so disgustingly cheerful so early?"

"All right, then. What's new with the mob?"

"The trouble with you, Liv, is that you're so damned focused. But, as I've been telling you all along, my patient is squeaky clean. And that must make him the black sheep of the nefarious Benedetto clan. Besides, he's very debilitated by arthritis. I don't know if *whatsherface,* Yvonne, will ever get him to the altar. Although, with his money, I suppose the altar can come to him."

"Nothing at all, then?" Olivia could not conceal her disappointment.

"Well, maybe one *small* item worthy of notice. A rather unsavory visitor. Closeted in the study with Cesare B. for a half hour or so. I had the impression that my guy was being asked to give this beetle-browed gorilla type some advice."

"Impression?"

"Okay, okay. I listened at the door. I'm taking my unofficial informant status seriously."

"And you found out ... what?"

"I found out that oak-paneled doors are really solid. I wouldn't want to have to break down one of those babies. *But* the visitor got agitated and raised his voice—something about a computer disc. Whatever C. B. murmured in reply I couldn't hear. Also I was interrupted by his housekeeper, the redoubtable Mrs. Gunner, and had to move along with my little tray. I noticed, however, that their conversation seemed to have an energizing affect on the visitor, who stalked out purposefully from the conference—you know, the way gorillas do, knuckles dragging on the floor—with a most formidable and determined look on his mug."

"Can you describe him—I mean, other than 'gorilla'? Happen to notice his car?" Olivia was getting an eerie feeling about this encounter.

"Absolutely. About five feet two, heavy-set muscular frame, square face, dark-browed, heavy stubble—looked as if he'd been sent down from Central Casting to play a pint-size King Kong. And I think I know where you're going with this. Did I notice the car, you ask? *Of course* I ran straight to the window and took a look, but it was entirely nondescript. Old, black, maybe a Chevy."

"Did you at least get the license number?"

"Sorry, I didn't have anything at hand to write with, and when I did get to my bag, I could only remember it began with 67."

"I think that may be the same guy who broke in and threatened me. He reminded me of a fire hydrant. Apparently he and the guy who got shot are brothers, Ben and Moses Klein.

"What's with the passive tense 'got shot'? *You* shot the bastard, girlfriend."

"Okay, then, the guy *I* shot. And by the way, I hear that Moses is recovering nicely and will live to serve a long, long term in prison. But Lily says the one I have to watch out for is some badass kid named Bobby."

"Oh my Gawd. You're still chatting with your girl ghost! But tell me, Liv, what's the scoop on that worrisome evidence you passed on to Dave?"

"It's a long story. I'll tell you later, okay?" Olivia promised.

"Oh, sure. You wring all the dirt out of *me*, then *you* clam up. False friend. When?"

"Soon. Gotta go now. Thanks, Jamie—you're wonderful!"

"I *know* that. Do you want me to report the guy I saw at C.B.'s to your boyfriend?"

"I'll tell him. With full credit given to you, of course," Olivia said. "Dave got the last part of this Klein guy's license number the other night, Z2, so maybe we're on a roll. And you will be careful, won't you? Wouldn't want Mrs. Gunner to catch on."

"Soul of discretion! And plan on my coming by for drinks some evening this week. I am *not* satisfied with crumbs."

ꙮ

Although not a Catholic himself, every Sunday Dave took his wards to St. Timothy's, as Alice had asked him to do. Sometimes Kevin got surly about going along and contemptuous of the Church itself, but Dave still had sufficient authority to enforce compliance, although he wondered how long that would last. Occasionally, if there was a really good reason, Dave let Kevin off the hook. This Sunday, Kevin wanted to rehearse with his friends—a confluence of bodhran, flute, fiddle, and accordion—for a performance later that evening at the Sons of Erin Hall, and Dave agreed. Moira and Danny, however, received no such dispensation.

While the O'Haras were in church, Dave had his own Sunday ritual. He bought the Boston Globe and brought it with him to the nearby Starbucks, where he relaxed with a mug of richly-flavored black coffee and a cranberry muffin, the South Shore's favorite flavor. He scanned the headlines and did the crossword puzzle. The kids knew just where to find him when they were ready to go home. The time varied, depending on what classes they were taking and whether they attended mass. To Dave, these Sunday excursions were a little oasis of calm and indulgence in his hectic weekly schedule. But this Sunday, the hour of serenity lingered a shade too long. Dave glanced at his watch. *What the devil is keeping Danny and Moira?*

∾

When Moira and Danny emerged from catechism class, the boy jamming a bright Red Sox baseball cap on his head, a black Chevy was waiting for them by the side door. A stranger leaned out the open window and called to them. He was a dark-browed man, ugly even when he smiled. Moira tried to hear what the man was saying, but Danny held back, having seen that car the night before.

"Your Uncle Dave has been in an accident up the road," the man said. "Hop in and I'll take you there." He reached over the seat and opened the back door.

"No, Moira, no," Danny whispered.

Scowling with suspicion, Moira hesitated for a moment. But then her imagination leapt wildly on the horror of smashed-up cars, Dave lying on the road somewhere, injured and bleeding. What if something terrible happened to Uncle Dave as it had to their father? Their only living relative was the grandmother who never even knew they were born after Teresa Sullivan fled from the FBI, disappearing into Alice O'Hara. Now living in a nursing home, Mary Sullivan was too senile to care for or about anyone.

With an iron grip, the girl pulled her younger brother into the car.

But Moira was no fool. It didn't take her long to realize her terrifying mistake. It felt like a cold fist squeezing her heart. They were going too fast and too far to be responding to an accident "right up the road."

"I *tried* to tell you," Danny whined, hanging on to his sister as the Chevy rattled down the highway at seventy and then eighty miles an hour.

"Stop this car and let us out!" Moira pounded on the driver's shoulder. "If you don't stop this minute, my Uncle Dave will put you in jail."

The Chevy squealed onto the road's shoulder as the driver slammed on his brake. Moira and Danny fell against each other. Before they could recover, the man pulled a gun from under his jacket and pointed it right at them. Cop's kids, and a murdered cop at that, knew what guns could do, and they froze right where they were. The man took a roll of duct tape out of his glove compartment, grabbed Moira, and made her get out of the car with him, pushing her out of sight of passing drivers, of whom there were few. Despite her struggles, he was too strong for her; he taped her hands behind her back. When she screamed, he taped her mouth, too, and pushed her back into the car. Danny, who had been cowering and whimpering in the corner of the back seat, was much easier to subdue and restrain; the man didn't have to tape his mouth to shut him up.

The man restarted the car and, driving slower now, seemed to be looking for something, but there was nothing to see, just uninhabited woods. Finally he swerved the Chevy into a dirt road that Moira could barely make out. She was sure he planned to kill them once they were out of sight of the main road. Although gagged by the tape, she silently recited the Act of Contrition.

O, my God, I am heartily sorry for having offended Thee, and I detest all my sins, because I dread the loss of heaven, and the pains of hell.

༄

The cell phone clipped to his belt buzzed him. He flipped it open. "Yes?"

"Lowenstein?"

"Yes. Who's this?"

"This is a friend. Listen up, buddy. We know you got to that bank and found something that belongs to us." The voice was harsh and deep, vaguely accented. It wasn't a voice that Dave recognized, except as a type. "Now you got two choices, hotshot. Get the stuff back or see it's wiped clean. If you want your little family to stay in one piece."

"*Where are they, you bastard? Are they all right?*" Dave was suddenly as frightened as he'd ever been. He might have known they'd come after him through the kids, should have stayed right there at the church door to watch over Danny and Moira. Already, he was out the door of Starbucks, scanning the street between the coffee shop and St. Timothy's

"Oh, they're all right *this time*. Maybe shook up a bit though. Maybe don't know their way home too well."

"*Where are they?*" Dave yelled angrily. He ran toward the church, the phone pressed to his ear.

Earlier, while Dave had been serenely enjoying his coffee, clouds had gathered, and now the threat of a spring storm was imminent. The sky was completely overcast, and thunder sounded in the distance. Parishioners coming and going between masses were picking up their pace and looking up at the heavens. None of the children Dave could see around the church looked like Moira and Danny. But maybe someone saw something.

"You know what you gotta do, right?"

"It's out of my hands."

"Not yet, it isn't. You get your butt down to the station and take care of what you got. Won't take much. Ask your girlfriend."

"I can't do that. The evidence isn't in my custody."

The rough voice laughed, not a pleasant sound. "If I was you, I'd figure out a way real quick. Tom O'Hara's brats, aren't they?"

Dave felt so chilled that the blood must be freezing in his veins. "No. They're my kids."

Another brutal laugh. "The little bitch sure can scratch. Won't do her any good, though. So why don't you save yourself a shitload of grief, Lowenstein. Just make sure that stuff never leaves Plymouth County." The phone screen went black; call ended.

Waving his identification, Dave began to question every youngster he saw outside the church. His manner was so distraught and anxious that some parents reached out to draw their children away from his path. Everyone was shaking his head negatively. No one had seen Moira or Danny O'Hara since C.C.D classes.

Dave sank down on the church step; all the energy had drained out of his body. If he sent out a general alarm—an Amber alert—he'd be in the spotlight himself; he wouldn't get a chance to steal back that evidence, or destroy it. And if it was coming down to a choice between nailing the Benedettos and saving his children, would he go against everything he

believed in and toast Rossi's disc? He thought about that
copy he made, one the Benedettos knew nothing about. His
lock box was such an obvious hiding place. He had to find a
safer place to conceal it. If he could bury that evidence for a
while, maybe later he could get it to the Federal prosecutor
through Lee Washington. No glory for his boss, but that was
the least of Dave's worries right now. His whole body went
icy with terror. *Where were Moira and Danny?*

Maybe don't know their way home too well, the thug had said.
That suggested what? Moira and Danny must be wandering
around lost in a place where there were no people to ask for
help and no phones to call Dave. Woods, then. Fairly deep
and impenetrable. Or maybe a boat drifting somewhere.
Never had it been so important that he guess right the first
time. Cell phone still in hand, he punched in Olivia's number.
Waiting for her to pick up, he sprang off the stone step and
paced back and forth.

"Liv, I need help," was the first thing he said when
she answered. Olivia had just finished showering and was
hopping into black chinos and throwing on a red-striped
shirt while she listened. In a few tense sentences, Dave told
her that the children were missing, probably lost in a place
where they couldn't find their way home, and that he'd
been given orders to destroy the evidence. "I know this is
absolutely nuts, but do you think ... is it possible that those
vibrations or whatever that you've been telling me about can
point us in the right direction? The trouble is, my kids could
be anywhere."

"Maybe. I can try. But Dave, what are you going to do
about the disc locked in the evidence room?"

"What do you think? My choices are not great. By the
way, this guy seemed to think *you'd* know how to erase the

data. Then I could leave the disc right where it is—perfectly useless."

"I do know. I have something called a bulk eraser. It's a hand-held electromagnet with a hefty field. Erases sensitive data you don't want read by others. But it's getting rather obsolete now. I have a write-over program that's more reliable. No time for that, though. You need something portable and quick—the bulk eraser is the way to go. And this would probably be a good day to do it, right? Sunday. Skeleton staff, am I right?"

"Right. But not until we find Moira and Danny."

"Let me call you back. I promise it won't be long. I'll try something here. Where will you be?"

"In the car, heading for the state forest. Could be they've been dumped somewhere in there."

"Why don't I meet you there? Wait for me by the main entrance. I'll bring the dogs, shall I?"

"Worth a try.

❧

After Ben Klein discovered that the dirt road ended abruptly between two ancient cranberry bogs, he cursed violently as if he'd hoped to drive deeper into the woods. Then he lit a cigarette and gazed thoughtfully into the brush while the kids cowered in the back seat, wondering what would happen to them next. At last he threw the cigarette through the window and jumped from the car. He strode over to the edge of the clearing and made a call on his cell phone. The youngsters couldn't distinguish much of what was said, but Moira did hear the man laugh in a nasty way and say "save yourself a shitload of grief" before he hung up. Then he opened the back door and pulled Moira and Danny out onto the ground, Moira thought, *this is it then. I'll never see my mom again.* Danny was crying, big gusty sobs. Moira commenced a silent Hail Mary—*pray for us sinners now and in the hour of our death.*

Seizing both children by the backs of their necks, the man pushed them ahead of him into the woods. Moira didn't know how long they walked, just that the brush scratched their skin and tore their clothes. Finally the man threw them down near the base of a large oak tree, took a roll of duct tape out of his pocket and bound their ankles. He lit another cigarette and glared at them menacingly. "Tell your Uncle Dave he was lucky this time," the man said. Grabbing Danny's Red Sox baseball cap, miraculously still clinging to the boy's head, the man stuffed it in his pocket and laughed. "Thanks for the souvenir, brat."

∽

When Olivia hung up, she raced upstairs to her office. "Lily! Lily!" She couldn't imagine that she was asking a ghost for help. Weird times call for weird measures.

But Lily in her Art Deco frame was missing again!

Olivia wailed loudly. When she stopped wailing long enough to catch her breath, she heard a small tapping noise. It seemed to be coming from her bookcase, the one that had so recently toppled to the floor. Lily's photo was sitting there on the bottom shelf, grinning at her.

All right, now what's this game, Olivia thought, crouching down to see what was going on. Lily's photo was sitting in a mess of books that Olivia hadn't sorted out since Jamie stuffed them into the bookcase just to get them off the floor.

She spotted her Rand McNally Road Atlas shoved in with some pamphlets, its pages folded over awkwardly, a sure way to ruin a good book. Olivia pulled out the atlas to straighten the pages and it seemed to leap right out of her hand. An assortment of Arrow road maps—Plymouth, South Shore, Southeastern Massachusetts—fell to the floor. Olivia picked them up and fanned them out like a hand of cards. She opened the Plymouth map and studied the Myles Standish State Forest, which sprawled across the middle of the town. *So many possibilities*

The other two maps rattled as if someone had opened a window and an east wind were blowing into the room. Southeastern Massachusetts flipped open a fold. *Woods*, Olivia thought. She pushed the Plymouth map aside and spread Southeastern Massachusetts across her lap. What if that Klein hoodlum or that other guy—the one Lily had warned her about—dropped those children somewhere within that desolate stretch along Route 44. She was guessing Middleboro. Or was she guessing?

Yesssssssssss. Olivia heard a hissing that could be an affirmative from Lily. She smelled a drift of the familiar exotic lily perfume. *Oh, why can't that ghost speak up when it counts!* In some dim recess of her mind, Olivia was aware of going off the rails here, but she didn't care. Those poor little kids! That son-of-a-bitch!

"Come on, you guys—let's go!" Olivia jumped up off the floor, maps in one hand, and headed for the back door. She grabbed her bag and cell phone, clipped leashes to Sadie and Bruno's collars. Picking up on her excitement, they were positively dancing on their paws with anticipation. The van was standing handily in the driveway as it had ever since that irate ex-employee Ray Chance had torched her garage. She flung open the van's back door and the dogs jumped in. Only when she was behind the wheel gunning the motor did she take out her cell phone to call Dave.

"Lowenstein," he answered, sounding both wary and angry.

"It's me, Dave. Where are you?"

"Heading to the state forest, as we agreed. Jesus, Olivia, this is crazy. Maybe I'd better just start the Amber alert."

"I had some strange phenomena at the house. Might have been a message from Lily. I know this is mad, but ... how about that stretch of dense woodland along Route 44, somewhere near Middleboro. Any chance he could have dumped the kids in there? It would be on his way back to Boston."

There was a long silence on Dave's end of the line. Should he follow his own instincts or be guided by Liv's companion ghost, the one who got his family into all this trouble? *Lily*. Lily wanted to crush the Benedettos. If ever there was an uneasy vengeful spirit, it was she.

"Okay," Dave said. "I guess a wacky psychic lead is better than no lead at all. I'll meet you at the Middleboro line. Did you bring the dogs?"

"Of course. See you there."

৽৽

As suddenly as he had braked, the short, dark-browed man threw away his cigarette and crashed back the way he had come. The cigarette he'd discarded started a little blaze in a drift of old oak leaves underneath the new plant growth. Unable to call for Danny's help, Moira used the tree to ratchet herself up from the ground and began hopping on her taped-together feet to stomp out the small flame. At first her brother took that to be some kind of victory dance. Then he noticed the smoldering leaves under Moira's feet and rolled over to help. Sitting on the remains of the fire felt hot, as if he was burning his bum, but only the backside of his good Sunday pants got blackened. Dave was going to kill him for that.

Making unintelligible noises under the duct tape, Moira used body language to motion Danny into a back-to-back stance. Soon they were yanking and pulling and scraping the duct tape off each other's wrists. The tape was really tight, and freeing themselves took a long time, most of an hour, Moira thought. Her fingers being more agile, she got Danny untied first, but once his hands were loose, he soon got his sister's tapes off, too. All except her mouth. Moira pulled that off herself, and the skin hurt bad.

Last of all they unwound the tape around their ankles, and Danny took off the compass clipped onto his belt and shook it. He wasn't terribly sure how it worked. Making a scornful noise, Moira started off in the direction the man had taken.

Olivia didn't remember exactly where the Middleboro line was, except that it was someplace along Route 44, so she drove a bit slower than usual, looking for Dave's car. At last she saw the Bronco pulled up on a grassy shoulder near the Middleboro-Plymouth sign. Dave, who'd been pacing around the car watching for her, nearly stepped in front of her Chevy when he waved her to a stop. She slammed on the brake and swerved to avoid him, hearing the dogs bump around in back, trying to keep their balance.

"I've been up and down this road looking for access. Damned hopeless." Dave shouted by way of greeting. "Jesus, I hope they're all right." His face looked ravaged with worry.

"Some of those old dirt roads are so overgrown, they're barely visible. Hop in my car and let's have another look. Less time if we don't have to move the dogs to the Bronco." Dave jumped into the passenger seat and leaned forward as if he himself was stepping on the gas. Olivia took the hint and floored it, leaving the dogs to knock around in the back as the van raced along Route 44.

Finally, as they hurtled in the direction of Boston, Dave made out what looked like an abandoned cranberry bog access road. Olivia slammed on her brakes. On closer examination, Dave saw fresh tire tracks. This road had been used recently.

"He'd have had to drive a long way into the woods if he wanted to confuse the kids. Maybe he even blindfolded them," Dave muttered.

"Too bad it's so overcast or Moira surely would have taken her bearings from the sun," Olivia said. "She's a plucky girl. If anything can be done, she'll do it." For all her crossness and bossiness, Moira had qualities that Olivia admired. Funny she'd never realized that before. She felt a terrifying vulnerability, cold fingers of fear shutting off her breath. *Those poor innocent kids! Is this what it's like to have a family?*

A few minutes later, about a quarter of a mile into the woods, they came to a clearing, just room enough to turn a car around, where the road ended. "Are you sure you don't want to call for help?" Olivia asked as she looked around at the thickness of trees and underbrush. This was too serious to mess around like amateurs.

"Yeah. I guess that's the only way to go," Dave agreed. "Let's get out for a minute, though."

Olivia turned off the motor and pocketed the key. "Okay, you grab Bruno's leash and I'll take Sadie. They hear things we never would, and smell them, too."

Standing in the clearing with two confused dogs, they felt like fools. Dave's hand was on his cell phone, ready to call in the alert. But Bruno, who'd been sniffing the air uncertainly, suddenly put his head down and surged forward so unexpectedly, he almost pulled Dave off his feet. Sadie barked sharply twice, then threw back her head and howled like the Hound of the Baskervilles.

"Do you suppose they're on to something?" Olivia asked. But she was talking to an empty clearing. Dave was being yanked through walls of brush by the intent muscular shepherd. Olivia followed with Sadie, getting thoroughly scratched in the process.

From somewhere within the woods, they heard a shrill and welcome whistle.

"Hey, Uncle Dave. Hey, we're over here," Danny called out.

"Dave!" *That was Moira*! "Are you there?"

A moment later, they were reunited with inarticulate cries of joy on all sides. Dave was kneeling on the ground, hugging both the children, not saying anything for fear it would come out with a sob.

Danny wiggled free and pointed to the compass he was holding in his fist. "See, Uncle Dave, I got this here. But Moira had to figure it out for me. She said we ought to head East back to the main road. Then, after a while, we heard Bruno. Good boy, Bruno. You knew where to find me, didn't you, boy?"

Moira looked at her brother scornfully. "Blackberries. That's what we really need."

"Blackberries?" Danny said wonderingly. "I'd rather have hot dogs."

"It's a cell phone with a direction finder," Olivia explained. "And a damned ... darned good idea." There was duct tape still hanging from Danny's wrist, and Moira's mouth looked raw. Their arms were crisscrossed with red scratches. The sleeve of Moira's pink church dress was torn half off. Danny's pants had a long rip down one side and looked as if he had sat in charcoal; his cap was missing.

Dave's face was still screwed up in a painful way so he wouldn't cry. Having no such male compunction, Olivia let the tears flow down her cheeks and wiped them away with the sleeve of her striped shirt. Evidence of recent tears also streaked Moira's face, which nonetheless wore its usual angry expression. Taking the handkerchief out of her pocket (Olivia always carried the real thing), she dabbed at the dirt on Moira's forehead. Snatching the embroidered square from Liv's hand, Moira spit on it and scrubbed her face, even her obviously sore mouth.

Sadie and Bruno attempted to knock everyone over with an excess of enthusiasm. With all that was going on, it took a while to get the youngsters' story. Especially since Dave interrupted them from time to time with heated questions and sanitized curses.

൭

After they told their story, Moira wanted to know why the man kidnapped them, and what was Uncle Dave going to do about it? Danny said it would be better not to tell their mother because she had enough worries. Moira asked if the kidnapper was the same man who'd shot their Dad.

Close enough. A lucky hit, Olivia thought. *Or a psychic flash.* She never used to believe in such things, but life (or death) in the person (or hallucination) of Lily had taken hold of Olivia the way a terrier grabs a bone, and was giving her conventional views a good shaking up.

"I don't know for sure who shot your dad." Dave put a hand on Moira's shoulder, and arm around Danny, who leaned against him. "But I'll never give up trying to find whoever it was and make him pay. And I'm going to do all I can to prevent anything like this from ever happening to you again." Promises that may have reassured his wards, but Dave himself was not convinced.

His eyes looked haunted, Olivia thought, as they gazed at each other across the youngsters' heads. What now? Should they destroy the evidence they'd gone to such pains to find? How to protect Moira and Danny—and themselves—if they refused to follow the Benedetto mob's orders?

"I've got to do it," Dave muttered to Olivia.

"Let's go back to my place," she said. "I'll give you a crash course in erasing data. But what about the other ... ?" She didn't finish the sentence.

"I'm working on a plan." Dave's look told Olivia *not in front of the children*.

∽

As soon as Moira and Danny were brushed off, washed up, and their scratches and cuts medicated, Olivia let Sadie and Bruno run ahead to do a ghost sweep of her living room. Apparently, it was clean. No vibrations of Lily to spook the sensitive canines, so Olivia settled the two children on the couch with sodas and the TV. Over Moira's complaints that she had a meatloaf all ready to go into the oven at home, Olivia insisted they'd have Sunday dinner with her. Silently, she did a quick mental review of the remaining foil-wrapped blocks of food in her freezer. That large oval one might be a braised chicken. She would find something.

Meanwhile, she and Dave snuck upstairs where she instructed him in the use of the bulk eraser. "How will you get into the evidence room? Oh God—what if you get caught? This could ruin you. You'd be fired, maybe arrested."

"You've got to know, honey—I despise cops who tamper with evidence. But this threat to Tom's kids has upset everything I believe in," Dave confessed. The line of his mouth tightened with resolve. "They are my first concern now."

"I know what you mean. Nothing is the same as it was for me either. I mean, before Lily. But the important thing right now seems to be—can you do it?"

"With luck, I think I'll manage it. Not the first time evidence has been meddled with, you know."

An avid reader of true crime stories, Olivia did know. "Please, please be careful." Olivia hung a camera case over his shoulder containing the bulk eraser. She felt as if she were helping Dave to strap on armor like a medieval knight being suited up for battle by his lady. She threw her arms around him in a passionate farewell.

"There's one more thing we have to do," Dave murmured against her cheek.

"We?" Olivia didn't know if she herself were up to any actual criminal activity.

"The other disc. The copy the Benedettos don't know about. I need a really good place to hide it for a while. You don't think I'm going to let these bastards get away Scot-free, do you?"

"I'll think of something," Olivia promised. She hoped that Lily would not be too disappointed that she had to wait a while longer for her revenge. After all, spirits were supposed to dwell in a timeless realm, weren't they, so what should a few weeks or months matter? Because it wouldn't do to have a ghost pissed off at you. Perhaps she'd better consult Florrie Mitchell on that point.

The oval aluminum package turned out to be a nice stuffed pork shoulder, very savory once she got it thawed and reheated. Having missed their midday meal, the children ate ravenously.

Dave didn't return until dark; meanwhile, Moira and Danny had fallen asleep on the couch, well-fed, exhausted, and guarded by Bruno who never left Danny's side. Olivia was reminded of the travails of Hansel and Gretel. Saved from the terrors of the wicked old woman in the forest. Or in this case, from the Benedetto family. When you got right down to the wire, Olivia reflected, you had only your own skills to depend on in an uncertain world. All official sources of help somehow failed to protect people who are being stalked and harassed. She thought again about how reassuring it would be to own a nice ladylike little gun. It was a subject she planned to discuss with Dave—later.

Just as she was imagining a scenario where she shot an intruder in the leg—or would his knees be better?—Kevin called. He was on his way to the Sons of Erin Hall, but he wondered why Moira and Danny never got back from church and there were no leftovers from Sunday dinner. When Kevin missed dinner, Moira usually left him a plate of something to heat up.

Olivia would have liked to present the afternoon's exploits in the least alarming manner, but in trying to explain matters to the older boy, found that there was really no prettying up a kidnapping. So she explained as briefly and as reassuringly as possible.

"Jesus, Mary, and Joseph," Kevin exclaimed. "We never had trouble like this before Dave got mixed up with you."

Olivia wanted to tell him that, yes he did. His father had been murdered by the same family of gangsters. But she resisted taking the cheap shot.

After a space of mutual silence, Kevin sighed resignedly. "Sorry," he mumbled. "Tell the kids not to worry and not to go anywhere. After the show, I'll catch a ride there—take them home and look out for them."

Another complication, Olivia thought.

ᕙᕗ

Olivia was putting dishes in the dishwasher when Dave tapped lightly on the kitchen door.

"Shhhh!" Olivia warned, putting her finger to her lips and pointing toward the living room. Then she flung herself into Dave's arms, suddenly aware of just how worried she'd been these past few hours. In fact, she'd been hitting the red wine she had opened for Dave. Red wine always needs to breathe, and Olivia needed to take a few unworried deep breaths herself. "Tell me everything," she whispered in his ear. "Did you do it? Anyone catch on? Were you able to cover your tracks?"

"Easy, honey. I think we're in the clear. And I'm starved—did the kids eat? Good. Would you fix me a sandwich—anything you've got will be fine. God, I am so bushed. What a hell of a day this has been!"

Olivia filled a glass with wine and handed it to him, then refilled her own. "Well, go on," she said impatiently, while she took the roast out of the refrigerator and began to cut thick slices. "Let's have the whole story. Every last detail."

Dave said maybe Lily was sitting on his shoulder because he sure got lucky. The Sunday crew had been light. He'd muttered something to the desk clerk about finding some papers pertaining to court testimony he'd be giving the first of the week; after that, no one had paid him much attention. The evidence room was properly locked up, but its desk was unattended and Dave knew where the extra key was kept—in Lieutenant Badger's middle desk drawer.

"Oh," Olivia breathed. "Now you're getting into real trouble."

"I couldn't afford to think too much," Dave admitted. He'd palmed the key. Everyone had been in the conference room watching the Belmont Stakes race on TV, it being a light day for crime on the South Shore. Quietly, Dave let himself into the evidence room while his colleagues were lustily cheering the favorite. He helped himself to a pair of latex gloves from the box under the counter. But then, the first glitch. The disc was nowhere to be found. Had their boss finally got antsy about sitting on that hot evidence and sent it along to Boston?

Then an idea had struck Dave like a punch in the stomach. A sickening thought, but it had to be faced. With evidence so important, the lieutenant would want to stash it in the department safe, not in the evidence room where, locked or not, many a screw-up had occurred in times past. *Yes, that was it.*

The combination! Damn! How many times had Dave seen his boss dial that combination without registering the number and letter sequence? He tried to picture the lieutenant swinging his chair around to open the safe—then what? *No wait.* Something came first. Wouldn't the lieutenant usually shuffle through his right hand drawer and *then* swing his chair around? *Yes!*

Dave heard the guys still laughing and cheering in the conference room when he eased into his boss's empty office and shut the door, hoping no one would spot his moving shadow through the frosted glass. He opened the right hand drawer in the desk. It was easier than it should have been. When Dave pushed the stack of forms aside, there it was, neatly lettered on a piece of adhesive tape fixed to the back of the drawer divider.

"What a slipshod way to handle a safe combination. Someone should definitely file a complaint," Olivia interrupted. Her protocols for handling sensitive information were seriously offended by such carelessness. "But did it work? Was it the right combination?"

Dave nodded, then started in on his sandwich before continuing. Olivia opened another bottle of red wine.

"God, I bet I aged ten years opening that safe and searching through it for the disc. Judging by the silence down the hall, the goddamn race was over, but then someone turned on NASCAR and saved my bacon. Because I still had to work on that disc and put everything back exactly right. I hope to God I scrambled the data enough at least so the Benedettos will be satisfied."

"How will they know? I mean, to be satisfied that you've done as they ordered," Olivia asked.

He drained his glass. Olivia refilled it, reflecting that it was no wonder criminals so often became alcoholics. "It's apparent that the Benedettos can call in favors from practically any place, not excluding law enforcement and city government."

"This stress is too much to take," Olivia said. "Aren't you glad you're a cop and not a mobster?"

He was gazing off into space. "If this was successful, all I've bought us is a little time. I have to keep the kids safe. They have no other relatives besides Alice's mother, and she's in a rest home with Alzheimer's. And my folks are spending this month birding in Fundy National Park."

Olivia knew that Dave would never seriously consider his own mom and dad as an option for emergency foster care. One of those couples who value nothing so much as their freedom, Dave had said they'd never understood why he took responsibility for Tom O'Hara's family. Olivia thought of her mother Cecelia, the whiner, in her overheated, small apartment stuffed with too many pieces of furniture and her collection of angel figurines. No, that wouldn't do either.

And, *brainstorm!* Jamie's parents still live in Cleveland, too, in an old fashioned bungalow of the cozy thirties Sears' Catalog style. Jamie's mother Sandy was a practical nurse whose rosy cheeks might have been the result of taking frequent nips of whiskey in the kitchen while she cooked dinner; nevertheless, she was invariably merry and generous. Her father Artie was a security guard at City Hall. They were simple, warm people who had welcomed their daughter's high school friend with open arms.

"I have a swell solution," Olivia said, "but I guess it will have to wait until school's out. When is that? Just a few days more? And I have to check with Jamie first. A kind of homemade witness protection program. Oh, that reminds me. Kevin called. He said he'd get dropped off here after the show."

"You told him?" Dave pushed away his plate with a sigh of satisfaction.

"As little as possible. Only that some creep had driven away with the kids and left them in the woods," Olivia replied. "Not about the tapes you're being blackmailed into destroying. I *suggested* the guy must be some vengeful hoodlum who had it in for you."

"Okay, and your 'homemade witness protection program'—what's that? Jamie can't take them on. How many bedrooms can that town house have?"

"Not Jamie. I'm thinking of her parents in Cleveland. They're a really nice old couple in a roomy bungalow. Perhaps they'd consider taking in some temporary foster kids. As I recall, they always had someone extra hanging around their house. Sometimes it was me, when I was in high school."

"They'd have to be saints. I'd pay them, of course. We'd have to keep it strictly hush-hush. Wouldn't want to put Jamie's folks in danger for doing us a good turn. But what about the next couple of weeks?"

"I think ... I hope it will be all right. When the evidence against them isn't forthcoming, the Benedettos will credit you with destroying it." Olivia shivered as another thought rose up unbidden. But it was true, and she had to say it. "But it's really you who are in danger now. You know where the bodies are buried, so to speak. Now that you've done as they've asked ..." She couldn't bring herself to finish the sentence. "It's important, I think, that you don't tell the kids about this Cleveland plan. As soon as they're out of school, just get in the car, make sure you're not followed, and drive."

With an absent-minded expression—his deep-thought mode, Olivia had learned—Dave took his dishes to the sink and thoroughly washed them, ignoring the dishwasher. "I can take care of myself. It's a good plan," he said finally, still scrubbing the clean dishes. "When will you talk to Jamie?"

"Tomorrow. We're going to another auction, God help me."

"I can't take much time off without raising questions. But I can drive the kids to New York, get the first available plane to Cleveland, then take the red-eye home. If I don't get the tickets in advance, no trail will be left for the Benedettos. Once the kids are safe, we can bring out that one remaining copy of the Benedetto accounts and nail those bastards. Meantime, I need a safer place to keep it."

Olivia went to Dave and encircled him with her arms, drawing him away from the obsessive washing of dishes. "You'll need plenty of cash, no credit cards. As for the disc, take it with you. Before you leave New York, rent a post office box—there may be one connected to the airport. I'll check that on the Internet. Memorize the number and destroy the receipt. Then you can mail the disc to yourself from Cleveland."

He turned and hugged her, nearly taking her feet off the ground. "That's a pretty smart idea," he said.

"Well, I'm a records expert, you know. Options just naturally come to mind."

"And you won't buy any photos at the auction?"

"*Once is experience, twice is perversion,*" Olivia said, nuzzling closer. She felt his quick natural response to their closeness. Too bad they had this houseful of O'Haras.

But just then Kevin knocked on the kitchen door, and they sprang apart guiltily. Sadie bounded out from under the table barking furiously.

"I can't see Kevin letting himself be moved away from his friends—and his music—willingly," Dave muttered while she was pulling the dog back from the door.

"It's only Kevin, for heaven's sake, Sadie. You know his scent," she reasoned with the dog. Her hand on the knob, she whispered to Dave, "If you give him the idea that he'll be protecting Moira and Danny?" and opened the door. "Oh, hi, Kev. Are we glad to see you! Are you hungry? Want a sandwich?"

"I want to know what the hell happened to Moira and Danny!" he growled, patting Sadie on her big white head.

JUNE 2
Things to Do Today

Call Jamie re: auction
Don't forget magnet, magnifying glass, notebook, checkbook, sandwiches
Libr renew Your Troubled Teen, borrow How to Disappear Without a Trace
Call Kung Fu Studio, Kicks for Chicks
Call insurance re: garage—squeaky wheel!!!

"Jamie, I have a really big favor to ask of you." Olivia was surprised to feel a little nervous. After all, this was her best friend.

They'd finished reviewing the odd assortment of antiques, collectibles, and junk smelling of dust and mold that comprised this "estate" sale. Having reclaimed their saved chairs, they were sipping gins and tonic, studying their notes, and waiting for the auctioneer to quit glad-handing dealers and get this show on the road.

"More chestnuts you want me to pull out of the Benedetto fire? Didn't you have enough truck with them when Dave's kids went missing?" Jamie asked. "What do you think of that Limoges dinner set?"

"Yes, in a way, I *do* want something, or *someones*, pulled out of the fire," Olivia said. "As for what I think about the Limoges—one, it doesn't go in the dishwasher, and two, where would you put it? Your dining room cabinet is chockablock full of some very classy Mikasa."

Jamie sighed. "You're entirely too sensible. Well, maybe not *entirely* since you got yourself haunted by a dead dame and chased by some local gangsters. The Mikasa pattern is called Deco Platinum, very restrained, and I'm bloody sick of it. I'm into that Limoges rosy floral—Canterbury it's called. What's the favor?"

"Well, it's more a loan of your parents. You see, Dave needs a safe place to stash his wards for a few weeks as soon as school's out, and we were wondering if your parents might be interested in boarding them. They'd be paid, of course."

"Gawd, Liv! I'd rather not get my parents wasted in some mob war, you know. I mean, I may not get home *that* often, but I like thinking of them puttering around comfortably together in their Age of Serenity."

"Dave's got this plan to get the kids out of town without leaving tracks. The idea is, no one is to know when they leave, where they're going, and who's taking care of them."

"Yeah? I'd need to hear the details of Dave's plan."

"Poor Dave is beside himself with worry. Can you imagine how you'd feel if Mike got kidnapped and dropped in the woods in the wilds of Middleboro tied up with duct tape?"

"All right, all right—the tug on the heartstrings always works. If Dave's all hot to protect his little family, tell him to get them off from school as soon as they've taken their finals. Ask to have the report cards mailed. Say they've got to visit a dying grandma or some such. That should buy him a week."

"Oh, good plan, Jamie!"

"I'll give Mom and Dad a call when I get home tonight. Or better yet, you come in for a drink and get your answer right then and there. They always did like you—all those Sunday dinners scarfing up our roast beef and Yorkshire pudding—so they'll probably say yes, poor unsophisticated babies that they are. Oh, look ... Byatt's got his hot coffee and cold water. He's ready to go. What are you buying? More haunted photos?" Jamie chortled.

"Let's have an auction!" Bill Byatt shouted and held up the first item, always a loss leader. As it happened, it was a miniature portrait of a pale somber woman, a work of no particular distinction.

"Never, never again," Olivia whispered. There were only three items on her modest list, all of them safe, she believed, from being infested with ghosts: a Victorian sewing table, an ironstone platter big enough for a turkey (although come to think of it, when will she ever have that many guests at Thanksgiving?) and a flowered Roseville vase.

"Never say never, Liv!" Jamie leaned over to read Olivia's list. "I noticed that Roseville vase. Did you realize that the flower's a lily? Pretty, though."

"Oh, no! I think my subconscious mind is playing tricks on me." Olivia drew a line through the Roseville. "So...let's see your list." There were nineteen items on Jamie's list. Olivia hoped she wouldn't win all of them. It would take forever to pack the van. Might make it too late to call Jamie's parents.

Jamie saw her look of dismay. "Oh, Gawd, Liv—don't imagine that I'll be lugging all this stuff home. I just love the thrill of bidding, and sometimes when there's a lull, you can win some fantastic bargain."

Which is how it happened that they found themselves packing the 60-piece plus serving dishes of Limoges in newspaper and cardboard boxes provided by the auction. There'd been one of those unforeseeable moments when the energy in the room, the buying frenzy, suddenly ran out like water from a leaky bucket. Bidders got restless and went out for smokes or to the john; tough guys from New York bellied up to the bar for a cold one; wild women dealers got a sudden yen for hamburgers and fries.

Byatt never paid any attention to the chronology of lot numbers, so no one knew when any particular item would be up for sale, unless a special request was made. Probably the auctioneer was now kicking himself for putting the dinner set up at the wrong time. It was a steal, and Jamie stole away with it. Later, another surprising lack of interest among the dealers was responsible for Olivia taking home that lily vase after all, against her better judgment. It was being knocked down for a pittance. Who could resist bidding? Such a graceful shape, blue background with green leaves and an ivory lily. Did her weakness in buying a lily artifact constitute *possession*?

"Don't laugh—do you think I've been *possessed* by Lily?" she asked Jamie, while driving her and her numerous boxes of fragile dishes back to the town house.

Jamie chuckled. "You mean, like in The Exorcist? If you're going to turn your head backwards and throw up pea soup, don't do it on my wall-to-wall."

"Cut out kidding—I'm serious."

Jamie stifled herself not very successfully. "Of course not, you dope. I'd be the first one to know if you, like, did the Stepford thing, or got replaced by an alien pod. You're the same good-hearted, smart, over-achieving, anal-retentive gal you always were. And personally, I think if Lily has loosened you up some, it's all to the good."

"Oh, thanks a lot."

"Only, if a Richard-Burton type offers to exorcise your demon, I'd go ahead and give him a shot at it, if I were you."

After they lugged in the boxes of china, it was only nine-thirty, early enough for Jamie to call her parents, who nonetheless believed that any telephone call after seven in the evening surely would be a report of some devastating accident, life-threatening illness, or other catastrophe. After reassuring them that she was in good health and still gainfully employed, Jamie posed Olivia's request, underlining the board money that Dave Lowenstein would pay for their trouble.

"*Oh, lovely*," caroled Jamie's mom. "Dad and I were just talking about taking in a foster child instead of rattling around by ourselves in this empty house. We thought since Dad's working nights on security, and I'm only doing outpatient house calls two days a week, there'd always be someone at home. For a teen-ager, you know. Couldn't handle a little one."

Jamie motioned "thumbs up" to Olivia, who silently clapped her hands. "Okay, Mom. This will only be for a few weeks, you understand. And you'll be compensated. I know the kids personally, and they're not delinquents or anything. Oh, the older boy Kenny plays some kind of Celtic drum; could be a problem if Dad's sleeping daytimes. And the girl, Moira, likes to mess about in the kitchen. You can teach her to make Yorkshire Pudding. Olivia will be so pleased. Danny, the youngest, is just a regular kid; good with animals. He'll love Flo and Jonas."

"Nice resume," Olivia murmured. "Those the same cats?"

"Yes," Jamie mouthed, still listening. "Fat old hellions."

"They sound delightful, dear," Jamie's mother was chirping. "We'll get the two spare rooms ready. I'm afraid I've been using the guest room for sewing, but your old room is just as you left it. I'll put the little girl—Moira—in there."

"Great, Mom. Olivia sends her love and thanks you from the bottom of her heart. And she says she still thinks fondly of your Sunday roasts."

Jamie's mother giggled. "That poor little child had a really amazing appetite."

∽

A few days later, the evidence scandal hit the fan. Dave was so overcome with feelings of guilt that Olivia had to keep reminding him of why he'd destroyed data. Well, almost destroyed it. Having decided to send the disc to the Special Investigations and Narcotics Unit in Boston rather than to the Federal Prosecutor, Lieutenant Badger had taken the disc straight from his safe and sent it with a police escort, but without checking it in his own computer one more time. To his limited knowledge, the data had been gobbledygook anyway, although Dave had clued him in to their provenance and importance.

Soon after the package arrived on the desk of Detective Commander William Hill in Boston, the lieutenant got a call. "Damn it, Badger, this disc is no fucking good," the commander declared angrily. "Sure it's Frank Rossi, it's the Benedettos, and we can read a few entries here and there, but for the most part they're damaged goods. Where in the name of Christ did you keep it? On the radiator? You guys in the boondocks ..." and more in that vein while Badger's face turned apoplectic red at his end of the call.

Being at a loss to explain what had happened, Lieutenant Badger looked for someone to blame for this incredibly embarrassing screw-up. The problem was, this important evidence had been stored in the department's safe to which only he had the combination. So everyone who'd handled the disc before (Dave and his partner Mendez) and after (the uniformed cops who'd driven up to Boston to deliver it) came in for a share of verbal abuse. Did Dave accidentally hit Erase the last time he'd examined the data? Did the uniforms stop for coffee and slop it all over that irreplaceable disc?

Everyone claimed innocence. In truth, Dave reassured himself, Badger hadn't hit on the precise way that evidence got damaged. The mystery seemed destined to remain unsolved. Dave worked a deal at the schools and took off early on Friday to get the O'Haras out of town.

SPECIAL AGENT IN DEEP TROUBLE

"Jesus Christ, Washington, what the fuck did you think you were doing, bypassing me with that fucking so-called evidence you got from some stinking street bum," Glumm screamed, pounding on his desk with the rolled-up transcription of the Benedetto "hit list" disc that Lowenstein had handed over to Washington. "And I want to know the name of that fucking informant."

"You were on vacation in Barbados, chief, and I didn't think I had the clearance to decide what could or could not be held in my possession until you got back." Washington's tone was conciliatory, but he stood his ground, aware that he was towering over the rotund SAC, Special Agent in Charge. "The informant—if you'll just read the rest of that cover page—was not a street bum. The disc came into the possession of Lieutenant Badger of the Plymouth Detective Division, who had it passed on to me. Apparently, the Federal Prosecutor's office wasn't quick enough on the uptake, and Badger insisted that what he had was too hot to hang around in Plymouth." According to their agreement, Washington was keeping Lowenstein's name out of the limelight.

Washington had patiently waited for the few days until Glumm's imminent vacation, seizing the opportunity to disseminate the material to key higher ranking agents, thus preventing his boss from burying it in his No Further Action file. Washington had known, of course, that this day of reckoning would soon be at hand, but he could hardly be demoted any farther. He was already at the bottom rung of the FBI staff flowchart.

"Yeah? Well, bully for Badger. Those Federal Prosecutor fuckheads couldn't find their asses with both hands," Glumm said. "But you, Washington ..." The man was close to foaming at the mouth. His sunburned bald pate seemed to glow even redder. "You deliberately overstepped your fucking position in this office, and you'd better believe I'll see these anti-authority issues of yours get noted on your record in indelible ink. You can kiss your hopes of advancement in the Bureau good-bye, you ... you ..."

Black bastard? Washington felt certain that was the phrase Glumm was searching for, but he wasn't about to help the man find the right politically incorrect epithet to use. Meanwhile, interested, involved agents would be analyzing Rossi's cryptic notes on names, dates, and locations, comparing it to unsolved murders suspected of being Benedetto hits, maybe coming up with useful connections. Sometimes these crimes actually got solved, gangsters apprehended, mobs put out of business. Despite his three years working for Glumm, Washington still clung to a shred of the idealism with which he had begun his FBI career. *Dumb black bastard,* he griped to himself.

"This material could reflect credit on our regional office," Washington said in a conciliatory tone. "And you're the man, chief. Bringing down the Benedettos is going to be a big deal in the Bureau. And you know how the Director loves that sort of publicity."

Glumm smirked. "What do you think, you're some kind of fucking diplomat, Washington? All very well, if it comes to commendation. I've certainly provided the climate in which real investigation flourishes. But don't think for one fucking minute that lets you off the hook, you insubordinate sonofabitch. Just remember who's the SAC around here, and who's not."

Sad SAC, Washington thought. He remembered his last talk with Lowenstein. "More later," the man had promised. "Better stuff. Financial records." Then something about getting his kids out of harm's way first. Lowenstein's tone had been anxious, obviously stressed. Washington wasn't the only one with his feet to the fire here. He said a short prayer for them both. A little rhyme his great-aunt Marie-Josie had taught him. *Black man, white man, great and small, Bondye's justice bless us all.* He wasn't especially religious, but saying that prayer always gave him the feeling that his aunt was nearby, a warm breath of incense, a quiet touch of magic.

He shook his head to dispel that feeling. This was no time to get soft in the head. After all, here he was, literally on the carpet in front of Glumm's desk.

"All right, all right, get out of here," Glumm snarled peevishly. "Back to those wiretaps. And see that you don't miss anything at the Fruit Company. You never can tell when a conspiracy may ripen or a rotten apple show its spots." He laughed uproariously at his own pun, dropped the report in his wastebasket, and waved Washington out the door with a plump hand.

Washington wheeled around and walked out the door smartly, sensing that his erect posture and long-legged strides were anathema to Glumm. As quickly as he could, he dismissed the scene from his attention, busying his mind with ways to subvert the next handover from Lowenstein so that it would never get fouled in Glumm's grasp. It would be more dangerous the second time, but this might be the final punch in the Benedettos' ticket.

Bon Dieu's ... justice bless us all.

JUNE 12
Things to Do Today

J, rent van Quincy for Fri
Call F Mitchell, exorcise?
Libr return Your Troubled Teen, borrow Seven Habits of Highly
Effective Stepparents

Olivia thought it best not to burden Dave (who had enough on his mind getting his family safely out of town) with the latest weird events at her house. Lily had taken on a new personna, that of the classic poltergeist. Apparently the ghost was less than pleased about the damage to her precious evidence, the Benedetto discs for which she lost her life.

Olivia's wonderful auction buy, the Roseville lily vase, which she'd carefully placed on the fireplace mantel in her living room, got smashed to smithereens on the hearth. Okay, that could have happened by accident, perhaps moved to the edge by sound vibrations or vague earth tremors. But then two of the cobalt glasses—Lily's glasses, bought at her auction—mysteriously disappeared from the dining room cabinet and were found shattered against the French doors. Thankfully the glass in the doors survived. These disturbing incidents were followed by Lily's photo again turning itself on its head in the Art Deco silver frame. A *smile upside down is a frown,* Olivia thought, while a thrill of fright zinged from the back of her neck to the base of her spine. Until now, Lily had been a harrowing but benign manifestation. What scary phenomena might Lily have up her ectoplasmic sleeve now? It was time to get help. Olivia prayed that Florrie Mitchell would be able to guide her in dealing with Lily's temper tantrums.

By three in the afternoon on Friday, Dave's Bronco was in Olivia's driveway. The O'Haras spilled out and took characteristic poses: Kevin sullen and slouching, Moira scowling with carrot curls frizzled wildly, and Danny beaming with delight.

"Okay, everyone—get your gear out of the car," Dave said briskly.

The tips of Danny's ears sticking out through his blond hair were red with excitement. "Uncle Dave got us out of school early! He's taking us on a surprise vacation!" he cried. "He said *you got a half hour to pack, that's all.* Wow!" Danny was dragging a red canvas duffle bag, his Game Boy under one arm.

Bruno ran to meet his friend with a joyful canine grin on his face. Sadie, however, exercised her usual reserve. After sniffing the new arrivals in a disinterested fashion, she wandered over to smell the roses that Olivia had planted on each side of her front door, Cavalier crimson, Jane Austin gold and white, and Jacqueline pink. They were in their June glory now, scenting the air with romantic perfume.

"What about the eggs and butter I put out on the counter for the cake!" Moira continued a harangue that had been going on in the car. "They're going to go bad and stink up the whole kitchen. And I didn't have enough clean stuff. You should have told me we were going away." Carrying a battered leather suitcase, the kind that predated luggage with wheels, she was wearing red Capri pants and a purple tank top under which her breasts were beginning to bud. *When this is over*, Olivia vowed, *I'm taking that girl shopping for training bras.*

Dave reached into the Bronco for Kevin's bodhran. The older boy was leaning a shoulder against the car, his hands empty, all his possessions apparently stowed in his khaki back pack.

"And the second surprise is, we're going to travel in this spiffy rental van, save wear and tear on the Bronco," Dave announced, slinging Moira's suitcase into the new vehicle. The Chevy Astro Jamie had rented for Dave last night sported dark-tinted windows and a CD player. She'd furnished it with CDs that might or might not be appropriate for kids, including some Celtic music for Kevin, and a hamper of sandwiches, fruit, cookies, and soft drinks.

"I'm not stupid, you know." Kevin glared at the impressive black van suspiciously. "You're going to dump us someplace, so we'll be out of your hair."

Dave fixed Kevin with the practiced steely look of his profession from which the boy's gaze finally slid away. "What we're doing here, Kev, is protecting your sister and brother. Because of what happened last Sunday. I don't think this vacation will be too long. I'm hoping to wrap up things in a few weeks. But I'm depending on you to look out for Moira and Danny."

Danny was busy playing fetch with Bruno, but Moira listened intently to this exchange, even forgetting to scowl. "Dump us where?" she asked in a small voice.

Dave smiled reassurance; he leaned over to give the girl a swift hug. "Like I said, it's a surprise vacation, and I bet you'll never guess where. But I'll give you a clue—a river runs through it. There's a zoo with a real rain forest and chimps, a science museum for kids, and lots more."

"Can we swim, Uncle Dave? Gotta beach where we're going?" Danny asked.

Dave and Olivia looked at each other. She nodded imperceptibly. "Yeah, in a way," Dave said.

"And I need a computer so's I can play games," Danny's voice was reaching its whining pitch.

Again Dave looked to Olivia. She shrugged and lifted her eyebrows. "I doubt it, Danny Boy," Dave said brusquely. "Okay, everyone into the van. Double-time!"

While the O'Haras were arguing over who would sit in front, a tussle that Moira easily won, Dave took Olivia in his arms and kissed her with the ardor of a soldier leaving for the frontline, which somehow blended with the sweet breath of roses.

"You be very careful, darling. Be sure you're not followed," Olivia warned, thinking she was really taking coals to Newcastle here. This guy probably knew all about how to spot surveillance.

"It's going to be fine," he said. "You were cautious about the rental?"

"Jamie and I drove to Quincy last night; we used her I.D."

"I guess we've got everything covered. Thanks a million, honey—and *don't worry so much.*"

When the van pulled out, only Dave and Danny waved darkly behind the tinted window. Olivia went back in the house, emptier somehow than it ever was before.

Dave and Olivia had agreed not to call each other, in case someone else was listening. After the O'Haras got to Cleveland, he would ask Jamie's mother to call her with a prearranged message. Mrs. Andrews was to tell her daughter that she'd rented the spare room to a boarder, and he seemed very pleasant.

∽

On her way home from work, early on Monday, Olivia stopped at the Moon Deer. Skipping lunch and leaving at four had become her regular interpretation of flex hours. Fortunately, the new minimum-wage assistant, a young computer nerd named Norman Unwin, whom she hired after firing Ray Chance, seemed quite up to holding the fort, even from Emma Ridley's incursions. Norm's stocky body and round white face disguised a stubborn resourcefulness. He would not be budged or diverted from his task of protecting Mattakeesett's town records. In a way, he reminded Olivia of Sadie. Any employer with sensitive material to guard would be glad of an assistant who was a bit of a pit bull.

The little shop around the corner, Olivia thought as she wedged her van into a parking place on the charming side street that wound right down to the ocean shore. The Moon Deer was located half-way, between an antique clock repair place and a candle shop from which spilled out scents of all seasons. The Moon Deer's windows were as attractively arranged as before, but the display had changed to a Southwestern theme with a hand-woven Navaho rug surrounded by Ute pottery and carved Zuni fetishes. Olivia imagined stroking that smooth little black bear. A neatly printed sign read: *The bear person is strong and caring, a helper and a seeker after deeper knowledge.*

Florrie Mitchell was again sitting behind the register, this time reading *Barron's*. She looked up and smiled, her shrewd dark eyes lighting up with recognition. "Ah, Ms. Andreas, how nice to see you! Still having difficulty sending that poor lost soul to the West Wind? Come, sit down and tell me what brings you here looking so distressed." The Harvard-accented voice was welcoming and slightly amused. The elegant brown hand wearing the impressive diamond ring waved Olivia to a woven cane stool.

"Please, call me Liv. You're right about my ghost problems. There's something that Lily wants me to do that I haven't been able to manage—at least, not yet," Olivia explained, seating herself on the other side of the counter. "I can't go into detail, but I can say that the action Lily desires would threaten the safety of others at the present time and has to be handled carefully and patiently. But Lily is not patient."

"Perhaps she's eager to move on to a higher realm. Earthbound spirits are not peaceful souls," Mrs. Mitchell said. "How does Lily's impatience manifest itself? Broken crockery perhaps?"

"Is that the usual thing?" Olivia was impressed.

"It's a favorite attention-getter."

"But a recent development at my house, you understand. Just a few things broken but it definitely suggests a destructive energy afoot. A Roseville vase, which coincidentally depicted a lily, bought at a recent auction. I'd placed that on my living room mantel, and it simply moved to the edge and dropped onto the hearth. It could almost have been a regular accident—you know, some sympathetic vibration. But then there were the two wine glasses from the same auction where I bought Lily's photo. They transported out of a china cabinet and smashed against the French doors in the dining room. And something else that only happened once before. Lily's photo turned upside down in its frame."

Mrs. Mitchell gave her full attention when she listened, not interrupting, fidgeting, or glancing about. Now that Olivia paused, the other woman said, "How very intriguing. It does seem as if Lily is offering you ample evidence of her displeasure, and I imagine you'd like this damaging phase to stop. Perhaps if she knew your intentions. I take it that you do intend to execute her wishes eventually, but at the moment it's inconvenient and dangerous?"

"That's it exactly," Olivia said, thinking how gratifying it is to consult someone who really understood the problem.

"I think that from Lily's point of view, time is both concurrent and sequential. Apparently she's aware that 'time's a-wasting' in the chronological sense. Maybe if you assure her that you're moving in the direction of her interest, she'll relax into a simultaneous view of events. As a spirit, she should understand that things happening in the future have already happened in the eternal now."

Olivia was feeling a little out of her depth with Mrs. Mitchell's analysis of the situation. "How do I assure Lily that things will work out her way?"

Mrs. Mitchell reached across the counter to pat Olivia's hand. Her fingers were cool and consoling. "We could have another séance. You're a natural medium, although I don't think you want to know that. You can talk to Lily yourself. Explain the situation. Ask for her patience."

"Oh, a séance would be good," Olivia breathed with relief. "Would you?"

"It would be my pleasure. And besides, I really want to see that upside-down photo phenomena for myself. So I'm not going to charge a fee for my time. I'll chalk this one up to research."

Olivia thought she'd give Mrs. Mitchell a nice gift anyway, to show her appreciation. They arranged to meet the following evening. That would work out fine, because she didn't expect to see Dave before Wednesday, a meeting they prearranged to avoid discussing their plans by phone and perhaps revealing the Cleveland connection. Jamie had come by on Sunday to say that her mother had called. The cryptic message about the new boarder had been delivered, so it appeared that the O'Haras had arrived and all was well. Olivia felt that these precautions had covered their tracks pretty well, and whatever happened now, at least the children would be safe.

Before they parted, Mrs. Mitchell went to the window, picked up the smooth little black bear and handed it to Olivia. "Take this," she said. "The bear will give you its protection. You're clearly a bear person, my dear."

Olivia was not exactly surprised that Mrs. Mitchell seemed to be a mind-reader, along with her other talents. Remembering how cynical she used to be about the paranormal was like looking back at a less-dimensional self. The mysteries of life were its richness, Olivia decided. She might be grateful to Lily for the changes she had brought, providing the ghost stopped breaking up the house, and they all lived through their campaign against the Benedettos.

"It's a very appealing carving. I really love it, thanks," Olivia said, taking the bear. Her hand seemed to fit around it smooth surfaces just right, and there was a curious comfort in holding the fetish.

"You might like to keep that in your pocket and rub its back in times of stress," Mrs. Mitchell suggested.

JUNE 16
Things to Do Today

Mrs. M. 7 pm, tea tray, candles, table, Lily's photo
Clear out breakables
Brush S & B, doggie deo
Deadhead roses

Although promptness was not one of Mrs. Mitchell's virtues, she had plenty of others. *Who're you gonna call?* came to Olivia's mind. A good ghostbuster was hard to find. But when the black Lincoln pulled up in front of Olivia's house at 7:43 PM, she was over-prepared and edgy. Hearing a few joyous barks that signaled the arrival of a special friend, Olivia poured boiling water over the kava tea in the pot and hurried to open the front door.

Mrs. Mitchell was crouched down on the walk, crooning to the dogs in her low musical voice. "Good girl, Sadie. Good boy, Bruno. Don't you two look spiffy!" This new friend remembered their names; the dogs responded with low-throated yowls of excited welcome. Seeing Olivia at the open door, the visitor rose gracefully and, pausing to smell the sweet pink Jacqueline roses, swept through. She was wearing a dress of Southwestern design, a turquoise print with matching fringed stole.

After they'd exchanged greetings, Mrs. Mitchell looked around, her bright curious eyes missing no detail. "This séance should prove most interesting," she said. Olivia had placed and lighted candles in five places in the living room, and now she turned off the one electric lamp. Shadows against the wall replayed her every motion as Olivia brought in the tea tray and set it on the low table between the two wing chairs. Mrs. Mitchell was sitting in the one that Olivia now thought of as Lily's chair. She sniffed the air. "Ah, kava. Excellent. We'll have our tea and unwind before we begin."

"I'll just let the dogs in now," Olivia said. She excused herself and went into the kitchen to open the back door. Sadie and Bruno bounded into the living room and rushed over to be patted by the visitor. "They're so happy and content living with you, after all their previous misadventures, yet I'm sensing that Bruno misses the presence of children," Mrs. Mitchell said. "But he's made friends with a youngster recently?"

She reads canine minds, too? "Yes, my friend's ward Danny and Bruno have become great pals. I'm afraid my dogs are not always this friendly. Sadie especially tends to be reserved with new people. But they seem to love being with you."

"They'll skedaddle as soon as Lily arrives," Mrs. Mitchell said. "Sit now, my friends," she added as Olivia handed her a cup of tea. The dogs hunkered down obediently at her feet. No one else had quite this effect on these two ruffians, Olivia reflected. She wondered if it was a talent that Mrs. Mitchell could teach her, but she suspected that the woman's calm, assured manner and detached loving-kindness might be the qualities to which the dogs responded. And there was no school for that.

"Where is ... ?" Mrs. Mitchell turned in her chair and caught sight of Lily's photo, still upside-down in its Art Deco frame, which Olivia had set on the small table of Shaker design that they used for the last séance. "Goodness. Such an impressive manifestation. Lily, what a performer you are!"

On that cue, the candle flames flickered as if a door had been opened. A drift of lily scent wafted through the air. Simultaneously, the dogs lifted their heads and glanced around. Sadie sniffed the air. As if that were a signal, instantly both dogs scampered out of the room and up the stairs. Olivia could hear them dashing into the safety of her bedroom.

"Well," Olivia said with a rueful smile. "Apparently, Lily has arrived. She was a performer, you know. A show girl. Musical revues and the like. She had a nice amount of cash put away for herself, too, perhaps planning a fresh start before the Boston mob caught up with her. Then she fell or was pushed down the stairwell in her apartment building."

"Her uneasy spirit suggests that the fall was no accident. And she's counting on you to avenge her. Let's begin then," Mrs. Mitchell said. She rose and went to the Shaker table, where Olivia had placed two straight chairs. "It's time to reassure Lily."

They sat down and placed the tips of their fingers on the table, just as they did the first time they summoned Lily. Gazing at Mrs. Mitchell's mesmerizing diamond, Olivia was surprised at how sleepy and relaxed she felt, *must be the Kava tea*. When the raps came, one on the wall between the windows, and a second on the opposite wall, they hardly startled her. Even when the little table trembled, and Lily's photo gave a very small hop, Olivia remained calm and distant, floating on a cloud of serenity.

"Spirit in this house, spirit in this room," Mrs. Mitchell chanted in her musical tones, "tell us what is troubling you, so that we may help you to fly away, fly away with the West Wind."

What have you done with Frankie's book?

The voice seemed to speak right behind Olivia's right shoulder. It had a rich "whiskey" timbre, a voice that had spent many years in nightclubs. Olivia didn't turn around because she was afraid of what she'd see, whether empty air or a materializing form. Two of the candles hissed and sputtered out, leaving the room nearly dark. The tea tray slid forward on its table and the milk pitcher tipped over, spilling its contents onto the pale green rug. Olivia didn't know which was harder on rugs, dogs or a ghost in bad humor.

"Tell her," Mrs. Mitchell hissed. "Explain."

Olivia took a deep breath to drive out the icy snake of fear. "It's all right, Lily. Frankie's notes are with the FBI. His accounts are in a safe place for now. As soon as possible, we're going to see that they get into the right hands, too. The men who hurt you and Frankie will pay for their crimes."

The Shaker table on which the women were resting the tips of their fingers, suddenly tilted, causing Lily's photograph to fall face down. Olivia reached out to right it, but Mrs. Mitchell hissed at her again, "No, leave it be."

Promise, promise, promise, insisted the voice over Olivia's shoulder. Mrs. Mitchell stared at whatever was behind Olivia. Her serene features had taken on an expression of awe.

"I promise you those murdering mobsters will not get away," Olivia whispered, hoping this was a vow she'd be able to keep. Slowly she turned to see whatever it was transfixing

Mrs. Mitchell. Ah, there she was! The transparent figure of Lily seated in the wing chair recently vacated by Mrs. Mitchell. The shining blonde hair, the face turned away, the sparkling tennis bracelet, an impression of white skirts swirling around her legs. Yet everything amorphous, like an image on water that may any moment erase itself in rippling waves.

Be careful, careful, careful. The voice sank lower and lower with every word as the form faded into a gray swirl like smoke.

But Olivia wanted to keep Lily a little while longer, to ask for her aid. Surely ghosts must have special powers, rather like lower-rung angels. Urgently she pleaded, "Lily, please watch over Dave's children. Those men who hurt you have threatened the children, who have nothing to do with this. Will you help me to guard them?"

All trace of Lily's form had vanished, but from the far corner of the room her voice was heard becoming fainter, moving away. *I am here, I am watching, I am ...* For a long time afterward, the two women sat in the near darkness of a room lit by two candles, motionless in wonder. Olivia's skin felt prickled by static electricity, the energy passing through the room.

She turned back to the table where Lily's photo was still lying face down. When Olivia stood it up again, both women saw at the same time that the smiling woman was now right side up.

"*Geronimo*," Mrs. Mitchell murmured. Then she said some words that Olivia didn't understand.

"Is that a Wampanoag proverb?" she asked.

Mrs. Mitchell laughed, a pleasingly infectious chuckle. "We are very superstitious about death and bodies. It means, 'Do not touch the dead. Uneasy spirits thirst for living breath.'"

"Well, that's rather dark, isn't it?"

"Yes, it took me many years to overcome my people's fear of anything to do with the dead."

"Me, too. Not that I was taught to be afraid. I just never believed in an afterlife or ghosts or any of this stuff myself."

"And yet you kept Lily's likeness in that beautiful frame, which you could have used for another more personal photo."

Olivia was thinking that she'd had no one to cherish at that time. No family, no lover, no one whose portrait meant that much to her, but she said only, "It seemed the right thing to do. All Lily's things dumped in that dreadful auction. Apparently no one gave a damn."

"A life-changing decision. You couldn't know, but on some level, you did know."

∾

"Jamie's parents are such good souls, I felt a little guilty getting them into the middle of our troubles," Dave said. He opened the bottle of wine on the kitchen table, and poured it into two glasses while Olivia was making a salad.

She was so relieved to have him home, safe, mission accomplished without incident, that she couldn't stop smiling as she sliced the vegetables, thinking *we did it* with every chop of her knife. *We did it, we did it.* All her senses seemed to be keener than normal. The sharp odor of scallions and bell peppers, the brilliant rays of sunset gilding the kitchen windows, the quiet panting of the dogs under the table. She even felt the shimmer of the new silk underthings she was wearing under her shorts and T-shirt. Was this like the affect of drugs? Olivia might be the only college graduate in America who didn't know.

"Was it hard to leave the kids there? I suppose it must have been. But the Andrews are a dear couple. I'm glad you felt that, too. I remember how sweet and generous they were to me when I was in high school." She opened the oven to check on that reliable Beef Bourguignon, ready whenever.

"Oh, well, you know, Danny always tugs at my heart. But his having the two cats to fuss over helped a lot. Jonas and Flo. Funny names."

"Jonas Salk and Florence Nightingale. Mrs. Andrews always wanted to be a full-fledged nurse. The cats are named after two of her heroes."

"Oh, and another good thing—Artie was still puzzling over setting up his brand-new computer, and Danny was happy to help him cope."

A dark thought flickered through Olivia's mind, but it flew away before she could grasp its warning. *What? Bats in the belfry now?* "I'm just beginning to realize that Danny has his own special talents. Even though he often plays second fiddle to Kevin. How about Moira?"

"When I left, Mrs. Andrews—Sandy—was teaching her to make genuine Yorkshire Pudding. They seemed to be thick as thieves. Kevin, now, no doubt he's fidgeting and griping. But I put it to him that he's there to watch out for his sister and brother. He's a good kid underneath all that swagger and strut."

"Marches to a different bodhran, that's all. I never had any doubt of his fine inner qualities." *Well, that's not quite true*, Olivia thought, *but he's growing on me.* "How are things at work? Air still blue in the boss's office?" She left the vegetables and the chopping block to sip her wine and ended up sitting on Dave's lap. After a long while of kissing that left her breathless, he said, "You have no idea. Not only is Badger flaming angry, he's mystified as to how that disc could have been compromised while safely locked in the department safe to which only he has the combination. I'm expecting him to have a heart attack any day now from the sheer aggravation of losing this enormous boost to his career."

"Did you mail the other thing from Cleveland as we planned."

"I did. When we're ready, I'll go pick it up."

"And when will that be?"

"As soon as the Benedettos are satisfied that I fulfilled my end of the bargain."

"How will they know?"

"That's the thing, honey. I think we must have an ugly little mole somewhere on the force. How else could the Benedettos have found out that we were in possession of the Family's private accounts, thanks to Frank Rossi?"

"Shades of *Smiley's People*. Any ideas who?"

"Not yet, but when I find out, I'm going to beat the crap out of him. After I'm through with him, if there's anything left, I'll turn him over to Internal Affairs. In the meantime, the mole has his uses. If he's witnessed the Badger's explosion of frustration and all the shit the Lieutenant's been getting from the Special Investigations and Narcotics Unit, hopefully the mole has reported that back to the Benedettos. They'll know I got them off the hook in regard to their dirty money accounts and tax evasion. Once they believe I've knuckled under, we'll pick up that other disc and get it to my contact at the FBI. Could have been the work of Frank Rossi rising from the grave for all the Benedettos will know. Not so far from the truth, only it's Lily who's rising. Maybe the Benedettos will think that Rossi left a package with his lawyer, instructed him what to do, *in case*. At any rate, Rossi's evidence will find its way from the FBI to the Federal Prosecutor, who will then be in a position to put away the bastards who shot my partner. I'm really looking forward to that."

Olivia sighed and leaned her head on Dave's shoulder. She was thinking of her promise to Lily, but she didn't mention the séance. *Dave will follow through, the evidence will reach the right hands, Lily will rest in peace.* "You think we'll all be safe then? Life can return to normal, the kids can come home from Cleveland?"

"Yeah, I believe that," Dave said, his mouth traveling gently over her neck and downward. "Who needs dinner?" he murmured. "Let's go upstairs." His fingers reached under her shorts, encountered that Victoria's secret silk, caressed the skin underneath.

Olivia only paused long enough to turn the oven down. They moved up the stairs slowly, savoring every step.

ೲ

A full moon was rising when they finally had dinner. Olivia lit candles in the dining room, the better to enjoy the shimmering backyard. Now ravenous, Olivia and Dave, dug into the braised beef and hasty salad with the gusto of farm workers.

Feeling pleasantly irresponsible without his family, Dave stayed the night. The moon, now high above the trees, flooded the bedroom with silver, painting their naked limbs with luminous shades of pearl. The scent of roses drifted in through the open window. They moved from love-making to dreaming without being aware of the transition, the two states were one world. Their bed was a boat floating on the waves of the summer night.

In the seductive mood of June, Dave soon slipped into spending more and more nights at Olivia's. Several idyllic days went by before another fright jerked the lovers back to reality.

LILY

I have to admit I got myself into quite a temper over that dumb cop deliberately erasing Frankie's biggest coup, the Benedetto financial records. Another Learning Experience! This time I learned that getting Seriously Pissed makes it a cinch for Our Kind to cause a little mayhem. Crashed a few things around Liv's house. Made My Point.

But then Liv went to a lot of trouble to explain things to me, how there's a copy of the disc in a safe place, and all. She even got Moral Support from that old Indian dame, the one who keeps talking about the West Wind and the Sunset Path. The Guardians say that many people like to think about their loved ones going to a place like the Golden West or Heavenly Mansions or the Beckoning Light because it makes it easier for them to have a kind of future map in mind, that they can't deal with the notion of Spirit existing everywhere at once and always. Not sure I've got that one by heart myself, but the Guardians tell me I will "in time," although time is just a human construct. Talk about confusing. I feel as if fuses are blowing in my brain.

Anyway, I can stay on This Plane as long as needed to tidy up my affairs, which means shafting the Bs—Big Time. (But I'm warned not to get stuck here like those pale Civil War wanderers. Now that is scary.)

I guess Lowenstein is a good sort, taking in those three Irish hellions instead of letting them flounder in the foster care system. I'll bet their father is around somewhere giving Lowenstein the occasional thumbs up, but I couldn't swear to it—I haven't met O'Hara personally. It's just that I know now how hard it is for us to Let Go.

I'm glad that Liv's personal cop has decided to work through this Watusi Warrior in the FBI. LeRoy has some good instincts, not to mention his feisty auntie Marie-Josie looking out for his interests. Speaking of not letting go, if only we were allowed to give Certain People a shove under the wheels of a moving truck, Marie-Josie would have had her boy promoted to Big Wheel in no time. And I would have given those Benedetto goons a taste of their own castor oil. So much easier and quicker than waiting for Justice to Triumph, ha ha. But alas, it's for the living to sort out the living.

With a little nudge from Absent Friends, of course.

So I'm hanging onto my hope that soon, really soon, I'll be able to find Frankie and give him some very satisfying news.

JUNE 23
Things to Do Today

Chng bd, silk sheets
Libr: return Seven Habits of Highly Effective Stepparents, borrow
Joy of Sex
Casseroles: non time-sensitive stuff
Check track no. Vict. Secret order

Having warned Kevin not to use the Andrews' phone, or to allow his sister and brother to do so, Dave called from a pay phone every day, using a phone card. Sometimes he called twice, to check up on his wards' well-being. Surprisingly, they seemed to be having a fun time on this unscheduled vacation, even Kevin. The oldest O'Hara had found a Celtic group to hang with. On Sundays the Kerry Kids broadcast traditional and Celtic rock music on a local university's radio station, WJCB.

Actually, it was Danny who found the Kerry Kids on the Internet. Besides the pleasure of unlimited surfing on the Andrews' new computer, Danny thought gardening with Artie was cool, while Sandy was glad to give Moira a free hand in the kitchen.

"The Andrews have that quintessential Mom-and-Pop quality," Olivia explained to Dave. It was another gloriously sunny evening. They were sprawled in the Adirondack chairs, facing them away from the blackened ground of the old garage. "And their bungalow looks as if it had been created for a Disney film. Youngsters just naturally bloom in such comforting surroundings." She sipped her gin and tonic.

"Your idea, Liv, and I bless you for it." Dave drained the last of his bottle of Bud. "This is as relaxed as I've felt since that bastard kidnapped the kids. Really, the Andrews' place seems an ideal safe house."

"I've never understood why Jamie insisted on moving so far away," Olivia said.

"Oh, you know what youngsters are like. She probably felt stifled by all that charming hominess. Caught like a fly in honey."

"Yeah? Maybe you're right, but with my home life, or lack of it, I sure envied her. My mother raised the art of being aggrieved to a whole new level."

"Haven't you ever had contact with your father? Didn't he pay child support?"

Olivia nearly choked on the gin-soaked lime slice she was chewing. Sometimes she forgot that Dave hasn't absorbed everything about her by some kind of lover's osmosis. Despite their physical intimacy, she was still a closed book of which he'd only read the title and a few chapter headings. She'd never even told him that her father was an embezzler still wanted by the Feds. But since Dave had been bending the law himself, this might be a good time to come clean about her family.

"Guys who are running from the law usually don't pay child support. Wouldn't want to get caught leaving a paper trail," Olivia said.

"I see. Want to tell me the rest of the story?"

So she did. He was sympathetic and non-judgmental for a lawman. Olivia felt an invisible weight lifting off her heart. Later, in the caressing warmth of the summer night, they made lazy love, almost, not quite, cooled off in the shower, then stayed up late watching favorite *films noir* in bed. *The Maltese Falcon* and *The Postman Always Rings Twice.*

At first light, Sadie began throwing herself again and again against the closed bedroom door. Maybe she was just lonesome, Olivia thought, displaced from her accustomed sharing of the big bed. Rising with a languorous yawn and stretch, Olivia noted that Dave was still sleeping, prone on his stomach, arms and legs flung wide, looking like a castaway struggling to reach shore. She slid into her new green silk negligee and slipped out the door sideways so that Sadie couldn't enter. Bruno was waiting on the landing looking downstairs. Sadie gave one meaningful woof and trotted to the first floor followed by Bruno.

"Hey, you guys. Don't think these shenanigans are going to get you an early breakfast," Olivia scolded. She followed, thinking she'd just let them outdoors for a quick pee, then back in again before a dawn bark-fest could get well underway.

It was a lovely morning, albeit early. Infused with joyous energy, Olivia started the coffee, then went to stand on the kitchen doorstep breathing deeply from the diaphragm according to Zen teachings. She was feeling mildly euphoric for a gal intent on outwitting the local mafia. Stepping out onto the grass in her bare feet (while keeping an eye out for canine deposits) she practiced a few Tai Chi moves, *brushing the peacock's tail* and *parting the horse's mane*, inventing some of her own, naming this one *repulsing the thug* and another *sweeping evidence under rug.*

With front paws on the fence, Sadie was barking at Dave's Bronco parked behind Olivia's Chevy Van. And barking and barking. Taking instruction from the female as always, Bruno commenced running around Sadie and woofing in chorus. Olivia's idyllic interlude had definitely ended, and it was time to bring those guys inside before the neighbor whose son worked nights got on the phone. As Olivia's gaze traveled to the object of Sadie's alarm, she noticed something that wasn't there before. A Red Sox baseball cap on the Bronco's radio antennae, flapping around on the morning breeze as if at any moment it would take off on its own and fly away. Olivia raced into the house and up the stairs to wake Dave.

∞

Dave jumped into his jeans and dashed downstairs, calling the Benedettos every indecent name in his vocabulary, which was considerable. He rushed out the door to retrieve the cap, removing a square of paper pinned inside.

"Oh, God! What does it say?" Olivia cried.

Dave's expression was unreadable as he looked at her over the excited jumping dogs. He passed the note to her, and she read: *You did good. Give our best to the kiddoes in Cleveland.*

"Oh, God," she said again, this time in a frightened whisper. "How did they find out? Are you sure you weren't followed?"

"We took a plane, for Christ's sake. Do you think they followed in another plane?" It was the first time Dave had spoken crossly to her, but she knew it was only his terror. He'd failed at hiding the children. That must be hard to accept.

Olivia put her hand on his arm. "It's not your fault. Something weird must have gone wrong. Let's call and see if we can find out what's happened." It was only six in the morning, but maybe someone in the Andrews' house was an early riser.

Back in the kitchen, she poured them both a mug of coffee. It was a good strong brew that brought with it a jolt of clarity. And guilt, apparently. Dave was muttering, "I destroyed evidence, do you realize that? Important evidence. I could go to jail for that. And all for nothing. There's no safe haven for any of us."

"No one will ever know, and remember you did it for love," Olivia assured him. "How would they find out? The Benedettos aren't going to give themselves away. And besides, the evidence was not lost actually. We have our backup."

"I won't have my children going into the limbo of witness protection," he said.

She waited. She knew what was coming next.

"The only solution is to expose those sonsofbitches and put them away for good," he declared. "I'm picking up that package in New York and sending it to the Feds."

"What about the kids? Want me to fly to Cleveland and bring them home?"

"They might as well come back since the Cleveland deal is blown. I'd rather have them where I can keep an eye on them. That would be really good of you." He took her in his arms for a grateful hug.

"Maybe Jamie would like to go with me for a little family visit. I'm hoping the Benedettos will think your backup disc came from some other source, Rossi's lawyer maybe, if he had one."

"Okay. We might fool them. Look normal, that's the thing. You know what I'd like to do is go in there with an AK-47 and massacre that whole corrupt family of gangsters."

"Since the jig's up anyway, you may as well call the kids from my phone."

Artie and Danny were in the kitchen having breakfast so they could get an early start on weeding before the day heated up. Dave insisted on their waking up Kevin and Moira, then questioned each of the children in turn. Kevin, who'd been up late practicing with the Kerry Kids, was particularly surly. No one would admit to using the phone, and Artie Andrews backed that up.

"Tell Kevin he's off the hook, go back to bed. Then ask Danny about the computer," Olivia suggested. "You know, e-mail?"

Danny whined that he had "cross-my-heart-and-hope-to-sizzle" obeyed the phone rule, but reluctantly admitted he had been sending e-mails to his friend Vinny.

"Vinny who?" Olivia asked over Dave's shoulder.

Dave relayed the question calmly but he was clenching his free hand and pounding his knee. "Vinny Tornitore? *Vinny Tornitore!*" he repeated. "Who's his father?" The quiet tone was rising to a shout. "Tomaso Tornitore That wouldn't be *Cadillac Tom Tornitore*, would it?"

Olivia put a quiet restraining hand on Dave's arm. "The boy had no idea. These things happen. What's done is done." Despite these soothing platitudes, Dave's face was turning a mottled red. He passed the phone to her and muttered, "Here, you'd better say good-bye for me, okay?"

Olivia didn't know if she was pleased or concerned about this little audition for the Mom role. Maybe she shouldn't have been so quick to volunteer for the Cleveland trip. But she chatted with Danny for a few minutes about the computer and the early green beans he and Artie had been harvesting. She asked to speak to Moira who continued to mix pancake batter because "Mother Andrews just loves blueberry pancakes."

"I can tell she's going to miss you, Moira. So, are you guys ready to come home now? And how would you like me to be your trip escort? Your uncle's really busy at work, and so I offered. Friday, I think. I'll stay over, and we'll leave Cleveland on Sunday. Let you know as soon as I get our reservations."

After she hung up, Olivia told Dave, "Much as they love the Andrews, they love you more. Maybe there was a twinge of fear that you might decide to leave them there permanently. Resume your carefree bachelor life."

"As if the Andrews would have gone for that deal."

"Children can never be sure what might be arranged over their heads. Anyway, they're dying to see you. Moira, too. You're their security, darling."

"Well, that's something. But I'd really like to wring Danny's neck right now."

The sky might be falling, their beautiful plan wrecked, and the future uncertain, but they both had to get themselves to work. Monday morning, and it began to rain steadily and heavily. *Perfect timing*, Olivia thought. Now she wouldn't have to worry about everything in her garden turning brown while she shuffled off to Cleveland.

JUNE 25
Things to Do Today

Research kennels—outdoor runs, exercise, diet, air conditioning, music, aromatherapy
Reserv Cleveland
Make arrang with Norm, cover Fri, poss Mon
Pack for trip
Google Cadillac Tom

Last minute reservations were pricey, but Dave insisted on paying the entire tab for this unscheduled jaunt to Cleveland, including Jamie's fare. Despite the discomfort of air travel, going anywhere with Jamie made the trip a party.

When the beverage cart came by, Jamie ordered gin and tonic. "You can't get a decent martini on an airplane," she explained as she poured the nip of gin over ice in a plastic glass. "I'll just pretend I've ordered extra-extra dry."

Olivia had brought her own a bottle of water. It was important to stay hydrated on planes, where the air was so dry. "What, no olives? Here, let me have that tonic if you're not going to drink it." Olivia grinned at her friend, grateful to Jamie for agreeing to make this jaunt on such short notice. She was glad, too, that their tight schedule would not permit visiting with Olivia's mom, who was still urging her to move back to Cleveland. After all, there was no real reason Cecelia even had to know that Olivia had been in town.

"Olives we have." Jamie fished out a small baggie out of her Dooney and Bourke handbag. "Ugh, how can you drink that tonic stuff plain?"

"I like it. A bracing, bitter flavor. And I won't reek of gin when your mother hugs me."

"I make it a habit never to fly perfectly sober. Gin deadens my basic distrust of men and machines. Which is also why I have generously given you the window seat," Jamie said. "And speaking of men, every time I've called you at home in the last two weeks, Dave has been beside you breathing heavily. I guess he's more or less moved in. So aren't you two going to miss honeymooning when the O'Haras get home and he has to assume his Daddy role again?"

"Yeah. It has been idyllic—so idyllic that I'm rather afraid he's on the verge of proposing," Olivia confessed. "And frankly, I don't know what I want. I mean, I know I love Dave and all that, but I can't say I love his kids, and they're certainly cool towards me. A household with teenagers is bound to be chaotic. And you know me, I'm fairly set in my ways, and I like things neat and tidy. Organized. So the big stumbling block is, getting married would mean our living together."

What was there about being closed inside a steel cylinder zooming far above earth that brought about the urge to share one's innermost secrets? Olivia had not planned to discuss her worries about marrying Dave at all, not wanting to have to listen to her friend's predictable encouragement. Yet here she was, blurting out everything.

"Well, yes, usually marriage does mean living together. But maybe the kids could stay in one house and you and

Dave in the other?" Jamie took a long thoughtful sip of her martini. "No, I guess that wouldn't work."

"You admit, then, that there are insurmountable problems?"

"Are you crazy? You should be thanking your lucky stars that a cute, wholesome guy like Dave wants to sweep you off your feet and into holy matrimony. Get him to the altar, I say, and figure out the rest later."

"I *knew* you would say that. Even though you yourself have been divorced twice and are now looking for a decrepit millionaire to wed. How wholesome is that?"

Jamie sighed. "But wouldn't it be heavenly to be taken care of financially for a change? Sleeping as late as I wish, no more 6:00 AM shifts, ringing for service instead of being rung for, buying all the shoes I fancy ..." She gazed down at her pretty blue Ferragamo drivers that were getting a little worn at the heels.

"You're *not* thinking of trying to ace out that determined little fiancée of Cesare's, are you?" Olivia protested.

"No, dearie, I don't poach. And besides, I'm not as sure as I used to be that C. B's clean in respect to the family business. Oh, Gawd, here comes the cart again. Would you buy me another gin and tonic? I don't want the stewardess to think she's got a lush on her hands."

"Okay. I hope to hell she has peanuts this time. Boy, am I empty. So what brought you to this conclusion about C.B.?"

"Don't worry, you won't be starving for long. Mom's sure to be rustling up your favorite roast beef and Yorkshire pudding. Anyway, the tip-off was the hoods."

"Hoods? Do you mean neighborhoods?"

"No, I mean slant-browed Neanderthal types. Meetings with hoods behind closed doors, one of whom, as you noted when I described him, looked remarkably like the thug who threatened you and probably snatched the kids, too. The trouble is it's awfully hard to hear through that damned oak door with Mrs.Gunner breathing down my neck But apparently, C. B.'s arthritis is not too painful for him to pound on the library table with his fist and shout out orders."

"Wouldn't it be ironic if we find out that it's Cesare Benedetto who is secretly running the rackets under that real estate front? Well, if things go according to plan, we should soon be rid of the whole damned family."

"Sure. And how often do things go according to plan? Aren't we taking this exciting little trip because those wiseguys found out where you stashed the kids?"

The beverage cart rolled beside their seats. "My friend would like another gin and tonic," Olivia told the stewardess. "She's afraid of flying. But don't worry, I'll help her wobble off the plane."

"Oh, thanks a lot," Jamie said, twisting open the little bottle cap as soon as the stewardess departed. "It will be you who wobbles if you keep swilling down that quinine water. It messes up your equilibrium, you know." She poured the gin into her new glass of ice. "So then, girlfriend ... you haven't explained why Dave was unable to make this trip. Or for that matter, why he didn't just let the kids travel by themselves. Kevin's old enough to look out for them."

"Dave's got something he has to take care of, something that may bring an end to the Benedetto empire in Boston. And as for the kids flying home by themselves, have you ever let Mike make the trip to Cleveland by himself to visit your parents?"

Jamie was adding more olives to her drink. "Mmmm. *Yes*." She took an appreciative sip. "I mean, no. I've never let Mike travel alone. Point taken. But I suppose that day is coming if my ex moves out of state. So, this *something* that Dave's doing, is it a sanctioned police action or a rogue mission of his own devising?"

Olivia drank some more tonic. "I wouldn't put it just that way. I'd say it's a solo mission. Lily's mission, actually. She'll never rest until we bring the Benedettos down. Here, let me have a swig of that martini, will you?"

∞

"The strangest thing," Sandy Andrews exclaimed while Jamie and Olivia were helping with the dinner dishes. "A young man's been hanging around here for the past two days. I didn't notice, but Kevin—he's such an observant boy. He said to me, 'Mom Andrews'—I asked the children to call me Mom, makes them feel more at home, you know—'Mom Andrews, do you know that character in the Toyota? He's been parked across the street all day.' Well, that was news to me, so I told Kevin, 'No, son, but maybe he's waiting for one of the Goldberg girls.' Three attractive young women live in that house across the street. So Kevin says, 'He keeps looking over here, Mom.'"

"Could you describe him, Sandy?" Olivia asked. She was peering out the window into the darkness. No one was parked under the streetlamp now.

Mrs. Andrews was wrapping up the remaining slab of roast beef. "You'll have to ask Kevin, dear. Kevin borrowed Archie's digital camera and took a picture of the young man in the Toyota through the upstairs window. Used the zoom lens, he said."

As soon as the dishes were finished, Olivia rushed upstairs to the bedrooms where the O'Haras were packing for tomorrow's trip home.

"Dave really, really wants us back!" Danny exclaimed excitedly. "I knew he would miss us."

"Danny, did Kevin transfer the digital pictures he took to the computer?"

"*Kev!*" Danny shouted.

Kevin slouched in from the hall where he'd been sitting on the top step, beating a soft fast rhythm on his bodhran. His packing had been swiftly accomplished, since he'd brought so little with him.

"Kev, Liv wants to see the pictures you took, okay?"

"I suppose *she* wants to see that jerk who's been staking us out. Okay, so show her. Maybe *she'd* like the license plate on the Toyota as well? I got that, too." Never looking at or addressing Olivia personally, Kevin slumped out of the bedroom he'd been sharing with his brother and went back to his music.

Hopeless. This family is just plain hopeless, Olivia thought.

Jamie came upstairs just then, skirting around Kevin. Seeing Olivia's dour expression, she whispered, "Don't worry, Liv. Things have a way of working out. Remember there's always military school."

"Good tip. Come and see the photos with me."

The two women followed Danny to a little open sitting area located directly above the front door. It was furnished with a desk looking out at the street, and a couple of cushioned cane chairs. "This used to be my *honest-I'm-doing-homework, not-watching-for-boys-to-come-by* spot," Jamie said.

"I remember," Olivia agreed.

Danny was booting up the computer, opening the Kodak program to the page where the latest digital photographs were stored. They appeared to have been shot from the bow window in this sitting area. Although Kevin had zoomed in as closely as possible, the stranger's picture, taken as he sat behind the wheel, was grainy, and the license plate difficult to decipher. Seeing Olivia peering at that one in particular, Danny clicked on Open and the photo filled the screen.

"Son of a gun, that's Ray Chance!" Olivia exclaimed. "That's the guy who probably burned down my garage!" She jotted down the Toyota's license plate on a scrap of paper and tucked it in her shirt pocket. "What's he doing in Cleveland?"

"Your garage *and my first Thunderbird*!" Jamie screamed. "Is that the same goon who worked as your assistant and disappeared after the fire? Jesus, Liv! I've seen him before. He's been in and out of Cesare B.'s several times lately. If I'd only known he was the firebug—wouldn't I like to get my hands on that bastard and rearrange his face!"

"Small world. It's lucky he'd never met *you*," Olivia gave Jamie a not-in-front-of-the-kid nudge in the ribs. "Hey, Danny, would you mail these photos to my home computer. Here, I'll write down my email address."

Later, when Dave called on what they hoped would be a secure connection—his phone at police headquarters to her cell purchased just before the trip—Olivia told him about recognizing Chance. "As we guessed, the Benedettos must have caught on to this place through Danny's slip-up and the Tornitore connection. I looked up Cadillac Tom by the way. I guess you never ran into him at the PTA."

"Don't make me feel any worse than I do already. I have to admit I don't know the last names of half my kids' friends. Careless as hell for a cop. But from now on, they'll have to submit a dossier for every one of their pals. Coincidental to have that Ray Chance character show up. And I don't believe in coincidences. After what he did to you, I sure would like to throw his ass in jail."

"And to Jamie. It was her car in there, remember? I can't believe Ray is, as they say, connected. He strikes me as being more like one of those wannabes who hang around mobsters hoping for small jobs. But of course he does have some demolition expertise. Maybe he was so eager to fetch and carry, they sent him to watch the house, see if the kids were really being hidden here. He's gone now, though, or I could have reported him to the police. But Kevin's photo got the Toyota's license plate. You can check out that when you get back to work. So how are things with you?"

"All set. No need to talk about it now though. In fact, I could meet you at the airport. What time is your plane arriving?"

"7:15 PM, if it's on time. But there's no need of your getting jammed up in Boston. Jamie's car is parked in the airport garage. She's transporting us home in her new Thunderbird. It's a convertible. Ice blue, very classy. The kids are delighted. We should be home by 8:30 or so. Oh ... you could do something for me."

"Anything ... after all this."

"Good. Take a ride over to the Pampered Pet Vacation Villa in Hingham and spring my pups, will you?"

"Oh, okay. I was hoping for a mountain to climb or an ocean to swim. But transporting two annoyed dogs is almost as daunting. I bet they despised the Villa. I'll wait at your place then? And even bring dinner. Pizza or Chinese?"

"Chinese. I'm not that much into Italian these days. Great idea, though. I don't think we're going to get anything on the plane but a few peanuts. And gin for Jamie, of course. I can't wait to hear ... well, you know."

"If we get a minute alone..."

"Yeah, things will be different now."

"Different, but better. Wonderful to have us all together again. I missed those little guys."

Dave sounded so happy, Olivia stifled her sigh. "Yes, wonderful."

∽

There was precious little time for Olivia and Dave to confer, but they did manage a few minutes alone in her office. Jamie was in the kitchen helping Moira to clean up after the Chinese buffet, and the boys had taken Sadie and Bruno for another turn around the backyard.

"Picked it up without a hitch," Dave was saying. "And I'd wager my professional reputation that I wasn't followed to the P.O."

"I was a little worried that the package might have disappeared," Olivia admitted. "So many strange things have happened lately. Those gangsters always seemed to be way ahead of us."

"I'm going to look into that. I still think *someone in the office* ... That's why it's just as well we're going this route. So anyway, I've handed my package over to my contact in the FBI for better or worse."

"And you didn't leave, like, any fingerprints or saliva or anything that could be traced to you?"

Dave laughed affectionately, sitting on the edge of her desk. It seemed to Olivia that Lily's portrait, now positioned in lonely splendor on a nearby shelf, was watching him and that he was unaware of it. "You read too many crime stories," he said. "Yes, everything's cool. And my contact knows what he's got and what to do with it. He impresses me as not being stupid or careless. Now what about Ray Chance? Did you say you have the license plate number of the car he was driving?"

Olivia took the slip of paper out of her desk and tucked it into Dave's pocket. Somehow this resulted in her standing between his legs, and he folded her into his arms for a long tantalizing kiss. "Jesus, I wish I could stay," he murmured into her neck. Olivia wished that, too.

Lily's portrait fell flat on its face. "Oops, I guess I knocked Lily over," Dave said, righting the frame.

"She knocked herself over to give us some privacy—she's being discreet," Olivia said.

"Oh, sure," Dave said.

⁂

Finding the children hanging around the living room in various attitudes of exhaustion, a look of guilt passed over Dave's face; he declared that it was past time for him to drive them home. Kissing Olivia lightly on the forehead, he whispered in her ear, "It doesn't always have to be this way. Someday we'll all be at home together," before he departed.

Jamie came out of the kitchen with the remaining bottle of chardonnay that Dave had brought with the Chinese food. "Did I give you guys enough time? Did he ask you? Did you say yes?" She laughed, a deep bawdy chuckle.

"No, he didn't ask, you irredeemable matchmaker and all-round busybody. But he did sort of hint. And that's all you're going to hear from me."

"Okay, okay. Here, let's have a glass of wine. You're far too sober. And the other thing, Dave's secret assignment, how did that go?" An eyebrow raised questioningly, Jamie filled the glasses and handed one to Olivia.

"Sorry. Best you don't know. But here's one little clue. You may be looking for another nursing situation soon."

❦

"I need to see you," Dave said as soon as Olivia answered her cell. It was Saturday, and Olivia had been thinking that, with the O'Haras newly returned from their travels, she'd be on her own for the weekend, a prospect she viewed with mixed feelings. On the one hand, the opportunity to catch up on chores. On the other hand, no tumultuous love-making. What she didn't figure on was a preemptory summons like this one. *Nothing in life is predictable anymore,* she thought, with a little frisson of satisfaction.

"What's up, honey?" she asked.

"I'd rather discuss this in person."

"Okay. I'm in the middle of cleaning, so if it's not an emergency, I'll be there in an hour or so."

Olivia continued to mop and dust throughout the house. She watered and pruned the houseplants and folded the last load of washing. Just because she was caught in a mob war, there was no excuse to lower her standards. She did, however, skip the ironing, not her favorite job. Fortunately, with the advent of miracle fabrics, there was less and less of that odious task.

❦

"What's up?" she asked again, when Dave pulled her into his bedroom for a private embrace.

"It's been too long," he said. The white linen shorts she was wearing gave his hands an invitation to caress the inside of her thighs. Her response was too quick and hot for comfort. She pushed him away slightly.

"We were together just yesterday, honey. Was this summons a ruse, I hope?" Her tone was teasing, but she kept a discreet space between them.

"Never together enough. But no, not a ruse at all. I heard from Alice. Teresa, actually, but I knew her longer as Alice. A collect call, which is the only kind they can make. She was mildly hysterical. It seems she had a visitor Thursday. Some 'little bozo with a peacock strut' came to tell her that she'd better keep me in line if she didn't want her kids to end up like her husband.'" He sat on the bed, still holding her hand.

"Oh, that's fairly chilling." Freeing her hand gently, Olivia moved away from Dave and his bed toward the door of the room, the better to think calmly. "That description sounds a lot like Ray Chance. After his successful sojourn in Cleveland, maybe he was given another opportunity to prove himself worthy. The guy really does have a strutting peacock aura, always presenting his bundle to the female gaze."

"You never told me that."

"Because I could manage the situation myself. So what did you tell Alice-Teresa?"

"I told her I'd done everything those sonsofbitches asked me to do, the kids are fine, enjoying their summer vacation, and I will continue to keep them safe. I said that her visitor was just a hanger-on, no one for her to be concerned about."

"Did that make her feel better?"

"No. Would you have felt reassured?"

"I guess that worrying about one's children goes with the territory," Olivia said.

"You'd make a wonderful mom, do you know that?"

"Yeah, but not right now, honey. Right now we're going downstairs before things get out of hand and those children discover us in *flagrante delicto*." Olivia felt that she was skating nimbly over some very thin ice here.

SOMEBODY UP THERE
LIKES AGENT WASHINGTON

Washington leaned back at Randall Glumm's desk and sipped an iced tea sweet enough to carry him back to New Orleans. The house wine of the South. Moving an issue of Firearm Times closer, he used it as a coaster. No need to mar the sacred mahogany surface. He gazed at the prominently displayed photo of his boss chumming with President Bush at the Texas White House. A glorious moment in a rather inglorious career.

A miracle, that's what it was. Special Agent in Charge Glumm stuck in the hospital with a hemorrhoid flare-up (anal retentive tight-ass, if ever there was one!) leaving Washington a clear field with this latest dynamite from Lowenstein. Washington had personally shepherded the evidence upstairs as far as possible, out of Glumm's purview, to the same people who had welcomed his initial investigative efforts.

From their first contact, Lowenstein had seemed a straight enough guy, yet Washington had harbored the suspicion that the promised financial evidence might not be exactly sensational. The advance billing had seemed just too good to be true. *Wrong!* Now that the forensic accountant had a chance to evaluate the material, the highly confidential analysis suggested that Rossi's records would be the downfall of the Benedettos. It couldn't have happened to a more deserving crime family, Washington crowed to himself.

And more than that, Washington's initiative had earned him a nod from an Assistant Director in Charge, Bill Wright, at FBI HQ. The man had all but guaranteed Lee that he would be transferred out of Glumm's reach into an assignment more worthy of his talents as an investigator. Wright implied this could mean a promotion to the FBI Organized Crime Program in New York City.

Lowenstein had done some bypassing of his own with the Rossi material, letting Lieutenant Badger believe that the original disc in the Plunkett safety deposit box had been flawed beyond redemption. Bill Wright had agreed to give Lowenstein the status of a confidential informant known only to himself, Lee Washington, and the Director.

Washington was intent upon there being no repercussions to Lowenstein and the O'Hara family to come out of the ensuing investigation and prosecution. Not even Glumm would know from whom the FBI had obtained the Benedetto accounts. It was only fair after Lowenstein had put his own career and his life on the line. When the dust settled, Washington would even look into the bogus charges of drug dealing that had followed Tom O'Hara to his grave.

Smiling to himself, Washington drained the iced tea and placed his most recent summary of the Benedetto Fruit Company tapes at the exact center of Glumm's handsome desk. Other than a little chicanery over lacing a rival's shipment of seedless red grapes from Chili with a trace of cyanide, not much was going on with the first family of Boston crime ... yet.

JULY 3
Things to Do Today

Picnic 4th consult Moira
Check Jamie Mike Norm
Mole consult F. Mitchell

"Is there any way I can contact Lily on my own?" Olivia asked Florrie Mitchell. She was in her home office but had chosen to use her cell phone. "Do you think that she might be able to tell me the name of the person who keeps leaking information, jeopardizing ... well, the thing Lily wants us to accomplish so that she can travel that Sunset Path on the West Wind, or whatever."

"That's okay. I understand there's something going on with Lily that you have to be vague about," Mrs. Mitchell reassured Olivia. "I guess the gist is that you need Lily's help to unmask a spy."

"Yes." Olivia glanced at Lily's photo on her desk. It was giving off no vibes at all, no change of expression.

"Get yourself in a meditative state and talk to her."

"How do I do that meditative thing?"

"You've never meditated?" Mrs. Mitchell's tone was incredulous as if asking, *What, you're still a virgin?*

"Nope. I've read a lot of Zen theory though. I like that serene view of life."

"It's time to dangle your toes in the river, Olivia. Sit comfortably and quietly. Center yourself. Breathe deeply and evenly from the diaphragm. Push away intruding thoughts. If you wish, you may repeat a simple sound—*Om* is traditional. I usually say *Imi,* but that's Wampanoag. When you feel peaceful and detached from worldly concerns, try speaking to Lily."

"Okay, I'll try it. Do you charge for phone consultations?"

"Sometimes. But not this time. You and Lily are a special case, my dear."

"Well, at least we didn't have to build a sweat lodge." She and Mrs. Mitchell laughed together like two old friends. Olivia thanked her, and they said good-bye. Yet there seemed to be a faint echo of their laughter somewhere in the corner of her office, up near the ceiling.

Sitting in her Stickley rocking chair, Olivia followed Mrs. Mitchell's directions to the letter, but after ten minutes found herself becoming irresistibly sleepy. Perhaps this was as meditative as she could get. "It's in your ballpark now," Olivia said to the photo of Lily. "So how about giving me a clue as to who in Dave's department is talking to the Benedettos? Just make a few notes right here while I brew myself a cup of coffee." She left a little white pad of paper and a pencil conspicuously in the center of her desk.

When she got back to her office, Olivia couldn't help glancing hopefully at her desk. The paper was still blank. But as she turned to leave, Olivia noticed that the Marshfield phone book she kept in the bookcase has slipped onto the floor. The yellow pages were lying open. She picked it up, keeping her finger in the open place, and sat at the desk to study it. Under the page heading *Beauty Salons,* she read through the listings from Gail's Nu-Concept Nails to Sheila's Shear Pleasure Spa without a glimmer of understanding. Perhaps the book did just fall open on its own. Books did simply drop out of shelves sometimes, didn't they?

No! Not in Olivia's house, they didn't. She was not a careless shelver. Every book was lined up in perfect order one inch from the edge.

Olivia read through the page again. And again. She thought she remembered a name. An inspiration snaked through her consciousness. *Could it be? So simple and yet so awful.* Not a good idea to call Dave at work, because that was the heart of the problem. "How about another little hint, Lily," she said to the portrait, which was still looking glossy and inert

"Okay, once more then. If only because I don't think I have a meditative personality." Olivia perused the yellow pages again and re-read one particular ad. Then she laid down the cumbersome book on the desk, picked up her cell, and punched in a number.

"Gloria's Cutting Edge Coiffures. Walk-ins Welcome. How may I help you?" sang a young woman's voice. Olivia asked if they were too backed up with the Fourth to give her a quickie trim this morning or early afternoon. She was invited to come along right now, and they'd squeeze her in. Glancing in the mirror, Olivia noted that her former Joan of Arc buzz, which she'd been letting grow longer, had indeed reached a very shaggy stage. A little shaping wouldn't hurt. She grabbed her shoulder bag and headed out to the van.

On the way to the salon, she called Jamie on her cell. "Mike's coming with you to Dave's tomorrow, right? Picnic at Dave's, then Kingston to watch the fireworks over Plymouth

Bay. Moira's cooking her heart out. I invited Norman Unwin, too. Poor guy looked lonesome."

"Okay, but I trust you weren't thinking of fixing me up with that nerd, right? Sometimes I wonder about your hiring skills, girlfriend. First, that bastard Ray Chance and now creepy Norman Unwin."

"Gosh, and I thought you two would really hit it off. If he were old and rich, I bet you wouldn't find him so creepy."

"See you tomorrow. With Mike, under protest. He's afraid that Moira will come on to him," Jamie said.

"Mike can hang with Kevin. He'll like that, if Kevin's in a decent mood. Gotta go. I'm having my hair styled."

"What hair?"

Gloria's Cutting Edge Coiffures had a steamy atmosphere that smelled so strongly of hair and nail chemicals, Olivia thought they should be giving out gas masks at the door. Soon she was swathed in plastic and seated at a station with "Kandy," who pointed to the name embroidered on her smock and said, "Kane. Kandy Kane. Bet you can guess when I was born." She was sporting a hair cut so uneven it looked as if it had been executed by a deranged Edward Scissorhands. Even though various posters indicated this was, indeed, the cutting edge of fashion, Olivia was tempted to snatch off her protective cape and run for her life. Only the pressing need to fulfill her mission kept Olivia in Kandy's clutches.

"I'm letting my buzz grow out," she explained. "Just shape it a little, okay?"

"Sure, honey. Let's shampoo and see what we've got," Kandy said. "That's a nice rich color, but you ought to consider highlighting. We do it so's it looks real natural. You'll love it."

Tipped backward under the spray, Olivia began her campaign. "Is Gloria here today?" Kandy shook her head. "No?" *Good,* Olivia said to herself. "I think we may have gone to school together. Was she Gloria Johnson?"

Kandy laughed and rubbed a dab of conditioner onto Olivia's hair. "No, honey—that must have been some other gal. Gloria was Gloria Turner, now Mendez. She's married to a cop here in town—well, he's a detective now—Hector Mendez."

Turner! Thank heavens, Olivia thought. She'd be glad to be proved wrong here. Otherwise, it would be so demoralizing for Dave. "So she's not Italian then?"

"Gloria? Oh, sure she is. Turner's just the name that her folks got given at Ellis Island. *You gotta Americanize*, they were told. Her father was afraid if he complained, they'd send him back."

"Rather high-handed of that immigration official."

"Yeah, well some of them were like that, you know what I mean? His brother, Gloria's uncle, came over a year later and had no trouble at all. A perfectly decent name, too. Pietro Tornitore.

Olivia's heart plummeted. Was it possible Dave didn't know his partner's wife's was related to the Tornitores? She was not going to enjoy telling him about this unhappy coincidence. This could be the departmental leak, simply a family affair. "Any relation to Tomaso Tornitore?"

Kandy chuckled and slung a towel over Olivia's head. "Cadillac Tom? Sure. Gloria's his cousin. Comes in here all the time for his haircuts. We're unisex, you know. Hot-looking guy, you know what I mean? Head of hair guys his age would kill for, and a great tipper. Always drives a brand new black Caddy."

As soon as she got out of the salon and into her van, Olivia called Dave at work. "Hi, honey. Listen, can you meet me for just a few minutes? Maybe a cup of coffee? How about that Starbucks near St. Timothy's?" After they hung up, Olivia had another look at her hair in the van's lighted mirror. Not too bad—still very short but beginning to curl in an attractive way, enhanced by Kandy's skillful hands. Maybe she'll go back to Gloria's, if only to keep abreast of the Tornitores.

Dave was waiting for her at Starbucks, with two coffees as simple and black as the coffee shop produced in its various hissing machines. "Hey, babe, you're looking great."

"You like the curls? I just came from the hair salon. Gloria's Cutting Edge Coiffures. Ring a bell?"

Dave looked bemused. "No, should it? Oh, is that Hector's wife's place."

"Yeah. Sorry to be the bearer of upsetting news, but this you have to know."

"What? *Gloria?* Oh, you're kidding. You think Hector's the leak? Not a chance, honey. Hec and I have been through a lot together, and I think I know the guy better than anyone." Dave was immediately defensive of his partner. That inevitable male-bonding thing. But Olivia had steeled herself for this confrontation.

"Hear me out for a minute. Suppose that Hector does tell his wife, as men often do, how his day went, interesting things that happened at the department. Like, for instance, about you and he scooping up that disc implicating the Benedettos? And then the story of Lieutenant Badger going ballistic when, for some strange reason, the disc got erased while in his sole custody? Isn't that conceivable husband-wife chit-chat? Just like you told me about the very same incidents?"

"Well, that's different. You're up to your pretty neck in this mess. What makes you think, anyway, that whatever Gloria was told ever got passed on to others? I know Gloria—she's an okay gal. A little loud, likes to sing *That's Amore* at department parties and dance up a storm. But a good wife and a devoted mother."

"Do you know Gloria's maiden name?"

"Sure. Turner."

"Which is, as it happens, an Americanized version of Tornitore. Two branches of the same family. In fact, Cadillac Tom is Gloria's cousin." Having delivered the final spear into her lover's chest, Olivia sat back and sipped her coffee. It was very good. "Is this Arabica?"

Dave's skin paled under his tan. He looked thunderstruck, his normally warm brown eyes had suddenly turned chilly. Olivia laid her hand consolingly over his on the table. "Christ almighty," he whispered.

"Keep in mind that there's no way you could have guessed this."

"*You* guessed it."

"I had help. Lily's help. What a researcher *she'd* make." Olivia told Dave about the question she'd asked, and how the yellow pages had fallen open to Gloria's page.

"But you figured it out. You put two-and-two together."

"I admit a few ideas popped into my head. Maybe you mentioned Gloria's salon sometime in the past, and it was lurking down there in my subconscious just ready to surface. Or maybe Lily was whispering in my ear, at a decibel beyond ordinary hearing, like a dog whistle. *Whatever*. The thing is, we know now there's a connection. So you have to be super careful that Hector doesn't know that you copied that disc. You never told him, did you?"

"Thank God, no. It was so against regulations that I didn't want to get him involved, get him into trouble. Deniability, you know."

"Good. We're safe there then. Now what about that package you just gave to your friend at the FBI?"

"Hec hasn't a clue. So, what you do think—Gloria has regular tell-all chats with the mob? Like she doesn't know or care that her husband could be compromised by her blabbing whatever he tells her in confidence?"

"No, honey, I don't think it's anything like that. The leak could be perfectly innocent. Cadillac Tom has his hair styled at Gloria's salon. Maybe while she's giving him a "cutting edge" haircut, she tells him a few things she thinks may interest or amuse him. Probably he chuckles in a sexy way and asks a few provocative questions. I hear he's a good-looking guy, and after all, he's family. What kind of car does Gloria drive?"

"Oh, shit. Of course. *Hec* drives an ancient Ford Taurus but his wife sports a Caddy convertible. 'Business must be great at the salon,' I ribbed him once. And he said, his wife knew the dealer, that he's an old friend who always saves one of those special trade-ins with low, low mileage for her."

"It all fits, I'm sorry to say." They'd finished their coffee, and Dave had to get back to work. As they were walking out to their cars, Olivia said, "Please, whatever you do, don't let on to Hector that there's a problem. We'll talk more about this tomorrow. Looking forward to the party. I sure hope Moira will let me help, though."

"What burns my ass," Dave said, "is that Hector's wife, with her big mouth, put my kids in harm's way."

"It's a sobering thought. Just be careful. And remember, that none of this is Hector's fault. If it were any other case, there would be no problem at all. You don't have to stop trusting him."

"Yeah, maybe."

"You just have to keep cool about this business."

Dave was quiet and thoughtful. Olivia knew he was probably thinking over every conversation he'd ever had with Mendez about the Benedettos, what slips he may have made. He gave her an absent-minded kiss and headed back to work.

Sorry as she was to have ruined her lover's day, and maybe his relationship with his partner, it was a relief to know that Dave hadn't given Hector a clue that another computer disc existed, Frank Rossi rising from his untimely grave to finger the Benedettos' finances. At least she hoped not. Partners could be so very close that they almost read each other's mind. But Olivia didn't think that could really be the case with Dave and Hector. After all, Dave had never caught on to the Gloria connection.

Later that night, while Olivia was making a flag cake for the fourth, the one dish that Moira had reluctantly delegated, Dave called her new cell phone from his desk at work. His voice sounded a bit unsettled. "That guy I know sure moved fast," he said

"You're working late. What happened?"

"The prosecutor brought the evidence to a Federal judge, following which the Feds took the senior Benedettos into custody last night. The Justice building was crawling with high-priced lawyers today, trying to get their clients out on bail."

"Successfully?"

"Not yet but probably soon. A grand jury will be convened to review the evidence and bring back indictments.

At least we know that Lily's stuff must have been compelling, even conclusive."

"They might have been working on this one for a long time. Maybe what you gave them is just the icing on the cake that was needed." Olivia spread the rest of the whipped cream with a flourish and began to make red stripes with sliced strawberries. "The records were fairly straightforward, but nevertheless I'll wager some forensic accountant was burning the midnight oil last week. Good show, I say, as long as none of this ever gets traced back."

"Yes, exactly."

"But what about Jamie's patient?"

"Not him. He's in the clear. Just a real estate mogul."

"I don't think so, and neither does Jamie. But let's not go into all that now. If the opportunity presents itself tomorrow, you might want to have a talk with her." Olivia didn't really think anyone could be listening in to her cell, but on the other hand, she preferred discussing sensitive matters in person. Perhaps she *had* been watching too many crime dramas.

After they hung up, Olivia finished the cake with a square of blueberries "stars", placed it reverently in the Frigidaire, and went upstairs to her office. She smiled to herself, realizing that she felt the need to tell Lily about this latest development. Sitting at her desk, she addressed the showgirl's smiling face. "Okay, Lily, the wiseguys who ordered the hit on you and Frankie are in custody. The FBI didn't have to be geniuses to know what they held in their hands with that disc. They've even shared it with the Federal Prosecutor's office in a prompt fashion. Your boyfriend's private record of the Benedetto finances is pure gold. Bottom line, your revenge is nearly complete now, so I hope you're a happy spook. You can pack your ectoplasm and get ready to drift away on the West Wind. I'll miss you, but I'll adjust, in time, to always finding things in the very same place where I left them."

The photo gazed back at Olivia impassively, but a drift of that exotic lily fragrance wafted through the room. Sadie and Bruno, who had been standing in the doorway waiting for whatever their person was going to do next, immediately skedaddled down the hall to the bedroom.

"You guys sure will be relieved when there are no more ghostly high jinks to drive you under cover," she continued talking as she got ready for bed, vaguely aware that she seemed to be rambling to herself. *But that's one good thing about having dogs around,* she thought. What might have seemed like an eccentric monolog could be justified as perfectly normal communication with one's companion animals, and no listeners could be more attentive. It's as if they almost understood and were trying hard to get it right.

Olivia opened the window—it was much too pleasant an evening to ruin with air conditioning—and settled herself in bed with *Step-parenting for Dummies.* She was glad the lily perfume didn't follow her into the bedroom so that Sadie and Bruno could get a decent night's sleep. Tomorrow's celebration of the Fourth at Dave's was going to be a bang-up day for them all.

∾

The next morning, the Glorious Fourth, Olivia was up with the birds, literally. On a hunch, she jumped into the van, and drove to the nearest convenience store to pick up the Boston Globe. The arrest of the Benedettos was emblazoned on the front page above the fold.

Drinking a mug of strong black coffee, Olivia, who had always enjoyed true crime dramas, reveled in her own secret connection to this big story. There was only one grainy photo of the three men, surrounded by an armada of agents and being hustled into a Federal holding facility. She thought of Lily's cruel death, hurled screaming down the stair well of her apartment building. No wonder she couldn't "rest in peace." Olivia smiled with grim satisfaction as she read:

FBI NABS MOB BOSSES. In a sweeping raid of the Sant'Angelo Social Club in Boston's North End and the Palermo Social Club in Newark, Federal officers arrested brothers Angelo Salvatore "The Angel" Benedetto, Rosario "The Rose" Benedetto, and their cousin Louis "Lou the Bull" Benedetto late on Friday night. Rosario Benedetto, is president of the Benedetto Fruit Company on King Street in Boston.

At a press conference yesterday, Federal prosecutor Sam Savage stated that it's taken the FBI five years to assemble the evidence in pictures, tapes, and financial records needed to put the Benedetto mob bosses behind bars. Attorney for the Benedettos, Paul Galante, issued a statement welcoming the opportunity to prove that his clients have been the victims of a FBI witch hunt, and declared that they will be found completely innocent of any and all charges.

Sources in the Federal prosecutors office claim that the charges against the Benedetto family will include loan-sharking, extortion, drug trafficking, tax evasion, and murder.

Other family members, Angelo Benedetto Jr., known as "Junior," and Cesare Benedetto, a well-known South Shore real estate broker, now retired due to failing health, could not be reached for comment. Another cousin, Dominick "Dapper Dom" Benedetto, is currently residing at his villa in Messina, Sicily.

THE BROTHERS BENEDETTO

Seated in his wheelchair behind an antique mahogany desk that once belonged to a Boston mayor, Cesare reached into the humidor, removed a Cuban cigar, and sniffed it appreciatively. As he went through the business of clipping and lighting it, silence was thicker around the two brothers than the aromatic smoke that soon encircled their heads. Leaning back, Cesare coldly eyed Rosario who was literally on the carpet before him, hat in hand. "Help yourself," he said, shoving the humidor toward his brother.

"This fucking Rossi thing has my nuts in a vise," Rosario complained, reaching forward to take a cigar.

Cesare slammed the humidor shut, nearly catching his brother's fingers in the heavy cover. "That's because you've fucked up from the start, Rosy," he shouted. "Whacked the two people who could have given up the evidence before it became a problem. So you never fucking found out where it was hid. Then you sent Angelo's kid, who's a fucking *idiota*, thinks he's John Travolta, to retrieve the stuff from the broad's auction, and who does he hire? The crazy Kleins, who routinely fuck up everything they touch. Didn't one of them get shot in the stomach by a girl, for Christ's sake?

Bottom line, the Feds got the goods on the family business now. You're all going to be indicted—you, Angel, and Lou."

Rosario stuck out his square jaw defiantly and threw himself into a leather chair. "Hey, you never know. Galante got me out on bail over the prosecutor's dead body. We're gonna owe Norm Millhouse on that one, big time. I had to give up my passport, but ..."

"Yeah, well, don't worry about that. You'll be getting a passport with a new name, Rosy, and you'll be going on a trip home. You're going to join Dom in the family olive oil business. That way you won't be tempted."

"Hey, what are you talking? Me? Never. Besides, I could beat this. I mean, how many times have they tried to make some garbage stick to us, and we got acquitted anyway. Evidence disappears. Witnesses get cold feet. A hold-out screws up the jury. Hey, Machiavelli said it, people are fickle by nature. Their convictions are easily weakened. And you ... you're my brother, my own blood. You should be helping me get off, persuading witnesses, paying off some judge."

Cesare sighed. "I'm doing this only because of Mama, God rest her soul. I'm getting you out of the country before you bring down the *la famiglia*, you asshole."

"Oh, no, you're not. I hate that fucking Messina, nothing to do, no place to go. You got Dom out of the way because he was going *pazzo* with the Alzheimer's, but me, I'm still sharp. I'm not gonna let you dump me."

Cesare smiled, the first time he'd smiled since they'd closeted themselves in the library. "You're not gonna let me? Who the Christ do you think you're talking to? Who the fuck is the boss here? There's not one of you got the brains that God gave fava beans. You, Angie, Lou—the three stooges of King Street. If it wasn't for me, there wouldn't be a fucking family business. And I'm not going to see all we achieved go down the toilet. I gotta think of the next generation. Angelo and Lou will be all right. They'll keep their mouths shut and do their time. But you ... you Rosy ... you're a royal pain in my ass, the way you swagger around, acting the *capo de capo*, just because I'm keeping a low profile. Which I do to protect *la famiglia*. So someone will be around to run things when the shit hits the fan. And this shit sure is flying. No, Rosy. I don't trust you. You got allusions of grandeur."

"I think big because I am big, Cesare. You imagine I'm going down quiet? Not a fucking chance. I've got a detective under my thumb who will go to the wall to protect his fucking family. All I got to do is motivate that guy, and who knows?"

"I tell you what, Rosy. You get out of this mess without an indictment—however you do it, I don't want to know— I'll let you off this time. But if you screw up now, believe me, you're on the next boat to the old country."

JULY 4
Things to Do Today

To hell with this, just have fun for once!

Olivia turned over the To-Do list with a flourish and picked up the newspaper again. "Your turns are coming," she promised the gray picture of Junior smoking a cigarette behind a wall of melons, and the slick photo of Cesare B. accepting a "Realtor of the Year" award with glittering blonde Yvonne looking on.

"Have you seen the Globe?" Olivia asked Jamie when she called later that morning.

"Oh my Gawd, yes. Guess it will be all gloom and doom at C. B.'s today. Yvonne is planning a gorgeous little party with a fireworks finale at midnight. No problem for the Benedettos getting all the fireworks they want. The family imports them. Anyway, I'm glad I won't be there."

"Why don't I pick you guys up?" Olivia offered. "You don't want to bring your lovely new Thunderbird to the fireworks display over Plymouth Harbor with all those cars parked every-which-way and streets closed off so people can watch. Dave will take the O'Haras in the Bronco. You and Mike and Norm and I and the dogs will travel in my van."

"Oh, lovely, Liv. Put the dogs between Norm and me, will you? But listen, we need to talk. Just you, me, and Dave."

"Okay. First chance. You know, Norm seems like a really nice person. A bit shy and reserved, though. All those hours at the computer, I guess."

"Sounds like your friendly neighborhood ax murderer."

Olivia ignored that and continued, "But not old enough for you, that's for sure. A guy has to be in his dotage to be in the running for your hand in matrimony."

"Seventies with a seven-figure income. See you at three, then."

❧

"I love fireworks, don't you," Norman Unwin said. His round white face was shining with excitement. Olivia thought he resembled Sadie somewhat, except that her tongue was longer, and at the moment, lolling out of her mouth with joy as Mike scratched her big head between the ears.

"Gawd, Americans do love their explosions, don't they?" Jamie said.

"*I* think fireworks are cool," Mike said. "Better than a lot of other national celebrations, Ma."

"Like what, kid?" his mother asked.

"Like the running of the bulls in Spain. Or Guy Fawkes night when they light bonfires and burn effigies to celebrate a traitor."

"This is the problem with educating children," Jamie complained.

"Another good thing about dogs," Olivia said. "You don't have to endure smart answers. Way to go, Mike!"

"Dogs are natural protectors and guardians," Norman said, putting his arm around Bruno, who was leaning over him, sniffing his breath. "As soon as I get a place that allows pets ... where did you say you got these two, Liv?"

"Shawmutt Dog Pound. Might as well rescue one of those death row inmates, Norm. Most of them are already housebroken, too."

"And they come with their very own rap sheets," Jamie said.

⁓

"Gawd, what a pow-wow was going on at C. B.'s last night," Jamie said in a low voice to Olivia and Dave. "With all those weird customers slouching in and out, his library looked like the bar scene in *Star Wars*."

It was their first opportunity to talk privately since the cook-out, at which Dave had grilled chicken and sausages, and Moira had outdone herself with salads and side-dishes. Olivia's flag cake had been generally admired and demolished. Now they were getting ready to depart for the Kingston vantage point where the Plymouth Harbor fireworks could best be viewed. Meanwhile, Danny had shanghaied Norman into troubleshooting some of his computer snafus, and Kevin was playing Celtic CD's for Mike's edification. Moira, still in the kitchen, was putting away leftovers according to her own rigid system that brooked no assistance—a protocol that Olivia understood, being somewhat inflexible herself. But Moira was not alone. Sadie had sidled into the kitchen to keep her company and clean up any leftover tidbit of sausage or chicken that happened to fall to the floor.

"Is there actually a bar in Cesare B.'s library?" Olivia asked.

"Oh, Gawd, girl—it's bigger than the bookcases. Plus a temperature-controlled wine cabinet and a whiz-bang espresso machine. The library might be described as C. B.'s personal social club, since he's pretty much housebound with RA. Anyway, Mrs. Gunner was on patrol in the hall, so I couldn't hear much. My duties were simply to dispense medicines, administer a shot if needed, and respond to any emergencies. My shift was 3 to 11, but C. B.'s body man, the Incredible Hulk, was away on some nefarious errand so I was asked to stay over for extra pay. I could catch a few winks in C. B.'s dressing room, where the Hulk's cot had been freshly made up for me. *Okay*, I thought, *what a chance for me to snoop.*"

"Jesus, Jamie," Dave said. "I hope you didn't get caught— or even suspected. This is no Nancy Drew game, you know."

"I wouldn't have guessed you even knew Nancy Drew."

"Moira is devoted to her, second only to Julia Child," Dave said.

"So, what *did* you get yourself into?" Olivia demanded. She knew that cat-got-the-canary look on Jamie's face too well.

"Yeah. Just wait until you hear. About three AM, everyone was well and truly asleep. And I could vouch for C. B. there. The shot I'd given him to ease the pain practically guaranteed he'd be out of it for four hours or more. So I decided to take a look around the library. I just wanted to see what he might have on his desk, or his appointment book, something like that."

"I can't believe this," Dave said.

"So, anyway, I creep in with my trusty penlight and have a look at the papers on his desk. All perfectly straightforward real estate garbage. The drawers are locked, no appointment book in sight. I'm beginning to think I'm wasting my time. But speaking of 'wasting,' it occurs to me then to check the wastebasket as well."

Olivia and Dave both groaned in different decibels of dismay.

"But, alas, the wastebasket turns out to be a paper shredder. I'm actually thinking I'd better get back to my little cot, when I catch sight of a crumpled piece of paper that seems to have escaped the shredder. It's fallen under the desk where I doubt that anyone as crippled at C. B. could ever reach it. So I pick that up and flatten it out."

Jamie paused and took a long thirsty drink of the Chardonnay in her glass. She knew her audience was in the palm of her hand. "I'm staggered to think you created those sculptures, Dave," Jamie digressed, looking around the backyard in the fading rose light of evening. "If you ever get thrown off the force for your unorthodox methods of police work, you should seriously consider an artistic career. I know a gallery that would just love ..."

"Okay, *what?*" Aware that Jamie was purposely trying her patience, Olivia still couldn't help herself.

Jamie's smile had an air of triumph. "It was a scrawled note. Not C. B.'s handwriting. No salutation, but I think one of the thugees brought it in hand. It said, 'Pop says the Feds got a copy of Rossi's shit and they're running with it. Anyone you want me to contact? Say the word.' And it was signed, 'Junior.'"

"You're right, Jamie—this C. B. is no innocent bystander," Olivia said. "I wonder what Junior—Junior Benedetto, I assume—means by 'say the word.'?"

Dave slammed his hand on the picnic table. "They'll want to burn someone for bringing evidence to the Feds. I'd sure like to know who they suspect. Do you have the note?"

Jamie looked down into her glass. "Eh, no. Sorry. You see, just then Mrs. Gunner shows up in her bathrobe. Says, 'what in the name of all the saints are you doing in here, Andrews?' So I say, 'I'm looking for a book to read. Couldn't sleep.' Then I drop that note right back where I'd found it. I don't think the old harridan sees me, either. Anyway, she gets a real nasty look, like she doesn't believe one word, and she says, 'If you want a book, Andrews, take some of Yvonne's trash from the bookcase in the living room. No one is allowed in here *ever*.' I leave of course—better part of valor, and all that. I think she may even have locked the library door after me, but I don't look back. I go to the living room and get some dreadful Hollywood novel, and then I have to read the damn thing, because I really can't sleep a wink after that run-in with Mrs. Gunner."

Dave and Olivia looked at each other. This does not sound good, but neither one of them wanted to frighten Jamie any more than she was already.

"Mrs. Gunner will report this episode, you know, and they'll get rid of you,"

Dave said.

"*Get rid of me?*" Jamie's voice hit a slightly higher pitch. She drained the rest of her wine.

"Fire you," Olivia said. "So if I were you, I'd beat them to the punch. Call the placement bureau for a substitute. You can say it's for health reasons. The flu, or some such. Or maybe TB."

"It *is* for health reasons," Dave said in a low commanding tone. "I want you out of there, Jamie."

"Ooooh, I'm all shivery. Is he always this forceful, Liv?"

Before Olivia could answer, Moira appeared in the doorway of her kitchen kingdom with Sadie close by her side.

The three adults huddled over the picnic table looked up at the girl in her oversize chef's apron, frizzy hair emphasizing her pale face, like a young Elizabeth I. "Uncle Dave, if you don't mind, I think I'll stay home tonight. I got a headache and a stomach ache."

"I'd better see what's going on with her," Jamie volunteered, and without waiting for an answer, went to Moira and put an arm around the girl, leading her back into the house. Sadie pattered after them, shaking her big head like an anxious nursemaid.

"What do you think?" Olivia asked

"I'll follow up on Cesare Benedetto, but it's true that the man's record is squeaky clean. Meanwhile, you've got to keep Jamie out of there."

"Right. She'll protest but she'll listen to me."

They were still discussing their strategy when Jamie came back. "You'd better let her rest, poor little girl. It's not the cooking, you know, so don't get all guilty, Dave. She loves feeling responsible and grown-up, queen of the kitchen. The problem is her age, probably the onset of menses, which she knows all about. I checked. Anyway, I gave her some Tylenol and a cup of sweet tea. Talked her into watching TV in her room with her feet up for a while. Sadie's up there keeping her company. She'll be fine."

༄

The light faded from rose to purple. Soon they were surrounded by Kevin, Mike, Danny, and even Norm, all eager to get going "before everyone else gets the good parking places." With Moira opting out, and Sadie content to look after her, Danny invited Bruno to ride in the Bronco. It was only a few miles to Kingston where they would watch the fireworks show that began at nine over the bay. The yearly event was always a big draw, and Dave had to do some fancy maneuvering, with Olivia's van right on his bumper, to park where they would get a good view. The air was filled with laughter of all ages, shouts across the street, everyone knowing everyone, and the smell of French fries emanating from the one busy food stand. Children were sitting on rail fences or running around, little ones whining with impatience. Dave and Olivia had brought some folding chairs, and Jamie was carrying a cooler with soft drinks and wine, waving off Norm's offer to help. Bruno, confined in the Bronco for his own safety, barked in protest out the open windows.

"Those stars have any fireworks quite outclassed," Jamie said, leaning back in her chair the better to observe them. It was a clear, bright night, a half moon like a tipped silver bowl far up in the sky, cool enough to be comfortable, just enough breeze to keep mosquitoes on the move.

"Perfect," said Olivia.

"Perfect," Jamie agreed.

Dave's cell phone rang, an official insistent sound that jarred their relaxed mood. He smiled ruefully, and answered, "Lowenstein," listened a minute. Looking at Olivia, he mouthed, "It's Hector," and made a face, expressing the new doubt and dismay he felt about his partner. Then the expression changed, hardened to anger. "Jesus. When did this happen? Did anyone see who did it?" A pause. "A damn cigar? Right. Right. Any witnesses?" Dave listened without speaking for what seemed like too long a time. Olivia and Jamie were waiting apprehensively—what bad news was this? "Yeah, I'll tell her. As soon as possible, then. Thanks, Hec."

The phone report having ended, Dave looked down for a minute, then straight up at Jamie, his eyes now full of kind sympathy, his deep sigh a wish that he didn't have to be the bearer of ill tidings.

"*What happened!*" Jamie and Olivia cried out in unison.

"I'm so sorry, Jamie. It seems that your car has been involved in an explosion. You parked it in The Willows parking lot, right? A new light blue Thunderbird? Mendez checked the plate—it's yours, Jamie. Thought you'd want to know right away, and maybe the two of us should get over there and have a look at the damage."

"Oh my Gawd!" Jamie screamed. "Why the hell didn't I bring it with me tonight! I should know better than to listen to you, Liv! Remember the time you advised me to keep my car safe in your garage? Another disaster!"

"Jamie," Dave put a gentle hand on the excited woman's shoulder. "We are all grateful *you* weren't in the car. I think we know why this happened, don't we? And it's Cesare Benedetto you should be blaming, not Liv. My guess is that Mrs. Gunner made her report. Maybe even found that note you were reading."

"Oh, damn it, Dave, can't you see I don't want to be reasonable? Okay, let's go then."

"What about the children?" Olivia protested

"*For your sins,*" Jamie said, "you get to stay with the kids. And don't tell Mike anything yet. I'll tell him myself later." She pulled her white jacket closer around herself as if the balmy July evening had suddenly turned chilly. "Damn it! With my insurance history, I'm doomed to be an assigned risk forever."

"Insurance is the least of your problems, my dear," Olivia said. "What you've got here is a strong hint from Cesare B. and his friends to mind your own business. A hint I hope you will heed." She hugged her friend and looked at Dave over her shoulder with an apprehensive frown.

"The pot calling the kettle black," Jamie muttered. "Okay, let's get going,"

Olivia looked with dismay at the hodge-podge of vehicles parked behind them. "Dave, I don't know how you're going to get the car out of here."

"Hec is going to pick us up in ..." Dave glanced at his watch, "any minute now." He tossed her the keys to his Bronco. "Here, in case you need to move my car before we get back."

"Hey, hold on a minute. I want details. Didn't anyone see anything? Like, who did this?" Olivia demanded.

Dave smiled—the kind of Clint Eastwood grim smile that's guaranteed to strike fear into guilty hearts. "Oh, yes, he wanted to be seen. That's how we know it's a warning. A woman walking a terrier and a guy jogging each saw something. A slim dark man in jeans and a denim work shirt over a white tee. He was smoking a cigar and fiddling with the car door. It looked as if he was using a key. When he succeeded in opening the door, he stood back, lit something with his cigar, then tossed the package inside the car, after which he moved away briskly. The jogger saw him clearly when the man sped down the hill toward, he thinks, a Toyota, but the witness was distracted by the explosion that followed. Can't confirm the man's car's make or license plate. The woman and her dog were knocked across the lawn by the blast, but they're both okay. She's the one who observed the dark young man light the fuse."

"Ray Chance?"

"The woman said the man had a nasty look about him, tight jeans and evil eyes."

"Oh, shit, shit, shit." Jamie was crying now. "If I don't go back to C. B.'s, won't that look as if I'm feeling guilty about snooping?"

"No matter, you're not going back," Dave said sternly. "And after I drop around to question them, they'll be too worried to concern themselves with what the nurse did or didn't observe. Hey, I think that's Hec down the street. Let's get going, Jamie. Liv, I don't know if we'll be back before the display is over—I'll try."

"Fireworks?" Jamie spat out the word. "A little anticlimactic, wouldn't you say?"

Sniffing out trouble, Danny, Kevin, and Mike gathered around them. "Hey, Mom," Mike said. "Where are you going?"

"I'll be right back, honey. Don't you worry. Aunt Liv will be looking out for you." Dave and Jamie ran off into the darkness leaving Olivia with a barrage of questions and no answers. Fortunately, just then the first rocket shot into the air with a cascade of blue and red sparks. All heads swiveled to the glory of the skies.

Bruno howled with dismay. It hadn't occurred to Olivia that her dogs might be spooked by fireworks. She was glad now that Sadie had stayed with Moira. A nice quiet evening for them both. Moira was an unusual girl, Olivia reflected. Seemingly able to cope with the most adverse events. Talented and independent. Qualities that Olivia admired. It might be fun to see how Moira turned out when she grew up, to help her rise above that tragic family history.

The dazzling fireworks continued, diverting the youngsters' attention from Jamie and Dave's odd departure. Norm clapped enthusiastically after each sally. In the intervals between gorgeous displays over the bay, teen-age boys set off illicit cherry bombs in dark corners. The sweet evening air that had been perfumed by the blossoms of surrounding gardens began now to exude the sharp odor of explosives. And yet, in the midst of that acrid smell, Olivia sensed the aroma of lilies. *Lily! Lily is here! Why?*

Anxiety drenched Olivia like a bucket of cold water. What if there was more than one target tonight? What if Dave's anonymity at the FBI had been compromised? Or the Benedettos wanted him to destroy more evidence? What about Moira alone at home? The fragrance of lilies intensified, and with it Olivia's agitation, to the point that she knew she must take some action. Lily didn't kid around. Something was terribly wrong.

"Guys, listen up," she yelled at the startled youngsters. "I have to leave you on your own for a little while. This is an emergency, so I'm depending on you to be very grown-up and responsible for one another. Stay by the van with Norm. I'll be back just as soon as I can."

"You're going in Uncle Dave's car?" Danny quavered.

"Yes, I'll need to take the Bronco to break out of here. And Bruno will go with me, if only to get him away from this earsplitting noise." As if to emphasize her point, several rockets soared up at once in a rainbow cascade of sparks and war movie sound effects. Bruno howled mournfully.

As she jumped in, Olivia was analyzing the parking situation. *Impossible!* But ever since the first whiff of lilies, she'd been anticipating this situation. "Okay, Bruno, I don't know if you're going to like this any better." Grabbing Dave's flashing red and blue police light, she slapped it on top of the roof, searched around for the siren, turned that on full blast, and revved the motor.

"Police emergency, *police emergency*," she yelled out the window. Drivers ran back to their cars and those who were obstructing the transformed vehicle moved out of the way. "Thanks ...thanks ..."

When she looked back to her own car, she saw the white faces of the boys and Norm gazing at her in amazement. With a reassuring wave, she tore out onto the main road, tires squealing. Less than a half hour later, she was at Dave's house, where her worst fears became terrifyingly real.

None of the outdoor lights at Dave's house were on except for solar torches in the back yard. The Bronco's headlights caught two figures standing outside Dave's house. Olivia immediately stomped on the brake before even entering the driveway. She recognized the stocky intruder as Ben Klein and the slim figure as Ray Chance. Reaching for her handbag to call for help, her heart turned to ice. In her rush to get out between the jammed cars, she'd completely forgotten to grab her handbag out of the Chevy van. "Now what!" she whispered to Bruno. The moment she opened the car door, the interior light was going to reveal not a possibly armed policeman and irate foster father, but only herself, an unprotected woman.

Before she could decide whether to face the intruders or cut and run—leaving Moira in the house defenseless, which simply wouldn't do—she was skewered where she sat by the brilliant gleam of a high-powered flashlight.

"Well, look who we have here," Chance chuckled evilly. "It's the frigid bitch from Mattakeesett." Immediately, Olivia locked all doors of the Bronco, but before she could get the window closed that she'd left open for Bruno, Chance's hand snaked into the car to grab the door handle.

"Hey, I know that gal," Klein growled. "She's the one shot Moe, the bitch."

Ray Chance cursed loudly and pulled his arm out of the window with difficulty, since Bruno was trying to clamp his jaws around the intruder's wrist.

Ben Klein drew a gun. "I know that fucking mutt, too," he muttered.

"No!" Olivia screamed. "Down, Bruno. Stay." She jumped out of the car before Klein could take aim, leaving Dave's keys in the ignition. *Got to distract these guys*, she thought. *Best defense is ...* She positioned herself between Bruno in the back seat and Klein on the front lawn aiming his gun. "Just what are you gentlemen doing here? You'd better leave immediately. I've already summoned the police, and they'll be here any minute."

Ray Chance swaggered over to her. He was wearing something like a camera case over his shoulder, but with his customary tight clothes, it was evident that he was not packing a gun like his partner in crime. As usual, he stood too close. She could smell him, a mixture of sour masculine sweat and cigar smoke. Glaring at him, she refused to step back. He laughed, moved quickly to one side, then behind her, grasping her arms.

But Olivia was a broad-shoulder and muscular woman. She rammed her regrettably low heel down on his foot and threw her arms up, breaking his hold. Darting to one side, she began to back up toward Dave's car. Chance moved slowly, following menacingly, smirking, his eyes giving off frost like dry ice. Olivia thought about jumping in for a quick getaway, at least as far as the nearest phone. *But where is the nearest phone?* She'd have to bang on a neighbor's door. Probably they'd all be out watching fireworks tonight.

But escape was not an option. *Moira and Sadie!*

As if on cue, Moira appeared at an open upstairs window, her face pale as moonlight, her hair standing out like a rosy aureole. "Hey, what's going on out there?" she called in her little girl voice.

The two men and Olivia looked up at the window as Sadie's square white face appeared under the girl's elbow, snout on the windowsill, eyes hard with canine suspicion. She barked once, twice, and Bruno in the car lifted his head, obediently joining the alarm with his deeper *woof, woof.*

"Oh, fuck," Klein muttered. "The kid's here. Thought you said everyone would be at the fireworks. We ain't supposed to … Just the fucking house."

Olivia continued slowly backing up to the Bronco while Chance's attention was distracted. At least she could blast the horn. Maybe someone would hear her and come to help, or at least call the police.

"Hey, cover the fucking broad." Chance motioned toward Olivia, and Klein pointed the gun her way. She froze.

Chance was grinning. "So much the better with the kid. This is supposed to be motivation, isn't it? Get this guy in line to help us out. So, I'm for making it a real deal." He took a half-chewed cigar out of his shirt pocket and lit it. "And later, I'll do her, too." He nodded his head toward Olivia, then removed a bundle out of his camera case. *It looks like dynamite!* Olivia's thoughts screamed.

"Oh, please," she said.

"*Oh, please,*" Chance mimicked her. He strode over and with a single kick, pushed open the front door of the house, directly under the window where Moira was standing.

"*Moira, get out of there!*" Olivia screamed. Moira moved back out of sight. *Will she get far enough away?*

Still grinning, Chance puffed his cigar to a glowing tip, then used it to light the fuse on the bundle. He tossed the lit dynamite into the house. The moment of quiet was like eternity, but instead of an explosion, there was a streak of white flying past them. *It was Sadie!* And she was carrying the dynamite in her big terrier jaws, the lit fuse dangling down like some obscene firework.

Olivia screamed and screamed. Piercing soprano screams that could shatter fine crystal. Finally the command she needed emerged from her frozen brain. *"Drop it, Sadie! Drop it!"* she shrilled. Sadie stopped in her tracks, peered around for Olivia. The habits of obedience kicked in. The dog opened her mouth and let the bundle fall at Klein's feet.

"Fuck! Fuck! Fuck!" the man shouted, stamping around to douse the fuse, as if dancing some kind of frenetic jig.

He looked so funny, Chance doubled over with laughter but dashed to safety across the street. "Throw the fucking thing back into the house, you fuckhead," he yelled over his shoulder. Sadie stood between the dancing man and the running man uncertainly. Klein was attempting to retrieve the dynamite which he had kicked into a bush.

Urgently, Olivia whistled for the pit bull, the sharp two-finger whistle that Danny had taught her. Sadie shook her head as if trying to understand. At that moment, Bruno howled his heart out, and hearing him, Sadie trotted over to Dave's car.

Sirens in the distance! *Oh thank God*, Olivia thought. Moira must have called 911.

But not in time to prevent what happened next. An ear-splitting explosion slammed Olivia and Sadie against the Bronco, which rocked like a ship in high seas. And that's the last thing Olivia heard for some time, but what she saw was the disappearance in a puff of fire of Ben Klein and Dave's front porch.

Moira, where was Moira?

Everything that was Klein and the porch seemed to be crashing down on them. Police cars were careening into the yard, slamming to a stop behind the Bronco. Fire trucks followed, and a rescue wagon.

Moira came running out of the backyard and threw her arms around Olivia and Sadie. She was crying, but Olivia couldn't hear what she was saying. Olivia was crying, too, as she hugged the girl back tightly. Moira alive, that was the wonderful, amazing thing.

Looking over Moira's shoulder, Olivia saw a bloody object that looked like a man's forearm and hand. A gun lay nearby, clean and unmarked by the explosion. About ten feet away she spotted a leg, a foot, a shoe. Screening Moira from the gory remains, Olivia stumbled painfully around to the other side of the Bronco with the girl in tow. Being smashed against the car has had its affect; Olivia felt bruised down one whole side of her body. Sadie crept after her, shaking her big head as if not believing the silence of her ears.

Olivia got Sadie into Dave's car where Bruno greeted the pit bull with anxious sniffs of her head and chest. He probably whimpered, too, but Olivia could hear nothing. She imagined that the dogs were exchanging their tales of misadventure and left them to it.

Still hanging on to Moira, Olivia moved toward the rescue wagon. Maybe something could be done for her hearing. When she reached a paramedic, she pointed toward her ears plaintively. Having seen her slow progress, the man appeared to be more interested in her arms and legs, checking for sprains or breaks. But medical attention had to take second place to insistent questions from the police officers. She pointed to her ears again and shook her head. One of the officers wrote questions in his notebook, then handed her the page to read.

"Yes," she told them. "There is another man. He ran away into the woods across the street, I think. His name is Ray Chance, and he's the one who threw a bundle of dynamite into Dave Lowenstein's house." It was weird speaking without hearing her own voice, except for some faint vibrations in her head. She didn't know if she was shouting or whispering.

Officers were hurriedly dispatched to look for Chance, but the hastily scrawled questions continued. "Well, no, the dynamite was in the house, but one of my dogs carried it out." Why did the officer look so incredulous? "Yes, my dog Sadie brought it out in her mouth. She's all right, though— see, that's her, the pit bull in Detective Lowenstein's car. I yelled to her to drop the dynamite, but unfortunately, when she let go of the bundle, she was standing near the other man, and it exploded. I don't know where that man is, but his arm and leg are over there near where the porch used to be. And his gun. That's there, too." Olivia wondered if they would find any of these remains, what with the firemen trampling over everything to put out the fire before it took the house.

Poor Dave, she thought. *While he was worrying about Jamie's Thunderbird, look what happened to his place.* Then she thought, *Where the hell is he? Surely someone has called him. And I need him here* now, *dammit.*

Another paramedic, a woman, was wrapping Moira in a blanket. It wasn't really cold, but Moira was shivering uncontrollably. Olivia wrapped her arms around the girl, and they sat together on the wagon's tailgate, waiting.

"YOU'LL PROBABLY BE HEARING OKAY IN ABOUT AN HOUR," the paramedic shouted. She could almost hear, reading his lips. There was a new screech of brakes that Olivia didn't hear, but Moira did. Moira looked up hopefully and squeezed Olivia's hand. It was her Chevy van and Dave running toward them. And right behind him, a crowd of concerned faces: Jamie, Norm, and the three boys. They might have been speaking all at once, but it was lost on Olivia. Not lost, however, were the big warm hugs and the kisses of relief. Norm was grinning all over his round face, leaning against the van. He said something she couldn't make out, but the thumbs-up hand gesture was clear enough.

"I thought you'd never get here," she said. She couldn't hear Dave's reply, so she repeated the sign language for "ears not working" and motioned to the notebook in his breast pocket. Moira, wedged under one of his arms now, told him something, probably about her deafness, because he took out his notebook and scrawled. "Thank God, you're all right. I love you. Now I'm going after Ray Chance."

All she had for comfort were his words on the page, because Dave immediately took off in the Bronco with one of the officers. Kevin's expression showed how edgy he was. He wanted to get into the house, to see if his stuff was okay, Olivia deduced, and she knew that Jamie was arguing with the boy, telling him he had to stay put until the fire has been contained and the house was safe to enter. Jamie's expression was full of authority, the scolding nurse who will not be contradicted by a mere kid.

"We're going back to my place," Olivia said firmly. She was assured of no back talk because she couldn't hear it anyway. "Everyone will stay with me tonight. Tomorrow we'll see what we can do, Kevin. Jamie, can you ... ?"

Jamie shook her head. Of course, how could Olivia forget that the lovely ice-blue Thunderbird had gone up in fire and smoke just like Dave's porch. "I'LL DRIVE THE VAN," she mouthed at Olivia. Soon after they were all wedged into the Chevy, the two women and Norm in front and all the youngsters and dogs in back

Looking back, Danny said, "Wow, what a mess!" Olivia nodded and smiled, not understanding a word.

"Even battlefields become meadows again, eventually," Jamie said as they drove away from the disaster scene. When she dropped Norm off at his house, he thanked them all for a great time, except for the explosion, of course. He'd never had such a fun Fourth.

Moira repeated Jamie's line about the meadow to Olivia later, when around eleven that night she began to hear again, albeit with bells and whistles.

Meanwhile, Jamie had made a restorative pitcher of martinis and a large pot of tea. Moira turned out a platter of sandwiches from whatever she could scrounge out of Olivia's Frigidare, and found some Cokes there, too.

Kevin was moaning about his bodhran, and Danny worried about his computer. "Oh, stop fussing," Moira said tartly. "I don't think the fire got very far into the house. It was mostly the porch. And the firemen soaked that good. Our bicycles, though—they're toast. But you should both be grateful that your wonderful sister is okay. I expect you'll both want to light candles to say thanks to the Holy Mother next time we all go to St. Timothy's."

With her hearing slowly coming back, Olivia settled Kevin and Danny into the larger of her two guest rooms, and Moira got the smaller one with pink flower-sprigged wallpaper. The kids were exhausted. Mike, too, was drooping over the kitchen table.

"You'll have to take my van," Olivia said to Jamie. "What a muddle everything is!"

"No, you may need it—this isn't over yet. I'll call a cab. You're a lucky gal, you know." Jamie hugged Olivia. "Dumb and Dumber wouldn't have left a witness to the bombing of Dave's place. I hope that's the end of them. And I hope the Feds bury the Benedettos in the deepest dungeon the law allows. Or better yet, fry them."

Olivia heard most of that. "Amen," she agreed. She noticed that Jamie's eyes were moist with tears, possibly due to too many martinis as well as a threat to the life of her oldest friend. Olivia grinned, feeling her own eyes well up with emotion.

∽

Lying on the sofa in her living room, cell phone at the ready for a call from Dave, Olivia studied the wing chair where Lily had made appearances in the past, all white and gold and diamonds. "Aren't you going to say good-bye?" she asked. "And I think I deserve some kind of an award, don't you? *La Croix du Spectre*, perhaps." Olivia laughed, aware that she was talking to empty air again. No way to tell if she was truly alone, though, because her ghost-sensitive dogs were bunking upstairs with the O'Hara kids. "Fair-weather dogs," she muttered to herself, but she would never forget the sight of Sadie dashing out of Dave's house with the bundle of dynamite in her mouth. Did the dog know? Would she have allowed herself to be blown up to save Moira? Olivia guessed the dogs were now making the point that they wanted to be part of a family with youngsters. Never mind her feelings might be hurt by their defection. Dogs never dissembled for the sake of good manners. "All right, you mutts," she said. "Have I ever denied you anything?"

Maybe she shouldn't have finished Jamie's pitcher of martinis. Slow tears leaked under her closed lids as she drifted into a dream. She was outside Dave's house, wearing a heavily laden carpenter's apron. With nails in her mouth and a hammer in hand, she was putting the finishing touch to rebuilding his porch, only she noticed that it was a lot bigger than it used to be. The L-shaped farmhouse now had a two-story addition. "A first-floor bedroom, that will be ideal," she said. "A little privacy for us newlyweds."

"How about French doors leading to a hot tub?" a woman's voice said. Olivia turned and saw Lily sitting on a swing that hung from the giant beech tree. Wearing a white dress and her diamond tennis bracelet, she was trailing a long white mink on the bare earth under the swing.

"Not my style," said Olivia. "I thought you'd left already for the Sunset Trail, or wherever you're going."

"Oh, Livvy. Not without saying thanks! And not without leaving you a good-bye gift."

"What?" Olivia said ungraciously, nervously. She was not at all sure that she wanted a present from the Other Side.

Lily began to reply but her words came out garbled and jangled. Olivia woke up and realized that her cell was ringing.

"Got him, the little fucker, trying to get into C.B.'s house. Robert Ray Chance is locked up good and proper." Dave said. "I'm coming home now."

Bobby Ray, Olivia thought, as the obvious connection finally clicked into place. *Of course, Lily.* "No, we're all at my house. The kids are asleep. What time is it, anyway?"

"It's three. I know where you are, and that's home to me." His voice was deep and warm and full of intimate possibilities.

"Hurry, darling," she said. "I'm keeping the sofa warm for you."

"The sofa?"

"Proprieties will be observed while the children are here in the house. And God only knows when your place will be habitable again."

"Well ... we'd better get married as soon as possible, then."

"Yes, we'd better." Olivia felt herself rushing forward into a delightfully unknowable destiny. The only thing certain about her future was that it would bring change, surprise, and, with luck, exquisite new joys.

❦

One of those surprises was Ray Chance's decision to become a witness against the Benedettos. But in a way, it was predictable. The Feds offered him witness protection with a walk on extortion, arson, and attempted murder in exchange for his testimony on matters of racketeering and murder. Chance was even able to implicate the real boss, Cesare Benedetto.

"It was a no-brainer for that little weasel," Jamie declared. "I'm only sorry that Cesare B ... I mean, I really liked the old bastard. And he's not a well man."

"So he's saying, over and over," Olivia rebutted. "Too frail to stand trial. And it wouldn't surprise me at all if Paul Galante succeeded in pulling that off. So I hope to God I don't have to live in fear for the rest of my life."

"They'll be too busy following the trail of Ray the Informer, my dear. The long arm of the Benedettos will reach out into his secret new life, and someday, when he least expects it—*Ka-boom!*" Jamie chuckled wickedly.

In another not-so-surprising twist of fate, Jamie was on her way to Newport to "special" one of the Vanderbilts who was undergoing prostate surgery. "He's a minor Vanderbilt, but still, I bet he'll be really grateful to the nurse who can help him recover his full manhood."

"Don't settle for anything less than a cottage-mansion on Ocean Drive," was Olivia's advice.

Other revelations lay in wait for Olivia. She experienced moments when the O'Hara clan did not drive her absolutely crazy, when a feeling of fulfilling a good role in the lives of these children suffused her being. Maybe that feeling was fleeting—until the next major clash of wills—but it was heartwarming while it lasted.

And then there was the real shocker. One afternoon, while the repair of the Lowenstein homestead was still in progress, Danny raced down Olivia's upstairs hall in pursuit of Bruno, who had stolen his sock. Catching the fringe of a scatter rug, Danny swerved out of control into her office, banging his body squarely against her desk and smashing to the floor the Art Deco frame in which Lily's photo had held court these past months. The portrait was silent now, finished with its former mischief-making, simply a smiling unknown woman whose life force seemed to have departed this plane. But the frame was broken cleanly into two pieces, like slices of bread in a sandwich. And inside, between the layers of silver, was a cleverly constructed secret compartment, a groove just large enough to hold several gems.

"That's okay, Danny," Olivia assured the boy magnanimously. "Accidents happen." He took off guiltily for a romp with Bruno.

"Lily's little nest egg," Dave said in wondering tones. "Remember that dream you told me about?"

"You think it's her gift to me. You, a sterling representative of the law, think it's perfectly all right for me to keep—wow! Look at that ruby!—these amazing gems rather than returning them to the Plunkett estate? Is that what you're saying?"

"If Lily's family—which, you remember, included that nasty piece of work Bobby Ray Chance—wanted these diamonds and rubies—how many you got there? Five? God love Lily! If the Plunketts had wanted these, all they had to do was to keep their third or fourth or whatever cousin's photos instead of unloading them at an auction."

"So that's a yes?"

"That's definitely a yes, sweetheart. I'm not quite the same man I was before I met you."

"Me neither," Olivia said. They kissed for a long time, a kiss aware of lovely possibilities and the time to savor them, then she said, "Do you think there's enough here to build an addition on your house? I'm thinking maybe a bedroom on the first floor—for you and me."

LILY

*Hey, You Can't Take It with You, the saying goes. And as the
Guardian is fond of adding, you won't want it when you get there,
anyway. Maybe. I did love those precious gems I stashed away
for a Rainy Day. Got the trick frame specially made for me by a
silversmith who crafted one-of-a-kind jewelry, high-class stuff, so
refined that no one would guess it cost big bucks.*

*Frankie used to lecture me about retirement funds accruing
interest and all that garbage, but I'd always say, Frankie, don't
you worry about me, Hon, those little stones are my IRA, and what
do you want to bet they'll increase in value lots more than some dull
treasury fund? Of course, Little Did I Dream that I'd die so young
(relatively) that my stash might be Lost for All Time, geeze!*

*Anyhow, I just gave Danny a bit of a push so that my treasure
would fall into Liv's hands. And I got back a real feeling of pleasure
like I haven't enjoyed since the last time I smoked some high grade
Acapulco Gold. Liv deserved a financial break much more than those
greedy, bitching Plunkett cousins. After all, she really Put Her Life
on the Line, and the life of her family, and even her dogs, for me.*

*Well, a big part of my satisfaction is my knowing those bastards
the Benedettos won't get away with what they did to Frankie and
me, and who knows how many others? In a way, I'd like to stay
around and watch them sweat when the judge sentences them to grow*

old in Federal prison, but the Guardian says I'm looking a bit worn around the edges, I'd better move on before I get Too Thinned Out to leave here.

I'll miss Marie-Josie, spunky old bird that she is. We got thrown together over the Benedettos, but it turns out she's a gal after my own heart. We've had a few laughs, all right. She introduced me to some fine saloons of yesteryear where we drank excellent bourbon and listened to blues played by the saints who've already marched in. But I don't know if she'll ever move on after she pulled that stunt with the hemorrhoids. Tricks like that are strictly forbidden here. But M. J. says whatever happens to her was worth it. Her handsome boy needed An Intervention, as she calls it. Says she'll be okay, she's aiming to be L'wha herself. That's Vodou for Guardian.

And maybe I'll miss hanging around Liv's place and spooking the doggies. But I know in my bones (ha ha) it's time to let go. Anyway, I've wrangled a promise—sort of Transition Bonus—that Frankie and I will have a gorgeous holiday together, better than Las Vegas, Havana, and Disneyworld all rolled into one. And after that, as they say around here, The Sky Is Not the Limit.

DECEMBER 15
Things to Do Today

Call Jamie re: Christmas auction
Give up listing in the New Year? Learn to go with the flow!

"Now this is my idea of a *real* auction." Jamie said, picking up an ornate sterling silver-backed hand mirror and studying her face in its fading, mottled reflection. "Gawd, it makes me look like a ghost, but, hey! Being a ghost is better than not being at all." She laughed raucously. "Let's have a look at the jewelry. Don't you just love Victorian jewelry? Some of those brooches can look really smart pinned to a suit jacket, don't you think? And the pearls! Ladies all had their pearls in the good old days. That's what I need, an old guy who dotes on draping me in pearls."

They were milling around with the other auction-goers reviewing what had been advertised as "Victorian Antiques and Collectibles from the Berwind Estate with some additions." The sale items were densely packed, all the carved mahogany whatnots, feathered cloaks and fruited hats, gilt-framed portraits of unsmiling ancestors, tasseled table covers and embroidered linens, amber and jet beads, fine crystal and Canton-imported china, pale porcelain dolls, leather-bound books, painted vases, and silver-chased perfume bottles that one hall could hold.

"Okay, but I'm not going to bid on any mourning jewelry," Olivia declared. She studied her notebook. "I'm only interested in Christmas gifts for Dave and the kids."

"How about a nice Christmas gift for yourself? I always include myself in my Christmas list. Santa would have wanted it that way," Jamie said.

"Oh, look at this!" Olivia exclaimed. Something about the portrait of a young man in World War I uniform brought tears to her eyes. Its somber silver frame was nowhere near as elaborate as those that encased other portraits, and underneath there was an unassuming silver medallion inscribed: *Lieutenant Hugh Berwind, 1890-1915. Eldest son of John Jacob Berwind. Bravely strode through the front lines cheering on his men until the last moments of his life.* "How could the family part with this?"

"Times change, memories fail, affections fade," Jamie said. "Please don't be tempted to buy this."

"Not to worry, my dear. *Once burned*—or should I say, *exploded*—*twice shy.* Now what do you think about this lovely set of molds for Moira? Too elaborate?"

"Nah, she'll love them. She's probably at home right now studying her incarcerated mother's recipe for salmon mousse that would mold perfectly in that copper fish. And you might want to check out the fiddle over there. I don't know a whole lot about fiddles, but that one has a provenance with it, belonged to Liam O'Leary. Might be just the ticket for Kevin."

Olivia viewed both of these items and added them to her notebook with firm prices, *this high and no higher,* which in the heat of the auction she often ignored. "Danny, of course, is another country entirely. It's right on to *Comp USA* for his gift. I'm thinking along the lines of a digital camera."

"Hmmm. Nice. Now for *my* gift from Santa, I've got my eye on that sapphire ring—did you see it?" Jamie dragged Olivia away to the locked jewelry case and asked the young lady in attendance please to allow her to see it more closely. "Byatt guarantees precious stones and gold," the young woman said, handing over the ring. Jamie tried it on with a sigh of delight. It fit perfectly on her plump finger.

"As long as you have the case open," Olivia said, "may I look at that silver locket?" As large as a pocket watch, but oval and slim, it rested smoothly and comfortably in the palm of Olivia's hand. The initials carved upon it were too elaborate to be deciphered easily. There was no attached chain, but that could be added, Olivia thought. "This really appeals to me. An indulgence, though. It will probably go too high," she said. She tried to open it but broke a nail. Nevertheless, she marked down the lot number, 43. She hoped it would come up early and not go much higher than the paltry $10.00 she jotted beside her description.

"Pretty piece," said the attendant, slipping the locket and the sapphire ring back into their boxes. "Sterling silver, too."

About an hour after the auction began, Lot 43 came up. It was another of those unexplainable hiatuses when interested parties wandered away to the bar, the water cooler, the rest rooms, or outdoors for a smoke. "Who will give me ten?" the auctioneer asked. Olivia glanced around; no one was signaling. She raised her card to indicate she would bid. "I've got ten, who will make it fifteen? Ten going on fifteen. Ten going on fifteen. What about twelve? Beautiful sterling silver locket here, belonged to the Berwind family. You may never see another one like it. Are you all done at ten then?"

the auctioneer pleaded. "Going, going, *sold* to Buyer number 662 for ten dollars."

"Wow," Jamie said. "I did think that piece would go at least thirty-five. People just don't care about silver jewelry any more. But I think it's lovely. I wonder what those initials are? I couldn't read them, could you?"

"Nope, but it's not important. A long gone story," Olivia said. "Anyway, for only ten dollars, I can afford to add a nice silver chain. I'm thinking thirty inches or more."

"Sure, let it dangle right into your cleavage, that's the ticket," Jamie agreed. Olivia thought to herself that Jamie had the cleavage; all she had were broad shoulders and an A-cup bra with clever underwiring. But still, the locket with its pure, clean lines (apart from the initials which were more like a design element than real letters) and cool smooth silver surface somehow was Olivia's style.

Later, as they were loading up the van, hefting a three-paneled screen with Chinese figures that Jamie bought, she said, "If I keep buying stuff like this, I'm going to have to auction off my own 'estate' to make room for new acquisitions. But you did pretty good yourself, Liv." They jockeyed in a fireplace screen with an intricate wrought iron design depicting a hunter and his hound. "Dave is going to love this—it looks like some of the iron sculptures he makes, doesn't it? And Kevin will be wild over that fiddle. Liam O'Leary is quite well known, you know. Then you got the copper molds, too! For a bit more than you figured, though. Too bad that frantic dame bid against you on that lot, but, hey, that's the excitement of auctions."

"Better than the Mohegan Sun, as far as I'm concerned," Olivia said, who had never put one dollar in the way of a gamble, not even on lottery tickets. Before she started the van, she took the little blue velvet box out of her handbag and removed her locket. She stroked the inviting cool surface. "It's almost as if it was meant to be carried in someone's pocket."

"So, open it," Jamie urged. "You can put a nice little photo of Dave in that. Or if you prefer, Sadie and Bruno. *A chaque son gout.*"

Although there was a nearly invisible lip where a fingernail could be used to open the locket, it didn't come apart easily. Olivia's blunt nail got chipped again before she succeeded in looking inside. Lying flat as a tiny book, there were two miniature silver frames with real glass. Under one was a tintype of a young woman with a cloud of dark hair and a wistful smile. Under the other was a tiny lock of hair tied with a rose ribbon.

"There's an inscription under the hair," Jamie said, hanging over Olivia's shoulder to examine the inside of the cleverly hinged locket. She turned on the van's overhead light.

Olivia picked up the magnifying glass pendant hanging on a chain around her neck, gingerly opened the second frame and lifted up the lock of hair. She peered at the words closely. "For Hugh from his Rose. *I shall but love thee better after death*," she read aloud.

"Oh my Gawd," Jamie said "Is that romantic or what?"

"Elizabeth Barrett Browning. She was all the rage." Olivia carefully put back the lock of hair, clicked the frame into place, and closed the locket. She slipped it back into its case and started the motor. Time to get Jamie home and unpacked. Already Olivia was missing Dave, eager to get home to her new bridegroom in their newly rebuilt farmhouse. With luck, the kids might be occupied elsewhere. That was one good thing about teenagers—they were often out and about.

About a mile later, "Say," she remarked to Jamie, "do you smell roses? Or is that my imagination?"

"Yes, I smell roses. The scent is quite overwhelming. Before you ask, I am not wearing any rose cologne. And you've got on your usual minimalist White Linen or something," Jamie said. "So I just want to point this out to you—this is December. What do you make of that?"

"God gave us memory so that we might have roses in December," Olivia quoted absently. She was often surprised by what she remembered. So many records stored haphazardly in her mind, everything she'd ever experienced, learned, or even glimpsed once in passing, much of it inaccessible and unruly with emotions, never to be put in the perfect order she valued so much. She supposed she'd just have to accept the chaos of life and hope that it turned out to have its own intrinsic pattern, too large perhaps to be seen from where she was now, like the Bronze-Age white horse inscribed on the hills of Oxfordshire.

"Is that all you've got to say?" Jamie said. "I don't mean to be fanciful, but didn't you perhaps notice that the rose fragrance seemed to float out of that locket the moment you opened it?"

"I must remember to send Mrs. Mitchell a little note at Christmas," Olivia said. "A gal never knows when she might need a good American Indian shaman channeler. In case we have to encourage someone else to lift off with the West Wind."

After she helped Jamie carry the Chinese screen and other auction purchases into her town house, she said, "So, you won't mention this to Dave, okay?"

"*I* will be as silent as the grave," Jamie promised. Then she laughed, her most wicked laugh. "I don't know about Amityville Rose, though."

The overpowering fragrance of roses, deep and sweet, continued to swirl around Olivia all the way home.

∾

CPSIA information can be obtained at www.ICGtesting.com
Printed in the USA
LVOW10s1453250516

489934LV00020B/620/P